Slitherskins

MARTHA GILSTRAP

Martha Gilstrap
Slitherskins

ISBN: 978-0-9887500-6-7

Slipaway Trail Publishing
Copyright © 2014 by Martha Gilstrap
Cover © 2014 by Amy Moyer

Acknowledgments

As always, my first acknowledgment must be directed toward my sister-friend, Carol Englehaupt, who writes as CL Roth. Our discussions and her ideas added greatly to the quality of this book—in spite of the fact that she has no use for snakes (or slithers, their intelligent counterpart).

I also received wonderful support, encouragement, and feedback from my writers group, The Summit Scribes, in Lee's Summit, MO. Stephanie, Jennifer, Dave, Edwin, Jerry, and everyone else, thank you from the bottom of my heart! Especially for your help in setting up the library in my basement. That was above and beyond!

Kudos go to my editor, Deb Courtney, who had to be really frustrated with the mishmash I sent her to start with. With her help I cleaned it up, made sense out of the sections that didn't make sense, and otherwise made it a readable book. She never went easy on me, and I could almost hear her eye-rolling . . . but it was worth it to tell the story I wanted to tell, in a way people could relate to.

As she did last year with *The Slipaway Trail*, Alicia Howie did a fine job of formatting *Slitherskins*. Luckily for me, she's not only talented but easy-going (by her own admission), which makes her a joy to work with.

Slitherskins received fabulous cover art, created by Amy Moyer, whose sister, Jennifer, was right to tell me Amy can do *"anything."* Amy's snake tokens got Alicia excited, and her cover creation has put me in 7th Heaven! The view of the Rainbow Sands from the Slipaway Trail is detailed and wonderful, providing a visual link to the previous cover (for *The Slipaway Trail*).

I'm lucky and blest to be surrounded by such talent. I truly couldn't ask for more from any of these wonderful people. Thank you all, from the bottom of my heart.

1. Visitors

Snake gazed out his window at the swirling snow that obscured jagged mountain peaks, missing the warm sands of his childhood. Sometimes he imagined mounds of sleeping snow to be dunes of pure white sand.

The wounds of his body had healed long ago, even before his mother had moved them from the desert to the high, cold Kingdom of the Snows, where there were no slithers—or snakes, their distant and mindless kin.

Here, his real name wasn't known. People knew him as Snake—for the tattoo on his right biceps—and he'd never mentioned slithers to anyone here except his friend, Kayde.

"My lord, you have visitors."

Snake sighed in exasperation, though it wasn't the servant's fault. "Show them to the fountain and let my mother know they're here," he directed. "She'll want to speak with them."

He called this time of year the season of envoys, at least in his own mind. Someone arrived every year about this time to plead for his return to the white sands.

It twisted his gut to allow them inside his home, but he wouldn't deny his mother the chance to visit with them about the friends she'd left behind.

As usual, his mother's husband was away on business, so decisions fell to Snake. He didn't mind. Atalas had been good to both of them, taking in Senyr as a washerwoman when they had no place in the world. And now they were part of a family–a noble family, no less. When they'd first arrived, he hadn't even known what a "noble" was.

Snake unfurled his long, lanky frame, rising gracefully from the carved wooden chair with leather seat and headrest. He picked up his sword and scabbard. The sword would emphasize the difference between the boy who fled and the man he'd become. He slung the harness across his back and buckled it into place. His linen shirt covered the tattoo on his right biceps–the reason everyone here called him Snake. Covering it hid the only visible vestige of Snake's origins.

The house on Atalas's modest estate wasn't huge, and the distance to the fountain in the central courtyard wasn't far, but dread dragged at Snake's heels, slowing his normal brisk stride.

Who had they sent this time? Usually it was one of the three chief priests, accompanied by one of Snake's boyhood friends. Men with whom he had nothing in common now, whose faces he didn't even recognize.

And yet, just knowing they were here made his palms wet and his mouth dry. He blocked old memories that clamored in his head for attention.

And it was about to get worse. He'd have the usual nightmares tonight.

Big, tough warrior, he scolded himself, and you're cut off at the knees by something that happened twenty years ago, halfway around the world. Grow up!

The scolding only distracted him for a moment, and then he reached the fountain.

The modest pedestal fountain stood in a pool in the middle of a small courtyard open to the sky. The low wall about the pool provided seating, as did the marble benches lining the four short walkways leading from hallways to the water.

As Snake expected, his two visitors sat on the pool's edge, fascinated by the water. Their hands trailed in the cool liquid, their eyes wide in wonder at so much water, so easily available that it could be spent for no other purpose than peace and simple beauty. Rapt, they didn't hear his feet on the marble path over the gentle sound of splashing.

He politely cleared his throat and stepped more noisily as he moved past red and purple flowerbeds.

His visitors stood and turned, dropping their cloaks' hoods onto their shoulders. Chief Priest Evron, of the Praise, looked old. Gray lines and wrinkles checkered his face like cracks in dry brick. His desert robes were threadbare and grayed with dust from the journey. The edges of hem and sleeves and neckline were frayed. Hard times, if even a chief priest looked so shabby. Or perhaps they'd simply suffered a sandstorm on the way here.

The other was a tall woman about Jynx's age, a few years younger than Snake. Her unbleached robes were as threadbare as Evron's. Long black hair cascaded over her shoulders below shapely features and startling, light blue eyes shaped like almonds in an olive face. Chin held high, haughty set to her mouth. Who was this!

Snake tried a welcoming smile but it didn't stretch far. "Evron, it's good to see you again," he lied. He owed them courtesy. What had happened twenty years ago was not the fault of either of these people. He stepped forward to clasp forearms with the old man, equal to equal.

"I'm pleased to see you looking well," replied Evron in his smooth, rich baritone. "May I present to you Queen Shyriel, who speaks with the gods?"

Queen! This was the human queen of the People? Here? So far from the sands?

And he thought of Ick, the slither queen who now lived with Jynx in the tallgrass, far from here. She wasn't supposed to leave the white sands, either, her presence on this continent a riddle he'd never solved.

For an instant, Snake wondered about correct protocol. He'd never met a queen before–a human one, anyway. But this wasn't *his* queen. After a brief hesitation, he offered the same short bow he would offer any noblewoman.

"Kneel!" snapped Evron. "She is your queen!"

Startled, Snake stared at him. "Not *my* queen, Evron. Mine lives here, in the Kingdom of the Snows." He tried to keep an edge out of his voice.

"You are of the People! She *is* your queen!"

Snake relaxed, as if entering battle. He shifted some weight forward to the balls of his feet and met Evron's angry gaze. Strange, to realize he was several inches taller than the chief priest. "I am not of the People anymore, and have not been for most of my life. My allegiance is sworn here. I have great respect for the People, and for Queen Shyriel, but my life and my loyalties are here."

Shyriel–he refused to name her queen in the privacy of his own head–stepped forward and touched his arm. "I understand, Kyr, and I am not offended. You suffered much in the white sands, and no one blames you for fleeing. I have come only to speak with you, to know your mind first-hand. What I know now is only story."

Snake barely heard her. He'd suddenly realized that there was likely some kind of protocol for one queen entering another's kingdom–and Shyriel hadn't followed it. What kind of trouble was she making for him, just by her presence?

The back of Snake's neck prickled. "That's less than honest, Shyriel." He ignored Evron's gasp of outrage. "You also share the inherited memories of the slither queen."

Too late he realized what he'd said, saw the pain in her eyes. She had no slither queen to rule beside her. But if Shyriel was–what, sixteen?–then Ick was older than he'd realized. They'd been born on the same day. The queens always were.

But she'd had years with Ick before the slither had followed Jynx out of the Rainbow Sands. She'd shared Ick's memories. There would be no hiding the truth from her.

A servant appeared on one of the marble paths, carrying a tray of meat pastries and fresh fruits, as well as a ceramic pitcher of iced fruit juice–apricot, it looked like. Or maybe peach.

Snake forced himself to relax, to step down from his initial reactions. "I beg your pardon for my lack of manners. Please, sit. You must be hungry and thirsty. My mother will come soon, to speak with you about her home."

More servants entered, bearing a small table for the tray and cushions to sit on. As they left, Senyr entered, her green eyes lighting up at the sight of Evron.

As strong and straight as ever, she greeted Shyriel and Evron warmly, apologizing for not kneeling to Queen Shyriel. "I cannot," she explained with a smile, "as I am sworn to this kingdom. All nobles must swear fealty and provide support to the throne as needed." And she proceeded to put the visitors at ease, talking about life in the Kingdom and asking for news of the Rainbow Sands.

Snake ate with them, but he spoke little, watching his mother weave her magic. She was so likeable, so beloved of everyone who met her! Dark, almost black hair like his, strong and slender frame, animated eyes and gestures... but to Snake she never aged. He'd never noticed the gradual appearance of lines in her face, wrinkles on her neck, graying strands of hair. Until now. A pang of fear shot through him, a knowledge that someday she would be gone, leaving him without his anchor.

As Senyr at last rose and took her leave of the visitors, Snake caught the look she gave him. A reminder of her wishes–wishes he'd ignored for years. A plea to help them, or at least to truly listen and to consider their request, the same request they always made.

This was the time to listen, while she would be here to know he'd done what he could. No, that wasn't in her look. But it was in her heart. He knew what she wanted.

Servants cleared trays and table, and the adversarial atmosphere left with them.

When they had gone, Evron spoke first. "We must speak of things I know you would prefer not to remember. We have spoken of this before, and others have spoken with you in other years, but it becomes more important with time, not less." He stopped when Shyriel held up her hand.

"You are the one foretold," she said to Snake. "Twenty years ago Queen Tchenya spoke to you—the only male of the People ever to hear the voice of the slither queen. This alone is the fulfillment of prophecy, confirmed by the memories of the next queen—and my partner—Erilya."

Erilya. Ick's true name. Snake felt sick to his stomach. Ick—Erilya—shouldn't be in the tallgrass but in the white sands. But neither should she be separated from Jynx, who was bonded to her, too. He swallowed before speaking. "Tchenya said nothing that could affect the future." He spoke with more steel than he'd intended. "She called me names. That hardly qualifies for a history-shaping prophecy."

"The importance is not what she said but that she spoke directly to you, and you heard her. It marks a change for the People, for good or ill."

"I know," Snake said. "'A male of the People will hear the voice of the queen, earn the highest of all honors, and forsake the sacred slithers. The future of the People will change forever because of this.' It's required memory work for all acolytes."

"You heard Queen Tchenya's voice." Shyriel spoke with passion restrained to civility. "You earned the hero's tattoo for saving Slyn's life..."

Snake muttered, "That aberrant little worm!"

Shyriel shot him a dark look. "...And you forsook the sacred slithers when you and your mother left the white sands."

Evron's pacing stopped. "And the future of the People *has* changed because of it." His sonorous voice intoned the words like a threat.

Snake turned his back, intending to walk away. He couldn't bring himself to do that, so he turned again, taking a deep breath to calm his agitation. *Calm,* he told himself. *Calm. You're a Wolf Guard warrior, one of the most feared warriors in the world*. He relied on that training now to restrain the jumping nerves that forced his pacing. Aloud he said, "What's the connection with the People's future? Which of the things you mentioned has caused the changes you see in the People's fortunes? I see no connection between my almost being swallowed by the queen when I was a child and the future of the People of the white sands. Draw the lines for me, to show why you think I bear *any* responsibility here!"

Snake took a deep breath, trying to regain the calmness he'd just lost again. He'd been nearly shouting. Shyriel's chin lifted and her gaze felt like needles piercing his brain. He clamped his teeth over an apology. He owed them nothing!

Then Shyriel's shoulders relaxed, slowly, as if it took effort. Her voice, when she spoke, was calm and reasonable. "Please. Sit, Kyr. I will tell you of recent events, and you will see the connection."

He hesitated, then remembered his silent promise to his mother. This time he would listen. As distasteful as it was, he would listen.

~~~

Shyriel leaned forward, elbows on her knees and hands clasped in a very unqueenly pose. Her gaze turned inward, toward memory, and silence hung heavy for a long moment.

"I'm unsure how much you know of events in the white sands," she said slowly. "I know that every year we send people to talk to you, and every year you turn them away, refusing to hear them. They speak with Senyr, instead, knowing there are people she misses from the sands. We have urged her to speak to you on our behalf, but she will not 'take sides,' as she calls it. Still, she may have told you of some events, leaving me unsure where to begin."

Evron spoke, his volume as low as the queen's, as if in solidarity. "The People have fallen on hard times since your departure. We have become poor, with little wealth and fewer prospects. Our waters are receding, and we had little enough to begin with. The decline in our fortunes began with your departure, and Tchenya's final prophecy foretold that you must return to the white sands before life could return to normal."

Snake couldn't help himself. "And you blame me? It seems the true culprit is the drought."

"It is beyond that," said Shyriel, still staring at the flagstones in front of her knees. "We are forced to buy water and other staples from neighboring tribes, because our production of slitherskins is low, as birth rates have declined. Also because many slithers are being stolen from us. And the thieves are becoming bolder."

Evron opened his mouth to speak but Snake cut him off. "Wait! Wait! Production of slitherskins? What are you talking about?" Removing skins from the slithers? Just the thought nauseated him. Henth immediately came to mind, the gentlest and most beloved of his nest.

Shyriel sat up straight, eyes wide, staring at Evron, who stared back.

And Snake knew he'd stumbled onto some terrible secret, something they didn't want him to know. Something shameful? Elation soared, a vindication that he'd been right all these years to shut them out of his life. "What awful secret have you been hiding from me?"

Shyriel's mouth dropped open, and then she burst out laughing. "You don't know?"

Evron's startled look gave way to a smile of his own. "Please forgive us, Kyr. There is no secret, only assumptions on our part. Because you are of the People, I assumed you knew of adult things, although you were only–what, eight?–when you left. Even though your family was not directly involved in commerce."

Anger flashed through Snake at the laughter, replaced by more confusion. Commerce? "Then tell me."

Shyriel's laughter had stopped with Snake's anger. She

stretched a hand toward him. "I'm sorry to have laughed, Kyr. I was only startled because, in my mind, you are a legend, larger than life, not a boy who didn't complete his education in the sands. Please forgive me."

"And allow me," said Evron, "to help you make sense of what's happening in the Rainbow Sands."

Snake felt the heat in his face. Anger burned more brightly for his ignorant mistake. He worked to squelch it.

"What is the one thing the People have that no one else does?" said Evron, clearly not expecting an answer. "The slithers, messengers of the gods. As a People in a dry land, our possibilities for commerce with others, both within and beyond the Rainbow Sands, is limited, and is mostly in trade, rather than sale. We have a few women who weave baskets from the water reeds. We have one or two who make potions and medicines that include a drop of slither venom, although that's carefully controlled. We have a small amount of jewelry created from the odd cast-off slither scale–a queen's scale commands a good price. And we sell prophecies. If a prophecy affects other tribes, we offer to share it with them for a price. These are not common, but they do happen."

"Do you remember," said Shyriel, "as an acolyte, how you carefully oiled the slithers in your nest?"

"Of course. The importance of skin care was heavily stressed," Snake said.

"Did anyone explain why?"

Snake frowned, thinking. "For the benefit of our young godlets. For their health and comfort."

"What did you do with the skins they outgrew and left behind?" Shyriel's voice was soft now, and patient.

"We took them to... somewhere. I don't remember."

Evron spoke again. "The most valuable thing in our tribe is the slithers, and our relationship with them. Yet we would never think of selling them to other people, although we receive many requests."

"We do? ...you do?" Surprise made Snake's tongue careless.

He caught a glint of satisfaction in Shyriel's eyes and swore silently. "Why would anyone else want the godlets?"

"I don't think you realize how valuable slitherskins are." Evron's voice took on the lecturing tones of a teacher. "Our primary commodity for sale or trade is fiszt, a drinkable antidote to almost any poison—slithers, scorpions, Canba beetles, dicklebush thorns—just about anything. Its primary ingredient is the cast-off skins, crushed to a fine powder."

"In fact," said Shyriel, "we have made some bad enemies because of the potion's value. There are those who would like to have their own slithers to create their own fiszt. And so they raid us and take our slithers."

"If that were all, you wouldn't be trying so hard not to tell me. What are you holding back? And why?" Could he trust anything they told him, even now, if they were being so careful with their words?

Shyriel shot to her feet, fists clenched. "Isn't that enough? We have lost dozens of slithers, and all their cast-off coils that feed us, and all their unborn children, and all their prophecies! This is a tremendous blow to the People!"

"You didn't send the Protection after them? That's certainly enough to warrant your warriors attacking another tribe."

"We did," said Evron, his voice half an octave lower. "We lost eight warriors and the remainder were forced to retreat. Only one slither recovered, and she speaks to no one, immobilized by fear. Henth was one of our most beloved slithers, too."

Henth! Snake's breath caught in his throat. Henth was a part of his nest, a sweet, gentle slither of whom he had only good memories. "Did they hurt her?" No, no, that tone cared too much, gave these people a weapon. Distrust hammered at his heart. They'd brought her up on purpose, knowing she'd been one of his nest.

"Not physically, no," said Evron. "Not that we can tell. She doesn't much like being touched anymore."

Early days in the acolyte precinct. Henth "giggling" with

him as they struggled to understand each other's thoughts through their emotions. Henth coiled up against his bare belly, inside his robe, as they slept. Henth's coils massaging his arm as he tried to massage scented oils into her skin...

The spark in Evron's eyes told Snake he knew what Henth was—had been—to Snake. He'd used her name deliberately.

Snake roughly shoved those memories aside. "It does seem the People have come upon hard times, and I'm sorry for it. But you still haven't said how this is a direct result of my hearing Tchenya's insults as a boy. What do I have to do with any of this?"

"Tchenya's prophecies were never wrong. You are the one foretold, the only one who can restore us to what we were, put things back to rights," said Shyriel. "Your leaving was foretold, and so was your return. I believe that you were led *here*, to the high mountains, by the gods, and that your life here has prepared you to aid us in this crisis."

"I don't believe any such thing," Snake retorted.

Shyriel took a deep breath, surprising Snake with its shakiness. "Our story gets worse," she said through a tight throat. "They took our queen, Erilya. Yet the Protection did not find her when they went to retrieve our slithers. Several other slithers were also missing. We don't know what the Children of the Night have done with Erilya and those others. If they'd killed her, I, too, would have died, so I know she lives, but our queen is lost to us."

A chill ran down the back of Snake's neck. Shyriel was talking about a queen to whom she was bonded for life.

She was talking about Ick.

~~~

Snake knew what he had to do. He just didn't want to do it. He lay awake most of the night, wrestling with questions of duty, responsibility, love, debt, and prophecy. All the questions felt nebulous, none of them had good answers, and they soon whirled inside his head in a maelstrom of doubt and confusion. He swore aloud at himself, called himself names, decided to think logically, and carefully started to sort everything out, one at a time. But it seemed as if no question could be answered until all were answered.

Ick was Erilya. The People needed their slither queen and her prophecies. She belonged there, and her absence would be devastating. It had nothing to do with him. Except that he was by blood one of the People. And he could restore their slither queen to them. Easily.

Except that Jynx was the woman he loved. And she was bonded to Ick. If he took Ick back to the People, Jynx would be devastated.

He had no idea what Ick would think. Until he asked her, at least.

Snake gave up and got up. He wasn't sleeping, so he might as well find something to keep him busy. Maybe oil his leather. Check his weapons. Set out what he needed to take. With a sigh he reached for his leather and the oil.

Had he decided, then, to return with them?

The real question was Ick. Erilya. Would he tell them about her? That would be a betrayal of Jynx. Could he tell them, give them hope, and *not* lead them to the young queen?

If only he could talk to Jynx. She was so clear-headed and practical. *She'd* know what was right.

Besides, he wanted to see her, hear her bright laughter... and that led to unproductive thoughts. He shut them down with a sigh.

Why couldn't he decide? He was a captain in the Wolf Guard, for Baldair's sake! One of the fiercest, deadliest warriors in the world! This shouldn't be any different than any of the difficult battlefield decisions he'd made.

As first light grayed the mountains visible from his window, Snake at last slept, his head pillowed on his forearms, an oiled rag still in his hand.

No wonder he had trouble waking up when a servant

knocked at his door to call him to his breakfast.

Shyriel and Evron were already eating with Senyr in the intimate family dining room. This one, seating no more than a dozen people, was one of the friendliest, least formal rooms in the manor.

Something in Snake's confusion seemed to have solidified as he slept. He sat, waving off food, and both of his visitors gave him their full attention. Even his mother laid down her spoon to listen.

He spoke without greeting or preamble. "Your slither queen is alive and healthy. And quite spirited."

Shyriel gasped, eyes widening in delight, and a wide smile split Evron's face.

Before either could speak, Snake held up a hand. "I know where she is, and I'm riding out today to talk to her."

The girlish tone of Shyriel's excited voice surprised him. When her speech slowed enough to understand her words, she said, "How soon can we leave? I can't wait to see her!"

"We came on foot," said Evron, "but perhaps we could borrow horses? It would be much faster and easier."

"Whoa!" Snake raised his voice to be heard. "Wait! This will be done my way, or not at all." He didn't smile.

He tried not to show the dread curdling his stomach at the thought of facing a slither queen again. Even Ick. "I'm going alone. You two will return home and wait."

"No." Shyriel's eyes flashed with queenly stubbornness. "I will *not* wait! I will see my queen as quickly as we can get there."

Snake knew a royal command when he heard one. He loaded his voice with steel. "Then it won't be done at all." He rose and started for the door.

"Wait!"

"No, you can't! Stop!"

Snake wanted not to hear the desperation, but it was inescapable. He hesitated at the door, then turned back. The visitors drew back at the look in his eyes. Good. "Your queen is bonded to someone else, Shyriel. I'm going to talk to her, see what she wants to do. Yes, I hear this queen, too. If she agrees, I'll bring her to you. If not, you'll never see her again.

"Either way, neither you nor any of the People will be welcome here again. I'm done with this." He spun on his heel and walked out, leaving stunned silence behind him.

2. Ick

The Beast kicked up his heels and ran. Snake let him. Few horses were faster or smarter—or had a wickeder sense of humor—than the ugly black gelding, and the day would be far easier if he allowed the Beast to get it out of his system now.

As if hearing his thoughts, the Beast shied abruptly. Twice. His ears drooped in disappointment when Snake stayed with him easily.

Early morning in late spring was still cold this high up and Snake had dressed accordingly, a light bearskin coat over leather over linen. His sword was strapped across his back, as usual, and he led a packhorse with supplies enough to reach Jynx.

He'd thought about asking his friend, Kayde, to come along, but Kayde had troubles of his own to deal with. Snake wouldn't drag him into this mess, anyway—not just to have his company on the long journey to the tallgrass. Besides, if Kayde came with them to the Rainbow Sands, so would Jynx's friend, Kahpur. And that was too big a group for traveling through the desert, where water could be a problem.

If it came to that. He prayed Ick would choose to stay with Jynx, and that no further travel would be necessary. That he wouldn't have to face the Rainbow Sands again. Contending with one slither queen would be easier than facing hundreds or thousands of slithers in the white sands.

His skin crawled. He'd have to deal with Ick again. Jynx insisted the queen liked him, but he shuddered, remembering the spike of fear when Ick had tickled the inside of his ear with her tongue. A "kiss, sort of," Jynx had called it.

He needed to move his thoughts elsewhere. Which meant directly to Jynx. He sighed happily and settled in for a few hours of dreaming and daydreaming. Happy memories didn't keep him from a sharp lookout, though he also relied on the Beast for alerts.

Thus he traveled for two weeks, with no mishap more serious than breaking three arrows on the hide of a giant bear early in his journey. Good thing he'd packed plenty of spices to tenderize and flavor the meat. And a good thing he had a packhorse to carry it. Leaving it would have been a waste of good food. Carrying it would postpone the use of penkin later on. The trail patties of meat, berries, and suet were tasty enough, but they became tiresome quickly.

He dropped down out of the foothills into the broad grasslands that covered half the continent, and within a few days rode from the short grasses to the mixed grasses, then finally into the tallgrass, some of the most nutritious pasturage in the world, where grasses often grew taller than he stood. The footing wasn't as good here, as above-ground root systems tugged at feet or hooves, but game abounded–when he could see it through the grasses. At least the land wasn't flat, although the hills would barely qualify for that name in the Snows.

The huge sky he'd grown used to when he and Kayde came through before was as overwhelming as the first time he visited the tallgrass. He could have hunted the strange deer that Jynx called "antelope," but it would be a waste, as much bear meat as he still carried. The gods frowned upon wasting food, especially meat. With a sigh, he resigned himself to living off bear meat until he reached the town of Sayvil in the tallgrass, where Jynx lived. With Ick, of course.

Pulse pounding with excitement and anticipation, Snake made camp, staked out the packhorse, and then took the Beast for a long, fast ride. When he returned to camp, the Beast was in his best mood of the entire trip.

So was Snake. Tomorrow he would see Jynx again. Maybe they could even spend some time together before he had to face Ick. That was the only part of this trip he truly dreaded.

What if she was off somewhere with Kahpur again? What if she'd found someone else while they were apart? Snake knew better, but he still couldn't settle down. Only after two hours of sword work was he worn out enough to sleep.

Dawn found him on the road again. At last, as the sun crept toward the horizon, he found the road to Sayvil.

He walked the Beast into town before dark.

~~~

Sayvil hadn't changed much since Snake's last visit. The potter's house had a fresh coat of paint on the eaves—the same reddish color as before. The streets were still as dusty as ever, but the porch rails of the Blue Goose Inn had been replaced with sturdier rails—probably because of a fight—and painted blue like the eaves. All roofs in town slanted to one side or the other to shed rain, a look that Snake still found odd. Smoke rose above the smithy, but both the building and the house next to it looked faded and in need of repairs. Beyond the smithy were horse pens, shared by Ell's Stable on the other side of them.

The stable was his first destination. He dismounted to lead the horses inside, where a young woman wearing men's britches met him. The shoulder-length coppery hair and green eyes belonged to Jynx's friend and the daughter of the stable's owner. "Hello, Kahpur," he said.

The woman jerked her attention from his horse; her eyes had lit up at sight of the Beast. "Snake!"

Clearly she'd recognized his horse before she did him. An

amused quirk tugged at one corner of his mouth.

Kahpur grinned and clasped his forearm as if she were a man. "What are you doing here? Where's Kayde? Does Jynx know you're coming?" She reached for the Beast's reins.

The brute's ears flattened and he showed his teeth. "Stop that!" she snapped, swatting his nose. "You know better than to misbehave around me!" The Beast's head drooped, ears wilting as if in apology.

Snake laughed. Kahpur was one of the few people who could handle the Beast with no trouble. He followed her into the cool, shadowed depths of the stable, inhaling the scents of fresh hay and grain. As they stripped the horses and put them into roomy stalls, he answered her questions. "Kayde's not with me. I'm on my own this time. Jynx doesn't know I'm coming, but I'll head over there after I get settled at the Blue Goose and get cleaned up. And don't you spoil the surprise!"

Kahpur laughed. "Then go on. I'll take care of these two. No charge for care or feed or anything else, by the way. I think you'll find the Blue Goose will have the same policy for you— and so will most of the merchants in town."

He stared at her, trying to make sense of her words. "Why?"

"You don't remember yours and Kayde's desperate ride to the Spring of Healing for the magic water that saved almost the entire town?"

Snake blinked. "Of course, but..."

"The townspeople know who brought them hope and health. We lost too many people to the epidemic as it was, and we all know it would have been worse if not for our two mountain warriors." She waved a curry brush at him, then turned away to apply the bristles to the Beast, who didn't even try to step on her foot.

Snake stood there for a moment, adjusting to the idea, then spoke quietly. "Thank you, Kahpur." He walked out into the bright sun and down the street to the inn.

Kahpur was right. He was welcomed warmly, given the best room, and informed he would be paying for nothing. Oddly, he found himself thinking, *So this is what it feels like to be a hero.*

He'd been more heroic than that many times, without such appreciation. He shook his head, nonplused, and took full advantage of the wooden tub filled with bucket after bucket of hot water for him. And then, of course, he felt obligated to eat dinner in the dining room, during which his ale mug was never empty. It was a long meal, with so many of the locals stopping to shake his hand, clap him on the shoulder, buy him a drink (the innkeeper did allow *them* to pay), and give him warm—and sometimes emotional—thanks.

By the time that activity simmered down, he was a wee bit tipsy. Not drunk enough to accept any of the feminine invitations, but too drunk to visit Jynx tonight. Besides, midnight was surprisingly near, and Jynx's family wouldn't appreciate a drunken warrior appearing at their door at this time of night. He fell asleep on top of the bed, boots still on his feet.

Only a couple of hours later, he became aware again. A board on the stairs had creaked. Was that what woke him? He heard a murmur of voices outside his door; all else remained silent. He strained to hear. The speakers seemed to be making an effort to keep their voices low and he couldn't quite figure out the words. Probably someone late coming in. He closed his eyes again.

Then two spoken words came through clearly: "Kill him."

And suddenly Snake was wide awake, grateful to be fully clothed and not bound to the bed by blankets. Eyes wide in the darkness, he listened, heart pounding.

The voices didn't change, didn't move on past his door.

Careful to avoid creaking the rope lattice on which the thin mattress lay, he sat up and swung his feet to the floor. He waited, to make sure no sound had alerted the speakers, then eased to his feet. He took his time with each step, and with drawing his sword silently from its sheath. Sword in hand, held to cover the center of his body, he faced the door and waited, breathing shallowly, a light tension radiating out from his belly. His grip on the sword was easy but not loose, ready for whatever came. He flexed his knees, adjusted his stance for easy movement in any direction.

And waited.

He heard no footsteps but the voices ceased. A long, slow breath helped maintain the calm in his muscles. Ready. Not tight. His ears seemed to ring in the silence. He strained to hear.

Nothing. Not even a creaking floorboard. They hadn't left. Why? What were they waiting for? He cleared his mind. Preconceptions could lead him to be ready for the wrong thing. Then he'd have to shift hands, or feet, or plans—and perhaps die for it.

The wait seemed forever. His eyes blurred with the need to go back to sleep. Surely by now it was safe. They'd probably left and he just hadn't heard them go.

He relaxed his shoulders, started to come out of his stance.

Someone knocked softly on his door.

He startled. A knock? From someone who might want to kill him? He hesitated, unsure whether to continue to wait, to answer the door, or to invite his visitor in.

He'd be a fool to relax too soon. "Come!" he called.

"Are you decent?" A woman's voice, speaking softly as if to avoid disturbing others. A voice he knew well.

Snake dropped out of his stance and set his sword aside. In two strides he reached the door and yanked it open. "Jynx?"

And backed up hastily as a sinuous silvery shape struck in his direction.

"Ick! Stop that!" scolded Jynx, stepping back to hold the slither queen away from Snake.

Cold sweat chilled Snake's arms and shoulders, but he made himself look directly at the slither—just not in her eyes. "Stop that!" he said, as if she'd actually obey him. He felt her laughter in his head, understood that she thought it was fun to surprise him with a sudden lunge. She bore him no animosity, had no intention of hurting him. But it was fun to startle him so.

He blocked her from his mind as best he could—she was so strong!—and turned his attention to her partner.

Jynx was as he remembered her: short, with an amazing figure and flowing walnut hair, beautiful from top to toe. The challenge in her brown eyes was typical, and he found himself grinning at her.

Then propriety caught up with him. He hastily glanced in both directions, saw only empty hallways, and grabbed her. "Get out of the hall before you're observed," he said.

She laughed, an easy laugh under dancing eyes, and allowed him to pull her inside and close the door.

"You do know," she said, "that my presence here is already known, since the innkeeper had to show me which room was yours." Jynx crossed the room to sit on the edge of the bed.

He sat, too, turned to face her. Wanting to kiss her, to put his arms around her. And more.

He didn't touch her. "It's the middle of the night! What are you doing here?"

One delicate eyebrow arched primly. "You told Kahpur you were coming to see me as soon as you got settled here. When you didn't, I came to see you."

Snake made note that Kahpur couldn't be trusted to keep secrets from Jynx. He shouldn't have expected it.

"I heard voices in the hall, something about 'kill him.' You could have been hurt before I realized who you were!"

"That was me, telling the innkeeper I was going to kill you for this."

"For what?"

"For not keeping your promise. Besides, Ick would have warned me if necessary." Jynx gently unwound the seven-foot slither from her waist. The beautiful silvery creature coiled comfortably in the middle of his bed and stared at him from emrel eyes. He felt her amusement in his head, in the same way he used to hold long conversations with young slithers.

"I could have killed her instead," he said, but his tone didn't convince even him. The strike had been so fast! And his terror had sent him backward, away from her, overriding the warrior's instinct to step forward into a killing strike. He shuddered, hoping Jynx didn't notice.

"So why didn't you come see me?" Jynx said.

He explained, shamed at having allowed the distractions.

Jynx just rolled her eyes. "Men!" But her smile held no irritation. It drew him in...

He reached for her hand and she gave it to him. Not a soft, delicate lady's hand, but slightly work-roughened, callused in unusual patterns from her work as an herbalist, and strong. Such a simple contact, to inflame such desire! He couldn't rush this woman, though, and valued her all the more for it. She was a bright gem, worth the time and effort. So for that night they talked, catching up on their lives for the year and some they'd been apart. Touches were limited to hands and faces—and a few soft kisses as morning neared.

She left as dawn's first blushes touched the sky, her lips brushing his in farewell.

He watched as she walked down the hallway, certain he heard Ick's approval in his head. She would support him as a mate for Jynx.

But he'd better not hurt her. Ever. In any way. Or he would once again face the wrath of a slither queen.

3. Queens

The conversation about Ick was perhaps the most difficult ever for Snake. He'd been born with the basic talent for Rapport with the slithers. Jynx hadn't. Yet somehow Ick had found and selected her for a partner. Somehow she'd managed a rudimentary communication with the slither anyway, as long as Ick did most of the work.

Jynx had told him in broad terms how she'd met Ick, but now he needed more details. How familiar was she already with the world he'd grown up in?

They walked together out into the tallgrass to gather herbs Jynx needed for cooking and medicines. To ease her burden, Snake carried the light satchel for plants. Truly, he should have carried the heavy slither instead, but he couldn't bring himself to offer her a ride. Nor could she keep up in the tall grasses on her own.

"We should have ridden," he said, trying to keep the irritation out of his voice. "It would be much faster and a lot less tiring."

Jynx arched both eyebrows at him. "It's easier to find what I'm looking for if I'm closer to the ground."

And that ended that.

So Snake felt mean and discourteous, while Ick rode wrapped around Jynx's waist. What he really wanted was to protect her from the slither, but Ick laughed at him for it. She seemed to think she was better for Jynx than he was.

"You met Ick in the Rainbow Sands, right?" he asked, turning his shoulder to the slither. "How did you end up there?"

"By accident. When Kahpur and I went looking for a healer, we'd never heard of the Slipaway Trail. We still hadn't figured it all out when it opened facing these beautiful golden sand dunes. We left the Trail to explore and it disappeared behind us. We had no idea where we were or how to get back to the tallgrass, so we just started walking."

Snake knew the Slipaway Trail from his and Kayde's travel with Jynx and Kahpur. Strange magic, there. The Trail changed destinations constantly on each end, and once on it, a traveler couldn't leave until he reached the other end. There was no control over the destination, so the knowledgeable traveler simply rode from end to end until he saw something that looked like it might be close to his destination and left its confines there. He could save days or weeks of travel—or take weeks more than expected.

"Just started walking? In the middle of the Rainbow Sands? I remember the journey my mother and I took when we left home. That's wicked traveling!"

"And Kahpur is so fair, her face looked like a glowing coal. We both blistered. My feet were practically shredded from popped blisters, until I couldn't even walk on them."

He could have lost Jynx then, before even meeting her! The thought left a deep crawling sensation in his gut. At least his mother had known what faced them and prepared them both as best she could.

They walked in silence for a while, with Snake trying to avoid getting close to Ick while staying close to Jynx. He tried to think how to tell her about Shyriel without just blurting it out. She knew the story of how Tchenya had nearly killed him, so she had some understanding, but she wouldn't be happy to hear this.

He wanted just to walk hand-in-hand with Jynx all day and never have to dull that brightness with the words he needed.

Maybe he would never have found them if Jynx hadn't given him an unavoidable opening.

"Why did you come?" she said, glancing at him from the corners of her eyes.

He felt the faint tension in the hand he held.

"Uhh..." *Great beginning, Snake*, he told himself.

Again she rescued him. "I know you said you'd be back if you could, but I think this trip isn't part of that promise."

The moment he dreaded, the one he couldn't put off any longer. He inhaled, long and slow, and took his time letting it out. "You're right. I came for another reason, and when I tell you, you may wish I hadn't come at all."

"Then don't pussyfoot around." She stopped and faced him boldly, but she didn't release his hand. "Just tell me."

Snake looked around hurriedly, hoping for a hilly outcropping or limestone bench to settle on, but there was nothing. He abandoned the idea and simply returned her direct look. "I came to talk to Ick."

After a brief, stunned silence, Jynx's eyebrows rose again. He felt Ick's buzz of interest in his head.

"Well, you certainly surprised me with that!" she said. "Why?"

He gathered his courage and suddenly remembered protocols from the white sands.

"Privately. It would be poor manners for me to say more without her guidance."

There. The hurt in her eyes he'd expected, and it hurt him to see it. Her face stilled as she turned toward Ick, hurt replaced by frustration. But apparently Ick got through to her on some level, because the buzzing in his head soon returned.

His reflex was to block it out, but he forced himself into Rapport. His alarm grew; he hadn't anticipated Ick's request.

He hadn't anticipated a number of things lately.

"She wants me to take her aside to talk. To actually carry

her away from you. Just for a few minutes. It won't take long. Rapport is faster than words." As if Jynx didn't know that.

She sighed. "This better be important, to cut me out like this." She reached for Ick's head to unwind her.

But Snake stepped up close to her, hands shaking, and Ick began to ooze from Jynx's waist to his. He closed his eyes and swallowed to avoid throwing up, trying to ignore Ick's amusement. Did she have to move so slowly? As if she wanted to prolong this?

Jynx's hands touched his face and his eyes opened. He bent to her waiting mouth and lost himself in a kiss that thankfully distracted him from Ick. Completely. Until Ick, her fun spoiled, "grumbled" that she was ready.

He even managed a big smile at Jynx as the kiss ended. Her eyes danced with mischief.

"We'll be just a few minutes."

"No hurry." Her voice sounded a bit husky. "I see a patch of feathertips I need to gather."

Skin crawling and the back of his neck cold, Snake strode away for a private conversation with the slither queen.

~~~

Snake walked downhill, toward the runoff creek at the bottom. There he found a fallen tree that looked fairly solid and sat on it gingerly until he knew it would bear his weight. Ick unwrapped herself from his waist—he shivered at the feel of her crawling against him—and stretched her length out on the trunk to bask in the sun.

Was she actually being kind? She could have coiled right next to him.

He felt her amusement in his head. For the first time he separated the "normal" feeling of Rapport from the crawling sensation of physical contact. If he didn't look at her, this might not be too bad.

Except that he still thought of her as a danger, and his

warrior instincts wouldn't allow him to turn his face away from danger. He compromised by looking elsewhere, with occasional twitches of his eyes to assure she hadn't moved.

"I had visitors recently," he told her. "Evron and Shyriel."

An explosion of wild joy rocked his head like a physical blow. He grunted, managed to keep his seat on the tree trunk.

"Ick, you're hurting my head. Calm! Please!" He felt her casting about for Shyriel, as if she were hiding nearby, in the tall grasses. "She's not here, Ick. I sent them back to the sands to wait."

Ick quieted a little, but he still heard the chaotic questions buzzing in his head. At least he had no trouble interpreting slither emotions in this Rapport!

His heart sank. If Ick chose Shyriel, the effect on Jynx... And for him to be part of hurting her so...

"Ick, I told her I would talk to you, that I would tell you what was said so you could choose." He closed his eyes, already feeling Jynx's grief and pain. "And then, if it's your choice, I'll take you back home to Shyriel. If you choose to stay with Jynx, they'll never hear from me, and they'll never trouble us again."

And he told the subdued slither everything that had been said, even the parts he was tempted to omit, about how desperate they were for her return.

When he told her about the thefts of slithers, her rage rocked him. He cried out, wrapping his arms around his head and toppled off the tree, moaning in pain.

The pain dropped to a hideous murmur as Ick controlled her reaction.

She had been one of the stolen ones. He should have remembered that sooner!

As she shared with him, Snake saw an image of a crate made of sticks, much too small for her size. She'd been cramped in the same position the entire time, with little water and no chance to hunt. She watched the other slithers die, but the thieves had no Rapport with which to feel the deaths, or the queen's anger. Then one came too close to an opening between the sticks of her crate...

With horror, Snake "saw" the strike with the tip of her tail into the arm of her captor, his fellows coming to help, two more quick tail stabs, the dropping of the crate as three men staggered away to die.

Fools, Ick said. *They knew of our venom but thought our fangs carried it, not our tails. Now they will never alert their friends to the truth.*

The men had died in the blue sands, and the next day Jynx and Kahpur had come across the bodies and rescued Ick, the lone survivor.

~~~

Ick gave Snake permission to share everything with Jynx, and he did. The blanched face made his beloved's eyes look larger than ever. She maintained the appearance of calm acceptance, but he read her pain in the tiny change in the tilt of her eyebrows and the muscle twitching in the side of her neck, beneath thick walnut hair.

She swallowed loudly. "Then I guess we'd better start early tomorrow and try to catch the Slipaway Trail. Maybe Kahpur will let us take the magic bowl with us, so we'll have food available. And I'll see if I can make an unguent to protect exposed skin from sunburn. And..."

"Jynx." Her name was a soft breath in Snake's mouth.

"You can't leave me behind!"

What could he say? That it was too dangerous? She already knew that. He searched her eyes, saw that she feared losing him as much as she did Ick.

Ick turned her emrel eyes on him and he dropped his gaze to avoid the hypnotic stare.

"Don't worry about that now," he told Jynx. "Ick hasn't said yet whether she'll go. Like a human being, she needs time to think about what she's heard."

"But she's so excited about reuniting with Shyriel."

"Of course she is. They bonded the day they were both born, and they've lived together every day since, until Ick was stolen in a raid. But you rescued her when she most needed you, even though you don't like snakes—which is how you saw her." He winced at the mental lash for calling the slither queen a snake. "You are bonded to Ick the same way Shyriel is bonded to Erilya, but without the background and training to ease the relationship."

"And no gift of Rapport."

Snake floundered for only a moment. "I disagree. She makes her will known to you, right? How could she speak to a stump? Clearly you have some level of Rapport, and probably a strong talent, to communicate with her at all, with no training or understanding of what you're doing."

Jynx crossed her arms in front of her. "You have a strong talent yourself, right? Will you teach me?"

Snake stared at her, speechless. "Learning to interpret slither emotions is a long process. No one is really considered fluent before reaching priest level."

"Priest level?"

"Acolyte, novice, priest, prophet. Priests are adults, at least twenty years old. I left as an acolyte, didn't even achieve novice rank. That means I'm almost as much a beginner as you are. I don't know how much I could teach you."

Then he saw her iron-jawed determination and sighed. "I can try. Just don't expect much."

"All I ask is that you try," she said. "It's important. After all, I'm going up against powerful competition."

With Ick riding Jynx again the walk back to town didn't take long, but it seemed to take forever. Jynx pestered Snake with questions the whole way, about the sands, and the three major clans—Prophecy, Praise, and Protection—about the slithers, the slither precincts and burrows.

He was amazed at how nebulous some of those old memories had become. And just as amazed at the startling clarity of others.

"Well, does the queen bear all the young, or can all the slithers become parents?"

He had never thought about it. But surely they all could create offspring.

"Do you get to name all the Youngens in your nest?"

No, they came with names.

"The priests name them? The ones in charge of the nurseries?"

Probably. He guessed.

"Why does the queen grow so much larger than the others? Why is her coloring different?"

How would he know? He was only eight when he left.

"Are they all as good-tempered as Ick?"

No.

"Did you ever have one that was mean?"

And he thought of Slyn. Lost, lonely, powerful, aberrant Slyn. Not mean, just difficult, and possibly a bit mad. The one he'd tried to protect by entering the queen's precinct, where he'd almost died.

Skin prickled and ice slid down his spine as he answered. And that was when he asked–insisted–that they change the subject.

Ick seemed to listen avidly but never joined the conversation. What was she thinking?

Twilight's deep color domed the world when he delivered Jynx to her door. He kissed her softly, feeling her hunger match his own.

"Snake," she said, "this should be your decision, too, not just Ick's. Perhaps it's time for you to return, to face your past head-on, so you can leave it in the past."

"I'll go if I have to, but only then. I've faced the past every day for twenty years and feel no need to return, except to keep my word–if it becomes necessary." And he silenced her response with another kiss.

But there was a price to pay for dwelling so much on his past. As expected, he paid it in nightmares.

~~~

Two days passed in quiet contentment—except for the decision hanging over Ick's head. Snake didn't hear her voice at all during that time, and even Jynx became anxious.

"I don't know what she's thinking, Snake. She hasn't really said anything to me, either." Jynx walked beside him, hand in hand, toward the upside down waterfall just outside of town. Even from here he heard the excited shrieks and laughter of the children riding to the top, then climbing out to race downhill and ride up again.

"I catch a little worry from her once in a while. When she notices me she sends her love and reassurance, but it's pretty non-specific. Mostly she's distant and absorbed, although some longing leaks out, too."

"She'll decide when she decides, Jynx. She's a queen, after all, and used to doing things in her own time and her own way." Snake's attention was drawn to a yellow-haired boy of about twelve who blocked the top of the waterfall, letting one of the little girls up only when she gave him a kiss.

Jynx laughed softly. "Stinky Pete used to do the same thing when Kahpur and I were about that age. Some things don't change, I guess."

She steered Snake past the waterfall, to where the river cut its way between grassy banks several feet high. A few minutes later the banks became overhangs and Jynx took him down a well-worn path to another grassy bank only a foot or two above the water.

Snake's eyes lit up. "What a welcoming place to spend a little time."

Jynx laughed again. "This is the town's trysting place for lovers. Secluded, comfortable, quiet, and of no interest to younger children."

"Really? I'd think they'd like it, like a hideout."

"There's nothing to do or see here that you can't experience in three minutes." Her eyes met his. "If you're a child. Besides, there are much better hideouts in other places." She drew him forward and settled next to him on the soft, springy grass.

Snake's heart quickened and he put a casual arm—as casual as he could manage at the moment—around her shoulders. She leaned her head against him.

"How likely are we to be discovered here?" he asked.

"I wouldn't worry," she said, meeting his blue-green eyes, "unless we get noisy."

He laughed, then, joy singing through his veins. And then he kissed her. And kept kissing as long as she kissed back. Which looked like it might be forever...

And then, just as things began to get interesting, Ick interrupted. *She's here! She's here!* was Snake's interpretation.

"Ouch!" Jynx sat bolt upright, holding her head.

Snake's heart sank. Of all the times for Ick to interfere. His body didn't want to be interrupted, and he groaned as he and Jynx pulled apart.

"What is Ick saying?" Jynx struggled to her feet, with Snake's help.

Suddenly the slither queen's "voice" disappeared.

Snake and Jynx stared at each other.

"Come on," he said, "We'd better check on her." He grabbed her hand and they started up the short path to the top of the bank.

"Is she talking about Shyriel? She thinks Shyriel is here? In Sayvil?"

Snake didn't know the answer to that, but he hoped it was no. Evron and Shyriel should be well on their way back to the Rainbow Sands.

As they neared the main street of the town, they heard screams and yells. Snake dropped Jynx's hand and ran, Ick's anger pounding into his head. Jynx hiked up her skirts and ran, too, but his long strides left her behind.

Ick lay coiled in the middle of the main street, not far from Ell's Stable. Two young men danced around near her, yelling, and another writhed on the ground nearby, screaming. Someone came running with a garden hoe, while Kahpur's voice cried, "Ick, what are you doing? Don't anybody hurt her!"

Snake burst into the middle of it and halted with one foot on either side of the queen. "Stop!" he commanded the man with the hoe. His battle voice thundered at the excited youths. "Get back!"

Kahpur arrived at the same time. "You idiots! This is Jynx's companion! Leave her alone!"

"It bit me!" screamed the youngster holding his arm. "I'm dying! It bit me!"

Jynx pounded up, hastily dropping her skirt over exposed knees. "What's all this about?" she demanded with admirable calm. "What's happened here? Potter?"

The man with the hoe dropped its butt into the dirt. "I heard screaming and saw your pet snake loose. It bit Loopy there, you can see the blood from here!"

Jynx turned her attention to the bitten youth. "She's not going to hurt you without a reason. What did you do to her?"

"Nothin'! I was mindin' my own business!"

The other young men joined in. "He was just walking past it, we didn't even see it, and it wham! Bit him!"

"I didn't even see it!" the injured youth echoed.

Snake gave him his best warrior glare—the one he used on new recruits while they were still stupid. "How could you not see a seven-foot critter winding along the street?"

"We was horsin' around, honest!" said another. "We wasn't looking down. Why would we watch the street for a giant snake?"

Giant? They had no idea.

"Loopy stepped on her." Jynx's lips thinned, anger glinting in her eyes. "On purpose, to see what would happen. She was defending herself." She gestured at the bleeding youth. "Come with me. I'll get that bite cleaned and bandaged for you."

"Is it poisonous? Am I dying?" His eyes were large with fear, his breathing rapid.

"She's not venomous. It just needs to be cleaned."

He followed her back toward her house. Potter walked away muttering, and Kahpur returned to the stable. The other two gave the still-coiled slither a wide berth and walked away.

Snake let down his warrior readiness with a sigh and addressed Ick. "What are you doing out here on the streets? People will be terrified of you."

He felt her satisfaction. Typical slither.

She turned emrel eyes toward him and he carefully didn't meet them. *I sense Shyriel.*

Snake must have misunderstood. "Shyriel is going back to wait, remember? I'm sorry I misunderstood, but please try again."

Her irritation came through clearly. And so did her conviction that Shyriel was here, in the tallgrass, and not too far away.

"If you'll allow it, I'll carry you and we'll go see. Have you told her where you are?"

No, she hadn't. She had given an image to Queen Shyriel but couldn't tell her how to get here from there. And yes, it would be faster if he carried her. And rode a horse.

Snake sighed. "It will take time to saddle the Beast." But he gave in to the sudden pressure in his head.

By the time the Beast was saddled, Jynx had returned from bandaging Loopy's bite. She wrapped Ick around her waist and Snake pulled her up behind him. They cantered out of town at Ick's urging. Apparently Shyriel was in some kind of trouble and needed help.

Snake couldn't get too excited about that, but he did have to react to it, to avoid the pounding headache that would come with Ick's "shouting." Within a matter of minutes she had them deep in the tallgrass, unable to see where they were going unless they found a limestone shelf or could see through the tall grasses from the top of a hill.

Ick's idea of rescue insisted on a straight line to Shyriel. They rode down steep banks, across muddy creeks and back up, instead of easy riding a hundred yards off this line, and there was no reasoning with her.

"What's that?" Jynx cried, grabbing Snake's shoulder.

"What's what?" Snake reined in sharply and the Beast half-reared in protest.

Jynx gasped and flung her arms around his waist, almost pulling them both off the gelding's rump.

The faint cry of birds resolved into a woman's cries and protests. Snake swung his head, searching for the source. There. To the northeast, perhaps a quarter mile.

Ick's mental shout hurt his head–and apparently Jynx's. She cried out, right in his ear. Snake winced.

Silence for an eerie moment. Not even a bird call or a whisper of a breeze.

A woman's voice shrieked, "Help! Help me!"

"Ick?" he turned the question, but the joy he felt from Ick was answer enough.

The woman cried out again. "Erilya! Help me!"

With an inner sigh, more annoyance than relief, Snake signaled the Beast forward. "Shyriel! It's Snake! Keep calling!"

But the voice that answered was Evron's clear baritone, and he called out every few moments until Snake rode through a thick patch of bright pink catclaw and found them.

Shyriel's long hair was caught in the branches of a scrub oak. Evron was trying to untangle the tresses but only made it worse, the fine filaments knotting as he worked. He had a knife in his hand, but the young queen kept slapping his hands away. "You will not cut my hair!" she snarled at him. "Don't even think you might!"

"My queen, you're caught!" Evron argued, still trying to reach a branch. "I can cut the branches if you'll just hold still."

Jynx slid off the Beast's back with the help of Snake's strong grip on her hand and started through the grasses toward the queen. Ick's head reached in front of her, toward Shyriel, weaving back and forth.

A sick feeling clawed at Snake's belly. He didn't want to see the two queens being reunited, or Jynx's pain when it happened. Helpless to prevent it, he dismounted and ground tied his horse, then followed Jynx. Slowly.

Jynx negotiated the thick grasses and thin branches easily. Nothing seemed to catch at her clothing and hair. Snake bulled his way through behind her, ignoring the small rips in exposed skin.

"Here, move back. Out of my way." Jynx pushed Evron aside before he even realized she'd taken charge. As he moved, she nipped the knife out of his hand.

Snake felt Ick's pride in her, which was gratifying. At least she hadn't pushed Jynx away to reunite with Shyriel.

Without asking and without introduction, Jynx deftly cut small branches from the scrub oak, freeing Shyriel's hair. "Now if you'll stand still, I'll remove these twigs from your hair," Jynx told her.

Shyriel's pale face took on some color and she quieted. Only a swipe of her hand and a quick sniffle revealed her tears of a moment before. The human queen's attention turned to the slither queen. She ignored Jynx as she might a servant.

Snake took warning from Jynx's lifted chin and tightened lips. Why didn't Shyriel see it? Apparently Ick hadn't made any introductions he hadn't been privy to. He tried not to sigh aloud.

"Shyriel, what are you doing here?" he exploded. "I told you to go home and wait."

"Your way," snapped Shyriel, "would have been an easy way to say no. I can't accept no." She turned toward Jynx, ignoring the woman and holding out her arms to the slither.

Ick practically threw herself from Jynx's waist to Shyriel's arms. Jynx gasped, eyes wide with shock, as the slither abandoned her.

The beautiful creature flicked her tongue against the human queen's cheek, her ear, her eyelids as Shyriel laughed in delight. Snake saw—and remembered—the caress of lightly squeezing coils, but the memory was overlaid by the feel of Tchenya's coils constricting. For a moment he couldn't breathe.

And then Jynx's small hand rested on his forearm. He felt the shame of his wince at her touch, followed by gratitude at how that touch stabilized him.

When the excited greetings finally began to calm, Shyriel spoke to Snake, still ignoring Jynx completely. "Now," she said, "we can go home."

4. The Slipaway Trail

"I haven't heard Ick say she wants to go home." Jynx's soft voice hung in the air.

For the first time, Shyriel looked directly at her, her eyes as flat and emotionless as a slither, as haughty as Ick. She deliberately looked her up and down, then turned away. "Kyr, you may send your servant away now. She's no longer needed for Erilya's transport."

Snake's mouth dropped open. He felt Ick's shock with Jynx's.

And then Jynx's small hand doubled into a fist and she punched the queen right in the mouth, her entire weight behind the blow, as Kahpur had taught her.

Shyriel flailed for balance and fell, her long tresses again tangling with scrub oak. She landed with a shriek and Ick went flying, landing on a small, bare hillock where she coiled and hissed at everyone.

"Don't condescend to me, Shyriel. Ick is as much my companion as yours. We've faced danger and hardship together. We've saved each other's lives more than once. That's a closer bond than you'll ever have! Far more than simply sharing a birthday."

Snake tried to sense Ick's reaction, but she wasn't sharing with him. He didn't doubt she was sharing with one or both of the women, though.

"Evron!" Shyriel shrieked. "Do something!"

Jynx didn't follow up her attack. Instead she stalked past the queen and went directly to Ick, who hissed at her.

"Do what, my queen?" asked Evron, spreading his hands helplessly. "Here, let me cut your hair loose." He closed his mouth before "again" escaped.

Jynx sat cross-legged near Ick, just out of easy range. Her voice murmured, but Snake couldn't make out the words over the sounds of Shyriel's anger.

He stepped closer to Shyriel. "Out here, you're not a queen. Out here there are no queen. Or kings." He hardened his voice and his eyes. "Out here you're no more important than Jynx or anyone else, including me, and you contribute a hell of a lot less to the world around you. You're behaving as no child older than three would ever behave here. Grow up.

"And if you disparage Jynx again, I'll leave you to find your own way out of the tallgrass." He glared at her another moment before joining Jynx near Ick.

The young woman's chin lifted. "I am your queen, Kyr, whatever you think," she called after him. "You will treat me with respect!"

"No, you're not my queen. I've told you before. And you will respect the life I've chosen."

A light touch on his arm drew his attention back to Jynx. She'd left Ick and come to him, and he'd not noticed. A slight tilt of her head, and he followed her away from where Evron still struggled to free Shyriel's hair. Away from Ick.

Her face was still, but the tilt of her eyebrows told him she wrestled with some trouble.

At last, sighing, she stopped to face him. "Poor Ick," she said. "She's caught between Shyriel and me. She's bonded to both of us, and we both want to remain her partner, and to live in our own homes, half a world apart."

"She'll have to choose soon."

"She doesn't see why she needs to choose at all."

Snake blinked in surprise. "How can she not?"

"I don't know. Shyriel and I seem to have become instant rivals, but Ick loves us both. Unfortunately for me, she also feels responsible for the People." Jynx wrung her hands at her waist. "She'll be returning to the People with Shyriel, to see if she can help set things right. That doesn't mean she'll stay; she hasn't decided on that yet."

Snake ran a hand through his dark hair, making his slither tattoo seem to snarl. "I know you'll miss her, Jynx, but I think she's made a good decision. Her appearance will give heart to the People."

Jynx laughed, but it held no joy. "I'm going with her, Snake. I don't trust either Shyriel or Evron to get her home safely. Shyriel is a babe in the woods. Or tallgrass. I want to be sure Ick is safe."

"I'm not comfortable with you making that trip, Jynx. It's long, arduous, and dangerous. You won't know anyone, and the language is different enough to make problems for you. Essentially, you'll be alone, except for Ick."

Jynx's smile lit up her eyes and she leaned toward him, lifting her face. "I was hoping you might decide to come along. To keep me safe."

~~~

Of course Jynx got her way. How could Snake say no to her? He certainly couldn't let her go to that place unprotected. He'd be beside himself with fear for her every minute of her absence.

He settled Shyriel and Evron at the Blue Goose, in rooms as far from his as he could manage. Ick chose to stay with Shyriel at night and Jynx by day, but even Snake could feel how torn she was between the two women. At least she'd informed Shyriel, including Jynx in the conversation, that as far as she was concerned, Jynx was as much a queen a the younger woman. After all, no one could bond with a slither queen but a human queen, and Jynx was bonded, just as Shyriel was.

Snake's thoughts turned to logistics. They'd need packhorses as well as their own mounts, and they'd have to find mounts for Shyriel and Evron. Kahpur could probably provide them. "I doubt Shyriel has ever ridden a horse, except in special processions," he told Jynx.

"Horses? In the desert?"

That sounded a bit skeptical. "Yes, there are some beautiful and intelligent horses that live in the Rainbow Sands—not just among the People, either—but so far few have been bred in the white sands."

They sat side by side on the stone wall next to Ell's Stable, the same wall where Jynx and Kahpur had spent much time in gossip. In a strange way, he could almost feel the echoes of her hours on this wall. Ick lay stretched in the sun on the other side of Jynx.

"Not having horses will be slower," Jynx said, "but having horses for Shyriel and Evron, who can't ride well, we'd be even worse off. They take a lot of food and water, and we'd have to haul it with us. Traveling by shank's mare would be just as fast, with much less to carry."

Snake snorted. "You just don't like riding," he teased.

One delicate eyebrow arched. "I like riding just fine. Kahpur taught me, you know. And you've seen me ride."

"There's also the question of what to do with the horses when we reach the Rainbow Sands. They need a lot of water, and there's not much available in the Sands, except for the blue sands. Besides, I won't trust the Beast to just any stable, and he wouldn't be safe for just any caretaker, either."

"Good. That's settled, then. We walk. I'll see about borrowing Kahpur's refilling bowl for food. Or water. Too bad Kayde isn't coming. He could be our packhorse."

Snake burst out laughing, in his mind a vivid image of his huge friend loaded down with packs and satchels.

Jynx grinned back at him. "So, when should we depart? Tomorrow morning?"

Snake sobered, nodding. "The sooner the better. I want to get this over with."

"Looks like I need to get busy, then," said Jynx. "And so do you." She looked over at Ick, as still as if she were listening. "Ick is excited to go back home," she reported. "She enjoys the sun-warmed stone, but she longs for sun-heated sand she can burrow into. And for her... palace?"

"The queen's precinct has a golden path leading up to the doorway and the entrance itself is begemmed. No human but the human queen knows what it's like inside, as far as I know. It's as close to a palace as you can get in the white sands."

"Poor thing has had to live in abject poverty this whole time." But Jynx's voice was light, and Ick stuck her tongue out at her–a disturbingly human gesture, though the tongue fluttered.

Jynx held her hand out to the slither, who tickled her palm with a forked tongue.

"Here comes Shyriel," Snake warned.

"There went that good mood. I'll bet she disapproves of the way Ick and I interact. And since I don't want to see her point her nose in the air and sniff, I'm off to talk to Kahpur." She stood. "Ick are you staying here or coming with me?"

Snake felt Ick's wistfulness as she coiled on the wall and watched Jynx walk away. The slither, to his surprise, was as accessible and easy to read–usually–as the slithers in his childhood nest. Or perhaps she was simply opening up to him more, now that he'd be taking her back to the warm sands.

A quick glance back at Shyriel showed that Jynx was right. She did have her nose in the air. He set himself to claim unequivocal leadership for this journey. With his military experience, Shyriel would have to capitulate, but she'd probably make him pay for it–maybe by pretending he worked as her servant, not as a temporary superior. He sighed and rose to greet her.

~~~

Finding the Slipaway Trail took days, but it felt like forever to Jynx. She sighed in exasperation, something she'd done often since they'd left Sayvil. Miss Priss, as usual, had her nose in the air, spoke to Jynx only when she had to—and then with a command in her voice—and expected everyone else to do all the work.

"A queen in the sands is highly respected, but she doesn't have servants," Snake muttered the first day out. "I notice she isn't quite so high-handed with us men. I wonder what's going on?"

"We're rivals for Ick, remember? Although I can't imagine that being an attitude Ick will put up with for long." Jynx strode down the road, moving freely in scandalous britches, while Shyriel struggled in her airy cotton robes. "And she's after you, as well."

"She calls me a 'man of destiny,' as if it's something to be proud of," he grumbled. "It's like she expects something of me but expects me to know what it is."

Men! They could be so obtuse! "Do you mean saving the People from a natural decline? Or do you mean her infatuation with you?"

"Her... what?"

Jynx couldn't help it. She giggled. "You should see your face! You really don't know that she's flirting every chance she gets? It's no accident she walks ahead of you whenever she can, or that she reaches for the apple in the bowl at the same time you do."

The look on his face was priceless. How many men had so little vanity they wouldn't notice a pretty young girl trying to get their attention? No wonder she fell in love with him— although they'd never used that word between them. Of course, his tall, slender body and graceful way of moving did set him apart. And so did those unusual blue-green eyes.

She cut off her thoughts before they could turn to daydreams.

The road northeast wound through hills of limestone and flint covered with grasses and a myriad of plants that drew Jynx's eye. Many were great for medicinal purposes, while others were simply beautiful. They grew in every color, from violet-striped pale pink beardtongue to deep gold paperflower to bright orange butterfly milkweed. She took a few minutes to dig up milkweed roots to supplement dinner tonight. A little could be kept on hand in case of medical need, too. She also collected a bit of hawkweed for indigestion or snakebite. Had Shyriel ever seen an actual snake?

"There it is!" shouted Snake.

Jynx looked up sharply as Snake bullied Evron and Shyriel into a run. Two tall sentinel trees guarded the entrance to a smooth path–trees too tall and sturdy for the tallgrass. Vines wrapping each tree bore reddish purple flowers that didn't exist in the tallgrass. She broke into a run, stuffing the hawkweed into her satchel as she ran.

An opaque, silvery screen suddenly hid the space between the sentinels. Golden sparks snapped softly as they approached.

Snake plowed to a stop as the curtain shimmered. His outstretched arms blocked Shyriel and Evron from darting between the trees, but Jynx had already slowed to a stop.

Then the trees disappeared, and the path between them. Once again only the tallgrass hills could be seen, big bluestem grass waving gently in a light breeze.

Shyriel turned on Snake. "We could have made it! Why did you stop us?"

His eyes were as hard as Jynx had ever seen them. "I don't know what happens if you're partly on the Trail and partly outside it when it shifts. I'd hate to leave part of someone behind."

Jynx knew by his prickled forearms that he remembered almost finding that answer the hard way. The Beast's speed was all that had gotten him back in time. Her own skin pimpled with the memory.

"Besides," he went on, "we'd have left Jynx behind."

Shyriel shrugged.

Jynx's anger surged.

"We leave no one behind." Snake spoke as sharply as nails being pounded into wood. "It's all of us or none of us."

Shyriel opened her mouth but Snake shut her off. "Or you can get yourselves home."

And part with Ick so soon? Jynx's heart almost stopped, though she knew he was bluffing.

Brief uncertainty flashed across the queen's face, gone almost before it appeared. "We got here without you. We can find our way home."

Now she was bluffing. Snake was part of a prophecy; she needed to take him back to the sands with her.

And Snake needed to go, whether he wanted to or not. He needed to face his past.

The buzzing in Jynx's head said Ick agreed.

The next days passed much like the first, with the addition of Shyriel's barbed comments aimed at Jynx's occasional side trips to gather herbs. Even though Jynx always caught up and never slowed down the group.

On the fifth day, they got a late start because Shyriel's feet hurt from so much walking.

Jynx examined the two tiny blisters and considered. She herself wouldn't have thought to complain, let alone hold up progress, for such small hurts.

She sighed heavily. She was a healer. She would heal. Good thing she'd been gathering herbs as they traveled—even over Shyriel's protests.

They stopped and built a fire, so Shyriel could get off her feet and Jynx could cut up and mash some yucca roots. She added a few drops from a glass vial in her satchel, slathered the paste on Shyriel's two blisters and tied a bandage around them. She added some downy milkweed seeds to cushion the queen's footsteps and they were soon on their way again.

And finally, that afternoon, they saw the Slipaway Trail again. This time it appeared between two hills, half a mile distant, and they ran. Even Shyriel, limping heavily, ran as best she could, until Snake swept her up in his arms and carried her.

This time deep purple flowers, almost black, vined the sentinels. As they passed the trees and stepped onto the path itself, Jynx smelled the faint odor of something dry and musty–and maybe rotting.

Then they were inside the Trail and stopped to catch their breaths. Shyriel sank onto the grassy verge with a groan, clutching the blistered foot. Evron leaned over, hands on knees, panting. Jynx breathed a little harder than usual, but it hadn't been that far. And Snake didn't seem aware of having run at all. Once again Jynx admired his strength and... well, masculinity, to be honest.

"Now what?" asked Evron. He was looking around at the tall trees whose branches met overhead, blocking much of the sunlit blue sky. And at the impenetrable brush filling all the space between the trees on both sides of the path. And beyond them, to the blank gray fog that, according to the stories, began an endless nothing–a place where nothing existed. Evron's eyes were large and dark, and Jynx understood immediately. Used to the much opener space of the Rainbow Sands, he looked trapped, hemmed in on every side.

Shyriel took it much better.

Due to her youth? Or to spending more of her life in enclosed areas like the queen's burrow?

"We make camp," Snake answered Evron. "At the least, we have a meal and a chance to rest while we wait."

"We have a choice," Jynx added, ignoring Shyriel. "We can stay here, waiting for the Trail to open somewhere closer to our destination, or we can walk its length to see where the other end opens. Do you prefer to spend your time waiting or walking?" She began unpacking what she needed to prepare a meal. Except Kahpur's magic bowl. No reason to reveal its existence until she had to.

"We will stay here," decided Shyriel. "We may have much walking yet when we leave the Trail, so we will rest up, heal sore feet and muscles, and be better prepared for the most difficult part of our journey."

Ick's buzzing in Jynx's head indicated agreement, so she wasn't surprised when Snake agreed, too.

"If we get bored, we can still travel to the far end once in a while." Snake settled on the verge next to Jynx, shedding his packs.

Jynx stifled a sigh. She wasn't good at either sitting or waiting. Add in Shyriel's constant presence, and this could be the longest part of the journey, from her perspective.

5. The Rainbow Sands

Snake was bored. He'd been on the Trail often enough it no longer seemed fascinating. He admitted to curiosity about that strange fog beyond the enclosing brush, but he had no tools to chop through to it. And he didn't care enough.

"My feet hurt too much to walk to the other end just for something to do," Shyriel told him, nose in the air, when he suggested hiking to the other end.

But this sitting and waiting was tiresome, and he felt himself becoming grouchy. He tried to hold it in, but he could tell by Jynx's face that he seldom succeeded.

The Trail first opened on water as far as they could see. Gray waves slapped at the trunks of the sentinel trees but didn't enter. The sky was leaden, with black clouds to the... south? Direction had no meaning here. Wind howled and screamed but also remained outside, as if the Trail held some invisible barrier there.

Snake glanced at blue sky overhead, visible through the over-arching branches of the trees. As if the Trail were separated from the rest of the world and set apart, a little world all its own. He shuddered. Nothing ever changed here, not even the scars on the trees or the packed dirt of the path. He could see their footprints now, but if they went to the other end and returned, the prints would be gone. The impossibility of it made him uneasy.

The shimmering silver curtain closed the view of the sea. It reopened a few minutes later on a flat, hard-baked plain under a powerful sun. How could life exist here?

The next opening revealed farmland, with sturdy crops in neat rows and soft smoke spiraling up from the chimney of a well-cared-for house. He thought he saw chickens in the yard before the Trail closed again.

A distant view of a village with dusty streets.

Rolling hills covered with bison, which he'd heard of but never seen. Jynx knew of them, though, and named them for him. They weren't close enough for a good look, although here the Trail remained open for hours before moving again.

Jagged snowy peaks, caught in a winter blizzard. The Kingdom of the Snows? The shape of the peaks indicated a different mountain range; these weren't tall enough.

The top of a waterfall, where a single step out of the Trail would send a man plunging a hundred feet or more, carried by thundering water.

With an irritated snort, Snake rolled up in his blanket, turned his back on the opening, and slept.

In the morning—if that's what it was—he grouchily roused everyone and pushed them to walk, Shyriel's tender toes be damned. At least walking was something to do, and it was good for their muscles. And for his mood.

The far end of the Trail opened atop the land bridge—a natural arch formation that spanned the distance between two continents.

"What do you think, Snake? Is this a good place to leave the Trail?" Jynx had appeared silently at his elbow, as if she'd been there all along.

He shook his head. "We're still too far. The white sand is near the south end of the continent, so we'd have more than half the continent to travel yet. We can't even be sure which end of the bridge this is."

Jynx tucked her hand into his elbow. "I'll be glad when we

get close enough to leave the Trail. Her royal prissiness is getting on my nerves. Evron spends a lot of time rolling his eyes, I rarely get to visit with Ick anymore, and you're grouchy all the time."

Snake looked at her, offended. "I am not grouchy. Just bored. I'm not used to such intense... inactivity."

"I'm surprised you haven't been practicing your sword forms. Is there not enough space here?"

Snake studied the path and its grassy verges. "You know, I could. I'd have to adjust some of my foot patterns and use both verges and the path itself, but I could do that." Why hadn't he thought of it?

And so at least twice a day Snake took his sword a little ways from the group and trained until sweat rolled down his bare chest and back in rivers and his muscles blazed with an aching fire.

He always felt better afterward, physically and mentally, and besides, he liked seeing the heat rise in Jynx's eyes as she watched.

Too bad he could do nothing about it here.

Too bad Shyriel's reaction was similar. That complication he could do without.

~~~

In the evenings, Evron sang. His rich baritone was deeper than Snake's and he had a seemingly endless list of songs. Many were songs of praise for the gods and their messengers, the slithers, but he also knew some secular ones. Snake taught him some bawdy drinking songs from the Snows. Evron learned them in one hearing.

A tiny triumph tickled Snake's throat. Evron's grasp of the language was thin at best; he'd be shocked if he knew what the words actually meant. So would Shyriel.

In exchange for the new songs, Evron spent some time teaching Snake and Jynx some of the polyglot spoken between the various tribes of the Rainbow Sands, a patchwork of languages, accompanied by gestures, and Snake recognized bits of it from his childhood.

Conversations between Evron and Shyriel brought back language skills that he'd thought lost many years before. Since Evron didn't seem inclined to teach that language, he taught what he could to Jynx, along with teaching her what he could about communication with the slithers and the culture of the white sands.

"Thank you," she said, heart in her eyes. "It's thoughtful of you to include me, when those two prefer a private language."

"Private language?" Snake turned the magic bowl upright and watched it fill with wild lettuce, mashed roots, and juicy fruits, exactly like the ones it had held before. Jynx had given up hiding it the first day out. Too bad there was no meat to be had. He might have to produce the penkin, just for the venison.

"They like being able to talk without fear that I'll know what they're saying. Ick has taken Shyriel to task over it, but she won't budge."

"You're telling me it's a deliberate act, aimed at you." Snake felt a surge of anger of Jynx's behalf.

"It's fine," Jynx assured him. "It irritates me that they do this, but Ick has begun translating everything they say for me. Without telling them."

Snake had to laugh, then pretended not to see the questioning look Shyriel sent his way. "Good for her. I could almost grow to like her, if she weren't a slither." He suddenly grabbed his head with both hands. "Ow!" And felt Ick's smugness at chastising him so... appropriately.

For a moment neither spoke. Then Snake met Jynx's eyes, serious again. "I wish we'd find the opening we need. I'm tired of this Trail. It's beginning to feel too confined, like there's no room to move and very little room to breathe."

Jynx nodded. "Me, too. I'm not looking forward to the sands, but after a while the Trail is just plain boring."

"I almost wish we'd brought horses after all. The Beast would have kept things interesting." He smiled, remembering some of the Beast's favorite pranks, like chewing the fletching off Snake's arrows if he forgot to secure the quiver properly. The smile only applied to memories, though. The Beast rarely got that reaction in real life.

"By the time we get back, he'll be a different horse," said Jynx. "Kahpur won't put up with his tricks. She'll have turned him into a well-behaved, biddable mount by then."

Snake grinned. "Even Kahpur might not manage that!"

As always, he was careful to sleep across the fire from Jynx, just to avoid temptation. One of these days, though... He fell asleep to dreams of Jynx's beautiful smile—and more.

He awoke with bright sun on his face. He started to roll over, away from it, but his eyes blinked open and he forgot about sleeping.

"Up! Everyone up! Hurry!" He bounced to his feet, grabbing his belongings. Jynx was snatching satchels before she was even on her feet.

Shyriel groaned and turned.

Snake saw the set of Jynx's jaw and left the queen to her. He held out a hand to Evron and hauled him up. "We've got to go!" he shouted. "Now!"

Jynx dragged a protesting queen to her feet and shoved her toward the Trail opening, where fresh sunlight poured over coppery sand dunes. Then she wrapped Ick around her waist before bolting off the Trail and onto the sand, under an enormous sun, followed by the men.

Behind them, the Slipaway Trail disappeared.

~~~

Stepping off the cool, shaded Trail into the Rainbow Sands shocked Snake's senses. Above, a blazing blue sky seemed to shimmer in the hot air that crushed his lungs. The white-yellow sun, the blue-white sky, and the metallic copper dunes splashed brilliant color across the world, accented by the sparse browns and greens of vegetation.

He wanted to bend over beneath the pressure of heat and light, to duck back into the cool Trail–and might have, had it still been there. If he'd thought the tallgrass was overexposed to the sky, this was worse. Little shade existed anywhere, except in the shadow of the undulating dunes.

As his body began to adjust, he straightened his shoulders and breathed more easily. He looked for Jynx.

For the blink of an eye he thought he saw fear in her eyes, but he must be mistaken. Jynx had never been afraid of anything in her life. Not even when he'd abducted her, the first time he saw her.

"Which way from here?" he asked Evron.

The priest looked around uncertainly. "South, if I can figure out where south is."

Snake and Jynx looked at each other then together turned and pointed. "That's south," said Jynx.

Shyriel's nose went up. "Are you sure? How do you know, if you've never been here before?"

"Oh, I've been here. This sand is a perfect match for my friend Kahpur's hair." Jynx smiled. "I poured some on her head just to be sure. But direction is a gift of the sun's position, not of the sand's color."

"Thank you," said Evron, striding in that direction.

Shyriel stared at Jynx for a moment before falling into step beside him.

"She really doesn't like you," Snake murmured to Jynx as they followed. "Don't turn your back on her."

"I try not to take it personally," she replied in the same low tone. "I'd probably feel the same way if I grew up with Ick and then she bonded with someone else."

In mid-afternoon, before they crossed into blue sand, Jynx made each of them a lidded jug from copper sand. They were a little lopsided and uneven, but they were secure. Three steps into the skystone-blue sand, she filled all the jugs with blue sand.

"For now," she instructed them, "you can drink by putting handsful of blue sand in your mouth. It will turn to water. Later, we may need to rely on whatever blue sand we can carry in our jugs."

Shyriel laughed, unbelieving.

Jynx's eyes narrowed. "The blue sand is where we met Ick."

Shyriel started. "Here? This is where you found her?"

"Well, not right here. I don't think. But in the blue sand, at least."

Shyriel made a face but Evron's hand on her arm stilled her. And maybe Ick's buzzing in her head. Apparently she liked the idea of drinking sand even less than Snake. Who knew what had crawled over or through the sand, after all?

"We rescued her from a crate made of sticks. The dead men nearby carried waterskins filled with blue sand. That's how we discovered it would turn to water in our mouths. Trust me. It's real water, and it can keep us alive."

Shyriel and Evron looked at each other, as if sharing an important private thought. Then Shyriel spun on the blue sand and walked off. Or tried to spin, at least. Sand sprayed out from her feet as she turned, pulling her off balance. She staggered before hitting her stride, cheeks red.

Snake glanced at Jynx, who struggled to keep her face neutral. At least where the queen could see.

As they had in the copper sand, the group rested often in whatever shade they could find at the foot of blue dunes. Jynx insisted they drink plenty of blue sand. "After all, water is the most essential part of maintaining good health."

"And what's the second most essential?" asked Shyriel, challenge in her tone.

"Exercise," said Jynx. "The more physical labor we do, the better our bodies function. Unless we overwork the body until it breaks down, of course. That's why servants and laborers are likely to outlive their less active masters."

As Evron guided the queen out of shade and back into sunlight, Snake murmured, "Is that the real answer? I saw you start to say something else."

"For her? The real answer is 'keeping your mouth shut.' What do you bet that by the end of the day she'll want someone else to carry Ick for her?"

Snake laughed softly. He glanced at the others from the corner of his eye. Since they were paying no attention, he lightly kissed the tip of Jynx's nose, then grinned at her, pleased to see her cheeks turn pink and her eyes light up. Her beautiful smile warmed his heart as they followed the other two.

The texture of the blue sand wasn't the same as the finer-grained copper sand. The copper's tiny grains were almost like powder, while the more granular blue sand grains were still tiny enough that they weren't too scary to throw into the mouth.

Snake learned fast that he would be wise to allow the grains to sit on his tongue for a moment before swallowing, to allow the sand to transform. He suspected Jynx had deliberately withheld that detail when Shyriel choked on a handful of sand before it changed, then spewed water. Jynx's twinkling eyes gave her away.

Jynx also had two... veils? Headdresses, at least, with shoulder-length veils down the back and sides to protect head and neck from the sun. She wore one and gave the other to him.

He discovered the lower part of the veil could be pulled across the lower face for protection from wind-driven sand, too. Where had she gotten them?

"I made them, based on the ones on the bodies Kahpur and I found in the sands. I knew they'd be valuable, so I made sure we had them," Jynx told him.

"You didn't make enough for all of us?" Snake asked. As usual, they climbed and descended dunes well behind the queen and the priest. He suspected Jynx managed that deliberately, to let them break trail.

She shrugged. "They're from the Rainbow Sands. I assumed they'd have their own headdresses. Veil things. Whatever they're called."

One corner of his mouth quirked up. "And other supplies and equipment, right?"

"I'm feeding everyone, with Kahpur's bowl. But I don't see them providing anything at all for us. Except orders perhaps. They weren't even going to mention that blue sand is drinkable."

"They may not have known. After all, they came by ship."

Jynx looked up in surprise. "By ship? From the desert?"

He had to laugh. "They walked south from the white sands to the hills in that area and rode a river barge to the west coast, where they caught a sailing ship north, under the land bridge, to the Kingdom of the Snows."

She stared at him, then smiled ruefully. "There are no ships or barges in the tallgrass, except on the river that runs through Brizze, and honestly, it never occurred to me. We just don't think in terms of ships, living so far from the coasts."

"Sun's coming up," he said, watching a pale streak of sky to the east. "Time to find a place to sleep for the day."

"I hope that woman is taking good care of Ick. If anything happens to her..."

"Ick's fine, Jynx. Shyriel has been raised with slithers, especially Ick. She knows how to care for her partner."

Jynx's mouth tightened. "*My* partner. As much as hers."

"Just... try not to punch her again, no matter what she says or does."

"Want me to whistle them to stop and wait for us?"

She was changing the subject. He'd never met a woman so obstinate! Or so good-hearted and caring. With an inaudible sigh, he nodded.

Jynx put two fingers in her mouth and whistled.

"Aaggghhh!" Snake slapped his hands over his ears. "You should have warned me!" Kayde probably heard that whistle all the way up in the Snows.

Ahead of them, Shyriel and Evan stopped, glancing at the sky, then began searching for a sheltered place to spend the day.

The best they could do wasn't ideal. They had to settle for dune shadows, and twice during the day they had to move when the sun did. Sleeping in such heat provided little true rest, but at least they didn't waste energy walking directly under the sun's malevolence.

As the sun at last disappeared behind the blue dunes, leaving a cerulean sky behind, Jynx once again brought out the bowl and they all helped themselves to breakfast–the same as supper last night and lunch the day before. As they ate, Shyriel took a deep breath and addressed Jynx directly–and civilly, for once. She still didn't call her by name, Snake noted with irritation.

"Tell me everything about finding Erilya," she commanded. "How many slithers, how many men, where they were from, what they wore, every detail you can remember."

Jynx's eyes lit up and Snake could almost see the wheels of curiosity turning. Come to think of it, why was Shyriel just now asking questions Snake would have asked long since?

Evron watched her closely, as if watching a daughter do as he'd coached her to do. Given the queen's obvious dislike for Jynx, it had likely been necessary to get the questions asked at all.

"Didn't Ick tell you everything?" Jynx asked.

Shyriel bristled. "Please use her real name, not that stupid nickname you've given her. She is royalty!"

Jynx shrugged. "If she minded, she'd tell me."

The flash of tightening lips revealed Shyriel's anger, or at least irritation. "She has told me what she can, but a slither perspective is not a human perspective. You may be aware of something she wouldn't notice."

Snake was pleasantly surprised at the insight, then wondered if that had come from Evron, too. Maybe he simply hadn't given Shyriel enough credit for intelligence.

Jynx looked at Ick, where she lay coiled next to Shyriel. The slither queen politely didn't meet her eyes, lest Jynx be unable to think or move until released. But as the look held on, Shyriel's face grew darker and darker.

At last Jynx looked back to the human queen. "I can't add a lot to what she's already told you. There were three men, as I've said before. They all wore similar desert robes and headdresses like ours, but the fat man's clothing was of a finer weave. We called him the Leader because he was at the front of the group. Four or five crates made of sticks sat nearby, each with a dead snake–slither–in it, except the largest crate, which held Ick. That's pretty much all I can tell you that she hasn't. Oh, and the men all died of poisoning."

"Poison?" Shyriel's eyes widened, then narrowed. "Are you sure? How do you know?"

"Their tongues were black. That generally signals death by poison."

Shyriel's face blanked, as if she turned inward. Communing with the slither again. Snake knew that look well.

He spoke to Jynx in a low voice. "So Ick killed all three of the men? I wonder how she managed that, confined in a too-small crate."

"Ick killed them? How? She's not venomous!"

"Of course she is! All slithers are, although the venom doesn't come in until they're about six feet long."

Jynx's skin visibly prickled. "Well, it's a good thing she'd never bite me, then."

Snake hated to break the news to her. "Slithers' venom isn't in their fangs," he told her. "It's in the tip of that pointy tail."

She swayed where she sat and he put a hand on her arm to steady her, glad for any excuse to touch her. "Jynx? Are you all right?"

"And I carried her all that time? Wrapped around my waist? Crawling all over me?"

"Jynx, relax. You're blocking her out and it worries her. She's getting frantic." Not that she could tell by looking, of course. He was the one Ick was pummeling through their Rapport. "And she would never hurt you anyway, by tooth or tail." He glanced at Shyriel from the corner of his eye. "Don't give her the satisfaction," he murmured.

Jynx straightened her back and shoulders. Her face regained its normal calm and color returned. "She hears Ick's reaction, too?"

"No, Ick was talking to me, not to her."

"So, Ick can talk to anyone?"

"Anyone with a gift of Rapport, yes. Evron doesn't have it, but the rest of us do."

"Hold on a moment." Jynx's eyes lost focus as she dropped back into Rapport to reassure Ick. "As we walk, she'll fill me in on everything she's told Shyriel."

Snake nodded, face barely visible as darkness covered the sands. "We need to be on our way," he announced to the group. "We're getting a late start as it is."

"I can carry Ick tonight," Jynx offered to Shyriel. "I know she gets heavy after a while."

Shyriel regarded her regally, then nodded. "I think I will like having a servant," she commented. "You will carry Erilya for me from now on. Do not take that as permission to speak with her."

Jynx flared, close enough to losing her temper to make Snake wince. "I don't need your permission to speak with my friend. You're not my queen and I don't take your orders."

"She is my partner, not yours." Shyriel's eyebrows almost met above the bridge of her nose.

"That's still to be determined, isn't it?"

Snake and Evron simultaneously stepped between the two women, took an elbow, and started them in the right direction. Ick was wrapped securely around Jynx.

Snake thought her colors seemed paler than usual. Perhaps she was just torn between the two women who loved her—and hated each other.

6. Black Sand

They spent four days in the blue sand but saw no sign of other people. Evron assured them the Pomlo people occupied these sands, but it was a small tribe and they might not encounter any of its people.

Jynx found that disappointing. She and Kahpur had met no one during their trek through the Rainbow Sands–it was a huge place, filling almost half a continent–but her curiosity ate at her. How would people flourish in a place like this? She imagined them as a relatively wealthy tribe, since they controlled access to so much water, but what did that mean out here? Fine fabrics? Fabulous gems? Money?

When she asked, Evron said, "The Pomlo sell water to other tribes throughout the sands. I've been told they're a happy, generous people, but the borders of the blue sand are heavily guarded."

"They are? I've seen no guards."

"I have."

Jynx's head swivelled, looking for them.

Evron smiled. "As I said, they're generous. They don't mind those who travel through helping themselves as they go. They're guarding against raiders who would come prepared to steal wagon loads of blue sand."

"So, when I explained that blue sand can be drunk, you

already knew that but said nothing."

He smiled again and shrugged. "I had nothing to add. You were correct."

Jynx decided she liked Evron. That had been thoughtful of him, and something she'd never have expected of Miss High-and-Mighty.

She went back to her daily inventory of medicaments. She'd made so much unguent for sunburn and salve for blisters they weighed down her satchel, but they were disappearing fast. Especially the blister salve, to her surprise. Everyone needed that, even Snake. Sunburn should have been the larger problem, in her opinion, but their clothes didn't leave much skin exposed to the sun, and hers was the only complexion fair enough to burn easily. The others' skins had darkened, but they suffered little reddening.

Laughter pulled her attention from nibbling worries. That damn Shyriel was flirting with Snake again. For some reason it hurt that, with little prompting, he shared childhood stories with her–stories he'd never shared with Jynx. The queen was so young, so powerful, so beautiful! Any man would want to spend time in her company.

But it left Jynx feeling very alone, in an alien place far from home and family.

~~~

Snake saw the look of dread on Jynx's face as they approached the end of the blue sand, but not until they crossed into the black sand did he understand.

Here the black dunes stretched twice the height of the blue dunes or more. He'd imagined glittering black, but the flat black that met his eyes seemed more ominous than beautiful, as if something living hunched its shoulders and leaned toward them, daring them to enter. The warrior went on alert without thinking, his eyes flicking everywhere in search of threat or trap.

"What's wrong, Snake?"

He jumped, startled by Jynx's voice. He blew out a long, slow breath. "I don't like this, Jynx. The shadows hang above the dunes, thick and dark, and I don't like how they obscure any threat or danger. It just feels *wrong*."

"I've been a little jumpy myself, but I didn't expect it to affect you so much. You're a lot braver, and used to danger," she said.

Though grateful that Jynx walked a little closer to him than usual, he didn't appreciate that Shyriel clung within inches, constantly touching his arm for reassurance. It annoyed him. How could a queen have so little courage? He wanted to pull his arm away from the constant touching, but it would be obvious and rude.

The farther they walked into the blackness, the more uneasy he became. He checked often to make sure Jynx was still next to him, although he could feel her presence there.

Shyriel slipped her hand through Snake's elbow. "This is fearsome," she whispered loudly.

Evron, walking behind them, cleared his throat but she didn't catch the hint Snake knew he'd intended. Shyriel's behavior wasn't just annoying but potentially dangerous. If a predator—human or otherwise—came at them, he had no chance to free himself of the women and draw his sword in time.

Snake stopped. "Shyriel, would you walk with Evron, please? I need my arm free for my sword, in case of trouble."

"Or," she answered brightly, "Jynx can walk with Evron and I'll remain on your left, so your sword arm will be free."

"No." His voice was flat. "I don't mean to be offensive, Shyriel, but Jynx is a better fighter than you are. She has much more experience. Between her, Ick, and me we should be able to protect you just fine. If you're safely behind us, with Evron."

"No one is in charge of a queen! I do as I please. Your task is to get me safely back to the white sands, not to give me orders. You promised to bring Erilya safely home. You did not put conditions on that!" Shyriel's voice rose to match his.

"If we run into trouble," he said, "I'll be protecting Jynx and Ick. You and Evron can protect yourselves. I didn't promise to keep you safe, only to take Ick home. You aren't even supposed to be here. Any aid we give you is out of the goodness of our hearts, nothing more." Hearing Shyriel's shocked hiss, he scowled at her. "Just be aware that if I need my sword, you'll be sent flying to get you out of my way. You're on your own, except for tagging along with Ick.

"And at any time I choose, I'll hand you Ick to take home yourself, while Jynx and I return to the tallgrass. And that's the end of it." Behind him Jynx gasped, but he couldn't look at her right now.

He strode forward, Jynx at his side. Evron and a pouting Shyriel fell in behind them.

He felt a tickle in his mind that felt like Ick, chuckling.

He pretended not to see the fear in Shyriel's eyes, now that she realized she was responsible for her own safety. She *should* be afraid. Of course he would try to protect everyone, if it came to that, but he would never tell her that. Better she learn the consequences of not following his instructions. She could have been safely home now, waiting for Erilya.

Come to think of it, he could insist that Ick remain with Jynx, even if Shyriel changed her mind. And in exchange he could require Shyriel to take on some of the camp chores Jynx had been doing, to better balance the workload. He grinned to himself. This could actually be fun.

~~~

The storm came in the night, blackness out of blackness. It caught them in a flat bowl among the dunes and happened so fast that everyone disappeared from Snake's eyes in an instant—except Jynx, who clung to his left arm, face against his biceps. Wind shrieked in his ears, whistled around his head.

The screech of wind and the hissing of hot tornadic sand blasting skin and clothes would have kept him from hearing Jynx even if she'd been shouting directly into his ear.

He curled one arm around her and pulled her protectively against him and headed for higher ground, where they'd be less likely to be suffocated by sand. He thought he'd seen a large rock thrust up from the sand—big enough to provide a little protection, as long as they stayed on the lee side. Pulling cloth from his pack, he wound a length around Jynx's head, leaving a single layer of cloth over her eyes. Then he did the same for himself.

Surely Evron and Shyriel had also headed for high ground. They lived in sand; they knew better than he what to do. He put them out of his mind.

The wind slashed at them with sandy knives. Snake could hear it, but even eyes squeezed shut accumulated grit so that he could see nothing. When the noise seemed muffled, he tried to dig the sand from his ears. And his clogged nose. He had to breathe through his mouth, trying not to inhale any more sand than he could help. He felt it gathering in every opening of his clothing, abrading the skin. How much worse for Jynx, with her delicate skin?

They reached the outcropping he'd seen and hunkered down next to it for as much shelter as they could get.

"Wouldn't it be safer on the lee side of the rock?" Jynx shouted into his ear.

"No," he shouted back. "If we're on the leeward side of the dune, the high winds could pick up huge amounts of sand very quickly and bury us under it."

They pulled the veil-things over their faces, especially nose and mouth. The veils included enough cloth that they were able to wrap their eyes and noses, too.

Where was his pack? He'd dropped it just a moment ago. How deeply buried could it be already? Jynx's satchel was even more important, as it held the magic bowl, the source of food.

And then he stopped thinking and just endured, enclosing Jynx and Ick in his arms as best he could. He'd have to worry about the packs later.

He drifted. Thick sand muffled the sound of the wind and provided a thick, warm blanket Perfect for a good night's sleep. Jynx hadn't stirred in his arms for some time, so she probably slept, too. He snuggled more firmly into the sand, tightening his arms around her just a little.

Something sharp stabbed into Snake's arm. He jolted awake, found himself unable to move for the suffocating weight of black sand.

Another stab.

Jynx moaned.

The feel of a wriggling body didn't fit with the dreams that still lingered. His mind felt muzzy. He was under the blankets, but they were too heavy to throw off. Trapped! Panic sizzled upwards through his veins.

Hush! Ick's fear filled her "voice," but she wasn't panicking.

He felt her intent to dig out. Sand stirred around him as she moved through it. For a long, frightening moment he neither heard her not felt her movement.

A sudden gush of air struck his face as she reached the surface. He felt her summons and reached upward. Cooler air brushed his fingertips lightly.

Knowing he could reach it poured energy into his body and he thrust himself toward the surface, into an invisible dawn, with chill night air wrapping him. He pulled the kerchief from his eyes, having almost forgotten it was there.

And then he dug Jynx free as well, helping her with her kerchief.

Then he coughed and spat, coughed and spat. He stomped as best he could to shed sand, dug the wretched stuff from every entry point into his body. The stuff scratched and abraded him painfully. He snorted, blowing sand from his nostrils, roughed his fingers through his hair to scatter the sand from it. He sat and pulled off his boots to empty them.

And then his shirt. Forgetting Jynx for the moment, he ripped off his britches and brushed sand from his naked body, frantic to be rid of the stuff. At least he remembered to keep his back to her to allow her a bit of privacy, too.

Even so, he almost turned back too soon, but Ick "slapped" him with her irritation and he froze, to await her "all clear."

The desert night chilled him as he waited, now that he could spare it his attention. He took his time shaking out every bit of clothing thoroughly before dressing again. As he snatched at one leg of his britches, he caught a glimpse of Jynx behind him, discreetly turned away but just as naked. It was all he could do not to turn and stare, or worse, walk over and put his arms around her. Best he keep his back to her for a bit, until he regained control. While waiting, he rummaged for their buried packs and shook as much sand off them as he could.

When he'd finally dressed again, he turned his attention to Ick. He brushed black sand from her coils gently, hands shaking and stomach tight in dread. At her insistence, he even wiped her eyes free of sand, although he wanted to throw up. Shyriel should be doing this, but he didn't see her at the moment.

He couldn't bring himself to get close to Ick's mouth at all, even though she was seven feet long, not twenty-five. She'd have to wait for Jynx. Her annoyance came through clearly.

Even Jynx had trouble with that, but loyal friend that she was, she curled her lip, swallowed hard, and cleaned grit from the queen's mouth, muttering, "Ick! Ick! Yuck!" After all, the slither had no way to spit it out herself. Her hands were shaking when she finished, and Ick gave her a slithery kiss on the cheek with her tongue.

Snake would have laughed, if he'd had the energy.

7. Lost

Wind-thrown sand still stung Snake's face and bare arms, though it was almost a caress compared to the storm. Between the still-moving sand and the dunes' black shadows, he couldn't see more than a few yards.

"Jynx," he called, "do you see Shyriel and Evron?" He kept his ears pricked, half expecting them to cry out when they heard his voice.

Jynx squatted nearby, pulling things out of her satchel and shaking sand from them. Her head came up and she glanced around, then stood. "No, I don't. Let me whistle for them."

Snake barely got his hands over his ears before her loud, shrill whistle rang his ears.

No response. No sound, no movement.

Jynx stepped up to his side, slinging her satchel over her shoulder. "How do we find them? Dig into every new bump of sand we can see?"

"They may not have stopped and dug in like we did. If they kept going, they could be anywhere, especially since they couldn't have seen Katinga's Eye to guide them."

"They could even have gone in circles," said Jynx.

"Let's assume they headed more or less in the right direction and go that way. We can check anything that looks like they might have dug in, and we can call and whistle as we go, too." Snake didn't mention that they could already be dead–or simply impossible to find in such vast sands. Jynx already knew that, and saying it aloud could only worry her more.

"Wait just a moment. Ick may have an idea." Jynx stopped moving, squinting in the way she usually did when using Rapport.

Snake had to grin. He'd done the same thing in the early days of his Rapport, making it harder than it really was.

Then Jynx looked at him, eyes wide in dismay. "Ick can't hear Shyriel. She says she's alive, though, because she'd know if Shyriel died."

"Then we search."

Shielding their eyes from the blowing sand, they walked through the area, calling out for their missing comrades–and each other. Once in a while Snake would dig into a pile of sand, just in case, but two hours of calling and searching brought no result.

At last, tired and discouraged, Snake sat on a small, rocky outcropping.

What do we do now? What makes sense? He was a Wolf Guard captain, promoted into Kayde's place when he was exiled last year. The captain was supposed to know what to do, to give orders that had the best chance of bringing the most men home safely while accomplishing strategic objectives. But his training hadn't included anything like this.

Jynx wasn't one of his men. More like a partner, actually. "What do you think?" he asked her. "Any other ideas on how to find them?"

She had to be as troubled as he, but her face remained smooth and calm.

"Perhaps," she said, "we don't even attempt it. Beyond what we've already done."

Snake's face tingled with shock. "Abandon them? Just... go on, as if they didn't matter?" He heard the accusation in his voice but he couldn't seem to quell it. "Jynx, they could be dying somewhere close by, just needing a little effort on our part."

"If they were alive and nearby, Ick could have established Rapport with Shyriel. She couldn't, so they're either dead or far away."

"Or Shyriel could be dead but Evron in need of rescue. How do we go forward without knowing?" Disbelief pitched his voice higher.

Jynx frowned at him, impatient. "We've searched the area already. And remember, we're not responsible for them. We've already been through that."

"The Wolf Guard doesn't leave men behind. We find them and if they're alive, we bring them home. If they're not, we bring their bodies if we can."

"We're not Wolf Guard." She didn't raise her voice, but her tone took on a steel edge. "Or at least I'm not. If we take more time to look for them, *we* may not survive. Our supply of blue sand is limited and we have a long way to go."

Could this be the soft-voiced, gentle healer he'd fallen in love with? "Jynx, we *have* to find them!"

"And if we die trying, Ick doesn't get back to the white sands and Shyriel and Evron don't get found by anyone. And if we die, Ick will mostly likely die, too. While I admire your ideals, you're not being very practical." She folded her arms atop Ick's wrapped coils and glared at him.

Snake floundered for an answer. He'd been raised in a kingdom of heroes and fighters. He couldn't just quit trying, stop looking for them. But Jynx was right, too. He struggled to find a way to compromise, to have both worlds—his ideal one and her practical one. But no answer presented itself.

Jynx shouldered her satchel. "We can still try for the white sands. Maybe we'll catch up with them on the way." She started walking south.

Snake glanced at the sky, where dawn paled the edge of the world. He couldn't see Katinga's Eye through the haze, but Jynx seemed to be going the right direction. His mouth tightened in irritation. In two strides he caught up to her and lifted the satchel from her shoulder. "You've got enough to carry, with Ick." He fell in beside her, squelching the hollow feeling in his stomach.

In his warrior world, women didn't make strategic decisions. He knew exactly what his men would be calling him behind his back, if they knew. He sighed, too soft to be heard, and fell into step with her.

~~~

They did search as they went, even going out of their way to check areas that looked likely. Since Ick couldn't "hear" Shyriel, Snake assumed they were looking for bodies.

Nor was he certain their progress was in the right direction. They now traveled in daylight, so Katinga's Eye couldn't guide them. Using the gray sun, seen through the shadows that clung to the dunes, didn't reassure him because it wasn't in a fixed position.

They could only do the best they could and hope for success.

When he found half-filled footprints in the sand, he halted in disgust. "We've gone in circles, Jynx. These have to be our own prints."

"How can you tell? They're holes in the sand, not real prints."

"Well, if they're not ours, they're Shyriel's and Evron's."

"Or someone else's, someone we didn't know was out here."

He thought about that for a moment. "It's likelier to be the ones we know about. I want to follow them a ways and see if we find them. Do you want to wait here for me or come along?" Not that he could bear to leave her alone out here, but he doubted she'd push him that far. She'd come along, at least for a while.

She gave him a long, steady look, and for a moment he feared she might elect to wait, after all. He controlled his sigh of relief when she began walking again, next to him. With Jynx, he never knew the lengths she would go out of sheer stubbornness.

By noon, Jynx began to ration the blue sand. Perhaps she hoped to have some left if they caught up to Shyriel and Evron, but she didn't say so.

An hour after that, Snake squinted ahead of them. "What is that? That bluish thing?" Had they circled inadvertently back to the blue sand? The color seemed much darker, and he thought he saw black sand beyond it.

The tracks they followed turned parallel to the blue, to his frustration, and he eventually touched Jynx's elbow and left the tracks to cut across the flatter area dividing them from whatever it was.

Not even in his own mind did he allow the word "river." Not, at least, until they came close enough to be sure.

Unlike the rivers in the Snows, this wasn't a frothy, fast-moving tumble over rocks. Nor was it a deep, slow, muddy river like the one in Sayvil, or a broad, relatively shallow one like he'd seen in the Dark Wood when he'd last traveled with Jynx. But it was a river nevertheless, shallow enough to wade across without wetting their knees. Narrow enough to cross in less than a dozen steps, with a sandy bottom. But it moved, albeit in a lazy trickle, and it was wet. He even saw two tiny fish darting busily through its ripples. They were too small to eat, but they might be a good size for bait—if any larger fish lived in this river.

Jynx dropped to her knees on the sand, next to the water. "If you want a drink of real water," she told him, "go upstream. I'm going to wash up here." And she reached into her satchel for a cloth, which she dipped into the water, then used to wash her face, the back of her neck, her hands and arms...

Snake had forgotten how much women liked being clean. Smiling indulgently, he walked upstream a dozen yards for a drink. He couldn't resist ducking his head into the water to get the last sand out of his hair, but he wasn't happy about banging his nose into the sandy bottom when he misjudged the depth. With a surreptitious glance in Jynx's direction, he decided she didn't need to know about that.

But he did enjoy watching her roll up the legs of her britches and step barefoot into the water downstream, a delighted grin on her face.

Snake rejoined her. "Do we have a way to carry water with us?"

She splashed out of the river and sat on the black sand, legs outstretched to dry. "We have waterskins, but they're full of blue sand. I'm reluctant to pour it out and replace it with real water."

"People tend to settle where there's water," Snake mused. "That means there's likely a village or settlement next to this river, and the footprints we've been following are probably headed for it."

"Which means it's someone who knows where they're going—and that means they're not Evron and Shyriel's prints."

"Likely not."

"Could this be the village that took Ick and the other slithers?" Jynx said.

That didn't sound right. "Why do you think so? Didn't you find her in the blue sand, not the black?"

"Well, yes. But I have a hunch..."

"The black sand feels evil, so the people here must be the thieves?" Snake tried Jynx's trick of lifting an eyebrow. It didn't work for him.

Jynx didn't notice, thank the gods. He felt foolish for the attempt.

"Let's at least be cautious approaching the village," she said.

"Of course. I know better than to walk into a strange place openly, without reconnoitering. I'll want to see what type of place it is, how heavily armed, their defenses, whether there are soldiers or warriors..."

"And whether the women and children move about freely, without fear."

What? "Of course they do. It's their home."

"If the men are harsh with women and children, we'll see it in their faces and bodies, right? Cruelty isn't that easily hidden. That will tell us something important about the place, too."

She was so matter-of-fact, as if it were a normal type of observation! That hadn't been part of Snake's training, and it wouldn't have occurred to him to look for it. He wanted to think he would notice something so unusual, though. He nodded instead of speaking.

For the third time Snake took a long drink of real water from the river. To conserve the blue sand for when they had no water, he told himself. Never mind this tasted much better. And then he had to duck behind a nearby dune to rid himself of the excess, only then realizing how little excess there had been in the last few days.

As they followed the river toward the hoped-for village, the wind finally died down, leaving shadows but no sand hanging in the air. He began to keep a closer eye on the surrounding dunes, but the farther they walked, the uneasier he became. Maybe Jynx's hunch was correct.

Was that a thin column of smoke hanging in the air? "Jynx, it's time for more caution. We're getting close to the village." He moved them a quarter mile back from the water, orienting on the smoke instead.

They didn't speak much, though Jynx and Ick might be talking. Still no sign of Shyriel and Evron, but Snake carried some small hope they might have found the village and safety.

Ick would find Shyriel first, if she still lived. But Ick seemed morose and unhappy. She hadn't teased him once since the sandstorm–a bad sign.

The hazed sun slid well toward the horizon before they found the village. The sound of people's voices and a braying donkey rose into the dunes to announce its location. Snake murmured to Jynx and they dropped to their bellies to crawl up a dune for a look–after an irritable Ick uncoiled like a whip from Jynx's waist to slither up the hill on her own.

"Not to the top," he whispered to Jynx. "Around the side, where we won't show up against the sky so easily."

She nodded and followed his lead. For a change.

Every few feet Snake stopped to listen, then crawled forward again. A stealthy approach couldn't be rushed, although Jynx's mouth reflected impatience. Still, he was comfortable with the approach he found; it should allow them a look into the heart of the village without exposing themselves to view.

They lay flat on the sand and crawled the last few feet. Ick shoved between them, her emrel eyes even with theirs, tongue flickering to taste the air. Together they peered over the sand into the black village.

8. Wohim

"Does Ick sense Shyriel in the village?" Snake whispered. His eyes never left the unexpected scene before him.

Jynx shook her head without looking at him, attention riveted on the village. Apparently she was as surprised as he was.

In the midst of the darkness, in obscuring shadows and black sand, color exploded. Fabric tents in a mad splash of hues filled the spaces between dunes. Solid saffron or red or pale blue tents sat side-by-side with tents bearing pictures and patterns. Here a tall, sturdy green tent bore stripes of pink and yellow, while a nearby sky blue tent was decorated with white clouds and trimmed in deep violet. Children playing with pebbles in front hinted that these could be homes. Their loose, unbleached robes looked cool and comfortable, similar to what Snake remembered from his childhood.

Closer to the center of the village, a fabric door flapped in the breeze. This tent was much larger. Inside, small groups of people sat cross-legged on colorful cloths. They seemed to be bargaining with whoever sat across from them. A bazaar or marketplace, perhaps.

Several women emerged from a large tent striped in red and pale blue. Bangles encircled ankles and wrists and throats, glinting in sunlight. The older, tall one carried her chin high, a large red gem adorning her throat. These women wore soft colors and finely woven robes. They disappeared as a group into another large tent, this one set back from the others and higher among the dunes.

"What now?" Jynx breathed in his ear. "Do we walk casually into the middle of town and introduce ourselves?"

Snake shook his head. "Not yet. Let's watch awhile first."

"And hope no one comes up behind us and wonders why we're hiding? Or spying?"

"In a few minutes I want to work our way around the village perimeter, get a better look at everything. See how big the village is. I can't tell from here."

Jynx nodded—and glanced behind her again. She made a good rear guard.

She frowned, craned her neck as she looked down into the village. "What's that smell?"

Snake lifted his nose into the air and sniffed. "I'm not sure." He frowned, trying to think where he'd smelled it before. It hadn't been recent, but he definitely knew the scent, faint as it was, if he could just place it.

No use. Its origin eluded him and Snake let it go with a sigh. "Come on. Let's circle around."

Staying low and moving carefully, they spent over an hour working their way around the village, Ick once again wrapped around Jynx. As they neared the area farthest from the river, the odor strengthened—musky, overlaid with a faint sweetness. It was so familiar! Why couldn't he place it?

Then Jynx pushed past him on hands and knees, intent on a plant he didn't recognize. The odor became momentarily overpowering.

Memory slammed through him, raw and visceral—a nest of youngens slithering over his arms and legs and belly, constricting in play or affection. A pot in his hand, a palm full of dripping oils in the other as he laughingly tried to rub the stuff into all his slithers at the same time...

"Slithers!" he hissed, dropping flat.

Startled, Jynx also flattened, pinning Ick abruptly to the sand. The queen hissed.

Snake forced his breathing to slow. "That's the smell of several slithers together in one place. They've been oiled, but not in the last few days. The scent is too shallow."

"Oiled? The kind of oil Ick is always moaning about?"

"It seems you were right about this village. They shouldn't have *any* slithers, let alone enough to smell from this distance. Come quietly. We need to find them, see how many and in what condition."

Heart pounding, he led the way more cautiously than ever. How many slithers would they find? Dead or alive? Surely they weren't being slaughtered here, within the village. His belly clenched, even as he realized he smelled no blood. *That* scent was distinctive, instantly familiar to all warriors. He thought of the berserker rituals in the Kingdom of the Snows, and the blood-soaked Tears of Heroes at the center of them. And shuddered. He pushed the thoughts away.

On the far side of the village he found the working beasts— tall, bad-tempered camels and a handful of beautiful desert horses with their oversize nostrils and the extra membrane they could close across their eyes without fully giving up the ability to see. The grass was pale and sparse, but both hardy species of beasts could survive on it for weeks at a time if necessary, so long as water was also available. The People had few such animals, but he remembered them clearly.

Beyond the working beasts he saw a wooden structure. Why would a nomadic tribe want a wooden building? Every time they moved they'd have to tear it down and rebuild it in their new site. It had to be where they kept the slithers—or slaughtered them.

Snake turned to Jynx. "Wait here," he murmured. "I'll be back in a few minutes."

Jynx was staring at the structure. "Good. I don't want to go any closer. But you'll have to take Ick. She's determined to reach the slithers there.

"No! Ick needs to stay with you. I'll take a look and report back, so we can plan."

Pain exploded in his head as if he'd been struck by a cudgel. He curled into a ball, arms wrapped around his head, struggling not to scream. The pain receded just enough to recognize a queen's roar in his head–a sound he had never managed to get past.

Terror soaked through him like volatile oil, needing only a tiny flick to burst into agonizing flame.

Jynx's hand covered his mouth, muffling his gasping, squeaking voice. Hot breath covered his face, shut off his air. Through barely cracked eyes he saw rows of back-curved teeth within inches of his face. He thrashed, trying to knock the horror away, to escape.

Suddenly the weight of Ick's presence was gone. He rolled away, got his knees under him, and scrambled.

"Snake!" Jynx cried. "Stop!"

He didn't. He couldn't. He got another dozen feet before sense began to return. He rolled onto his back, hands and feet coming up to fend off an attack.

No one was there. Blinking stupidly, trying to reorient, he felt the worst tremors begin to quiet inside him. He lay panting another moment, then sat up carefully.

A dozen feet away Jynx lay flat in the black sand, pinning a furious Ick with her body. The determination in her hard eyes and tight jaw would have chilled him if he hadn't been so grateful for it.

She glanced at him, still concentrating on Ick. "Did she bite you?" Steel in that voice. For Ick, not for him.

Snake checked himself hastily for tooth marks. "No. I don't think so." He barely got the words out.

"Stay where you are," she ordered. "Ick and I are going to have a private conversation."

Ick didn't seem to agree. She thrashed twice but Jynx held on. "Shame on you!" she gritted. "Leave him alone! You're coming with me!"

She and Ick wrestled for control, but in the end she grabbed the slither by the tail—clearly forgetting the venom it held—and dragged her backwards through the sand until the shadows swallowed them.

~~~

It hurt. Snake was so strong, so fearless, so self-assured. Jynx couldn't have imagined him as a gibbering ball of fear under any circumstances, if she hadn't just seen it. It was painful to watch, all the more because she knew the story behind his terror.

Ick knew the story, too. She'd tried to recreate it.

Why would she do that? She and Snake were friends! Jynx had watched her tease him. She'd seen him coax her back to consciousness after the cyclone the year before. She'd watched him, sword drawn, protect her and Ick from Slaughter's gang. They were friends! Of a sort, anyway.

And yet Ick had deliberately terrorized him, bullying him to do things her way.

Well, Jynx wasn't a queen, but she knew how to handle the haughty and the naughty. Ick was going to get an earful! As soon as she found a good place to talk, well away from Snake.

She kept a careful hold on Ick's tail, making sure it couldn't be used against her. Ick would never stab her with it—Jynx couldn't even imagine that—but accidents could happen and she wasn't taking chances.

Thinking about the tail, she almost didn't see Ick's head lift and arc over her back, teeth bared as she struck at Jynx, hissing.

Reflexively Jynx swatted at her head and missed, as Ick snapped her head back out of reach.

Emrel eyes caught Jynx's gaze and held her, frozen into immobility, at the slither queen's mercy.

Anger swept through Jynx. She sought Rapport with the queen. She may be physically unable to move, but she could still let her will be known.

To her relief, Ick was willing to talk and released her hypnotic hold.

The queen was furious and terrified to the point of panic. These were *her* slithers, *her* "people." She had to get to them before they were slaughtered. How could Jynx stand in her way? How could Snake? *Nothing* was more important than freeing them and returning them home—not even Jynx's life. *Ick* was queen, not Jynx! A mere human had no right to stop her. Unless she wanted to become Ick's enemy, she must release her now! And aid her in freeing the slithers. Now! Hurry! Let go!

Such a pounding! Eyes squeezed tight against the onslaught, Jynx released Ick to cover her ears, even though the drubbing was inside her skull and it wouldn't help.

When she opened her eyes, Ick was swimming across the sands in Snake's direction, as fast as she could move.

Still pale, Snake was on his feet. Instead of stepping out of her way, he stood in front of her and held up a hand to stop her.

This was the bravery Jynx expected from Snake. But pitting himself against a slither queen? Two of the souls she loved most in the world were about to fight, and one or both could be hurt. Jynx couldn't bear the idea. She ran as fast as she could through deep, soft sand.

But Ick stopped and lifted her front end off the sand, facing Snake. He avoided her direct gaze but otherwise stood his ground.

Panting, Jynx slowed, then paused. She was picking up some of Ick's side of their conversation.

Ick made the same desperate pleas of Snake. Help. Save my slithers. Don't get in my way. *Help. Save my slithers. Don't get in my way.*

Jynx couldn't hear Snake's side of it, but she knew when Ick relaxed.

Good. Ick controlled her panic now, and they could all three work together to help the captives. Jynx heaved a huge sigh of relief, hoping Snake had a plan.

~~~

Queen Erilya lowered herself to the black sand, her mottled colors beautiful even in the perpetual shadows. Her agitation still showed in the slashing of her tail across the sand.

Snake couldn't think of her as Ick right now. Her demeanor and its implied threat reminded him too much of Queen Tchenya, who had almost swallowed him whole.

Jynx sat in the sand next to the queen, one small hand on her scales. She had absolutely no fear of the slither queen. So what did that make him? His skin still prickled, just looking at her. He could feel his fear in the sweat of his armpits.

Snake wished he had direct Rapport with Jynx, as he did with Erilya. A three-way conversation would be so much easier. Still, this was better than nothing.

"What do we do first?" Jynx spoke quietly, although they were far enough from the village that no one could hear her.

Unlike his own screams a few minutes ago. He kept an eye out, just in case someone came to investigate. "I need to reconnoiter. We have to know what we're facing before we can make a coherent plan. Erilya cannot be part of the reconnaissance. She'd attract too much attention and can't move fast enough to escape men, even men on foot."

He saw understanding in Jynx's eyes. If the news was bad, they needed to prepare Erilya as best they could. Jynx wouldn't be strong enough to deal with her, and he... wouldn't be much help. Shame hunched his shoulders. He forced them loose again. *Warrior*, he thought. *Wolf Guard. I can do what I must.*

Jynx reached into the satchel slung over her shoulder and removed a pottery jar with a tightly stoppered lid. "Ick, how about an oil rub? You have some loose, dry skin that needs to come off, and something pleasant will distract you until Snake gets back."

Ick's fury began to build again.

"Stop that!" Jynx scolded. "Save your energy for when it's needed. Let's see what's what, first, then plan the best rescue we can. I promise, we will not abandon your slithers here."

Ick's tail lashed—hard. But she kept it well away from Jynx. She allowed Jynx to slather a handful of scented oil on her scales and begin a slow, luxurious rub.

Reassured, Snake turned toward the wooden building a hundred yards away. He approached it carefully, bending lower to reduce his outline against sky or sand. The building was silent, though plenty of daylight remained.

The musty smell of slither became thicker, and now he noticed other scents—oils, or ointments, maybe metal hot from the desert heat, old wood from the building itself. No movement was a good sign—until he realized he should hear slithers crawling, or at least hear a questioning mind or two. Or not. He couldn't be sure. Dread crept up from belly to shoulders.

He made his way to the far side of the building to put it between him and the village. The Wohim village. That's what Evron had called the people of the black sands.

The building surprised him. On this side the top half of the wall was open to the desert air, with wooden posts supporting the slanted room. The only light inside came from filtered sunlight. Snake bent lower and approached cautiously, although no sand had been disturbed and no sounds or movement came from within. Not knowing what he'd find, he sealed off his Rapport from both Erilya and any slithers inside.

Just as he reached out a hand to touch the wall, he recognized a smell that was half covered by other odors. Blood. Old, not fresh, but unmistakable this close. Thank the gods his Rapport was closed off! Erilya would have thrown herself furiously in this direction, regardless of Jynx.

Snake's hand crept to the top of the half wall and he eased to his full height. His hand encountered a door latch as he stood. Darkness and shadows waited inside. He paused for his eyes to adjust.

Then he eased the latch, pulled the door open with a faint metallic click. He reminded himself to breathe as he stepped across the low sill into the building. The floor was sand, of course. A thin wall divided the interior, running from front to back with open doorways at either end. He forced himself to relax and stepped into the room to the left.

Dismay and horror engulfed him and he hastily assured that all connections to Queen Erilya were tightly closed off. For this she would destroy. There would be no limit to her fury.

The floor was half covered with mounds and tangles of slithers. Black, ropy creatures with red eyes—those that still had heads. Cutting implements—knives, cleavers, flensers, and others. Empty bowls with dried blood streaking the insides. Still-warm ashes from smoky fires.

A slaughterhouse. Here the Wohim killed slithers and preserved the meat. These were intelligent, self-aware beings! They were messengers of the People's gods, and the queens co-ruled all the People! Couldn't these... these... Wohim see that? Didn't they know what they were destroying?

These were newly dead, meat not yet harvested or skins preserved. Someone would be here any minute to work.

Filled with sudden urgency, he made a rough estimate of numbers and darted into the other room.

No slither bodies here—only skins. Paraphernalia for scraping and sewing, oils and potions for treating the skin, as Evron had told him to expect. These skins would be formed into protective clothing or armor. But there, by the far wall, he saw grinders and such that would turn dried skins into fiszt, a potion to be taken internally for poisoning. A handful of slitherskins were stretched on the far wall, drying. Not dry, sloughed skin offered by the slithers. Taken skins.

Snake's stomach bubbled up. No rituals of consecration and thanksgiving here—only slaughter for commerce. He swallowed repeatedly, trying to hold his gut in place, then fled the building.

Dropping to his knees beyond a low arm of sand, he retched. And sobbed. And retched more, still sobbing, barely able to breathe.

As a warrior, he'd killed plenty of creatures and many men. He hacked men apart like animals, to survive. But he'd never been affected like this. Cutting up men trying to kill you was one thing. But this was like killing innocent children.

How would he tell Jynx about this? How could he tell Ick?

At last he crawled away from the vomitus, pushing sand over it to hide it. He found a cranny that felt as blackened as his heart and curled up in it, wallowing in misery until he felt in control of himself again. Hours passed as he mourned the passing of the slithers, wondering which of them he might have known in his childhood.

And then he started back to Jynx and Ick, taking a longer, roundabout way.

9. Captive

For once, Jynx was grateful for the black sand's constant shadows. She and Ick wouldn't be as visible to anyone from the village. Although they awaited Snake in a low area between dunes well away from the colorful tents, she felt vulnerable without him there to protect her. And irritated with herself for that. She'd been learning how to fight from Kahpur, who had learned from her mercenary brother, but she didn't have much confidence in her skills.

Mostly she just wanted Snake to hurry up. But he'd been gone a very long time. Could something have happened to him? The wooden building wasn't that far, and it wasn't that big. He'd had plenty of time to look it over and return.

Longing pulled at her. She needed to go after him, make sure he was all right. Yes, Ick must be kept away until they knew what they faced. But what if there had been people– warriors, even–in the building when he arrived? He could be hurt, or captured, or worse.

But she had no safe way to leave Ick here alone, and no safe way to take her into danger, or into a situation that could send her into another rage.

How would Shyriel handle this? She shuddered at the thought of asking her.

Impatient buzzing filled her head. That was easy to

interpret! With a sigh of capitulation she spoke aloud. For her, it was easier than mental discussion. "We promised to wait."

Her head hurt suddenly, "All right, I promised that we would wait."

Ick's response could only be heard as, *Why?*

"We don't know what we'll find in that building. It could be dangerous. There could be people inside."

Kyr will subdue them. Ick's tone was confident. Nevertheless, she coiled next to Jynx, touching her as if for reassurance. *We know my slithers are there, but I can't reach them.*

When did Ick start using Snake's childhood name? Jynx squelched her irritation at the knowledge the slither had picked it up from Shyriel. Ick *knew* what a snake was—and didn't think something so stupid was a good name for him. She told Jynx she just hadn't had anything else to call him.

Jynx forced herself to remain relaxed, not wanting to deal with an alarmed Ick again. "Why can't you reach your slithers?"

Ick's agitation increased. *I don't know!*

"Dear one, it could be something innocuous, like being asleep."

I would still hear their slumber.

"...or it could be worse, even something dreadful. I want to know what we face before barging in."

Ick's tail flicked sand against Jynx's arm. *I'm going to go look. Clearly, men can't be trusted to do as they should.*

Where did that come from? It certainly wasn't how Jynx thought! Most of the time. She lurched to her feet to follow Ick, who wound her way toward the wooden structure at top speed.

Even if she were twenty-five feet long instead of seven, Ick wouldn't be able to move over the sand faster than Jynx. She caught up in a few steps and slowed, uneasy at approaching the building so openly. "Let's slow down and try not to be seen," she said.

Too late. Just as they rounded the corner to the open back of the structure, a man stepped out of it and halted, staring at them with wide eyes and open mouth.

Jynx drew as much courage into her lungs as she could.

The man spoke, his tone sharp, but she didn't understand anything he said. Probably something like, "Who are you?" Or perhaps, "What are you doing here?"

He shouted, and two more men and a woman came running from the structure. All four wore unbleached robes, two of them streaked with red. Like blood. The man jibbered, pointing not at Jynx but at Ick.

"Ick, I don't think I like this." Jynx stopped, ready to flee. Ick ignored her.

One of the men darted back inside, emerging again with a noose on a pole. Without hesitation he ran toward Ick as the other three spread out, half surrounding the slither queen.

They ignored Jynx as if she didn't exist.

Ick rose above the sand, hissing, Suddenly the man with the noose stopped, unable to move, frozen by Ick's direct gaze.

With a yell, one man snatched the pole from his hand and started for Ick in his place.

Jynx charged forward. "Stop! Ick, stop! All of you, stop!" She placed herself between Ick and the Wohim.

Ick's voice roared in her head. *Move! My slithers are dead! They've killed them all! You're in my way*!

The excited jabbering from the Wohim rose. The man now holding the noose approached cautiously.

Ick struck, so fast Jynx barely saw her move.

Jynx grabbed the pole, a move that so startled the man she was able to pull the pole from his hand. She swung the hard end at him, striking his arm when he jumped back too late.

The four began to surround them.

"Leave us alone!" Jynx snarled in her best imitation of Kahpur. "What have you done with our slithers?"

But they couldn't understand her, either, and didn't seem to want to.

One of the men wrenched the pole from Jynx's strong grip. Ick struck at him, sinking two rows of back-curved teeth into his arm. The woman darted in, a length of cloth in her hand. While Ick's teeth still pulled agonized screams from the man, she covered Ick's eyes and tied the cloth in place. Jynx couldn't get there in time to stop her, and then couldn't get past her guard.

Even blinded by the cloth, Ick wrapped the man in thick coils. Blood ran down his arm, then from his nose, as she began to crush him, tightening with every breath he took. He panted heavily in panic.

The other two men dashed back into the building, re-emerging with weapons—an axe for one, while the other held a knife in one hand and a cleaver in the other.

Jynx's skin chilled at sight of the weapons.

She slammed her satchel down on the tall one's head as hard as she could, but it wasn't heavy enough or hard enough. He ducked and barely slowed.

"Ick!" she screamed. "Stop! Before they kill you! Stop!"

Never! They will die!

"No! No! *You'll* die! And that will kill me, too! Please! Stop!"

But stopping her wasn't that easy. Until the one with the knife suddenly changed direction and grabbed Jynx instead, holding a knife to her throat.

Angry tears rolled down Jynx's face as the men trussed her arms and looped the noose around Ick, just behind the head.

10. Rescue

Blackness swirled around him like a silent sandstorm and Snake spun in the darkness. His head didn't stop when the rest of him did and he staggered with dizziness. Disoriented, he sank to his knees, felt the graininess of black sand like pebbles indenting his kneecaps. A groan escaped but he bit it off so they wouldn't hear.

He couldn't remember who "they" were, but he knew they were evil. He felt their ropes about his wrists, the bruising from their fists. Lifting his arms hurt. His hands were cold from too-tight binding, but pain consumed his mind so that fear didn't touch him, even though he knew of men who had lost their hands from over tight binding left too long.

Vague memories began to trickle back, of wooden walls, of beautiful Jynx—what did she have to do with his pain?—of sand and wind, of breath closed off and clogged with scratchy grains. The old taste of vomit in his mouth. The smell of death that lingered in his nostrils. A giant slither, red mouth gaping above him—Queen Tchenya! Here! Then fear at last flooded through him, so that his shut-off hands prickled in pain. His breath came in short pants. No air. No air! Aaahhh!

Kyr.

He whimpered. Tchenya had never called him by name before, and he didn't like it.

Kyr!

His breath caught as he listened.

SNAKE!

He whimpered again, wanting to scream. He had no voice, could barely interpret her mind's collision with his.

Some warrior you are! It's hard to believe Jynx expects you *to rescue* us!

Body shivering, Snake swallowed his whimper, peered through the darkness. Sense drizzled back. "Ick?" His own voice felt loud in his ears, yet barely audible.

Who else would I be? Where are you?

An anchor. Thank the Bearslayer! Reality began to push forward, thrusting the darkness back. *I don't know. Somewhere dark.* Snake fell into Rapport easily, despite the distracting rustle of clothing nearby. *There are men here, and I'm bound too tight. I can't feel my hands.*

Ick replied, *I, too, am boxed and unable to move. Jynx is not with me.*

The cold gripped Snake's heart briefly. Jynx was in danger and Ick couldn't help her. But what could he do, from here?

"What do you want?" he asked aloud of the watchers in the dark.

A jabbering response came back, sharp and irritated.

Snake stayed on his knees. Clearly a response was expected, if only he knew what to say.

Movement startled him, and a brief flash of light nearly blinded him as someone left the enclosure. A tent, it seemed.

They'd done something to him, but he wasn't sure what. His head still felt fuzzy from it, whatever it was. Had he eaten or drunk anything since–

He tried to think back. He'd found the slithers. He'd seen... he'd seen... he closed his eyes and concentrated and at last the images trickled back.

The slithers had been butchered for their meat. But worse... the other half of the building. They processed sloughed skins there, gathered the dry paper skins and soaked them in something. And they collected... his stomach gnarled and bucked. They collected living skins, peeled from the struggling slithers. He swallowed vomit before it could rise. Sacrilege. Murder.

He remembered running, vomiting in the sand. And being awakened roughly, pinned to the sand and bound. And brought here. Did they give him water? He thought they had, given the strange, dusty taste still in his mouth. Not only water, to cause that disorientation.

Thank you, Ick. I'm myself now. I think.

A faintly relieved buzz–a very gentle one–tickled his head.

He squinted, trying to see the men who guarded him. How many? Warriors? Merchants? Servants? Too dark in here to know. He sank back on his heels. *Jynx is captured? Tell me what you know.*

She did. None of it was good. He shivered when she did, at the mention of their "breeding program." Poor Ick.

Fortunately, Ick didn't ask what he knew. He couldn't have shared that, and she'd have known he was holding back.

Why did you sleep, while we needed help?

I was drugged. Then he changed the subject. *Are you hurt, beyond discomfort, I mean? Is Jynx?*

No. We are both uninjured, except for a rope burn behind my head. She seemed more offended than harmed. Such things shouldn't happen to a queen!

He carefully didn't smile. She'd have heard it, and he didn't need her anger. The touch–even sight–of a slither still touched a cold core of fear.

The blinding light returned briefly as someone entered the tent. This time, Snake saw several indistinct men sitting between him and the doorway, but one of the two who just came in appeared to be a woman. Interesting.

After a brief, jabbering conversation, she came toward him, accompanied by a man carrying a long, curved knife. Long enough to cut someone's head off, if its bearer had the strength.

The woman turned her head and spoke to one of the seated men, who promptly jumped up and opened the door flap, hooking it in place. The angle of the light suggested late afternoon.

Snake turned his eyes from the sudden brightness, grateful to be able to see again.

The woman's long black hair and deep blue eyes accented robes decorated with blue and green. He watched her sink gracefully to her knees a few feet in front of him. Her eyes never left his face. He'd seen few women, besides Jynx and Kahpur, with such a direct gaze.

"Have you been harmed?" she asked. "Do you have injuries that need to be tended?"

She spoke his language! Some of her pronunciations were different, more like Jynx's, but very understandable.

The man with her was clearly a fighting man, with that long scar across his cheek. He remained standing behind her shoulder, long knife still in hand, eyeing Snake with distrust.

Rather than speak, Snake shook his head from side to side.

"I am Srika, the Malim of the Caretaker Guild. With me is Nerom, the Malim of the Warrior Guild. Directly behind us are Pesh, the Malim of the Harvester Guild, and Rhodor, the Malim of the Merchant Guild. Thus we are fully represented to make decisions here.

"Pesh brings charges against you for interfering with the harvest and disrupting the rituals. He claims that you entered Harvest House, and your presence tainted the work done there. Three living skins are now worthless, where they would be priceless if left undisturbed."

"Charges? What are you talking about? We were looking for our lost slithers, and when we found them, they'd been butchered!" Battle energy infused Snake's muscles with strength. "If charges are to be brought, it will be against the thieves who took them, stole the skins they sloughed, and murdered them all!"

Srika's head went up and her shoulders back, but her eyes

widened. She jabbered to the men behind her, then spoke again. "The snakes were found, not stolen..."

"Found in the white sands, not in Wohim territory!"

"...and murder is hardly an appropriate word. Humans may be murdered, but animals can only be harvested, as these were. We take only that which is given us by the god." Ice filled Srika's voice, and when she translated, angry murmurs broke out behind her.

"They're not mere animals! The slithers are as intelligent and thoughtful as humans, though their shape is different. They are sacred messengers of the gods, and we depend upon their prophecies for our survival. Stealing the slithers is an attack upon the People!" Snake fought to control shaking muscles, quelling the flicker in thigh muscles that wanted to leap to the attack.

Nerom the Warrior spoke and Srika took a deep breath before translating. "Nerom says that your gods are weak, as are your warriors. Our god in her might and mercy granted the battle to us, and ownership of your snakes with it. Even the silver snake has been given to us, that we may breed our own. Your people must make do with the snakes they still have—if any—for we have a god-given right to the ones we have, and to any we may encounter in the future. Blessed Night has gifted us, and if she has taken from your people to do so, that is between the gods. We will not spurn her gift."

Behind her Rhodor the Merchant spoke in his own language.

Srika nodded. "The Malim will now cast their votes for your fate, based on the charges brought against you. I, as Caretaker, will vote first." Chin high, she produced a blue stick from her sleeve and cast it down in front of Snake. "I vote for eternal slavery, rather than death, as your knowledge of these snakes could be helpful to our people."

Pesh stepped forward and, without speaking, cast a yellow stick.

Rhodor stood next and hurled a yellow stick point-first into the sand, more violent than might be expected of a merchant.

Nerom stepped forward, fingering four sticks–blue, yellow, red, and green. He spoke directly to Snake.

"You have the look of a warrior," Srika translated. "Out of respect for your calling, Nerom would cast the green stick, to spare your life, but he dare not. You are too dangerous."

And Nerom carefully laid the yellow stick with the others and returned to his place.

Silence stretched, as if giving the Malim a chance to change their votes. Then Srika spoke again. "It appears the other Malim disagree with me. The sentence is death."

~~~

The drums began sedately, just audible, but they caught Jynx's ear. It must have something to do with her, or with Ick. Or Snake. She knew Ick's situation, but her fear for Snake caught at her imagination. Why did she always assume the worst? Why did she have to scare herself with words like "dead"?

Ick buzzed in her head, a "voice" that expressed discomfort, pain, anxiety–and grief.

Jynx's fear spiked. "You've heard from Snake?"

He is in deep trouble. They will execute him for interfering with their slaughter of my slithers.

"You've spoken with him?"

Of course. Ick's tone was offended. *I can talk to both of you, but I do not know why Rapport doesn't work between you and him.*

Lightheaded, Jynx swayed where she sat. "Is that what the drums are?"

You must escape. Now. Kyr must live. His deeds have been prophesied, and if he does not perform them, the People will die.

"How soon? Where? What death do they plan for him?"

Now, I think. Follow the drums.

"*Can you guide me to him? I'll need your help.*"

No time. Go now! We cannot lose him!

Queen. For the first time Jynx understood what that meant. The queens lived for the People, and sometimes died for them. The tallgrass didn't have royalty, so it had never occurred to her they did anything but order people about. Another sudden insight: Among the white sands, humans and slithers together were the People–not just the humans. They didn't separate the two types of people in their thinking.

Jynx looked around, but no human shadows played against the walls of her tent. She dug through her satchel, found her small knife–she'd lost the large one–and slung the satchel over her shoulder. The skin filled with water tempted her, but she left it. The one filled with blue sand remained, the magic bowl was still in her satchel, and her packets of herbs and unguents. Nothing else really mattered.

She tried to walk casually to the back of the tent and sat. Keeping an eye out for shadows against the canvas, she slit the tent wall, ears pricked for any sound other than tearing fabric. Distant voices, the clink of pottery somewhere, a tent flap thrown back–nothing close, thank the One. She tried to swallow, but her throat was too dry.

She again checked for shadows on the tent walls, then thrust her head through the opening she'd made and popped it back inside. There. That was fast enough to be missed, unless someone was looking right at her. But it allowed her a quick look.

The drums still beat, slowly gathering intensity.

Jynx wouldn't get any safer by waiting. She set her satchel outside the slit, where it would be at hand. She couldn't stop the trembling, so she ignored it. Taking a deep breath, she crawled through the slit, shouldered her satchel, and began walking.

Her shadow would appear on other tent walls, so to avoid attracting attention, she'd have to be as casual and open as possible. Forcing herself to a nonchalant stroll was hard when she wanted to run.

The execution rituals were easy to find, right in the center of the village. A wide open space had been cleared and white sand layered thickly over the black sand in the center. A tall pole stood in the center of that, and Snake was bound to it, hands stretched above his head. Barefoot, bareheaded, and shirtless. The grimace on his face had to be from discomfort, as the bloody nicks across arms and shoulders were likely more annoying than painful. She hoped.

But she had no way to get to him across that open expanse. Especially through the crowd gathered to watch. No wonder she'd escaped the tent so easily! The whole village must be here, their chants blending with the drumming of four men seated behind Snake's pole.

Two men with knives danced into the makeshift arena and slashed Snake—one across the belly, the other across the forehead. These were longer cuts, a little deeper than the nicks.

What now? Jynx clutched her satchel to her side, tried to slow her breathing and with it her rising fear. She hated not knowing what to do. Remembering her patients back home, she forced the same calm she maintained when treating last year's flu epidemic.

Ick, I can't get to him without being caught, but I have an idea. I have *to have your help. Where are you?*

The frantic buzzing in her head quieted just enough for Jynx to find the path to the too-small box several tents away. The tent was unguarded, but the wooden box inside was locked. While she struggled with the lock, she explained her idea to Ick, and the slither began to calm.

Jynx broke the blade of her small knife forcing the lock open. But that was all right; she found a larger, fine quality knife, and then its twin, in the tent.

Someone's personal possessions lay strewn about the undecorated black floor. While Ick left the box and stretched the kinks out, she rummaged through them for anything useful.

A sword. Short and curved, not what Snake was used to. She took it anyway.

And then she changed clothes. Why on earth she had ever brought the hareem with her she had no idea. Gauzy and almost weightless, it had been no burden, but really!

When the gossamer, shade-sliding silver-blue hareem was finally in place, she checked herself over. Diaphanous material gathered at ankles and wrists and curved about her throat. Solid material covered her breasts and what Jynx thought of as her "private parts," but everything else was transparent. From experience she knew her deep cleavage, belly button, and the dimples above her buttocks were visible through the soft fabric. She felt naked, even though the essentials were well covered, but she had done this once before. She could do it now.

Besides, the thought of Snake watching... She shut the thought off so she could concentrate on what must be done.

She thrust the knives into her sleeves, hoping not to poke herself too badly with them. They'd be visible through the fabric, but no one would be looking at her wrists. Then she attached the tiny cymbals called "zills" to thumb and middle finger of each hand and wrapped Ick about her waist. She should add toe bells but didn't have time. The sword she carried across her palms.

"I hope this works," she murmured to the queen.

~~~

On her way out of the tent, Jynx snatched up a blanket and wrapped it about herself and Ick. She saw no sense in preparing people ahead of time by walking through the crowd in only the hareem and the slither. She muffled the zills in the edges of the blanket and on the way to Snake practiced the special way of walking that went with the hareem. Toes first, sedate and delicate, hips swaying.

To her surprise she drew attention as soon as she started through the crowd, which began to part for her.

Through the crowd she saw two knife dancers whirl near Snake again, slashing deeper. He bore several cuts that hadn't been there earlier, and fear clutched at her. How long before the ritual climaxed with Snake's death? How long would they make him suffer first?

Snake's face was frozen into a mask of anger and energy that would have been frightening had he been free to unleash them. Jynx saw no fear, and even pain had been blocked from his face. How did he do that?

She stepped out of the crowd into the arena, watching Snake's eyes change as he saw her.

The crowd murmured as she stepped forward, and the knife wielders paused, staring. She saw Srika with the men she knew must be the other Malim. All four were staring at her. They were her audience, although she'd rather dance for Snake.

Jynx controlled her shrieking nerves, stepped forward again, and dropped the blanket.

Murmurs rose around her and the crowd stirred. More importantly, Snake's eyes heated—a heat replaced by fear. For her. She swallowed, turned to face the Malim, and began to work the zills. She strutted to the center of the arena and stopped.

Ick unwound slowly from Jynx's waist, twisted down her hips and legs to the sand.

The crowd grew louder, a few shouts among the men, as Ick crawled across the black sand to the central white sand. She wound around the base of the pole and Snake's legs, up and up, draping herself across his shoulders. Jynx saw him shudder as she worked the zills and her swaying hips. The people seemed to think it part of the rituals. The Malim's reactions were guarded, but they didn't interfere–Jynx's greatest concern.

Ick's mouth opened, displaying needle-sharp teeth. She hissed at the crowd and the Malim. She encircled Snake's throat, and he groaned in fear as her tongue flicked his throat knob repeatedly.

Jynx began to dance in earnest, wishing for Kahpur and her tambreen to set the beat. She heard the jingle-tap of the tambreen in her head, set her feet and arms and hips circling and swaying, enticing and provocative. Sand, cool and soft, patted her feet, pushed between her bare toes. The movement drew her, the rhythm absorbed her. She closed her eyes, threw her head back to expose the graceful arch of her throat. Long walnut hair swayed just above her hips. She bent back farther. Arms circled gracefully above belly and breasts. Slowly she lowered herself, until thick hair swept the sand into tiny combed ridges.

Lost in the dance, she emptied her mind of all thoughts, all worry, all fear.

The tickle in the sand by her right foot would have startled her, if Ick hadn't warned her first. The slither queen's glide up her body was as sensual as Jynx's dance, drawing all eyes to wide hips, flat belly, shapely breasts... And then, as Jynx surrendered herself completely to the performance, Ick's face hovered over hers. Long jaws parted, exposing hundreds of deadly teeth, and Ick hissed. Loudly.

Silence, as the watchers held their collective breaths, and Jynx held her zills quiet. The deadly tableau held for a long moment.

Did you see me pretend to bite Kyr's throat? asked Ick, mischief lightening her voice. *I drew just enough blood to be convincing. And I got some of his ropes chewed within a strand or two. He'll break them easily when you signal.*

And then Ick flung herself from Jynx's body and slithered toward the Malim. Only Jynx– and maybe Snake–heard the embarrassing names she called them.

As Ick's body slapped into the sand, Jynx stood straight. Her dropped blanket was only three feet away. One graceful spin and she was there. She collapsed on the sand, body stretched forward and head down, fingers groping under the blanket. With a firm grip on the hilt of the short, curved sword, she spun on her bottom and back to her feet, flinging the sword in Snake's direction. It fell short by almost ten feet.

But Snake saw it coming and lunged forward against his bonds. The last strands parted. He landed flat out on his belly, fingers stretching to grab the sword. He rolled away from the converging knife men amid the screams of people getting out of the way and rolled to his feet, sword in hand.

Then Jynx lost sight of him as Srika and three other women ran toward her. They stopped abruptly, crying out, as Ick slapped Srika with her tail and bit another woman's ankle, leaving two dozen dots of oozing red. The last woman backed away fast.

A moment later Ick was wrapped around Jynx's waist as they ran toward Snake.

Jynx ducked under his raised arm and stood back to back, a knife in each hand. She cut and slashed, but the men's knives were longer and she took a painful gash along the ribs. Ick stabbed the man with her tail, and his falling corpse impeded others.

Snake grabbed Jynx's arm. "Run!"

She took two steps and changed direction. "My satchel!"

She snatched it up and flung it over one shoulder as Snake sliced a man's throat and pushed her in another direction.

They darted between tents, Snake almost stepping on Jynx's heels. "This way!" He pulled her to the right and they went between still more tents.

A man leaped from between the tents, curved sword swinging at close range, but Jynx got her knife up in time to catch his wrist with it. He screamed and dropped, holding the wrist where blood spurted rhythmically.

They seemed to run for an hour, though it must have been

only minutes, before Snake abruptly pushed her inside a blue and red tent painted with yellow stars. They flattened behind a pile of boxes and blankets and froze.

Feet ran past, men's voices yelled, but no one checked inside the tents. As soon as pursuit slowed, Snake sat up and gathered his scattered gear.

"This is where they held me to wait for the execution rituals," he told Jynx. "Hopefully, my sword is still here."

It was, along with his pack, where he stowed the curved sword. Jynx helped him into the harness for his own sword. They hid among the boxes, waiting for sounds of pursuit to fade. And longer.

Somewhere in the middle of the night, they slipped out of the tent and the village cutting across huge black dunes. They climbed up one side, sliding back a little with every step forward, then sliding down the far side on their buttocks.

Around midnight Snake found Katinga's Eye and they got their bearings, but they didn't stop to rest until the sultry rays of the sun peeked over the shadowed dunes.

11. Travelers

Daylight brought its own dangers in the Rainbow Sands. Snake and Jynx found a shady place on the far side of a sinister black dune, where an arm of sand curled around to form almost an enclosure. They dropped onto the sand, still panting from the exertion of climbing over the dune.

Unable and unwilling to stop himself, Snake put an arm around Jynx's shoulders and kissed her soundly. He half expected her to push him away so she could breathe. But she didn't, so he just kept kissing. His lips meandered from her mouth to her nose, her cheeks, her eyelids, her throat...

Her kisses were just as frantic, as if they might never have another chance.

Snake reluctantly forced himself to stop. Pursuit couldn't be too far behind. These people wanted Ick badly, and they'd want to eliminate their prisoners, too.

Still, better to stay ahead of the enemy if possible. The Wohim knew the area better and they were dressed more protectively. Speaking of which...

He started to comment on Jynx's provocative attire, to ask where she'd found it, but memory stirred. Last year, not long after they'd met, a bandit named Varid had made a suggestive comment...

"You got the hareem from Isyr," he said, trying not to make

it sound like an accusation. "She taught you to dance like that."

Jynx's eyes widened. "Yes, and yes. I told you about it. You said you didn't know Isyr."

Snake shrugged. "You didn't know I'd been born in the Rainbow Sands, and it's not something I share, generally. Isyr and I grew up in the same village, so we knew each other, but I was in the Prophecy Clan and she was in Praise. She was still there when my mother and I left. How did she end up in the tallgrass?"

"I don't know. When I met her in Irnia, she was their most notorious courtesan. She spoke of teaching me to be one, too." Jynx's eyes twinkled.

"A... whore? *Isyr?*" Snake still pictured her as a beautiful child, adored and destined for high rank in her clan. What happened to her?

And others he had known, children he'd thought of as lifelong friends. How had they changed? He might not even recognize the village when he got there.

Jynx picked up her satchel. "I'm going to change back to more protective clothing."

"Good. And then we need to move on for as long as we can."

As Jynx waded behind a dune to change, Snake indulged in a few moments of remembering her dance. So beautiful! Maybe one day she'd dance just for him. Privately. He deliberately changed his thoughts to something less affecting.

They experienced two more sandstorms over the next few days as they struggled south. Just before the first one, Snake glimpsed tiny dots—probably pursuers—crossing the slope of a black dune. He changed direction radically, wishing he knew a way to brush out signs of their own passage. No one caught up before the storm hit, and he didn't see them again.

Jynx pointed out the second storm as it approached. When Snake was sure it wouldn't bypass them, they changed direction again and ran for all they were worth, until stinging sand up the nostrils forced them to huddle next to another low stone outcropping.

When at last they emerged, spitting and wiping sand from eyes and ears, he felt confident they'd lost the Wohim.

"Just in case," Jynx told him, "I just thought of something we can try. Do you remember what Sprig told us about the magic in the different colors of sand?" Sprig was the Little Man who had guided their small group to the magic life-saving waters a year ago.

But Snake didn't remember that conversation. He frowned.

"Oh. Never mind. You were unconscious. He says the black sand hides people. Carry a handful in your pocket, to be hidden from sight. We can avoid the Wohim if they can't see us."

Snake's eyes snapped up to the dunes behind them and to either side. Was that why he hadn't seen their pursuers since the first storm? Of course they'd know the magical properties of their own sands. "Quick! Load your pockets and satchel with enough to hide you and Ick!" He scooped handfuls of sand for his own pockets and pack. "Will it hide our footprints, too?" No signs of movement, or footprints other than their own.

"Uh, I doubt it." She shoveled black sand into her pockets, even spreading some along the slither coils wrapped around her waist, to Ick's irritation. Eyes wide, she also glanced around.

Snake made another sharp change in direction, although it kept them in the sun—except for the protection of the shadows hovering perpetually over the sands. Within minutes he made another, and within an hour, one more. Whenever they encountered a particularly tall dune, they ascended it and stopped just below the summit for a look around. Always he saw their own tracks but no sign of the Wohim.

Had they turned back? Maybe, but tactically he had to assume the worst, not the best.

He pushed Jynx as hard as he could, until she began to glare at him every few minutes. His own calves were burning from the pace; hers must be much worse, though she made no complaint. But she would be safe, whatever the cost to either of them. So would Ick, for less personal reasons. He set his jaw.

Maybe he'd underestimated Jynx's durability on foot.

He thought about her dance again, a truly awe-inspiring bit of ingenuity. Maybe he'd underestimated her in other ways, too.

Different tools were available to women than to men, based on how their bodies were made. And yes, their different construction affected what things they were good at. He could fight; she could dance. And in this case, her way worked better than his. Even if only because it was so unexpected. So unpredictable.

The unexpected was always a good weapon.

By late the next day, with still no sign of the Wohim, Snake and Jynx shifted to night travel again. Although blurred by black shadows, the sunlight was burning Jynx's fair skin, and even Snake's browner hues turned darker. They sweated more by day and ran out of real water quickly. They began to ration their blue sand, even though the magic refilling bowl provided fresh, too-sweet melon slices to renew them whenever they wanted.

Snake took care not to mention Shyriel and Evron to Jynx. They were either too far ahead to encounter, or their bodies were buried in sand somewhere beyond the Wohim village. There was nothing they could do to improve that situation, so he wouldn't worry Jynx with it.

They soon developed a routine. They'd walk all night, then find a relatively sheltered place to spend the day. As they hunkered down, Ick left to hunt before the sun lifted above the dunes. Although the humans saw little wildlife, Ick fed on rats, scorpions, snakes, an unwary jackrab, lizards, and once even a small tanglecat just learning to hunt. That time they lost a full day while Ick stretched out in the sun to digest, demanding that Jynx oil her scales.

Before long the mother tanglecat came looking for her offspring. She might have taken on the sleepy slither, but the two humans added to the mix were overwhelming–and her tanglekit was already dead. She left with a lip-lifting snarl.

It felt good to be out from under the continual shadows, but the sun shone brighter in the sea-green sand than they'd become used to. Jynx soon brought out her salves and unguents for sunburn and blistering feet.

To Snake, the blisters were the worst. Sunburn hurt, but he didn't have to walk on his sunburns. Jynx was even redder, so he didn't complain. How did she manage to walk without limping? Pride kept him walking carefully, to show no sign of limping or weakness.

Occasionally he climbed to the top of a dune–these were shorter, overall, than the black dunes, to his relief–to check their back trail, but it seemed the Wohim had given up and gone home. Now it was just a matter of getting to the white sands.

~~~

Snake and Jynx crossed a narrow arm of sea-green sand in one day, so grateful to be out of the black sand that they slowed their steps to linger.

"So," Snake said, "what's the magic of this sand, according to Sprig?"

"He didn't mention this one," said Jynx. "I haven't seen it before, either, and had no sample to show him." She tied a handful tightly into a twist of fabric to show him if she ever had the chance.

Snake didn't remember the sea-green sand from his childhood, when he and his mother fled the white sands. Had he gotten them lost? Or were there other ways to the People than he'd left by?

He worried at this off and on all day, until he saw in the distance what appeared to be a strip of white sands. At last!

A terrible mix of emotions overwhelmed him: Excitement. Dread. An unexpected yearning for his carefree childhood, fear and loathing of the slithers who had both consumed and ended that childhood, curiosity about the friends he'd left behind. He'd always repressed that curiosity savagely, but this time he forced himself to leave the gate open for all these emotions to pour through.

Memories cascaded back, and to his surprise they were mostly good ones. Kicking over the copper sand boundaries between nests as he and Saam raced across the youngen precinct. Sleeping in his underground burrow with a dozen small slithers coiling and snuggling with him. The slow, boring voice of Sarro, one of his teachers and Father's friend, learning about slither prophecy. Breaking up fights between Slyn and Wint, then between Slyn and older slithers. Sitting by the palm trees with his father, watching the wading birds.

"Snake? Why are we slowing down?" Jynx's voice brought him back to the present.

"Sorry," he said. "Just gathering wool, as you flatlanders say."

She laughed, a light, tinkling sound that always warmed his heart. "Wool gathering," she corrected him. "And our land isn't flat. We have lots of hills and valleys."

He smiled at her. "To us Snows folk, everything else is flat."

"You seem happy to be returning here."

Snake had to think about that. "Not really. It's necessary, and I'm curious about some of the people. That's all." And about how returning would affect him, with slithers everywhere he went. Being sacred, they had the run of the village. He chewed his lower lip for a moment, made himself stop.

No, he wasn't happy to return. He truly hadn't missed this place, after the first few months of grief. But he did have some good memories, and he wouldn't close them off anymore.

Like putting a slither down Isyr's back. Who was his co-conspirator? Henth? He couldn't remember for sure. That had been fun!

Thinking of Isyr, he wondered how many other playmates had left for the wider world. Who? And why?

Jynx's touch on his elbow startled him.

"O mighty warrior," she teased. "It's a good thing you're so attuned to danger, to keep us safe."

His own smile was wry. "And a better thing that you're a sharp-eyed healer who keeps us safe *and* heals us of any hurts." He gestured ahead. "We'll soon enter the white sands."

She shaded her eyes with one hand. "Oh, good. Even my blisters are getting blisters." She slid her hand into his as they walked.

He couldn't remember ever feeling so... content? As if all was right with the world, no matter what trials might be ahead. Or behind, for that matter. He still wasn't confident they'd lost the Wohim for good. Even if they'd traveled many miles since seeing any sign of them. They just didn't seem the type to give up easily.

"What's that, Snake?"

"What's what?" He shed his contentment, eyes scanning the sands before them.

She pointed. "That."

Men. Maybe half a dozen, slipping in and out of the clefts between the dunes ahead of them and to the east. Wohim? This far out of their territory? And between them and their destination!

Ick hissed, raising her head as high as Jynx's shoulder.

"Snake, they're carrying wooden crates!"

He felt the slither queen's roar in his head, and then he was running. "Hide!" he called back over his shoulder, unable to stop running. From the corner of his eye he saw her start for shelter. He shrugged off his pack and let it drop where it would.

The line of men and crates dropped out of sight beyond a

sea-green dune and Snake redoubled his speed. Shouting voices floated above the sand as he spread himself flat near the top of the same dune. They hadn't gotten far, then. He crawled upward the last few feet and peered down at the Wohim.

So few? Only three men. No, four. Three danced around in agitation, wanting to do something... but unsure how to proceed. At this distance, Snake couldn't see well, but a square, dark crate sat on the ground near them. Several crates. The fourth man writhed on the ground. A long, sinuous shape lay next to him.

Was that a slither? Here? Snake "swam" downward through the sand on his belly, toward the scene ahead of him, stopping twice behind mounds of sand for a closer look.

A pale buzz in his head startled him. Ick! He opened to the slither, caught rage and despair but nothing coherent.

Then the queen's fury boiled in his head. One of her slithers was hurt! She needed to get to her. Now! Jynx was bringing her. *Kill them! Kill them all! Thieves! Murderers! Save my slithers! Go! Now! Hurry!*

Snake found himself on his feet, charging pell mell down the dune with his sword in his hand. He fell once in his hurry and the men at the base of the darkening dunes looked up.

One came toward him, drawing a short, curved sword from his sash. The other two just stared, mouths open.

The fourth lay still.

Snake bellowed a war cry from the depths of his gut. The swordsman had no chance against the longer weapon and went down in one clean, easy stroke. The spray of his blood looked black in the falling darkness. Snake snatched the curved blade from his hand as he fell.

The fat man—the one who did most of the shouting—seemed frozen in place. Only at the last moment did he try to run, but he was much too slow. His dead body slammed into the sand, rocking forward onto its face.

The third man held his hands in front of him, a futile barrier to Snake's charge. He jabbered frantically, then dropped face down into the sand, spread-eagled in complete surrender and submission.

Snake raised his sword for a killing strike, but suddenly Ick was gone from his mind. He caught himself, swaying and stunned.

This was Ick's doing. Her anger. Her orders.

And he'd blindly obeyed, as if he had no choice.

Did he have a choice?

He looked around. Six crates made of sticks lay scattered. One of them was shattered, and a young slither, only four feet long, lay next to it, red eyes gleaming in the darkness. She didn't move.

Next to her lay the fourth man. Dead. The slither's tail still protruded from the man's chest. Snake reached for Rapport with her. She was dehydrated and dying, too weak to pull her tail from her victim. And then Ick's buzz pushed Snake aside, out of Rapport, and she took over.

When he turned, she was just starting down the last dune, the one he'd raced down to kill two men.

Fortunately, one remained for questioning, if they could make sense of his language. But that could wait.

Snake leaped for the crates, released their latches as quickly as he could. From each he lifted a slither between four and six feet long and stretched it gently on the sand. The one with her tail stuck in a man's chest came next. He reached for the poor, valiant creature with his Rapport, reassuring her of his intent. Then he forced himself to slow down, to move quietly to avoid alarming her. Gently he stroked her tail, then reached for the venomous tip, holding his breath. He eased the tip free of its flesh trap and laid it carefully on the ground. She was so near death. Had he lost her already?

He heard a sound and glanced up. Jynx was coming.

As she approached, he said, "Jynx, we need blue sand for these slithers. They're badly dehydrated."

No answer.

He looked over his shoulder at her. "Jynx?"

She stood stock still, eyes wide and face white, staring at the black slithers.

He understood immediately. The only slither she'd ever met was the beautiful Ick. To her, the black ones would appear more sinister.

"Ooh, ick!" she said, lip curling. "Snakes!" She shuddered visibly and her knees twitched, as if she fought an urge to turn and run.

The same way he'd reacted as soon as Ick released their Rapport.

"Slithers, Jynx," he said impatiently. "Like Ick, only black, like my tattoo. They're dying. No one deserves to die like that."

She took a deep breath, then dropped her satchel and squatted to dig out bowls molded from copper sand. She filled them with blue sand from her waterskin.

Snake leaped to his feet and snatched the first bowl from her hand. "Thank you."

The hard part would be convincing a slither to swallow blue sand. He doubted his childish experience with Rapport would be enough to convey what he wanted.

But again Ick "pushed" him aside. *She* could explain to all her slithers at once what to do.

Then it was a matter of holding the bowl in front of the injured slither while she took a mouthful of sand, waited a moment for it to change, and swallowed.

The effect was immediate. She lifted her head and reached for more, already showing a little more energy.

Jynx joined him, moving from slither to slither with a copper bowl of blue sand—although she held the bowl at arm's length, by her fingertips.

Then Snake moved on to a thick-bodied adult almost ten feet long. Larger than the others—or even Ick—his red eyes turned toward Snake.

The slither suddenly tensed, and Snake fell back, buried under an onslaught of emotion. Frantic, he tried to stem the tide, to close the emotional floodgates–and abruptly he knew who this was.

Slyn, the aberrant slither whose trespass into the queen's precinct had almost gotten Snake killed.

12. Reunions

Snake felt Erilya's reaction to Slyn–irritation, caution, anger, frustration. All mingled.

Slyn's reaction to him was more complex. Exuberant joy and anger, loneliness and sorrow, suspicion and excitement battered at Snake as the slither threw himself bodily at the warrior. Slyn, who used to coil himself around Kyr's arm, now wrapped Snake from ankles to shoulders, squeezing lightly as in those early days. But a constrictor's instinct is to squeeze a little tighter every time its prey exhales, and in moments Snake's breath was cut off. He commanded Slyn to drop away from him.

He'd been good at command as a child, but he'd lost too much. His adult command was impotent.

Then Ick was in his head and Slyn's, as she gave her own imperial command.

Slyn ignored her! His queen!

Snake's world began to blacken. He would die here in the Rainbow Sands, destroyed by the one who had almost gotten him killed once before.

"Let go of him, you... monster!"

No, Jynx! With no breath, he couldn't stop her pounding on the big slither with her fists. He couldn't pull her off. He couldn't get between them. He gritted his teeth, hating that helpless feeling.

Ick hissed and launched herself at Slyn. Her teeth sank into his thick hide, leaving long, bloody gashes.

Slyn screamed in rage and struck at Ick.

Jynx hurled sand at his eyes, with no effect.

Bits of light sparked behind Snake's eyes. The pressure in his head built, as if it would burst his skull. One last try. He gathered himself as best he could, the berserker warrior who fought fearlessly against impossible odds, heedless of weariness, wounds, or the greater might of the enemy.

He shouted, a huge roar of sound pushed out from an almost airless chest, the sound heavy with the entire force of his being.

The world disappeared as he passed out.

~~~

This creature was huge! Jynx hadn't known snakes—slithers—came that large. Yes, Snake had said queens could reach twenty-five feet or more, but she'd assumed he spoke from a childhood memory, when the slithers would have seemed much larger to him.

She screamed every obscenity she knew, beating the slither with her fists, having nothing heavier at hand.

Ick lunged past her, hissing, and left bloody rents in the black slither's hide. *Slyn!* His name came from Ick in passing. She recognized the name. Snake's nemesis from his childhood.

Move!

Jynx obeyed Ick's command without thinking but her heel caught in the sand and she fell, still holding a fistful of sand. She scrambled backward, away from the slithers.

Sword. If she could get to the curved sword, she could free Snake. She turned onto hands and knees and lunged for Snake's pack, lying on sea-green sand a few feet away. Her hand closed about the hilt.

Something struck her in the ribs, hard. She grunted as she

flew through the air, but she held onto the sword. Slyn lashed his tail at her again as she rolled away and found her feet again.

The two slithers were intertwined now, black and silver, writhing and rolling across the sand. Ick's teeth had clamped near Slyn's throat and were slowly drawing his head toward her mouth, jaws alternating in their hold on his scales. He thrashed and the tip of his tail struck at Ick, but she batted it away with hers.

Snake lay unconscious a few feet from Jynx.

Jynx wanted to help Ick fight Slyn, but she hesitated, looking back at Snake. She needed to be sure he still lived.

She chose Snake because he was a lot safer and she knew what to do.

Her fingers against the side of his throat confirmed life. Thank the One! He breathed, his chest rising slowly as he inhaled.

She lifted his head and his eyes opened. He might not recognize her yet, but... ahh. Focus. Recognition. She helped him sit up.

For a timeless moment she held him, wanting only to be in contact with him. "Are you all right?" she asked.

He nodded vaguely without speaking.

The slap of scales against scales returned their attention to the slithers. Slyn lay on his back, stretched full length on the sand. Ick hovered over him, open mouth exposing her sharp back-curved teeth.

The silence in Jynx's head was deafening. She'd expected Ick's voice. Apparently this was a private conversation.

Slyn coiled in one sudden, powerful move, and so did Ick. Separated by several feet now, they stared at each other. Jynx began to think the fight was over.

Is Kyr all right? Ick's "voice" still felt tight with tension.

I think so. What was that about? Why did he attack Snake?

That's complicated, a story for another time, but it's all bound up in prophecy. Would you be so kind as to treat

Slyn's wounds?

Jynx stared at Ick, eyes wide. Ick's voice soothed her: *He will not hurt you. Go ahead.*

"Will you be all right for a few minutes, Snake? I need to treat wounds." She heard the quaver in her own voice and wished it away. It didn't go.

He nodded without speaking or meeting her eyes.

She shouldered her satchel and started slowly toward the big slither.

Show no fear, dear one. You are safe with me.

Taking a deep breath, Jynx walked resolutely to Slyn and examined his wounds. She soon forgot who her patient was, focused on her work. Mostly she found scratches, but two were deep enough to need stitching. She cleaned all the wounds, but it took a queenly threat before he allowed her to sew them up. "They'll heal cleaner this way," Jynx told him, as she would any patient. She had no idea whether he understood her, since they weren't bonded. And never would be, she thought, jaw tightening.

"How about you, Ick?" she asked. "Are you hurt? Do you need my attention?"

No, thank you. I have a few scratches, but none are deep.

Jynx went back to Snake, who got to his feet shakily. "Let me see," she said. It was an order, not a request, and Snake submitted, as he should. Trying to forget who her fingers touched, she checked his ribs and sighed in relief. "Nothing broken."

Her own ribs hurt where Slyn's tail had slapped her. It would be painful for a few days, but nothing was broken on her, either.

"I think," said Snake, "we'll stay here tonight and continue to the white sands in the morning. We could all use a rest after that." He looked a long time at Slyn.

Jynx touched his arm. His blue-green eyes met her brown ones, as if he searched deep. "How are you doing?" he asked.

Jynx held up a still-trembling hand. "Is it over? If so, I'm fine. If not, I may throw up."

Snake gave her a small smile. "I'm not sure what that was all about, but for now at least, it's over." For a moment he seemed lost in his own thoughts, his skin pimpling as if cold.

While Snake set up a simple overnight camp, Jynx watched Ick visit the slithers as if checking on them. She coiled next to each, as if offering reassurance. Or perhaps praying. The slithers were close to the gods of the People, after all.

To Jynx's surprise, it was Slyn whom Ick chose to guard the surviving human. The man had curled up in a ball, terror widening his eyes and whitening the hands that held his knees to his chest. He hadn't even tried to run away. As Slyn wove his sinuous way through the sand toward him, the man trembled violently and mewled like a frightened kitten. Slyn coiled next to his shoulders and opened his mouth, black tongue flickering inches from the man's white face.

Jynx almost felt sorry for him when she saw he'd wet himself. But he was a part of the cruelties visited upon the slithers by the Wohim. True sympathy was out of the question.

She did worry, though. She'd never seen this side of Ick before, and it frightened her a little. She watched Ick with her slithers. What did she say to them, and what would she do next?

That night Jynx slept in Snake's arms, the safest place she could imagine. Snake moaned once in his sleep and one leg kicked lightly, but otherwise his nightmares didn't disturb her rest. She had her own nightmares for that–images of a slither tail stuck in a man's chest, of dying slithers desperate for water, of what appeared to be an insane gleam in Slyn's beady eyes, of silver and black entwined in combat...

She awoke well before the sun poured over the dunes, feeling gritty inside and out. She'd gotten very little real sleep and debated whether to snuggle closer for a little longer. Just as her eyes began to drift closed, movement on a nearby dune popped them open again.

Two figures moved slowly through the deep sand, as if exhausted by the effort. Clearly, they saw the humans and slithers, for they came straight for Jynx and Snake.

Jynx sat up. Next to her Snake snorted and readjusted his position without waking. She reached out and touched his face.

He sat up abruptly, hand closing about the hilt of the sword he kept above his head as he slept. He looked where she indicated with a nod, and his shoulders dropped as he relaxed.

And then, as Jynx "tapped" Ick to awaken her, they both stood and waited for Shyriel and Evron to join them.

~~~

"What happened in the storm?" Snake asked. "We lost you, so we took shelter, such as it was, to wait it out, but we couldn't find you afterwards."

Jynx poured more strawberries, melon, and cheese from the small, wooden bowl onto a cloth. When she set the bowl down, it refilled with more melon.

Shyriel's fingers trembled as she reached for them. Evron got the next bowlful.

"We thought you were right behind us," Shyriel said around a mouthful of red fruit.

Evron swallowed a bite. "My guess is that we didn't dig in as soon as you did. With less experience in the sands, you probably thought the storm was worse than we did and stopped without realizing we didn't. When it ended, we backtracked a long way, looking for you."

"So how did you find us today?" Snake eyed a big strawberry but chose to leave it for the others. Had they even eaten in the last three days? At least they'd had their own waterbag of blue sand.

"We stumbled across a Wohim village and learned you'd been there." Evron's brown eyes searched Jynx's face. "They told us you stole something valuable of theirs and ran off."

Jynx snorted. "We stole Ick. As far as they're concerned, their god gave her to them for breeding purposes."

"Breeding?" The shock on Shyriel's face was almost comical.

I'll tell her. Ick curled up in Shyriel's lap, her mood as grim as Snake had ever heard it.

He nodded and turned to Jynx. She nodded that she'd heard, too.

Ick broadcast for all of them to hear, not holding back her anger. Snake winced, but he confirmed her words and added a description of what he'd found in the shed.

The roar that filled all their heads expressed shock, horror, anger, pain... and Snake remembered that she hadn't seen it— and he had deliberately glossed over it. Some of that anger was directed at him for withholding information.

"Erilya," said Shyriel aloud. "Calm. Please. This is a matter of terrible import, but neither you nor I may step again into that village. We will return home, and we will plan. We will make careful preparations. And then we will teach the Wohim a lesson that will be remembered for a thousand generations."

From her voice, Snake would never have known that tears ran in rivulets down the queen's cheeks. He glanced at Jynx's ashen face. Her anger and grief lay as deep as the queen's; she just didn't show it as readily on the outside.

"We'll need to carry the slithers and move as fast as we reasonably can," Snake said. "We don't have enough blue sand for so many for this length of journey. And that means traveling night and day until we reach... our destination." He'd almost said "home" but caught himself in time. Home was the Snows, and at the moment he longed for their cold, crystal clarity.

"I'll carry Ick," said Jynx.

Shyriel glanced at the slither queen and hesitated. "Kyr, will you carry Slyn? You're the strongest of us, and he's the largest slither."

No. No, and no. Not Slyn. But if he spoke those words, the slither would hear, and the situation would become worse, not better. He was grateful when Jynx spoke up.

"If possible, Snake should carry no slithers," she said. "We're not safe from the Wohim yet, and he's our only warrior. He may have to unburden himself quickly to fight. If he must carry a slither, let it be one much smaller and less important."

Jynx glanced at Ick, and Snake wondered if the suggestion had been the queen's. Was Slyn still going on about that old complaint of his, after all these years? Even as a youngen he'd been convinced he could match any queen. Snake managed not to roll his eyes.

"There are seven slithers and only four people," Shyriel pointed out. "One of the slithers is still at death's door, and only Erilya and Slyn would be able to fight alongside us. Kyr must carry one, and Slyn was once partnered with him. You will carry Razhra, the most injured; she can ride atop Erilya's coils to minimize the effort she must make. Evron and I will each carry two of them. I know they are heavy, but it is necessary." She stood.

Snake saw worry and sorrow in Jynx's eyes and knew his reflected the same, but he squashed it as best he could.

"I'll carry your pack, Kyr," said Evron. "You'll have burdens enough."

Snake nodded. "I'll keep my sword on my back, though. Slyn, if I tell you to drop off, do so without hesitation so that my sword is unencumbered." The buzz in his head felt familiar. Slyn hadn't changed much over the years. Still intelligent and a little wild. Unpredictable, to be polite. Aberrant, to be honest.

Ah, Kyr. I always knew you would return. You're in my prophecies, as well as the queen's. We are bound by destiny, you and I. Slyn crawled up his body and coiled three times

121

around his waist. *I have practiced fighting, so that you and I together can fulfill my prophecy by defeating the Wohim once and for all.*

Snake shuddered at the slither's touch. He tried not to, but he couldn't help it. His skin and scalp prickled, and he heard Slyn's amusement in his head. He forced himself to breathe normally, not in panic-stricken pants. Trying to be gentle and non-antagonistic, he closed off the link to Slyn except for the thready trickle that kept them barely in Rapport. He didn't want to talk, or to rehash old memories.

Evron led, Snake brought up the rear. Slyn tightened just enough to rest his head on his own coils in the small of Snake's back. He was their rear lookout–Slyn's idea, and a good one. But it didn't make Snake any more comfortable.

13. Warrior

They loaded their prisoner with Snake's pack and Jynx's satchel. At Shyriel's order, they also forced him to carry two of the slithers, hand-picked by the human and slither queens in consultation. The man's face turned gray, and Snake gave him as evil a grin as he could.

The prisoner's burden freed Shyriel and Evron of carrying more than one slither apiece. Jynx said something under her breath on the subject.

Snake didn't ask her to repeat it aloud.

If Snake had his way, their Wohim prisoner would be abandoned where he was, but prudence dictated taking him along. That meant he got a share of water, too. His irritation at having to share their precious blue sand dissipated when Evron found two nearly full waterbags among the Wohim's belongings. With careful rationing, that should get them to their destination deep within the white sands.

Snake deliberately stepped too close to the Wohim for the man's comfort. "Who are you?" he growled. His shoulders went back, his chin down, his eyes wide.

Seeing the man's sudden terror, he tried again without the posturing. He placed his hand on his own chest. "Snake."

He put his hand on the man's chest and looked a question at him, receiving a grudging "Morinl" in return. He put Morinl in the middle and himself and Jynx at the back, where he could keep an eye on their prisoner. Shyriel and Evron led; they knew the way. That was as secure as he could make them for this journey.

They ran out of water three days later, and out of blue sand two days after that. Progress was much slower than Snake had anticipated, and he ground his teeth with impatience.

Still, they had an unlimited supply of the juice from strawberries and melon produced by the magic wooden bowl. The humans managed on them just fine, but the slithers were all unhappy. They didn't like the juice, and some had upset stomachs. Given that their stomachs were almost the full length of their bodies, there was a lot of pain. And grumbling. And snappishness.

Especially for poor Razhra, who already hurt so bad.

Snake watched Jynx practically tiptoe through the sand, saw Ick support and protect the younger slither as best she could. But Jynx still got bitten twice and Ick once—a bite she returned with some vigor, accompanied by a severe scolding.

In fact, all the slithers became short-tempered. The bickering began when Slyn made a disrespectful comment to Razhra, who lost her temper at him. Slyn opened up Rapport with everyone and the bickering spread. Even Ick got into it when she'd had enough. When the humans tried to calm them down, it only got worse.

With everyone's attention on the squabbling, Snake decided later, no wonder no one saw, heard, or smelled trouble until it was almost too late.

The Wohim came from behind, so silently that until he saw Jynx's head turn, he didn't know they were there. Eight Wohim, carrying their short curved swords. These were warriors, dressed for action in short kilts instead of flowing robes, and they were led by Nerom, their Malim.

Even as the travelers noticed them, the attackers broke into a run across the face of a pristine white dune. The Wohim war cries were high and sharp, and their eyes carried no fear, only determination.

"Run!" Snake shouted. "Jynx, keep an eye on our prisoner!"

He saw Jynx push Morinl in the back to get him moving. She grabbed the short sword from Snake's pack and threatened her captive with it at every step. Good. He could count on her experience from previous adventures. Ahead of her and Morinl, Shyriel and Evron ran across the sand without looking back, freeing him to concentrate on defense.

He'd need to fight well, with so many opponents. Too bad the Beast wasn't here to fight alongside him. That would improve the odds!

The enemy spread out for room to fight. Or to break around him to attack his companions. If they did, he'd only catch a couple at best. Snake glanced around to see what the terrain could do for him. Not much. His opponents moved better in sand than he did, and only a few rocks and scraggly bushes broke up the sands in this area.

Could he lead them away from his group? Not yet. They had to have a reason to chase him first. Better to defeat them.

He chose intimidation as his first weapon.

The Tears of Heroes mushrooms would be helpful right now, but he had none with him. He'd have to become a berserker without the drug. Fixing his feet in a solid stance, knees flexed and weight slightly forward, he widened his eyes and snarled, his face a rictus of insanity.

He roared at his enemies. He stomped around like a bull ready to gore. He shook his sword at them. At his hint, Slyn reared his head next to Snake's and opened his red mouth wide, black tongue flickering.

His enemies closed the distance quickly, trying to surround him.

He waited... waited...

And attacked. A sudden leap at their leader, a berserker scream, his sword swinging in narrow arcs in front of his body.

The man plowed to a stop, bracing for Snake's strike. He lifted his curved sword to block the blow.

But Snake twisted his wrist. His sword dipped beneath his opponent's and up into his belly. He whirled away as the man clutched stupidly at his stomach, watching the red stain spread across the whiteness at his feet.

The enemy were too spread out to support each other. Snake slashed one's throat. Another's sword hand flopped onto the sand amid his screams.

The other five were regrouping fast, Nerom calling orders to the others.

Snake charged into the middle of them, sword swinging. Fear didn't exist. Pain could not. The blood on the sand would be theirs.

A sudden whirl, a twist of his hands, and the back of a man's knee collapsed. The sword continued behind his own shoulders to block the sword behind him. He spun, still holding the other sword, and twisted his wrists again. His blade followed the curve of the opponent's sword and struck into the man's face. The man's panicked cries of pain dropped with him to the sand, where he clutched at his eyes.

Snake didn't expect Slyn's movement, large enough to pull him off-balance. He turned his head in time to see the slither's venomous tail strike into Nerom's throat and back out, lashing at another fighter in the same move.

Only one left. Eyes wide in terror, the man turned and ran. Filled with the berserker rage, Snake could not let him go. He hurled his sword like a javelin. It struck the man in the back and he fell face first into the sand.

Still engorged with battle energy, Snake spun in a full circle. No enemy remained. All eight were dead or disabled. Snake lifted his fists in triumph, arching his back, chest thrust out. His victory roar echoed even among the soft dunes and went on and on... and on.

The fury took a long time to drain. Snake checked his enemies, finished off those still living. He stalked in huge circles, still screaming his victory to the hills of sand. He saw his group at a distance, the lone figure behind the others, walking toward the finished battle, her face white.

Thank heavens he had not partaken of the Tears of Heroes, for then he might not recognize his friends from his enemies. The thought was sobering, even in battle mode. He opened Rapport with Slyn. *Tell them to go on without me. I'll catch up soon.*

But Slyn was almost as crazed with battle ecstasy as Snake and ignored him.

I will, he heard from Ick. And a moment later Jynx turned back to the group, glancing over her shoulder at him.

The battle fury, especially in the aftermath, wasn't something he wanted her to see. And yet he smeared the blood of his enemies on his face and arms, and even drew a ring of blood around Slyn's neck, just behind his head. They'd earned these tokens. And they could be washed off later.

For a while he walked in a broad circle, growling low in his throat, working off the excess energy. He examined the dead, took weapons, waterbags, food items, and jewelry—all with a slither-head motif.

When he calmed sufficiently, he sat on the white sands, forehead on wrists that rested on his knees. Weariness soaked every ounce of his body. He had no energy to move, even to avoid the blazing heat of sunlight reflecting from sand. His stomach rolled with revulsion. With the Tears, he wasn't this self-aware for many more hours, and by then he had more distance from the battle. But this... He remembered the battle in agonizing detail, every stroke, every battle cry, every line of blood drawn. None of it his.

Eight men dead.

Why did the Wolf Guard even need the Tears of Heroes, if they could fight like this without it? Especially with the risk—a very small risk—that someone could become addicted to it? Like his friend, Kayde. Wearily, Snake pushed that thought away.

Slyn purred in his head, pleased with himself for the one death he'd caused. He, too, was a mighty warrior! He'd just proven once again that he was the equal of any slither queen—and he made sure Snake knew it.

The warrior ignored him. He could have reminded him he'd never take the place of a queen, but he wasn't up to an argument.

How far away had Jynx and the others gotten by now? He really needed to catch up to them as soon as he could. As their protector, not just for the solace of Jynx's presence.

What would she think if she saw him like this, covered in other men's blood? What did she already think, from seeing some of that vicious fight? Knowing that because of him, eight men were lost to their wives and children, and to friends, and to the tribe that depended on the contributions of every man? It didn't help much that he had no choice. And why was he so concerned about them, anyway? They were enemies! They were dead by their own choices.

Separating himself from such thoughts, Snake grabbed a handful of sand to scour the dried blood from his hands and face. Sand also scratched off most of the blood on his leather, but the streaks and splashes on linen would never come out. He had one spare shirt left in his pack.

Over Slyn's objections, he scrubbed the blood from the slither's neck, too, then asked Slyn to examine him for any remaining blood.

When he couldn't put it off any longer, Snake turned toward Jynx's footsteps. Slyn crawled up his leg and around his waist a few times, then stretched his head up by Snake's, balancing on Snake's shoulder near the sword hilt.

Further weighed down with the waterbags and other items he'd taken from the bodies, Snake started after the rest of his party.

~~~

Even with little blood still visible, Snake's party seemed unnaturally subdued by Snake's presence. Evron cut sideways glances at him but said nothing. Shyriel's wide eyes betrayed admiration and more desire than fear–but she kept her distance, nevertheless. Ick kept her counsel, saying nothing, so that Snake had no idea what she was thinking. The prisoner carried stark terror in every line of his body, from wide eyes and half-open lips that he licked often to the trembling in his hands and constant fearful glances, as if to be sure Snake wasn't about to kill him. Snake made no effort to discourage him, knowing fear would make the man easier to handle–even though he moved away every time Snake came anywhere near him.

Only Jynx seemed normal. But then, only Jynx had seen him fight before–when they escaped from the Wohim village.

When Jynx slid her soft little hand into his big, callused one, he was grateful for her touch. He ran a thumb across her palm, amused at himself. Her hands weren't lady-soft, only soft in comparison to his.

Her presence and her touch brought comfort and at least the beginnings of peace.

Besides, her grip helped him keep his feet when he tripped on deep sand out of sheer weariness.

The drain on his energy wasn't as severe as a true berserk, or he wouldn't be able to walk at all. Still, every step had to be forced, and the entire group was held to his sad pace.

Jynx kept a frequent lookout behind them, for which he could kiss her. If he had the energy. No one else even thought about an ongoing threat! It seemed unlikely to him, too, but this would be a bad time to abandon vigilance.

When they stopped that evening, the group enjoyed a water feast with their magically-produced melon, and everyone's spirits improved.

"A celebration of a great victory," Shyriel called it.

"It will take them awhile to discover what happened to their men," Snake said, "and longer still to replace them. If they can. My guess is that the People will be free of their raids for a time."

"You are already making a difference in the fortunes of the People," pronounced Evron. And then he began to sing, a melody he seemed to have worked on all day. His fine, rich baritone rolled across the white dunes, describing the fight and Snake's heroism in the face of great danger, and how prophecy's fulfillment had begun with today's horrendous battle.

How embarrassing! But Snake smiled and accepted it graciously, wondering how red his face was.

Next to him, Jynx giggled at his reaction to the song, which only embarrassed him more.

As a brilliant full moon ascended the steep banks of the sky, Snake had enough. He grabbed Jynx's hand and they went for a walk among the dunes, away from the noise of celebration and the giddiness of survival.

They walked in silence, Snake choosing easy paths as much as he could. They couldn't go far; the group needed not to be separated for the rest of the journey—a mind-set he couldn't release easily, although he knew it didn't matter as much as it had this morning.

"What do they expect of me, Jynx?" he asked at last, needing her sound sense and practical thinking.

"In what way?"

"Prophecy says my leaving as a child began the downfall of the People, and that my return will signal their recovery. But I don't know what that means. I don't know the details of the prophecy. If there are any. Or what they think I can do for them."

Jynx was quiet for a long moment, lost in thought. "I can't know, either, because no one has said anything specific. But I can guess. From the moment the earliest of your annual visitors discovered you're a warrior, I'd guess they expected you to rescue them, to lead them to some kind of glorious battle victory, to destroy their enemies and restore the world as it used to be."

"I can fight, if that's all they want, but I don't think it is. What if they want me to stay? A kind of talisman or icon for prosperity?

"How you respond to that is up to you, Snake. If that's truly what they want, you'll have to make a choice that may be as difficult as the one Ick has to make. It will be a choice you'll have to be able to live with the rest of your life, whatever the outcome."

Snake thought about her words. And about Ick and the choices facing her, and how that would affect Jynx.

How had he ever allowed himself to be pulled into this mess? Nothing good could come of it, for either of them.

He turned to Jynx and gathered her into his arms, holding her as tightly as he could without crushing her.

For a long time they simply stood there, taking what comfort they could from each other's presence.

He dreaded the choices that must be made, and the outcomes of those choices.

14. The People

"What are those?" asked Jynx, squinting into the distance.

Next to her, Snake peered ahead, too. "What are what?"

"Those bent sticks, the tall ones that look like broken windmills."

"What are windmills?"

Jynx laughed. She couldn't help it. "Don't you have windmills in the Kingdom of the Snows? To pull up water from underground, to water the fields and livestock?"

"What do they look like?"

"Just slats of wood, like a gray sunflower, on a tall wooden tower. You've seen them. I know you have, as much time as you've spent in the tallgrass."

"Ah." Snake smiled at her with that heart-stopping twinkle in his blue-green eyes. "I've wondered what those were. They draw water? How?"

She shrugged. "I have no idea. I just know they work. Those, off in the distance, look broken." She nodded her head toward them.

Snake burst out laughing. "Those are trees!"

What? Surely she'd misunderstood that. Jynx stared at him, hoping he'd elaborate before she had to expose her ignorance.

He obliged. "Palm trees, Jynx. The things that look like a broken windmill are the palm fronds. The branches. The part you called the 'sticks' is the trunk."

Jynx stared, trying to make out details as they walked. "That's the oddest looking tree I've ever seen." She tried to ignore Shyriel's superior smirk. Eavesdropper!

"In the desert sands, palm trees indicate an oasis, like a spring or pond. Most villages are built near one, because water sources are scarce here. In this case, the palm trees are like a welcome home flag. We'll reach our destination soon."

Jynx's stomach clenched. Suddenly the end of the journey was all too near. She laid a hand on Ick's coils at her waist. Ick would have to choose soon. If she chose Shyriel, such aloneness would be hard to bear. Their togetherness had been constant for over a year and she couldn't even imagine being eternally alone in her own head anymore.

Especially if Snake decided to stay, too. Or to return to the Snows, for that matter. A wave of melancholy swept through her.

Jynx cocked her head, listening to Ick. "Ick sent word ahead to one of the slithers... from her tangle?"

Snake nodded. "Like litter mates, for dogs. Her immediate slither family."

Ahead of them, Shyriel stopped. She turned to face them. "They will send the Protection to escort us into the village and there will be a crowd waiting to see us. I must clean up and dress as best I can to honor the People." She looked at Jynx, chin lifted. "It is expected of queens. You need not do so; your time could be better spent oiling Erilya's scales until she shines."

Jynx's jaw set. "I *do* need to clean up and dress. As much as you do, to make a good first impression. And then I'll oil Ick's scales."

Temper flared in the human queen's eyes. "Her name is Erilya! You will call her by her proper name and rank! This is *not* a place where your disrespect for a queen will be tolerated!"

Pouty child! Jynx lifted one eyebrow, her chin a bit higher

than it should be. Then she took three of the Wohim waterbags and disappeared behind a tall shoulder of gleaming sand, mumbling under her breath where Shyriel couldn't hear and hoping she'd left too little water for the queen to wash as she'd like.

Jynx didn't live in a kingdom but in free lands. She'd never thought of royalty as anything special, just people like anyone else. Shyriel certainly hadn't changed her mind.

She took her time at her ablutions, knowing it would irritate Shyriel, while Ick hunted. The slither returned soon and announced that she'd found a nice, juicy kangapak. Jynx knew right away what it was; Sprig had talked about his nephew's pet kangapak when she and Kahpur had visited his home in the Dark Wood with Snake and Kayde. Sprig had described the kangapak as a large brown rat with exceptionally long hind legs and a penchant for stealing things.

The slither queen seemed to think she had rid the world of something evil while filling her belly.

Jynx had to laugh. And then she oiled Ick's long, slender body with the queen's favorite scented oils, and applied a touch behind her own ears and in the notch of her throat. Then she dressed in the cleanest britches she had—not as clean as she'd like—and brushed out her long walnut hair until its deep reddish glints shone.

Only then did she awaken the slumbering Ick to return to the others.

~~~

Jynx got her first good look at the village of Farwyl from near the top of a mid-size sand dune. She caught her breath. This wasn't what she expected at all, despite Snake's descriptions. Certainly nothing like the Wohim village.

Her first impression was cleanliness and order. To her right lay the wooden buildings—homes, Snake told her, arranged in concentric circles about a larger wooden building that he referred to as a meeting hall for events that included the entire village, such as a queen's major prophecy. The sand in front of it was carefully raked into attractive patterns. Tall yucca, similar to that in the tallgrass, bloomed on either side of the entry. The main path to the entry was edged with small plants that Snake couldn't name for her. He did know that red or yellow flowers bloomed in the cool of the evening and closed up again as early morning warmed to the sun. Jynx found them fascinating and resolved to get a closer look later. She bit her tongue to avoid asking questions about their medical efficacy that he wouldn't be able to answer.

To her left lay larger concentric circles in the white sand, separated by narrow paths defined by pale green sand and edged with six-inch walls of pressed copper sand. Within each band, wedges were marked off with more low copper walls.

Confused, she looked at Snake.

"The slithers' precincts," he explained.

"Give me Erilya," Shyriel interrupted. "The Protection come now, to escort me in triumphal procession. The People need to see that Erilya has returned with me."

How rude! Were all royalty mannerless, or only this little girl? Shyriel just wanted credit for bringing the slither queen home. Jynx's lips thinned in irritation.

"When the escort arrives is soon enough," Snake told her.

He understood. Her time with Ick could be limited now, and her heart ached with the potential loss. He was protecting what time she had. She loved Snake more than ever at that moment.

Snake pointed to the center of the slithers' precincts. "That largest circle in the center is Ick's home. That's gold sand and real gems, forming the path up to the door." He stopped for a moment and swallowed loudly. "Do not set foot within the queens' precinct. They both live there, and it's forbidden to everyone else without specific invitation."

The place where Slyn had trespassed, where Tchenya had nearly killed Snake, when he entered to rescue the obnoxious young slither. Jynx shuddered. And shuddered again at the thought of living among so many snakes... er... snake-like creatures.

"The next outer circle is the Prophets' precinct, where they spend most of their time with the most god-touched slithers. Next outer are the Priests, then Novices, then Acolytes in the outermost circle, where my burrow was located. The copper walls line the paths between precincts–circles–and separate the burrows from each other within each precinct. A well-ordered People, as you can see."

Jynx opened her mouth to comment, interrupted by a weight at her waist.

Shyriel's hand lay on Ick's coils, as she prepared to remove the slither bodily. "They come! Give her to me!"

Jynx saw half a dozen men start up the dune, shields shining and spears exactly vertical. The one in front wore the skin of a large cat over his shoulders like a cape.

Evron, chief priest of the Praise, lifted his voice in a song that rang across the village.

Knowing the moment had come, Jynx stood and helped a reluctant Ick unwrap and transfer from her arms to Shyriel's. She felt Ick's sorrow at the parting, although she assured Jynx it was only for now. The queen was torn between two women she loved. Jynx determined not to make it worse for her. Removing her touch wasn't easy, though.

Snake's hand on her arm steadied her.

The warriors knelt as one before the queens, heads bowed.

"Welcome, Beyir," Shyriel's regal voice spoke with solemn formality, pitched to reach the wildly cheering People gathered outside the meeting hall to welcome her. "I have returned, triumphant, bringing with me the one who was foretold, and restoring to the People our lost queen!" She held Erilya above her head, the slither wound about and between her forearms. Erilya opened her red mouth and hissed loudly, announcing her presence.

Jynx wanted to cry.

"Kyr, come!" Shyriel commanded. Then she started down the dune in the midst of her honor guard, displaying Erilya for all to see.

With a helpless glance at Jynx, Snake joined her.

Should she trail after them like a servant? Or wait here for Snake to return for her?

Unthinkable, that she be seen as Shyriel's lackey! Sighing heavily, as lonely as she'd ever been in her life, Jynx sat down on the white sand to wait as the new arrivals entered the building.

Around her the earth was still. She heard an insect buzz somewhere nearby but didn't recognize its voice as one she knew. No wind wisped the sand for once. For one awful moment she seemed to be the only living person in the world, cupped between white sand and cloudless blue sky. She inhaled noisily and exhaled hard, just to hear something vaguely human.

Did Snake even realize she wasn't with them? It wasn't normal for him to ignore her and leave her alone in a strange place. The thought that she couldn't even count on Snake was hard.

And then she sat up straight and scolded herself. Never would she allow that bitch queen to make her feel so small, as if she didn't count, to make her feel sorry for herself! She straightened her shoulders as her eyes lit on fire.

Just in time. Here came Snake, dashing out of the building, eyes wild, looking for her. He slowed when he saw her where he'd left her, slogged his way up the dune to where she sat.

Without a word, he bowed from the waist and held out his hand. She took it, finding comfort in his warmth and strength.

Together they walked down the dune, still without speaking, and she knew he would be there for her, no matter what the rest of the day brought.

~~~

Jynx and Snake paused for a moment just inside the door of the hall to let their eyes adjust to the dimmer light. She hadn't expected a floor of tightly-joined boards, although she couldn't have said what she *did* expect. Colored streamers hung from otherwise plain rafters and broad stripes of matching colors had been painted on walls just below the ceiling. The People remained on their feet, abuzz with excitement, which was good since there were no chairs. A few stared at Snake—because they were trying to see the child they'd known in the adult before them? Or because his return had been prophesied? Or because he'd heard the voice of a slither queen? Two now, though the People didn't know that yet.

At Shyriel's gesture, they followed her through the throng, which parted before her, to a low dais at the front of the room. Tall torches stood at the corners of the dais, their colorful flames giving off sparks, each color exclusive to one torch—red, blue, green, gold. But the one that held Jynx's attention was the one in the very center of the dais, one with black flames dripping purple sparks.

Jynx and Snake stopped at Shyriel's low command to stand at the front of the crowd, below the dais. Still holding Ick above her head, the queen took her place before the black torch. At the back corner of the dais at floor level, Evron lifted his arms and sang. Even to Jynx, the stranger, it felt like a hymn of thanksgiving.

The crowd quieted as his voice filled the room.

Jynx sighed softly. Such a rich, beautiful voice! She never tired of hearing him sing. She closed her eyes to focus on the song and didn't open them until the last notes faded.

Shyriel lowered her arms to shoulder height and Erilya—Ick, Jynx corrected herself—lay across her shoulders in loops, from wrist to wrist, the end of her tail dangling almost to the floor.

The crowd quieted as Shyriel drew herself up, preparing to speak to them. She waited for complete silence before opening her mouth.

"Thank you, my People, for your warm welcome. Queen Erilya adds her pleasure to mine. Chief Priest Evron and I have endured a long, arduous journey to speak with Kyr, as our People do every year. As you all know, Kyr was foretold generations ago as the one whose leaving would begin the People's decline, and whose return would restore to us our prosperity—a return that has been sought every year since he left, until I personally prevailed upon him to come."

The crowd broke into wild cheering, and Jynx twisted to see ecstatic grins and wildly waving arms. She looked back just as Shyriel summoned Snake onto the dais with a small jerk of her chin. His thumb gently caressed her palm as he released her hand and stepped up onto the dais with the queens and turned to face the People.

Jynx saw the tiny tightness at the corners of his mouth that signaled his annoyance. She doubted anyone else did.

"There is a pattern here," called Shyriel as the escalated cheering began to quiet, "that demonstrates that the gods shape our lives and watch over us. Who could dispute the gods' hands in this, when the one sent to restore us is a man who was born of us and understands our ways, a man gifted with a strong Rapport, and a man who has become one of the most feared warriors in the world, as well as a leader of more such warriors. Even here, halfway around the world, we have heard stories of the fabled Wolf Guard in the Kingdom of the Snows!" She turned her beautiful, radiant smile on him and the crowd went wild when he smiled back.

Jynx inhaled slowly, hoping his smile was a reflex, not a commitment.

Behind her, someone spoke of "a fitting consort for the queen." Her heart sank. Yes, the queen was younger and more beautiful and much more powerful than she. Yes, they looked good standing together. *What am I doing here? I don't belong! And Snake looks at home, as if he'd never left.* She smiled at him bravely, hoping he couldn't see how much all this hurt. If he stayed, how would she ever get home by herself? And how could she survive his loss?

Shyriel released Snake, who rejoined Jynx, and the crowd quieted–although it took a few minutes, during which Praise singers in the center section of the room filled the air with thanksgiving.

The human queen waited expectantly until the last sounds died away. "I have more good news. As you can see, I have brought to you not only our prophesied warrior, but I have rescued and brought home my partner and sister queen, Erilya!"

More songs soared through the air–like a host of angels singing, Jynx thought. She barely heard the roar and the chanting of the People in the tiny space between outrage and resentment. Rescued? From her? Ick didn't need to be rescued, once *Jynx* had freed her from men she now knew were Wohim.

Praise singers flowed onto the dais from both sides, singing and swaying, feet dancing in praise of the gods for restoring both their foretold savior and their abducted queen. Jynx thought she might throw up. Someday, some way, she would get Shyriel for this lie.

Snake's quiet hiss made her aware of just how tightly she was squeezing his hand. As if it were Shyriel's throat.

Shyriel held up a hand, palm out to the crowd, and once again they quieted. She held their silence for a moment, then signaled Jynx with a jerk of her chin.

Of course, Jynx never considered that it was aimed at her, until the queen spoke aloud. "Jynx, will you please join me." It wasn't a question.

Startled, Jynx glanced at Shyriel, at the hidden darkness in her eyes, and then at Snake, who urged her forward with a hand in the small of her back.

Jynx stepped onto the dais reluctantly and turned toward the crowd.

"I have also brought us an important guest," said Shyriel.

Jynx suddenly understood. This was Ick's idea. No wonder Shyriel's smile looked just a bit forced.

"This is Jynx, a pastoral healer from the tallgrass. When Queen Erilya was lost and far from home, Jynx took her to the tallgrass and cared for her there until Kyr and I arrived to bring her back to the People. Queen Erilya befriended her and has a special relationship with her, and Jynx came with us to continue caring for our slither queen. For Queen Erilya's sake, please welcome her to the white sands and honor her with your courtesy and respect."

As more subdued cheering and acclaim ensued, Jynx had to smile at the crowd. Shyriel's praise might be niggardly, but she hadn't expected recognition at all!

"Tonight we feast in celebration!" Shyriel cried, echoed by the enthusiasm of the crowd. And Jynx was dismissed, now that Shyriel had done her duty.

Only the purr in her head, expressing Ick's gratitude and love, soothed Jynx's wounded pride. She returned the slither's love, tinged with sorrow at what was to come. Whichever way the decision went, Ick would be hurt, and Jynx hated the thought.

15. Celebrations

"Welcome," said a woman's voice at Jynx's elbow as the crowd slowly dispersed. "I am Lasyr, of the Prophecy."

Jynx squeezed Snake's hand and he turned from those trying to speak to him.

"Preparations for tonight's feasting and celebration have already begun," Lasyr told them. Her brown eye met Jynx's eyes easily, but the blue one seemed to be looking at Jynx's shoulder. Wander-eye, the healers called it. Jynx focused on the brown one. "If you would like to rest from your long journey, we have prepared a place for you to stay while you're here, and if it please you, I can show you there now."

"That would be lovely! A place to leave our belongings and perhaps wash would be appreciated." Jynx turned her beautiful smile on the young woman, whose shoulders relaxed, as if she were reassured by Jynx's friendliness.

Jynx and Snake followed Lasyr through the crowd, their progress interrupted every few steps by welcomers and well-wishers. Lasyr, smiling as brightly as any of the People, waited patiently.

The building Lasyr led them to appeared to be an empty home. Wooden walls were interrupted by shuttered windows on either side of the door. A low wooden porch welcomed them to come inside.

The home was completely unfurnished, although the walls were whitewashed. Jynx's heart sank. How would she get any rest, let alone sleep, on hard wooden floors?

Then Lasyr led the way to a second room Jynx hadn't noticed, and she changed her mind.

The outside of the building might be weathered wood, but this room and another next to it were thick with colorful pillows of many shapes and sizes, clearly meant to be arranged in whatever way made them comfortable. All shutters were open, allowing fresh air and sunshine inside. The soft scent of a spice Jynx didn't recognize wafted through the house from a small incense burner in each room.

"Please," said Lasyr, "be comfortable here. Tell me what you require and I will arrange it. The spring is near—only a short walk from the back door. You may bathe in the designated area there, or I can have a tub brought and filled for you."

Snake spoke before Jynx could even think. "The spring is fine for bathing, but I thank you for the offer."

"If you would like a guide to show you around, I can also arrange that."

Snake chuckled, "Again, thank you. But I think the village hasn't changed that much during my absence. We can find our way."

"If you need anything, send the nearest of the People for me and I will see you are accommodated. When the feast is ready, I will come for you."

And then they were alone, for the first time since their tryst under the riverbank in Sayvil.

Snake gave Jynx a mischievous grin, and she returned it.

For a little while, Jynx forgot she was in a very strange place halfway around the world from home.

As Snake's lips met hers, her last thought was, Shyriel would not approve. But Ick would.

~~~

Snake was in heaven. Jynx felt so good in his arms and they had their own private place. The colorful pillows configured to a large, luxurious bed. Her body was hard in all the right places and soft in all the right places. He himself didn't have any soft places at the moment. None. They had become explorers together, accomplices in their mutual delight. Maybe they'd even skip the feast and celebration, even if it insulted their hosts.

The gasping shriek from the doorway wrenched him out of his intensity as Jynx rolled out of his arms and sat up, eyes wide. She held a pillow like a shield between her and their visitor.

A middle-aged woman in full ceremonial robes stood in the doorway, fingertips across her open mouth and long lashes raking her eyebrows.

Praise be to all the gods that he still wore his britches! "Don't you knock?" he demanded.

The woman dropped her hand and squared her shoulders. Her chin firmed. She glared at them. "I am Delyna, of the Praise, assigned by the queen to be your protocolist."

"My what?"

"Protocolist. I am to help you understand and adhere to proper protocol. When you were shown to this house, the assumption was that you are a married couple, and if not you would correct us. Queen Shyriel assures me you are not married. I beg your pardon for our error in your housing, but we will correct that now."

"We're happy with this arrangement," Snake said, a worm of dread and disappointment crawling in his belly.

Delyna drew back, scandalized. "It is not considered proper here and will shame the queen who brought you home at great risk to herself."

Snake glanced at Jynx, who was tight-jawed with fury. Unfortunately, this was an aspect of the People's lives he knew nothing about. He'd have to take Delyna at her word. Somehow he didn't think that would douse Jynx's anger at Shyriel.

Well, he wasn't happy, either. Within minutes Jynx left with Delyna and he was alone in more house than he needed. He hoped Jynx had equivalent quarters. Likelier, though, Shyriel had specified something less desirable—even a dormitory for women, if such a thing existed here.

~~~

When an escort arrived to accompany him to the festivities—in borrowed finery—he discovered that Jynx had been given three attendants to care for her needs. And apparently to keep her away from him. At least one accompanied her at all times.

On the other hand, the soft, flowing garments clung to her body just right. Her face shone with cleanliness and her hair had been brushed until it reflected the sun itself. He got just close enough to scent the light fragrance she now wore, but he had no chance to speak to her, except with eyes and smiles. Her coy glance in return told him she still lived within the memory of the time in "their" house.

He sighed in frustration. That spoiled brat of a queen would probably assign him a female escort, too, just to keep him from Jynx.

His own finery of silk robes irritated him. How could anyone move, with the generous folds entangling his legs at every stride? His efforts amused his escorts, who hid smiles behind coughs or turned heads. He was forced to slow his pace and shorten his stride to little more than a shuffle to avoid the tangling, but the slow pace felt like wading through a foot of mud. He ground his teeth.

The feast itself seemed quiet and sedate to him, despite the constant sound of speech and laughter and people chewing palm nuts and drinking cocomilk. In the Snows, feasting meant shouting and loud boasting, bawdy singing, constant thunderous laughter, and the occasional fight. Here, someone frowned when he pulled apart a roasted fowl of some kind with his fingers, but none of the implements provided looked appropriate. Maybe Jynx fared better but she was seated six tables away—he counted them—with her back to him. He, of course, sat with Shyriel on an elevated platform set in the pristine sand. At her right hand, which had significance in the Snows. But maybe not here. Uncomfortable, he tried not to squirm.

Sugar-glazed palm hearts, sweet dates and figs, buttered snails, wine-soaked... whatever. They looked like the claws of the giant lobsters sometimes caught in the seas near the Snows, but tiny. Crawly daddies. Something like that.

The servers kept his cup filled until he covered it with his hand. It tasted delicate, spicy, and slightly sweet, and it went straight to his head.

"It's called perfayne," Shyriel told him, "a lovers' drink from the Crystal Mountains on the other side of the world."

He didn't touch it again. But he watched Jynx, to see if she did.

Strangely, he couldn't see that it was served at her table. Perhaps reserved for royalty? They had no nobility here, no ranks between commoners and the queens.

And no one explained anything, as if he already knew, from being born here.

As the feast wore on, Shyriel's eyes turned bright and glassy. The occasional light touch of her fingertips on his forearm became a hand resting on his wrist most of the time, then a hand on his shoulder. Desperation set in when she leaned her head against his shoulder and almost fell asleep there.

Snake shook her shoulder gently. "Shyriel? Awake! I must relieve myself of too much wonderful food and drink, and I don't want you to fa... be startled." He disentangled himself carefully, especially from the delicate hand resting on his thigh. Clearly he'd drunk too much, as well, if he hadn't noticed that! Thank Baldair Jynx couldn't see it!

He fled the table and the feast as gracefully as he could.

A few minutes later he found himself wandering along the edge of the spring. The spring held clear water, as still as the grains of sand that formed its basin. It made a perfect mirror for the palms to preen themselves in, and to reflect the soft glow of the setting sun.

What am I doing here? I should be home in the Snows, or in the tallgrass with Jynx, or at least trying to find where Kayde went in his exile. But he'd drunk too much perfayne, so that an invisible barrier separated his thoughts from his emotions. Nothing felt real. It bothered him, but he didn't know what he could do about it at this point.

He'd brought Shyriel, Ick, and Evron safely home, as promised. His obligation was done. He and Jynx could leave anytime, except for... what was he forgetting?

Here stood his favorite tree, the one he'd sat against next to his father many times to talk, to ask advice, to spend companionable time. Sometimes his mother had joined them. Sorrow for his father's loss trickled acid through his heart. He sat at the base of the tree and leaned his head back against it. He closed his eyes, felt them sting. Chest tight, he indulged in old memories, surprised at how many he had of this place and its people—and at how many names and faces he could no longer connect. What would he have been like now, if he'd grown up here instead of the Snows?

A soft buzz in his head turned his thoughts back to the world again. Ick's gentle tone, offering him friendship and solace. Of course she knew he was sad—and guessed why.

He looked around, half expecting to see her. Her amusement made it clear she kept Shyriel's attention elsewhere, so she wouldn't come looking for him. He sent his gratitude for her thoughtfulness.

And then the strangest message: An invitation to visit the queen's precinct, he and Jynx, with Ick as their guide. She very much wanted to show them her burrow and its riches, so he would understand why the queen was so protective of it. There was something else, too, but she was hiding it, like a surprise or a gift to be revealed only in that place.

Wondering if that was the perfayne talking, he agreed.

I'll get Jynx and we'll join you where you are, she told him. *I don't plan to tell Shyriel, though. She wouldn't understand.*

Then she was gone from his head. He wondered if the queens often kept important things from each other. And what would be the consequences for that.

Oddly comforted by her brief "visit," he dozed while he waited.

The breeze cooled his skin, then chilled him. He should have brought his bearskin coat, especially knowing how much snow lay on the ground. The ice across the pond before him wasn't thick enough to walk on, and the solid-ice wind-blown ripples were too rough for skating.

But the soft hand laid on the bare skin of his arm was warm.

"Snake? It's me, Jynx."

He blinked, saw the palm trees before him, and awoke fully.

Snake sat forward, ran his fingers through thick, dark hair. "I was dreaming." He blinked again, until the mounds of snow settled back into mounds of white sand, and shook his head ruefully.

Ick's laughter buzzed in his head. She was hanging loosely around Jynx's neck this time.

"Ick has invited us to visit the queen's precinct—even the queen's burrow."

Snake unwound his long, creaky body to his full height, stretching. "She told me. And I'm very interested in seeing it." A lie, but a small one. Curiosity wrestled with dread. That's where he almost died and where his father was killed. The restriction against setting foot inside those boundaries was stronger than ever, because of that incident, and he might have passed on the opportunity despite his curiosity, if it wouldn't make him appear cowardly to Jynx.

Maybe this was what she meant by "facing his past." If so, he was glad she would be there with him. He'd never admit it out loud, but he drew strength from her presence.

~~~

The raked sands of the slither precincts surprised Snake. He didn't remember them so painstakingly kept.

Only the prophets', the priests', and the queens' precincts, Ick told him. *It's partly rank but also because the acolyte and novice precincts house children. Keeping them raked would be impossible, so we indulge the children.*

Jynx nodded as if she understood, and Snake realized Ick spoke to both of them at once. Was that a talent of the queens only? Or could any slither speak to several humans at once? One more thing he didn't know.

The copper sand walls separating the precincts and the burrows within them were much shorter than Snake remembered. Hadn't he jumped them as a child? Now he could step over easily. By childhood habit, he stopped to rebuild a wall kicked over but not fixed.

They cut through the rings of precincts rather than following the longer walkways leading between them. Snake had to lift his feast robes almost knee high to step over, which annoyed him, but he made sure to watch when Jynx had to lift hers for the same reason. Was she deliberately lifting them higher than necessary? He caught the twinkle in her eye and felt a faint flush of desire.

Ick took them by the walkway around the queens' precinct, their soft slippers crunching faintly with every step. So far from the feast, the sky was thick with stars, and more appeared every moment as the sun's last rays faded. Faint voices from the feasting seemed as distant as the sun's last light. Jynx's tiny hand slid into Snake's and he cradled it as carefully as he would a fragile flower.

An approving buzz made him laugh quietly, as his heart filled with love and joy and contentment. He wanted to freeze time in this moment but could only freeze its memory.

They stepped onto the golden sand, the pathway into the queens' burrow. Snake caught his breath, remembering in spite of himself...

Tchenya, a twenty-five foot queen, eyes filled with emrel fire and hate, flowing like an avalanche from the doorway ahead of him. Between them, the juvenile Slyn who thought himself a queen's equal. Three running strides toward the queen, when he wanted to run the other way. Slyn's tail in his hand as he turned and hurled the slither to the frantic men outside the precinct—the ones who dared not enter...

Snake's insides turned to water. He didn't realize he'd stopped until he felt Jynx's thumb tracing gently—provocatively—across his palm. He made it four steps farther before the images swarmed him again.

The huge queen, mouth wide, ready to snatch him up and swallow him whole. *Vile! Insect! How dare you!* The voice of the queen, heard by no other human male in the history of the People. The fulfillment of Prophecy.

Sweat dripped from Snake's face, ran down his chest below the feast robes, trickled into his groin. He shivered, suddenly cold, and closed his eyes to force the images away.

When he opened them a heartblink later, his father raced across the queens' precinct, yelling and waving his arms to distract the queen. A deliberate sacrifice, to save Snake's life.

It had worked—and changed every moment of Snake's life from then to now.

The runnels on Snake's face were no longer sweat but tears. Silent tears, but sorrow and grief insisted on them.

Jynx squeezed his hand and he gripped hers so tightly he feared her bones would crack before he could make his grip ease.

They had come within a few yards of the entryway itself. Even in the soft light of the stars he saw the multi-colored winking of emrels, rubies, tauz, diamonds, skystones, and half a dozen other gems set into the gilded pillars that framed the doorway. As a frightened child he hadn't even noticed them. As an adult, he admired the richness and beauty of the burrow entrance.

There are no dangers inside for you, he felt from Ick. He turned to look at her, where her cheek nestled against Jynx's.

His breath caught in his chest. He felt the urge to protect the woman he loved from this... this...

Friend.

He swallowed, forced himself to nod.

Welcome to my home. Please come in.

He couldn't move. All he could see was Tchenya's giant form flowing through the doorway...

Jynx tucked herself under his arm and put her arm around his waist. She stepped forward, and he stepped with her, his arm encircling her shoulders, pulling her tight to his side.

They walked through the gem-dazzled opening together.

Inside, the burrow was not what Snake expected. Instead of low ceilings to crawl beneath, these were tall enough that even Kayde could have walked upright. Instead of one passage ending in a single large chamber as he'd naively imagined, the queens' burrow branched in several directions.

I would ask that you not speak of what you see here, to preserve the mystery and awe accorded the queens' burrow.

Ick directed them into the first left turn. A heavy wooden door studded with multi-colored sea pearls blocked the chamber at the end of the long hall.

The People's treasure. Ick burrowed into the deep, soft sand near the door until even her tail disappeared. Snake and Jynx looked at each other without speaking. And waited.

Ick's head thrust up through the sand and she rose on her tail as high as she could in front of Snake. Her red mouth opened.

A key lay on her tongue, on the other side of her back-curved teeth. She meant for Snake to take it from her mouth.

He could not. Not even with Ick, his friend, could he reach into a queen's jaws.

Jynx reached for it instead, but the queen's jaws closed. When the woman's hand withdrew, the mouth opened again.

A lesson in trust. And an exercise to move beyond his fear. Courage, he reminded himself, isn't lack of fear but being in control of your own reactions to it. *I* will decide, not my fear. He took a deep breath, eased his hand past two hundred deadly teeth, and daintily lifted the key from her tongue with hard fingernails. *This is Ick. She won't hurt me.* He even believed it, pretty much.

Her approval left him a little giddy as he turned the key and shoved open the door.

His jaw dropped in wonder. Huge piles of wealth rose from floor to ceiling, carefully sorted. Diamonds, rubies, pearls, opals, cinnabar, beryls, carnelian, jade, seastone, skystone, and many other gems, each in its own ceiling-high pile. Gold bars. Silver bars. Copper. Bronze. All segregated. Coins of many denominations and nations, each in its own pile. Gold in links, in vessels, plates, cups, statuary–and silver likewise. Lacquer ornaments and dishes, enamelware, fine leather, works of art Snake couldn't have imagined.

"What better place for this treasure than in the burrow of the queens, guarded by humans and slithers both?" whispered Jynx, eyes wide.

Snake understood from Ick's smugness that there was more to see. He locked the door behind them and Ick returned the key to its place under the sand. Jynx's hand swept it level again when Ick withdrew.

The next rooms were unlocked–meeting rooms, comfortable for both slithers and humans. Only the queens and the chief priests entered these rooms, and occasionally others needed for a particular topic, such as a report on a

Wohim raid or members of the Sett or Shabishosh tribes crossing the white sand, or trade dealings with other tribes.

Their huge bedroom was shared, and comfortable for both. It included a luxurious human bed, piles of soft sand for sleeping, chests of clothing and jewelry for the human queen, shelves of fragrant oils for the slither queen, and other features for their shared life.

One narrow hallway nearby was a locked escape hatch, so the queens could not be trapped inside their own home. Ick hinted at another elsewhere in the burrow but did not show it to them, apparently bored with the topic.

Two unopened doors remained. Snake's curiosity sharpened when he recognized Ick's hesitancy. Nor was he surprised when she swore them to secrecy, even knowing they would never speak of anything they saw.

Small creases of hurt bracketed Jynx's eyes at being asked to swear, but she swore firmly nevertheless, as did he.

She seemed confused when Ick identified the two rooms as the birthroom and the nursery.

For once Snake understood. "Jynx, the slither and human queens are born on the same day. Always. Any human mothers likely to give birth the same day as the slither queen are brought here to be with her. The new human queen will be whatever girl child is born the same day as the new slither queen.

"The slither queen does not lay eggs, as some snakes do, but delivers live young. At least one will be female—the next slither queen. The firstborn, in case of multiple female births."

"What if none of the human mothers has a girl?"

"Then she takes her new child home. Another mating must produce the new queens. It will happen, though, as the gods ordain. It always does."

She didn't look satisfied with his response, though, and he wasn't sure he was, either. He hadn't been with the People long enough to learn much about these things. Could two queens live at once, mother and daughter? He'd always thought not, but then how could a new queen be born? He turned toward to Ick to ask for better information.

Ick interrupted. *Dear ones, my sister-queen calls me. I will join her and the chief priests for a special, private celebration far out into the dunes. Our return is cause for sacred rites, where we mortals will commune with the gods in thanksgiving. And where perhaps I will find new prophecy in your arrival.*

Snake's shoulders sagged with relief. Shyriel would not be looking for him. One less problem to worry about.

Tonight, my home is yours, while I will rest among the dunes I've missed so badly. We will return at mid-morning.

Can a slither wink? Snake wondered. If so, Ick just did.

Ick moved toward the burrow entry, leaving them to themselves.

Snake looked at Jynx. She looked back, fearless and excited. They clasped hands as they watched Ick depart, and desire crashed through Snake. This was much better than the small house they started with. Scarce daring to look at each other, they started down the hall toward their own celebration of a different kind of homecoming.

16. Plans

Jynx studied the line of Snake's jaw, only inches from her face, noticing the shadow of morning stubble. A contented smile tugged the corners of her mouth. She laid her hand on his chest, her fingers teasing the dark hair there. She leaned an inch closer and blew lightly on his cheek, just to see what would happen.

The corners of his lips rose but his eyes didn't open. The arm on which she lay tightened about her and she laid her head on his shoulder. Such peace. Such quiet joy. Such belonging.

"How will we know when it's morning?" she murmured, wondering if he could hear her.

He opened his mouth to speak and kissed her instead—a long, hungry kiss. "Morning won't get here until after we've slept," he said, "although it wouldn't hurt us to sleep awhile now."

"Oh!" Jynx sat bolt upright, startled. "Ick!" She held up a hand to stop Snake's next words.

His reaching hand stopped just short of her bare breast as he waited. "I hear her." He quieted to listen, then sighed. "The rituals are complete and the queens are returning, exhausted. We'd better move."

Jynx was already rolling out of bed. "Is it already mid-morning?" She winced.

"Closer to noon," Snake confirmed. "And we need to leave without anyone seeing us in the queens' precinct."

"Is that possible?" All of Jynx's contentment and joy evaporated. "It will cause a ruckus, won't it? If we're seen leaving?"

"Yes, it will cause a ruckus. But we might have a way. Remember the escape hatch? It can't be hard to find and get through, if it can accommodate both queens."

"It's a tunnel, right? Where does it come out?"

Snake was already pulling on his britches. "I guess we'll find out. I hope it isn't locked."

They restored the bedroom as best they could, but what was the sense of covering their stay if they couldn't leave unseen?

The hatch was locked. Of course.

"Ick?" As usual, Jynx spoke aloud. This time that habit would include Snake in the conversation. "How do we unlock the escape hatch?"

Then they stared at each other as Ick replied to both of them.

"Six feet down, right in front of the hatch," Snake repeated as Jynx thanked her and asked her to delay their return if she could.

"Too late. They're stepping into the precinct now!" Jynx dug frantically for the key. "Six feet? We'll never find it in time!"

"Where's the other escape hatch, Ick?" Snake asked, pawing sand aside.

"This one's faster?" Jynx redoubled her efforts. "I guess they assumed the slither queen would be here to get the key."

Distant voices reached them from the entrance to the burrow.

Snake hung over the hole nearly upside down, Jynx grasping his ankles as sand slid back into the hole. At last his hand closed over the key.

Shyriel's aggravated voice reached them from a distance. "Delyna says Kyr and that common woman were both missing from their quarters last night."

Snake fumbled the key at the lock, dropped it. He scooped it up and a moment later the lock clicked. Half buried in sand, the narrow tunnel resisted his efforts to pull it open.

"What does he see in her, anyway?"

The door swung open and he more or less shoved Jynx through it.

She didn't notice the rough handling but pressed against one side of the tunnel to make room for him. She pulled the door mostly closed behind him, tossed the key into the hole.

"No," Shyriel replied to someone, "we don't need her for anything. Kyr's the only one who matters." She couldn't be more than a few steps and one corner away.

Jynx reached around the door of the hatch, hastily pushing sand into the hole and trying to smooth it.

Shyriel's footsteps crunched lightly in the sand as Jynx pulled the door closed. Snake's strong arm grabbed her by the hips and pulled her backwards down the tunnel with him.

"What's this?" Even through the thick door and all the sand, Shyriel's strident voice carried anger. "Someone's been here!"

Only I, sister-queen. Ick, broadcasting to Jynx and Snake as well as Shyriel. *After so long away, I reacquainted myself with my home before joining you. It's disturbed because I checked that the key is still in place, but I was late and hurried to bury it.*

Snake made a mental note. Ick was capable of lying to her partner.

"And was it still there?"

Of course. Although I rushed and did not rebury it deeply enough.

Shyriel sighed heavily. "Would you mind restoring this, sister, while I bathe?"

I will do that for you, dear one. You need not hurry your

bath, for I will bathe in the sand before you return. And then perhaps you would oil my scales?

The human footsteps faded, while Jynx and Snake huddled in desperate silence.

Jynx? Dear one? Go through the tunnel. It is long, and will leave you in the dunes. Go to your separate domiciles from there. I will see you soon.

Jynx nodded as if Ick could see her, wondering just how angry Shyriel would be if she caught them.

Very. She means to keep Snake, and she will not be happy you've stolen his heart.

Then silence.

~~~

Snake paced all three rooms of his guest house, worried and impatient. Unkind memory needled at him here. With Jynx now returned to her own sleeping quarters, he'd had no defender when the memories returned in nightmare last night.

He wanted to go home. He'd made no promises to fulfill prophecy, only to restore the slither queen to them if she was amenable. She was, and he had. He and Jynx could leave any time with a clear conscience. With or without Ick.

Yet only moments ago, Lasyr had brought him a summons from Shyriel, apparently for a council to discuss how he could save them and their way of life.

He didn't care about their way of life! Couldn't they see that? He didn't believe in their prophecy and wanted no part of it.

Yet every prophecy brought by the slither queen throughout history had eventually been fulfilled, despite occasional resistance by those destined to fulfill it. Or so he had been told as an acolyte.

Erilya would share a new prophecy with the council, and it involved him. Of course. And that meant it involved Jynx, too, as far as he was concerned. Yet these weren't her People; her only ties were to him, and to Ick. They had no right to involve her–or him, either. They weren't his People anymore, by Landir's tits! He didn't have to obey Shyriel's summons.

Better to pack up and leave, taking Jynx with him. They could go south, out of the Rainbow Sands, to the coast, where they could take a ship for home.

If Jynx would go. And that was what worried him most. Bonded to the slither queen, she likely wouldn't be ready to leave until Ick chose between her and Shyriel. Erilya would stay here, of course. She could make no other choice. Jynx would be devastated. What if she chose to stay here with Ick, to avoid a sundering that could kill her, as it would Shyriel or any other human queen?

What would he do if she decided to stay? He could never live here again, but the thought of living without Jynx... He shoved it away. Shyriel would never allow her to stay, but if Erilya demanded it...

He shoved the thought away again. This was stupid and useless. Why hadn't his escort come for him yet, so he could get this meeting over with? So he and Jynx could leave?

Delyna came for him a few minutes later, and he remembered for the first time that the People reckoned time by the sun's position, rather than by hours or minutes: Timid sun, cool sun, strong sun, warrior sun, calm sun, resting sun. How had he forgotten? Cool sun was a popular time for meetings, before strong sun and warrior sun made men irritable and disagreeable.

The protocolist arrived early–one more irritation he didn't need–and lectured him on proper behavior and ritual all the way to the queens' precinct, a place she'd never entered but he had. Somehow Snake hadn't realized the council would be held here.

She still lectured as they joined the three chief priests waiting just outside the golden path.

Evron chuckled. "Delyna, Kyr has already broken so much protocol with the queens that more will hardly matter. You may leave him to me for this meeting." His eyes twinkled.

She gave the chief priest a somewhat sheepish smile and left Snake in his keeping.

When she'd left, Evron said, "She takes her position very seriously but has little opportunity to apply it so thoroughly. She means well."

Snake nodded his understanding.

And then each of the chief priests in turn gave him their condolences for the loss of his talented father so many years ago. He would have been raised to prophet soon, with the potential to become a chief priest one day.

Snake hadn't known that. But of course so wonderful a father would have had the skills to lead an entire Clan. He blinked away the mist in his eyes and thanked them for sharing their sorrow with him.

These were good people, the kind he had learned to value over the years. He tried to let go of the old stains they'd carried in his heart just by being of the People. Hadn't at least one or two of them been there when Tchenya attacked him? He thought Harn, and perhaps Beyir, had come into the queens' precinct to help him. Chief priests must have more rights to the precinct than he'd realized. Or they'd taken an awful chance.

He felt Ick's buzz in his head just before Shyriel appeared at the entrance, the slither queen draped across her shoulders and outstretched arms. The human queen's chin was haughty-high, her back straight, and eyes as cool as a Snows river during spring melt. Begemmed rings in vivid colors adorned every finger and godtears were tied into the belt about her slender waist. She stopped in the entrance, her hand gesturing gracefully.

The chief priests stepped onto the golden path and Snake followed.

Wait.

A new slither voice. Snake's breath caught in his throat but he waited. He wanted no trouble with Slyn. He carefully controlled his surface thoughts and feelings. Shyriel's tiny nod gave permission for the long black slither to enter. As if he belonged there, he wound up Snake's leg and torso and wrapped around him, resting his head atop Snake's right shoulder.

Snake tried to hide his faint shudder but Slyn felt it and laughed in his head. Slither humor. His skin prickled, which seemed to amuse Slyn even more.

He crossed the threshold into the cool interior of the burrow and followed Harn of the Prophecy down the gently sloping hall and into one of the meeting rooms Ick had shown him and Jynx. Still blocking his thoughts, he sat on a red and gold floor cushion between Harn and Beyir. Slyn coiled on the sand in front of him, as Erilya coiled in front of Shyriel on the other side of the circle.

"Welcome, my friends. We have much to discuss," Shyriel said. "I have invited Kyr to be here because he is the key to our ultimate success, the subject of generations of prophecy. I have invited Slyn because no slither is likely to understand Kyr better. Kyr was the first acolyte to see into Slyn's soul and understand who he is, and I have to believe their partnership will be as important as mine and Erilya's."

Snake's scalp contracted. That hinted at more prophecy. Partnered with Slyn? That was not to his liking.

Shyriel smiled at Kyr, queen to subject. No flirtation this time, to his relief. "For us all, but especially for Kyr, who was gone for so long, a brief history.

"You were only a small child, Kyr, when Queen Tchenya renewed a prophecy of several lifetimes: 'A male of the People will hear the voice of the slither queen, and the People will change forever because of it.' This prophecy was fulfilled when you, at age eight, came into the queen's precinct to rescue Slyn, who was misbehaving badly. It was a terrible day, if necessary. You and your mother left the People in your grief and resettled in the Kingdom of the Snows."

Necessary? His father's death was *necessary*?

161

"Sometime after that, Tchenya brought us a new prophecy: *'The People's decline has begun, and their prosperity cannot be restored until the son of prophecy returns.'* It took us several years and the connecting of many smaller prophecies to clarify that you are the 'son of prophecy,' Kyr. That's when we began to send emissaries to you, pleading for your return." Shyriel drank from the golden flagon at her elbow, the one Snake hadn't noticed until now.

He found one at his elbow, too, filled with cool, sweet water from the spring, almost as good as the cold, icy water in the mountain streams at home.

Chief Priest Harn picked up the story. "The thefts of our slithers began during this time. At first, we attributed our losses to normal tragedies, such as a slither encountering a tanglecat, or dying in a sandstorm. Even when we lost two or three at a time, we thought it was from natural causes. When we began to lose several at a time, we realized it couldn't be natural. As the number of our slithers decreased, so did the amount of fiszt we could make with their sloughed skins. Slitherskins have always been our main source of prosperity.

"Finally a new prophecy, from Queen Erilya, revealed that the Wohim were the ones taking our slithers. They wanted the skins and sought to discover how to make fiszt from them."

Shyriel nodded at Beyir, who continued. "Eventually we tried to negotiate with the Wohim, offering fiszt at a reduced price if they would stop their raiding. Their only counteroffer was that they would take only a limited number of slithers each year if we taught them how to make the fiszt themselves. Or simply teach them how and give them a slither queen to breed their own slither supply.

"When next they raided, we were ready. We met them in the dunes, well before they entered the white sands, and a great battle ensued. We lost many brave warriors that day, but we were not able to halt the raids."

Evron's beautiful baritone carried sorrow as he brought the tale to its close. "Their next raid was deadlier than ever. Queen

Erilya disappeared. We searched, and raided, and searched again, to no avail. Desperate to find our queen and to restore our prosperity, we determined that we had no choice but to find the son of prophecy and bring him home."

"One of the prophecies during this time," broke in Beyir, "foretold that the exile of the son of prophecy from the People would be the key to restoring us to our former glory, that you would return to us with the skills we need to restore our way of life."

"And that," said Queen Shyriel softly, "is how Evron and I came to visit you in the Kingdom of the Snows, hoping to bring you back to the People. Now that you're here, and especially since you've brought our queen with you, the world can be righted again.

"At last we can plan how to retrieve our slithers and end the raiding once and for all."

~~~

Jynx sifted sparkling white sand through her fingers, admiring its cleanliness and beauty. Her bare feet cooled in the edge of the spring, toes digging into the sand on the bottom. In the shade of three palm trees she felt almost cool, except where the warm sand trickled through her fingers.

One morning without him and she missed Snake terribly. According to Lasyr, he had been summoned to meet with the queens and chief priests. A good thing the priests were there, so that little shrike would keep her claws off him!

Idly she began to pack white sand with just enough water to stick the grains together. As her pile of wet sand grew, so did her imagination.

She shaped it into a large sunflower head, carefully sculpting the "seeds" in the center, then the delicate petals. Too bad she had no gold sand for the petals or black for the seeds.

"Whatcha doing?" a small voice asked. A young boy,

curious as all children are, stood back watching her work the sand.

"I'm making a picture. See the flower? Do you sometimes make things out of sand?"

He shook his head no.

"Do you want to help me?"

His eyes lit up. How long had he been watching, that she hadn't even noticed?

"Come over here and let me show you..."

The boy carefully added a bit of sand for a seed as Jynx explained what a sunflower was. She guided his hand through uncertainty, then sat back to watch and encourage. This was more fun than working alone! She coaxed his name out of him–Damyn, of the Protection. Apparently everyone identified themselves by clan as well as name, a naming system that didn't impress her. Better to take a name that meant something, such as identifying your work–Potter, or Saddler, or Smith, or Farmer, for instance. That made more sense.

It didn't take long for a friend of Damyn to approach and ask what they were doing. And then another, and his friend.

Soon there were too many hands and not enough sunflower to go around, so she started a sand castle. A big one. None of the children knew what a castle was, or a king, so she told stories about castles to help her explain.

At last Jynx sat back and watched as the children laughed and squealed and built and made up their own stories.

Listening, she realized she hadn't heard this much laughter since she'd been here. These were such a solemn People! The laughter eased a tightness in her shoulders that she hadn't recognized. One of the best medicines in the world!

Laughter and children brought the women of the village to the spring. Some of them joined in the building. Others wanted to hear the stories explaining these strange things. And they wanted to know where she came from, and what it was like there.

In return, they taught her more of the polyglot language used among the tribes of the Rainbow Sands.

The women came and went as they needed to, but at midday–strong sun, they called it–they reappeared with food. Jynx feared to ask what any of it was. It could be something she'd throw up if she knew!

This one seemed to be a concoction of some kind of roots, mashed with a bit of milk and some spices Jynx didn't know. And here were unfamiliar dried fruits–dates, figs, and raisins. And... plums? In the desert? She tried a meat dish, also well spiced, although she chose not to ask what kind of meat they used.

In midafternoon she met two village healers and they began discussing their remedies and treatments. Suddenly Jynx's presence in the white sands took on new purpose. She felt comfortable with Sanshar and Pensai, and their healing techniques and medicines were exciting! They shared liberally, and she shared her knowledge as easily, and some interesting ideas began to trickle into her brain...

~~~

Once and for all.

An ending to the prophecies involving him. No more annual visits. Do this one thing and he could go home. And maybe Jynx would go with him.

"It's not my responsibility to save you," he heard himself say. "If I allow you to draw me into this, there will be a next time. And a next. I have done what I agreed to do. I have spoken to Erilya regarding her wishes and brought her back to you. The journey has taken me from home and family for weeks, even with the help of the Slipaway Trail. You have no right to ask more of me." He had already detailed the events in the Wohim village. They knew what they faced–and what they were asking of him. Not that they'd named their goals out loud, but he was sure he knew what they had in mind.

"But the prophecies..." began Harn.

"You *must* help us," said Evron. "You have seen the danger for yourself."

Slyn's angry hiss was drowned out by Erilya's roar in his head. Both slithers' emotions bombarded him, demanding, sometimes drowning each other out.

Snake covered his ears, but the noise was inside, and it hurt.

"The gods have promised us," said Beyir. "It has been prophesied, and it will happen. The only question is when and how you will recognize the inevitability of this."

"You think you can force me?" Snake's spine stiffened and he leaned slightly forward, eyes wide with threat.

Harn and Evron both started back. Beyir leaned forward, his own eyes widening, and the broad scar along his jaw whitening.

Shyriel raised a hand and all three priests relaxed back onto the cushions. Only Snake remained on edge.

"What have the People ever done for me that I owe them for? What have your gods ever given me that I should care about their prophecies?" Snake tried not to shout, but he didn't hold his temper. "I'm not here for your gods, who would use me without recompense. I'm not here for the People, who care nothing about me except that they can use me. This isn't my home, you're no longer my people, nor do I care for your gods. I have my own home, in a land I love, a people who have been good to me for no reason except that I exist. I worship other gods and obey different sovereigns. I'm not yours to use!"

In the stunned silence that followed, Snake did not abate the anger on his face. But he did note the anger and stubbornness of the chief priests. They'd heard the words but did not accept. And the slither assault of anger, disappointment, and disbelief had not eased. If anything, Ick's roar was louder. But Slyn's softening voice felt more menacing at the moment.

Snake did *not* want to get caught between Ick and Slyn. Slyn seemed closer to insanity than when young Kyr had been his handler; although he'd risen to prominence on the strength of his prophecies, he had not been raised to royalty, which was where he'd always believed he belonged. His resentment for that was an underlying current to all his words.

"You ask what our gods have ever done for you," said Shyriel quietly into the thrumming silence. "They have brought you into the world, as they do all healthy babies. They gave you loving parents without peer, something I have never known. They gave you a strong body equal to the tasks foretold for you. They gave you a strong gift of Rapport, which makes you well respected among the slithers as well as the humans. They have given you perhaps the most important role ever given to a child of the People, and they have led you to the Snows, to be trained as one of the most feared warriors in the world. Through trial and tribulation, through testing and training, they have built your strength of will, of body, and of heart, to prepare you for life among the slithers again. There's no man on this earth who is better prepared for this, Kyr. For all your troubles, the gods have given you many gifts. This is a debt that has come due."

All three priests were nodding, as if her words were the only truth possible. Beyir's nod was sharp and belligerent. Harn's seemed anxious, perhaps because Snake had been born into his clan, the Prophecy. Evron, who had traveled with him for weeks, looked troubled, but his nod was definite.

Snake sighed. "Do all prophecies come true? I tell you they do not. Small events and large, small choices and large, can change the course of history—and prophecy is only history that hasn't happened yet. So I was taught as an acolyte. Prophecies sometimes change or disappear for those reasons. This is one that must be replaced or updated."

Silence again, but Snake had the impression that Ick spoke privately to Shyriel. Slyn's annoyed petulance—and lashing tail—seemed to bear that out. No one spoke as they waited.

"Gentlemen," said the human queen, "we have spoken difficult truths that have revealed divided opinions. We will take a break, reconvening here at resting sun to continue our discussions. That will give us each time to reflect, to search our hearts, and to look for a course of action that will accomplish what we need."

The men rose and bowed–except Snake, who merely nodded at Shyriel–and departed as a group. Snake started for his house, glad for the break but only too aware this wasn't over. And that Ick would soon follow him for a private conversation.

17. Manipulations

Snake flung himself onto the pile of cushions in his main room to wait, knowing it wouldn't be long. But the first visitor wasn't quite who he expected.

"Snake?" Jynx's voice called from outside the door.

He bounced to his feet. "Come!" He felt a grin splitting across his face.

She entered, Ick wrapped around her waist, her own grin reflecting the joy in his. "You're back!" she said.

I invited her. Ick's intent was firm. *What affects either of you affects both, so both of you should be here now.*

"You're going to scold me in front of Jynx?" He tried to keep the growl out of his voice, but he was too irritated.

What I am about to tell you must not be spoken of to anyone, slither or human. Not even between the two of you, if any ears are within hearing—slither or human. Will you promise me?

Damn snake, he thought, rebellious and tired of being manipulated. Only he forgot to shut off Rapport first, and Ick's roar lashed through him so hard he almost blacked out.

When the pain abated enough to re-establish a sense of self, he stared at her, stunned.

I can do worse.

Jynx's brows wrinkled in puzzlement. She wasn't included

in the chastisement, then. "Of course we promise," she said on her way to Snake. "What's wrong? Where do you hurt?" She laid her small, cool hand across his forehead.

"I'm fine," he said, despite a desire to keep her hand on his face. "I was insolent. Ick reminded me not to be."

Jynx snorted, removing her hand. "Then you deserved what you got. She's our friend!" She dropped onto the cushions next to him and set Ick on a lovely purple one the queen indicated, pulling it in front of her and Snake for ease of conversation.

Ick coiled up facing them and opened Rapport to both at once. *I desired from the beginning to include you, Jynx, but Queen Shyriel and the chief priests consider you an outsider and not a part of this. With none present to object, I will tell you what Kyr now knows.* And she did, in great detail.

When she finished, Jynx looked at Snake, eyebrows angled in anxiety. "They expect you to save them? How? What do they want of you?"

"It hasn't been spoken aloud yet," Snake replied, "but I think they want me to use my warrior skills to stop the Wohim raids for good, to protect the slithers from theft and butchery, and thus restore prosperity to the People."

There is more I would have you know, said Ick, *but first I must tell you what is in my heart. Know that you are each precious to me, a part of my nest. I have come to value your thoughts and opinions, to envy your ability to choose your own mate, to trust you at all times and in all ways. This trust is the foundation of what I'm about to tell you, for not even Shyriel knows these things, nor should she. I can tell you only because at some point you will leave the Rainbow Sands and are unlikely to return, an additional assurance of your silence.*

Snake looked at Jynx, saw his own perplexity in her eyes. Ick trusted them above her own sister-queen?

And then he wondered if he and Jynx even understood Ick the same way. He'd spent his childhood learning to interpret slither emotions felt through Rapport. Jynx had no training at all, although she and Ick seemed to communicate just fine.

"I am honored by your trust, Ick," he replied. "And I pledge to keep your secrets, whatever they may be."

"I, too," said Jynx. "I'm proud to call you friend and to be so trusted by one so wise."

For a long moment no one spoke. Why did Ick hesitate? Was she having second thoughts?

Kyr, check outside to be sure none can overhear. Please. The last seemed an afterthought. The slither had shifted to her royal mode.

He obeyed, reporting that all was clear. No one showed any interest in his house, and no one lurked near enough to matter.

Still Ick hesitated, as if gathering her thoughts. And then she slowly began to tell them the truth. *It is true that the gods give information to the slithers, which we share with humans as prophecy. It is not true that the gods share everything with us, such as how an event will come to pass.* She paused, as if to take a deep breath, although no such inhalation was heard or felt. *It is not true that the gods bring about the events of a prophecy—at least not entirely true.*

She stopped again, as if unable to find the right words.

Snake glanced at Jynx just as she glanced at him. So she, too, found Ick's reluctance troubling.

This is so difficult! I break a taboo that comes from ancient times. Ick wiggled uncomfortably on her cushion, but her obvious misery hardened to determination.

Sometimes a queen does not merely pronounce a prophecy but is also responsible for ensuring that it comes true. This is only queens' prophecies, not the smaller prophecies of the black slithers.

Jynx's small hand slipped into Snake's and squeezed. She shifted a bit closer, until their shoulders touched. They waited.

And waited.

And then Snake prompted her. "What do you mean, ensuring it comes true?"

Guilt emanated from the queen. *It feels a little dishonest, especially since not even the human queen is aware. We must sometimes manipulate events to match the prophecy received.*

Queen Tchenya recognized you when you were a small boy, Kyr. She reiterated and added to your prophecy. You were the only one who did not bow as she advanced to the dais. From that moment on, she watched for an excuse to speak to you. She needed only for you to hear her voice to fulfill that prophecy; it did not matter what she said.

"That was contrived?" Snake sat forward. "Did the prophecy also require that she try to kill me?"

No. She would have killed you out of offended anger, but for the prophecy. Killing your father was necessary, however, and with a word in the right ear, your mother decided you two should leave the village. That word included a suggestion for the Kingdom of the Snows, since no snakes live in such a high, cold place. That made it an attractive suggestion to Senyr, who was as devastated as you. And it set up your warrior training.

A wave of dizziness and disbelief left Snake reeling as if his heart had been ripped out. *"You killed my father on purpose? To force me into what you wanted?"* Snake surged forward, reaching for Ick with both hands. At the last moment he averted his eyes from her hypnotic emrel gaze and closed his hands about her throat.

"Snake, no! Friend! Friend!"

He knew Jynx was there, tugging on his arm, but he ignored the sounds coming from her mouth. All he saw was a slither queen, a smaller version of the one who had murdered his father. To manipulate *him!* He spewed every nasty insult he could think of, as if the vitriol could etch away the horrible truth.

Such horror! Such a sudden drowning in the pain of that loss. Ick claimed to care about him, but she was a part of this manipulation! The roaring in his head meant nothing. The rise of a silvery tail was irrelevant. Nothing mattered but destroying this... this... worm!

Something struck his cheek, hard. He felt no sting and ignored it. Again and again his cheek was struck.

Fingers tangled in his hair, pulled up against the growth, and pulled his head back. He was helpless against the pull, and his throat was exposed. Ick stabbed her tail at him! He threw himself to one side, bowling Jynx over.

Still he didn't release his grip on Ick's life.

Jynx's knuckles slammed into the back of his hand. Involuntarily his hand opened, just as Ick's tail flashed over his shoulder, barely missing his neck.

Jynx smashed his other hand, forcing that release, too, and bodily shoved him back onto the cushions

He started to surge up, but Jynx's full weight landed on him. Something blurred his eyes, and grief ground through him as if his father had only just died. He heard the scream of anger and pain, didn't recognize the voice.

Jynx tripped him, shoved him down onto the pillows.

He buried his face in them, gripping them until his knuckles whitened. But he couldn't bury the heart-broken sobs that rose out of chest and throat.

He couldn't look at Jynx, wouldn't look at Ick.

Jynx's voice was right in his ear, and her words at last began to take shape in his head. "It's not Ick's fault! *She* didn't do this! She's our friend! She would never do such a thing to you! It's not her fault!"

As his sobs began to give way, her voice quieted, until only a soft, pleading tone remained. And then only soothing, like the gentle hand that smoothed his hair back out of his eyes, that caressed his face, that wiped away tears...

He swung an arm around Jynx and pulled her down on top

of him, wrapped both arms around her, and just held her. Warmth. Comfort. Love, unconditional. He held her desperately. Heal this, Jynx! he wanted to say. But this wasn't something she could fix.

~~~

Snake may have slept a little. He wasn't sure. He only knew that he felt wrung out, empty of energy. His mind moved as sluggishly as his limbs and an invisible wall separated him from... himself, perhaps. The world seemed dull and spongy, even with Jynx snugged up tight to his side, head on his shoulder.

When he moved, she sat up. Concerned brown eyes studied his as her hand caressed his face. Despite the anchors seeming to weigh down his body, he also sat up.

He looked around as if he'd never seen the room before. Gradually familiarity returned.

He wanted to continue his anger at Ick, who still coiled on the purple cushion, her mottled abalone colors gleaming softly. But even that had dulled. And Jynx was right. Ick hadn't done this. She had only revealed truth.

Ick's head lifted from her cushion and her emrel eyes met his blue-green ones.

He couldn't move, irritated at himself for not watching for that. But he couldn't blame Ick for protecting herself.

"I'm sorry," he said. "I know you weren't even born when that happened."

But I can't disagree with Tchenya's decisions, terrible as they were. They set the path for the prophecy's fulfillment. Her words carried regret but no apology. *The fulfillment of prophecy demands sacrifice from all of us, and none more than you.*

Snake glanced at Jynx, saw from her face that Ick had opened to both of them.

Could people open to more than one slither at a time? If so, how did they do it? Could only queens, or very powerful slithers, open Rapport broadly? He knew frustratingly little, for a man who had been born here.

Are you ready to continue? There is more I would have you know, but we are expected in a meeting before long.

No, he thought. I'm not ready. But he couldn't say that to Ick, not when she risked her sister-queen's anger and perhaps the fulfillment of long-term prophecy by speaking to him.

He nodded without speaking, reached for Jynx's comforting hand.

Ick released his gaze and settled herself more comfortably. *Queen Tchenya also suggested placing young Slyn in your nest.*

"Why? Did she already know he would lead me into her precinct?"

Jynx's hand tightened on his.

Ick paused, and he wondered if she consulted Tchenya's memories. *I don't think so, but I can't be sure. I believe she wanted to push you, to see what you could do and help you grow in prophecy. Slyn was aberrant from birth, and if you could handle him, you would be a fine candidate for your destiny.*

"And if she didn't like what she saw, she'd kill me?"

Of course not. She already knew you were the son of prophecy. Her intent was to strengthen you through challenge and hardship.

He ran his free hand through his hair. "What else? What other ways have I been manipulated?"

Ick's tail lashed. *Prophecy extends beyond the person at its center, Kyr. As I have said, others have also sacrificed for this prophecy.*

"Such as?" Snake tried to avoid belligerence, but he still winced at his own voice.

I have. My personal manipulation of events toward fulfillment of prophecy has not always been pleasant, although subsequent events have confirmed my actions.

Jynx broke in, squeezing Snake's hand briefly. "You're talking about your capture by the Wohim, aren't you? How did that happen?"

I'll get to that momentarily.

There was another prophecy I doubt either of you are aware of. It was Slyn's, and as confusing as he is. 'We will lose a queen to the son of prophecy.' Very strange, its meaning hotly debated among the highest priests in the Prophecy.

"Has this prophecy been fulfilled yet?" Jynx asked. "Does it have to do with you being gone so long and meeting Snake?"

I believe so, yes, although Shyriel believes it may refer to losing her heart to Kyr. Neither scenario quite fits, though.

As little as I like Slyn, his prophecies tend to be major ones, and accurate. Based on that prophecy and a few smaller glimmers I received directly, I accompanied a few slithers into the sands for hunting, knowing the likely result. Indeed, we were captured by the Wohim. This confirmed who the enemy was, as we had suspected from the first raid.

By the time my opportunity for escape arrived, we were in poor shape. The Wohim know nothing of caring for slithers—and don't want to. I knew when the voices of my slithers were silenced, and I grieved for their loss. The Wohim cared better for me—a little—and I killed them as soon as I could.

"I knew they died of poison!" cried Jynx.

Fortunately, you came along in time to free me, or I would have died there. I was, however, quite concerned to discover your dislike of snakes! Which you thought I was.

At first I was angry with both you and Kahpur; I was a queen! You acted as if your responsibility ended when I was freed! Why would you run from me? Couldn't you tell I needed help? I had no idea who you were, or that you had no idea who or what I am.

But at least we eventually encountered Isyr. She told you what I commanded her to tell you. After that, I thought we got along well. You even led me to Kyr.

She looked at Snake directly and he hastily lowered his eyes.

I didn't realize who he was, until he commanded me—me, a queen!—in the language of the People. His horse and sword confirmed that he had acquired the training prophesied.

And then, Kyr, I went about trying to win you over, to make you comfortable with me, to get past your fear of slithers. I succeeded fairly well, I think, although I underestimated the damage done by Tchenya's attack on you.

I'm still trying to make up for that, as best I can. I want your willing assistance in our fight for the survival of the slithers and our way of life.

Please.

18. Decisions

Ick left soon after her plea, to assure no one knew she had spoken privately to Kyr. Jynx watched as she left through the back door and burrowed into the sand.

"How far can she travel under the sand?" she asked Snake. "Can she breathe under there?" It didn't seem natural to her.

"Not far, without surfacing for air. There's some air trapped in the sand, but not enough for any real distance. The main thing is to be well away from this house before she's seen. She can do that in a couple of stretches."

"How soon is your meeting?"

Snake glanced at the sky. "I have time to walk you back to your quarters before Delyna comes for me."

They left out the front door, not touching as they ambled across the white sand. They had to keep up appearances, Jynx knew. It exasperated her, but it would be much the same at home in Sayvil.

"What will you do?" she asked. "You owe them nothing. You've kept your promise. Yet the People have meaning in your life. Will you forgive yourself if you just walk away?"

He shrugged. "Why not? They're not my people now. Their gods aren't mine, so I have no stake in their prophecies."

Despite his words, Jynx saw his shoulders squirm. He wasn't really comfortable with the idea of leaving without notice.

She walked in silence at his side, thinking. How like a man, to become obstinate about the wrong things! How could she get him to see? Lehrie, her years-dead husband, had been much the same in that regard.

Several of the People greeted them with smiles and bright words as they walked. They were good people, not all that different from the people back home, in the ways that mattered.

"They have their own warriors, after all," she agreed. "Let them fight."

"Their own warriors have been driven back by the Wohim every time they've clashed. They're willing enough fighters, but they've had little training—and none of that very effective."

"These are a peaceful People. Even I can see that, as an outsider. How could they even learn what they need to know, to stave off destruction?"

Snake didn't answer, but his mouth set in a thin, hard line.

Had she been too obvious? Was Snake angry at her? Or was he imagining, as she was, Beyir's warriors fighting the Wohim and losing everything they sought to save? After all, if the Wohim won, there would be nothing between them and the slithers they craved. Between them and Ick.

Snake stopped and turned to face her. "You're manipulating me, too, aren't you? You *want* me to fight the People's war for them!"

Her heart almost stopped but she stayed in control, having anticipated the possibility he'd see through her. "I'm only giving you something to think about. I worry that you might someday come to regret your decision here, because I know you're a good man and a kind one. A man of honor. You will decide as you think best, and I will support you in that decision."

She watched the hardness fade from his eyes.

"Here comes Delyna," he said. He leaned over and kissed her on the lips, his blue-green eyes oh, so close. "I must leave you here, but I promise to consider your words. Not because I love you, but because I've always admired your wisdom." His eyes shone.

Jynx laughed, her heart a bit lighter, and spoke her farewell just as Delyna came up to draw him off.

~~~

Snake hated meetings like this. Kayde had dragged him to a few on one pretext or another, but Snake suspected it was so he'd have at least one friend in the room. The bickering, the arguments, subtle back-stabbing, political intrigue—Snake hated all of it. Being nobility, of course, he couldn't always avoid it, but he would never like it.

At least this one didn't have the political factions, as far as he could see. With fewer people, there was one clear decision-maker. Well, two, but the queens would share only one decision with the group, he was sure. It wasn't like twelve or twenty men trying to agree on a course of action to recommend to the king.

He disliked it all the same. The atmosphere felt similar, although the distrust seemed aimed at him alone, as the unknown entity.

He had promised Jynx to consider her words, he reminded himself, and he did that as everyone settled in. Chilly silver goblets before each of them held clear, cold water that misted the outside of the cups. A tall silver pitcher, graceful in shape and devoid of ornamentation, sweated softly on the table within easy reach. Snake downed his first cup and poured more.

Erilya slithered onto the low table and formed a loose ring about the pitcher, to Snake's amusement. That would keep her cool!

He was less amused that Slyn attended, coiled before Shyriel as if he were her royal partner, not Erilya. Snake's belly tightened in dread. The aberrant creature still and always represented his own terror and his father's death.

Shyriel opened the meeting. "I trust that you have all benefitted from our break, and that you've had sufficient time to consider what must be done. Chief Priest Harn, let's begin with you. Has any new prophecy been shared that will shed some light on this difficult situation? Do you have any thoughts on an answer to our dilemma?"

Slowly the heavy-jowled priest shook his head. Then he looked directly at Erilya for a long moment. She appeared asleep in her cool ring about the pitcher, and he sighed. "Everyone here already knows Slyn's most current prophecy, which Queen Erilya shared with Kyr during our break. 'The People will lose a queen to the son of prophecy.' That prophecy is over a year old, with no additional information on what it means. Perhaps we should discuss it in depth now, and look at the ways it might apply to our current problem—putting a permanent end to the Wohim raids."

Shyriel's face became still, her eyes guarding her thoughts as a tanglecat guards its kits. "And how do you see that prophecy applied here?"

Evron shifted on his cushion, across the low table from Harn. "I don't see how it could, my queen. The prophecy says either you or Queen Erilya will be lost—stolen, abandoned, killed, or whatever—to Kyr. Not to the Wohim. It seems a separate problem entirely."

"Unless the son of prophecy will become a danger to the queen," interrupted Beyir, "perhaps as someone in collusion with the enemy."

"More likely," Snake said, "it refers to Erilya's capture by the Wohim, her rescue by Jynx, and the time when we all traveled together, with the addition of my friend, Kayde."

"Or," broke in Shyriel, "it may refer to me, rather than Erilya. If, for example, I chose to marry Kyr, I would have to give up my crown and thus a queen would be lost to the People."

Snake shuddered. Jynx was right. Shyriel had set her sights on him!

"Gentlemen," Snake interrupted. "This is easily settled. The Wohim were killing me slowly in one of their rituals. Jynx rescued me, with Ick—Erilya's—help. Erilya was there and can tell you the truth. Surely you would believe your own queen?"

"Unless Queen Erilya is also under your influence," Evron said.

I AM UNDER NO ONE'S INFLUENCE! Erilya roared, emrel eyes cold and hard. *I was there. I saw. Kyr is not our enemy, nor does he collude with our enemy. This discussion is insulting to him and to me.*

No wonder Snake hated meetings like this.

"Unless you have proof, not just speculation, gentlemen, let's move on." Shyriel's chin lifted. Her tone brooked no argument. "Anything else to be gleaned from prophecy, Harn?"

"No, my queens."

"Evron? Your thoughts on solutions to the basic problem?"

Helpless, the leader of the Praise lifted his hands palm up and shook his head. "I see no application of song or dance that could help us."

Snake chuckled, hearing Ick's echo in his head. "You should have been there when Jynx and Erilya rescued me from the Wohim, Evron. Dance was the key to that feat."

"How so?" Evron clasped small, soft hands below his beard, above a barrel chest meant for holding songs.

"Jynx wore a hareem, and she and Erilya broke into the center of the crowd and danced. She was taught by Isyr, so you know the dance was as mesmerizing as Erilya's gaze. Erilya freed my hands while the audience was entranced and we fled. The right distraction at the right time can make the difference in a difficult battle."

"Isyr? You have seen her?" Shyriel leaned forward, intent.

Once again Snake wondered when Isyr had left, and why. "No, I haven't. Jynx encountered her before we met."

And I commanded what she would tell Jynx and what she would teach her. Our performance for the Wohim was not our first together. Erilya told them smugly.

Evron sat back, looking thoughtful. And Beyir leaned forward, as if to ask questions, but he didn't speak after all.

"And Beyir," said Shyriel, "what ideas have you brought us?"

Beyir seemed to return from somewhere else. He shifted on his cushion, almost squirming. "My queen, I am at a loss. I was once accounted a fine warrior, but none of my efforts have brought the results we hoped for. I have lost warriors, so that the Wohim warriors well outnumber us, and they cloak themselves in darkness, even in brightest day, so that we do not see them. We are caught off-guard, no matter what we do or how we prepare. We are too few to protect the People as they should be protected.

"I had thought that the son of prophecy, a mighty warrior himself, would take this burden and so restore our People, as prophesied. Instead, I find that Kyr is among the most feared warriors in the world but no longer claims kinship with the People and will not help us.

"Forgive my bluntness, my queens, and the depth of my discouragement."

Shyriel nodded and looked form him to the black slither coiled before her. "Slyn? What can you offer to help us?"

Snake could almost feel Slyn's enthusiasm. This couldn't be good.

To his surprise, Slyn connected with him directly, which answered one question. Apparently only the queens could share Rapport with more than one person at a time.

He'd have to translate for everyone's benefit, but he saw Shyriel's eyes narrowed in irritation that he spoke to Snake, not to her. Erilya's tail lashed and he thought she said something sharp to Slyn, who wiggled his tongue at her, reminding Snake of a little boy sticking his tongue out. Both queens would consider this an insult.

But neither said a word, to his surprise. Perhaps they saved their words for a private chat later.

"Shyriel, Erilya, I will be glad to share Slyn's thoughts, but I'm very rusty and you will have to pardon any errors. Or perhaps Slyn should speak to one of you instead."

No. I will speak only to you. You can best express my ideas in warrior terms. Slyn's red eyes locked on his, but they had no power to mesmerize as Ick's did.

Snake sighed heavily. "He insists he'll speak only to me."

Slithers are taking the brunt of the Wohim's depredations, Slyn shared. *They should be heavily involved in this battle. Find a way to use our particular capabilities against the enemy.*

How might that work? Even as Snake shared Slyn's comments, his mind began turning over possibilities–and impossibilities. "A lot depends," he added, "on your willingness to sacrifice the lives of the sacred slithers to this battle. I can see some possibilities, although I don't know enough about slithers to know how practical they would be."

Beyir's head came up and he stared at Slyn. Perhaps this new line of thought would help him find his feet again. Snake hoped so; he was a good man.

"What other possibilities do you see?" Beyir asked. "How would *you* fight them, Kyr? Will you at least guide me in this, so that I don't fail *my* People?"

"Yes, Kyr," said Shyriel, her voice cool. "Your perspective is quite different from any of ours. Do you have any suggestions for us? Please share freely, even though you have no love left for your People."

She's sixteen, Snake reminded himself, *and used to getting her own way. That was petty and spiteful, and spoken out of fear for those she's responsible for.* "Have you requested a truce, to discuss it with the enemy? Perhaps a nonviolent way to peace can be found."

"We have. They sent back the heads of our delegates. We are a quiet, peaceful People, but they worship evil gods and have become bloodthirsty and stone-hearted. If we cannot even speak together peaceably, what hope is there for a meeting of the minds on the issues that divide us?"

"I assume you sent a punitive raid against them?"

"Yes." Beyir twisted the stem of his goblet, took a sip, and set it down again. "I took thirty warriors. Only fourteen of us returned, and most of us were injured, some badly."

Snake had to think. He turned inward, ignoring the others. He did *not* want to give these People any more hold on him. And yet he had always been a champion for the helpless and the overmatched. He was born here. They were no longer his People. He owed them nothing! But how could he refuse his help? Even Jynx, who knew him so well, and who loved him, knew he would hate himself if he walked away. But to give them a claim to him again? He felt like the butter in a churn, beaten and mixed until he didn't know which way was up.

He turned his gaze up and met Shyriel's eyes. The hardness there came from a queen desperate for her People's survival. She felt too much, agonized over the slithers she could find no way to help.

He knew now what Jynx had tried to suggest without saying it outright. He looked at Slyn, and at Ick, who purred softly in his head. She understood. So much like Jynx.

He opened his mouth to speak, closed it again.

And finally the words came. "I will train your warriors. I will not lead them; that is Beyir's work. But what I can teach them should make them a match for the warriors of the Wohim. That's the best offer I can give you."

They would have to be content with that.

19. Training

At timid sun, Beyir led Snake and fifty warriors away from the village, deep into the dunes. Snake ran them, but in soft sand it was a tough slog. Legs and wind should build quickly, though the first few days would be hell. And this was only the beginning.

Tomorrow they'd carry additional weight, and every day more would be added. Snake had a full waterskin slung over one shoulder, as did every man here—and it must last them until calm sun. He required them to eat before gathering, and they'd eat when they got home, but training allowed no time for food breaks.

With Beyir's help, he found a broad, relatively flat area surrounded by tall white dunes that would deflect prying eyes. The sun reflecting off sand burned a thousand times hotter than he was used to. The others, at least, were used to the sun here. He set the men to flattening the entire training area, down to the underlying rock base, for solid footing. "Learn it first," he told them, "and then we'll increase the stakes in deeper sand."

Warrior sun had arrived by the time the area met Snake's requirements. They had long since donned head coverings to avoid cooking their brains, but not one seemed aware of the wet, soggy feeling dripping down their cheeks, necks, and bellies. Snake pretended the same unawareness and pushed the distraction to the back of his mind.

Time to go to work.

Balance first, beginning with one of the most obnoxious exercises he'd ever endured.

"Line up!" he called. He arranged them in five rows of ten men each, properly spaced out. "This is what I mean when I say 'line up.' Now squat on the balls of your feet."

He borrowed the light fighting cane Beyir had brought.

"Do not let your heels touch the sand," he called, "or you'll feel the cane on your ankles!"

Within five minutes he'd whacked everyone's ankles at least once. As expected. He knew the pain in arches and ankles, but it was a great way to build balance—and the muscles necessary for it. He watched the grim faces, hard eyes, compressed lips. But to his surprise, he saw no anger, no resistance.

These were Beyir's finest, he knew without being told. His hardest, most experienced warriors, hand-picked for this training. And they knew the stakes.

He'd have to work with the remaining warriors later. And that meant these would need a subcommanders. Not Beyir, who would command all the forces. Who else?

Snake began to watch the warriors with an eye to leadership. Beyir would make the final choices, but Snake might put in a word for someone promising.

"Stand up and shake it off!" he called, noting which ones couldn't stand without using their hands to help them rise. The same ones, generally, who had the most bruises on their ankles, who needed the most work on this exercise.

This early in the day the men sweated freely, but he'd have to watch for those who stopped sweating. They might need more water breaks than he'd anticipated. He frowned, decided to enlist Beyir's aid for that particular problem when they took a break.

Should Curzon stance come next? They had no horses to ride, let alone Curzon war horses, but it would help them develop leg strength and balance. He nodded to himself and talked them through the details of getting into the stance correctly. Easier than the squats, it was still tough for those not used to it.

So he distracted them by showing them simple blocks to be performed while in Curzon stance.

Their surreptitious glances at neighboring warriors revealed how little confidence they had in what they were doing.

"Look at me!" Snake instructed. He faced the group, assumed the same stance. "I'm your mirror!" He began counting loudly as he performed the blocks, using the left arm as they used their right. If they all made the same moves at the same time, he'd see errors more easily.

They soon caught onto the "mirror" method. In minutes he'd taught them several basic blocks and showed them a routine that included all of the blocks–still without rising from their stance. Legs began to tremble and faces to redden before he gave them a water break.

Not one had given up or complained.

Snake sought out Beyir, who stood in the back now, watching his men as he learned from Snake.

"Impressive," he told the priest quietly. "You have good men here. Not one complaint for doing 'children's exercises,' as I've heard it called."

"They *are* good men," Beyir agreed. "Ask anything of them, and they will die trying to give it to you. May I make a suggestion? Allow me to send for more water. A small wagon on runners can bring two or three barrels. These men will break before they ask, but I would rather keep them strong in training."

"I agree. I underestimated the amount of water that would be needed, and it's clear they must have more."

Beyir glanced at a nearby warrior and nodded. The man began jogging back toward the village. "I'll make it up to him tonight when we return by showing him what he's missed."

"No, I'll do that. You'll need your strength for fighting, and this is my error." *Fair is fair*, he thought. *There goes time I meant to spend with Jynx tonight.*

A few minutes later he put the men back to work, this time on correct, powerful punches. The kind that would damage the opponent more than the warrior. He followed that with kicks. And at this, he got his first protest.

"Kicks?" called a man with a puckered scar across his forehead. "Only little girls kick in a fight!"

Snake grinned. "Then that gives us the element of surprise, doesn't it?"

But the sullen, insulted look on the man's face didn't fade.

"What's your name? Snake asked him.

"Brennet."

"Come on up, Brennet. This will be a good lesson for everyone." Snake kept his voice mild but couldn't keep the amusement out of it.

Brennet wasn't quite as tall as Snake, but he had a hard, stocky build. Not as beefy as Kayde, though. He shouldn't be any trouble.

Snake turned Brennet to face him, their shoulders to the lines of men. "Attack me," he said. Puzzlement and suspicion twisted Brennet's scar. "How?"

"However you like."

Brennet hurled himself bodily at Snake.

Snake stepped in at an angle. The toes of his right foot stabbed into Brennet's left inner thigh.

Brennet's left leg flew up behind him, pulling his right leg up, too. He landed flat on the hard surface and his breath huffed out. He rolled for a moment, trying to breathe, trying to get up.

Snake clasped his forearm to help him up, but even standing, Brennet stood bent, hands on knees, sucking in air.

"Would something like that be useful to you in combat?" he asked, loud enough for everyone to hear.

"How did you do that?" Brennet demanded with a deep growl.

"I'm just about to teach all of you."

~~~

By the end of the day Snake was teaching combinations of blocks, punches, and kicks. Not bad for the first day of training. Still clumsy and imprecise, they already had the general idea. He wandered among them, correcting the angle of a foot or the hand surface taking the brunt of a punch. "No, Gorf, point your knuckles more. Line it up, knuckles through shoulder, to get the most power with the least damage to you. Here, lean your entire weight on my palm, through those first two knuckles."

Gorf tried, but his elbow was up instead of under. His arm collapsed when Snake pushed back into his fist and he nearly crashed into Snake.

Gorf caught his balance, red-faced. "How long before we actually do some fighting?" He asked. "I'd do better at that."

"Not long. A few days. By that time it won't be anything like you're used to. Here, try again."

Snake glanced at the rest of the men. "Punch to the center!" he called. "Straight out from your own center!"

He stopped them to explain, shouting over the sounds of panting men. "We're most vulnerable in the center of our bodies, where heart and lungs and stomach sit. If you've done any hard fighting, you've seen that for yourself. Aim your punch here..." he pointed to his own torso "...to hit where you'll hurt your enemy the worst."

"If the weakest area is here, that's where the punch goes, not out here to the side. Work for accuracy, not just the general area." He paced from one side to the other, using up excess energy.

"For now your opponent is imaginary. When your punches are correct, you'll work with a partner for some real training.

Hopefully that will be in a couple of days.

"I'd rather train you every day for a year before you face an enemy, but we don't have that long. You will *not* be ready when Beyir leads you to war, but I will push you to be as ready as possible when that time comes."

He gave them a short water break then sent them back to their drills. He set Beyir to lead them as their mirror and to count the sets of strikes and kicks, then took his own place at the back to watch.

Beyir was the best of them. He'd earned his leadership position with his proficiency, and Snake already knew him to be fair and just, from the way his men spoke of him.

A little extra training for Beyir in the evenings would be good, a small reward that would keep him a step or two ahead of his men.

By the end of the day, Snake was as exhausted as the men. Perhaps more, as he was still adjusting to the dry, blistering heat.

As planned, when they returned to the village Snake spent training time with the man who had gone for the barrels of water. And then he spent an hour with Beyir, fixing up his blocks, punches, and Curzon stance. He'd do the same for the men tomorrow, except that he took pains to explain the whys to Beyir; he'd need that to continue training when Snake and Jynx left. Resting sun's last yellowish rays were fading by the time Snake started for his little house by the spring. He looked for Jynx, hoping she'd been watching from somewhere nearby. No sign of her.

Maybe she waited in his house instead.

But the house was dark and empty.

Snake's shoulders sagged. Now what? Maybe she got tired of waiting. Maybe she was waiting in her quarters, where other women also lived?

Suddenly that seemed a long ways away. He just wanted to sit and rest. Sleep, even.

She shouldn't be subjected to the smell of sweat rivulets

tracking down his exposed skin through layers of dust and sand. His nose wrinkled at his own filth and he headed out the back door for a bath in the spring, stumbling as he stepped down onto the sand.

He must be tireder than he'd thought, to miss a step like that, even in the dark. He took a step toward the water.

A low moan at his feet arrested the step and he launched himself forward far enough to miss the crumpled form he'd almost stepped on. His ankle twisted in the soft sand as he came down and he fell to his hands and knees. Without thinking, he rolled to one side and back up to his feet. And stopped. Waiting. Listening.

Nothing.

Distant voices in the village. Two women talking and laughing near the water some distance away. The buzz of some insect he didn't recognize.

Was someone waiting silently for him in the darkness? Or was the moan from someone who had fallen down the two steps from the house?

"Jynx?" he breathed. Fear drained the blood from his face.

This time the moan's feminine pitch was more audible.

He found her by feel, not wanting to stumble over her.

"Snake." A breath, barely heard.

His hand touched the robe she wore. He ran his fingers ran lightly over the nigh-invisible form until he found her face. "Jynx! Are you all right? What happened?"

She stirred under his hands but didn't answer.

"Where are you injured?"

Still no response, except a brush of fingertips against his arm.

Working by feel, he gathered her up and carried her into the still-dark house. He laid her on cushions in the largest room, then fumbled with the brazier to create a light. Even so, he could barely see her in the dimness.

He sat by her and brushed hair back from her eyes. "Where are you hurt?" he asked again.

"I'm all right," she whispered. "A moment, please."

He watched awareness return to her eyes as she pulled herself out of the shock of whatever had happened. He still saw no injury, and that frightened him most of all. "What happened?"

If she answered, he didn't hear it. Slyn's voice was in his head. *A meeting has been called, Kyr. We must go now.*

"No," he replied. "Please give Shyriel my regrets, but I can't come tonight."

This is not a choice. She has waited all day for your return, for this meeting.

"No. She's not my queen, Slyn. I don't have to obey her orders."

Please come, Kyr. Ick's voice this time. A request, not a command.

He sighed and slipped into Rapport with the slither queen to reply. "Jynx is hurt."

I'll send a healer to tend her. You can stay with Jynx until she arrives. Jynx will be in good hands, I promise.

"I'm still filthy from the day's training."

Come anyway. I'll assure Shyriel doesn't see it as an insult but as obedience.

No use. He'd have to go, although Shyriel likely wanted a report on the training. Which Beyir could give her.

Irritated, Snake held Jynx's hand, smoothing her forehead with the other. Despite coaxing from Slyn, he didn't leave until the healer arrived.

A woman's voice called from the doorway. "Healer Jonyl!"

"Come!" Snake didn't even look up.

The first thing Jonyl did was build up the light in the room, talking as she worked. "I met Jynx at the spring recently. So beautiful and full of life! And generous with her vast knowledge. I liked her immediately."

Flame flared up from several fire dishes Jonyl set out. She strode toward Jynx, seeming not even to notice Snake. "What happened?"

He told her the little he knew and she shoved him gently out the front door so she could work. "I will still be here when you return," she promised. "She'll be well cared for; do not fear for her."

Slyn prodded at his mind impatiently. *We must go.*

Snake waved his hand in irritation, then laid a gentle kiss on Jynx's forehead. "I'm coming, Slyn."

He'd find out more when he got back; hopefully this would be a short meeting.

The more interesting question at the moment, though, was why Slyn seemed so smug.

~~~

All the way to the queens' precinct, Snake asked Slyn questions, without receiving any useful information at all.

The slither hadn't been there when Jynx fell and had no idea she was hurt until Snake arrived.

No, he was aware of nothing of import that might have happened during the day to require a meeting.

He didn't know the purpose of the meeting, either. Yes, it could be for a report on the training, but after dark? Surely a training report could wait for the next day.

That matched Snake's thoughts, too. But he couldn't imagine why else there would be a late meeting that included him. Especially one when Delyna, the protocolist, did not appear to offer him guidance and reminders of etiquette.

The slivered moon provided little light to see by, but lit torches at wide intervals showed him the way. The slither curled across his shoulders gave him directions as well, but how he could see in the dark Snake had no idea. Maybe he smelled the way. He had a vague memory of learning that slithers had keen noses but poor eyes.

As long as he got where he was going, the rest didn't matter.

Torches set off the golden path into the queens' precinct and Snake swung onto it without slowing, ignoring Slyn's objection to the sudden change of direction. He wasn't in a good enough mood to care. Jynx was hurt, and he had to be here instead of with her. He felt tired and filthy and irritated with the whole world. Shyriel would do well to treat him with kid gloves this evening or he was likely to bite her head off.

He knew he was being petulant and unreasonable, but he didn't care. Couldn't, until he knew what happened to Jynx and that she was all right.

Shyriel's nose wrinkled at his smell as he entered the meeting room and a slight twinge of satisfaction tingled between his shoulder blades.

She didn't say a word. He was almost disappointed.

Slyn uncoiled from his shoulders and slapped onto the table top as Snake threw himself onto a cushion. Erilya, coiled in front of Shyriel, hissed at Slyn's bad manners.

No one commented on Snake's.

Then he saw the shackled man standing near the far wall. Morinl, the Wohim they'd captured. Snake had forgotten all about him.

Someone had beaten the man. On his brown face, black and purple bruises stood out clearly. His nose was pulped, one moss-green eye was swollen almost shut, and an angry half-healed cut above the eye gave it an odd slant, mismatching it with the other eye. His wrists were chafed raw, his fingernails broken, some still bloody. Undoubtedly other wounds were hidden by his robe. From here nothing appeared broken except skin and nails. When the force of the man's eyes touched him, they overflowed with hatred and contempt.

When he looked at Slyn, Morinl's eyes showed interest and avarice, perhaps even fascination. But when he looked at Ick, his eyes filled with awe—and fear bordering on terror.

Snake remembered charging down upon this man and the other slither thieves, sword in hand, intent on their deaths. He'd been under Ick's control. She'd released him just before he reached the last Wohim. The queen was different, beautiful and powerful. Morinl knew to fear her, even if he didn't understand why he did.

Shyriel sat forward. "It's time to turn our attention to our captive from the recent Wohim raid. Kyr, Evron, Erilya, and I encountered the thieves carrying stick crates with slithers crammed inside. One of those slithers was Slyn, who saw what was happening and fought back. He was captured, but he fought valiantly. Equally fierce, Razhra nearly died killing her captor. We did not save them all, but we brought most of them home.

"Unfortunately, it appears none of the Wohim bear the gift of Rapport, so that little communication has been possible. Also unfortunately, this one is a servant, with little information of value to us, although he has been questioned thoroughly.

"Now we must decide what's next for this thief. A private death? A public execution? Should he become a bloody message left at the doorstep of the Wohim? We cannot wait long to decide, lest his friends make a violent attempt to recover him, if only to protect their secrets. Your thoughts, gentlemen?"

This doesn't concern me, Snake wanted to say. But it did. Or it might. Could there be a connection to Jynx's fall? If that's what it was. *And why is it important enough for a night meeting?* he asked Erilya.

It's the only time you and Beyir are available, she replied.

He grudgingly admitted that made sense, but he was no happier about it.

Beyir shrugged, watching the man as closely as Snake did. "Perhaps we should skin him, as his people have skinned our living slithers, and leave him outside their village. That should be message enough. And tell them that for every slither they kill, we will skin one of their men. Until they repent of their sin against our gods."

Our men are nowhere near ready to take them on, Snake shared with Erilya. This was not something for the prisoner to overhear. *Perhaps in a few weeks, but it would be suicide now.*

Skinning their prisoner would be a savage message, one that could ignite fear in the hearts of the Wohim, but it might be necessary.

Her tone grim, Erilya shared his words through Rapport.

Beyir stood, slowly drawing a long, wicked sharp knife, eyes locked on the prisoner.

Snake tensed, ready to intervene, if necessary. *He's allowed to bare steel in the presence of the queens?* he asked Erilya.

He is trusted, she responded. *The steel is for the protection of the queens from those not a regular part of the council.*

He couldn't imagine that being allowed. It certainly wouldn't be in the Snows.

Beyir advanced on the Wohim and, grinning, pantomimed skinning him from top to toe and throwing him out in the sun to die.

Morinl paled, terrified, eyes darting everywhere in search of escape.

Beyir chuckled and sat down.

Chief Priests Evron and Harn looked as sick as Snake felt.

Snake sighed. The warriors' training had just taken on more urgency.

20. Slyn

Jonyl was still sitting at Jynx's side when Snake got home. Firelight flickered quietly around the room, and Snake started at once for the piled cushions where Jynx lay.

The healer held up a hand. "Go wash, Kyr. She can wait a few more minutes for you."

He ignored her, slowing as he approached. Jynx lay silent, eyes closed, her stomach rising and falling gently, as if she slept. He saw no immediate sign of injury. "How is she? How badly is she hurt?"

Jonyl shook her head. "As nearly as I can tell, she but sleeps. I have found no injuries, but neither can I wake her. For now, I tend her and wait."

Snake eased himself down next to Jynx. For a long moment he watched without touching, but she remained inert. He touched her cheek, fingers lingering. "Jynx?" No response.

For one awful moment panic caught him in a dense fog. What if she never woke? What if he'd lost her, so soon?

How could the gods be that cruel, to bring them together so sweetly, just to cast them apart?

He lay the flat of his hand on her cheek and closed his eyes, trying not to think at all. His thoughts were too painful right now. He was consumed by awareness of Jynx, by worry about undiscovered injuries, and by the memories he could cling to.

Jonyl opened her mouth, hesitated, then spoke. "I can think of only one possibility, though it seems unlikely. Sometimes a young child new to Rapport is–burnt out, for lack of a better term. They're not really ready for full Rapport and are asked to handle too much. But Jynx has clearly experienced much Rapport with Erilya, a very powerful slither queen, and she's an adult, not a small child." She sighed with heavy worry. "I'm sorry I have no better ideas to offer."

Illness. Like the flu that had killed so many in Jynx's hometown last year. Snake had spent many an hour at her bedside with Kahpur or with Jynx's mother, watching for her to pull through.

He mentioned that to Jonyl.

She shook her head regretfully. "There has been no such illness in the village for several years. And there would be symptoms to observe for a diagnosis. In some ways, it would be easier if she *were* ill. At least we'd know what we're dealing with."

A noise outside sent Snake to full alert, until he heard Shyriel's voice.

"Kyr?" she called, "May we enter?"

He relaxed back onto the cushion, hoping his irritation didn't show. "Come."

We have come to see Jynx, Ick told him, *at my insistence. How is she?*

Jonyl leaped to her feet and bowed to Shyriel and Erilya.

Shyriel waved her back to her cushion. "I'm pleased to see you here, Jonyl. Erilya tells me Jynx has been injured. If anyone can help her, it will be you. What's happened? What have you found?" Without asking, she settled onto a cushion near Snake.

Snake told them what they knew, with some help from Jonyl.

"She was conscious, just barely, when he found her," the healer summed up. "But she has shown no such awareness since I arrived. I have found no injuries. Nor has she any symptoms of an illness."

Shyriel glanced at Snake from the corner of her eye and he caught it. He wasn't surprised to hear her ask, "Will she live?"

Jonyl started to speak but he cut across her words. "Of course she will! She's strong and wants to live. So she will."

Shyriel spoke to the healer. "Have you considered poison?"

"I have, my queen. But again, there are no signs of it."

Cold trickled down the back of Snake's neck. Poison! Why hadn't he thought of that? "Did you look for punctures or other tiny signs?"

"Yes, I did."

Shyriel glared at him. "Of course she did! Jonyl is very thorough, our most respected healer!"

He'd been asking, not accusing, but he saw no reason to say so.

Erilya slid from Shyriel's waist and came to Snake, coiling on his lap. He felt the Rapport but she said nothing–the slither version of holding his hand while they waited.

He wanted to cry, simply from the kindness and understanding, aware of the irony that the cold slither empathized, and the warm human queen did not.

For the first time he wondered if paired queens always got along. He'd assumed constant harmony, the public face of the sister-queens, but what if they hated each other?

But he didn't care enough to ask.

Kyr, you smell. Wouldn't you like to be clean and fresh when she wakens? If you want to bathe, I'll stay here and let you know the moment anything changes.

He did smell. But leaving Jynx, even for a moment, was hard. Slowly he made himself move, stand up, walk toward the door. "I won't be long."

And he wasn't. Still, when he returned clean and wearing fresh clothes, he was surprised to find Slyn coiled next to Jynx, on her far side.

What was he doing here? He didn't care beans about Jynx!

The first fingers of timid sun were stretching over the horizon, and Snake needed to go back to work, to train Beyir's warriors so they could wreak havoc on the Wohim.

He felt sick of the whole thing.

He just wanted Jynx to get better. And to go home, taking Jynx with him.

~~~

Slyn rode Snake's shoulders on the long run out to the training area. He'd be more secure around the waist, but the big slither scorned such a safe perch.

And he wanted to talk.

Snake didn't.

He felt no special connection to this creature. Slyn had been trouble from the first day the priests had brought him to Kyr to raise and train. He was the third acolyte they'd brought him to. The first couldn't handle his strange thought processes and bizarre behavior. The second was damaged in some way never specified in young Kyr's hearing, though he'd seen adults circle a finger near their own ears when speaking of him. Crazy. Not right in the head.

Kyr had done much better and earned respect from novices and priests alike. Mostly he and Slyn got along well—except for the slither starting fights with increasingly larger slithers, and trying to enter the queens' precinct, and biting humans when they made him unhappy—even Kyr, his own handler.

Yet he was also known as powerful and astute. And ambitious. That ambition had almost gotten Kyr killed.

Snake, the adult, wasn't putting up with any behaviors that could get himself or anyone else killed. He no longer regarded the slithers as sacred; he wouldn't hesitate to kill this one or any other if necessary.

He guarded these thoughts carefully from Slyn, who seemed to think they were close friends.

Understanding Slyn didn't make them friends. It only made Snake wary.

Why did Slyn want to come to the human training today? Maybe he thought the hunting would be better this far from the village? Or perhaps he still sought a way the slithers could be part of the fighting.

He found Slyn a place out of the way, where he could see what was going on, and lined up the men.

The first three hours repeated everything from the day before, demanding more strength and more power. Then Snake added two new stances, which used different muscles and represented different movements. When legs trembled, he pushed harder.

He taught them to plant the front leg, knee bent out over the instep. He taught them to stretch the back leg behind them, knee straight. He taught them to slide the back leg forward to the front leg, knees touching first instead of just stepping straight forward. The knees touching allowed some protection for the groin from an opponent's kick

The sun and fine sand filled Snake's eyes and weariness dragged at him. Even a couple of hours of sleep would have helped. He could go without sleep if he had to, but with the sun's heat added in, his own legs started to feel rubbery.

As the men took their first water break, Snake asked, "Why take the time to move your knees together instead of just striding forward?"

"To protect our voices," called back a cheerful young warrior.

Snake was already grinning when an older man frowned. "Voices?"

"Yes," said the youth. "I, for one, don't want to be one of Chief Priest Evron's sopranos."

Good-natured laughter and ribbing broke out.

"We talked about the targets your opponent may choose to disable you quickly," Snake reminded them when the laughter died. "Including your knees–and your groin. You're moving a tempting target from where your enemy expects it to be, and you're protecting something you value." A few chuckles greeted this pronouncement.

"You'll learn to move easily this way, so it will feel natural, and you'll know when you need it. Not when you're advancing, or running, but when you're in close quarters combat. The movement can also set you up for an effective kick. Partner up with someone and I'll show you how it's done."

At Snake's gesture, Beyir came forward to partner with him for the demonstration. He'd shown Beyir this movement last night, so the Chief Priest of the Protection clan would look good to his men.

Somewhere close to mid-day–warrior sun–Snake noticed that Slyn was gone. Hunting, most likely. He'd show up when he wanted a ride back to the village–or make his own way back. Snake put the irritant out of his mind and set up the men to practice block-and-punch exercises with a partner. They weren't ready for actual bouts yet, but maybe tomorrow. These men weren't amateurs; they had good instincts and were simply learning new techniques.

As resting sun set the empty sky afire with a pinkish glow, he started the warriors back to the village, pleased with the day's work. Already they looked more confident, more capable. And in their fierce concentration he saw intimidating scowls. Even now they would make an enemy flinch. Give him six weeks, and they'd be ready to be tested.

Then his thoughts turned to Jynx and stayed there for the duration of their run.

~~~

Jynx knew who she was, nothing else. A gray fog of nothingness enveloped her, obfuscating the world–if it still existed. She wasn't sure. She floated, neither touching nor being touched. No physical connection at all. Awareness felt new, as if she hadn't had that for a long time. She tried opening her eyes, but they must be open already, as nothing changed. Her ears seemed stuffed with the wooly cloud enfolding her, blocking sound. She felt... empty. She inhaled. Such a strange sensation! Only a thimbleful of air, odorless and empty. She pulled in nothingness across her tongue but it had no taste.

The effort exhausted her.

When she became aware of herself again, she had a sense of time passing but not its length. She felt a pressure against her body. Not heavy. Maybe not physical. She thought she groaned but heard nothing. Her chest rose and fell as her breath sighed out. She sensed... something. A presence? As if she weren't alone here. Heaviness weighed her down, vised her head, sent the nothingness in waves, filling her. Replacing her.

Jynx. Jynx. She clung to self, fingernails breaking against the stone piled on her head. There may be nothing left of the world, but she couldn't give up who she was. She had to keep that, protect it.

And then she felt pain, followed by fear. She fell, and kept falling, through endless gray clouds, with nothing below to catch her.

She screamed, but she had not recovered voice or hearing. A silent scream, unfelt and unheard.

Abruptly she stopped falling. She didn't land, didn't hit anything, but the sensation broke off, leaving her dizzy.

She opened her eyes and swam in blue-green pools, felt rough calluses against her palm, hard fingers barely touching her cheek.

She blinked, trying to orient. She was still Jynx. Beyond that, she was no longer sure.

~~~

This time Snake went to the spring to wash first. If Jynx was awake, he'd rather she see him clean than looking like a shaggy manbear from the high mountains. Surely by now Jonyl had discovered what was wrong and treated the injury.

Anything else was unthinkable, but that didn't stop him from thinking about it. He needed to see her, to set his mind at rest.

If anything had gone wrong–and he wouldn't define "wrong" even to himself–surely they would have sent someone to him right away.

He stopped, almost in mid-stride. If Jynx died–a word he had trouble saying, even in his own head–Shyriel might believe him more amenable to leading the warriors into battle, and even to stay with the people.

No, surely Shyriel wasn't behind the attack. He was reading too much into it, from his own growing animosity toward her. Well, not really animosity. Distrust. He didn't trust her. Or any girl half his age who carried so much power.

He hurried toward the house as anxiety increased. He should never have left Jynx all day, even with a healer.

As he stepped inside, bare chest still shining wetly, he looked toward the cushions where he'd left her. She lay still, just as before, and Jonyl remained beside her, bathing her face with a cool, wet cloth.

And on a cushion just behind her head coiled Slyn, looking as comfortable as if he'd been settled in all day. Maybe he had. Maybe he hadn't been hunting after all, when he disappeared from the training grounds. Nerves spiked, emphasizing Snake's primal reaction to the slither.

Despite being the only acolyte able to form a bond with Slyn twenty-plus years ago, Snake didn't trust him any more than he did Shyriel–a thought he buried quickly. He didn't trust Slyn's manners, either. He was likely to connect through Rapport without warning. He shouldn't be able to read Snake's thoughts unless they shared Rapport, but Snake also didn't trust his own knowledge and understanding of slithers. He'd been a beginner, and it was a very long time ago.

"Any change?" he asked Jonyl as he settled onto a cushion next to Jynx.

"No, nothing. I've tried three different stimulants, hoping to prod her back to consciousness, but without success. I can't use more stimulants for a while–tomorrow at least–or I may do more harm than good." Jonyl rubbed at her lower back.

Her eyes looked tired and her face drawn. Perhaps she hadn't slept last night, either.

"Go home, Jonyl," he said in the gentlest voice he could find. "Get some rest. I'll be here, and you need to be your best tomorrow."

She nodded, relief showing in the corners of her eyes. "Thank you. I'll return at timid sun tomorrow, before you leave again for training. If anything changes, or if you need me before then, send Lasyr to get me. I'll send her over on my way home, so you'll have someone to help you, to bring you supper, to run errands, or whatever you need. You might see if you can dribble a bit of water into Jynx's mouth from time to time. I'm not sure she actually swallows, but unless it's too much and she chokes, her body could use the moisture."

"Thank you, Jonyl. For all you've done, for your dedication and excellent care of her."

She nodded again and climbed stiffly to her feet.

He watched her out the door; she stumbled once but caught her balance.

And then he returned his attention to Jynx. He slipped his hand into hers, than caressed her cheek lightly with the fingertips of his other hand.

Now he could only wait, watching her face for any sign of awareness.

Did her eyes shift behind closed lids? He couldn't be sure. Did her breath stop for a tiny interval? He wasn't sure of that, either, but it frightened him.

Slyn didn't move, either. Except that Snake felt his eyes following his tiniest movements. But that had to be imagination.

At last, in a low, quiet voice, he said, "Why are you here, Slyn?"

To offer my support. To see how she does, and to help if I can.

"Help? Why would you help Jynx?" He chose to ignore the distrust the question conveyed. He didn't really care what Slyn thought.

Because she is your mate. Because you are the only friend I've ever had, the only human ever to understand me.

Probably true. He was... very different from other slithers. Memory flooded back. *Fear. Loneliness. Sadness. Anger. Nobody liked Slyn and he didn't know why. They kept moving him; he had not felt secure and safe for a very long time. He didn't know who to lash out at. No one understood him.*

At the time, Kyr could only hang on and project as much acceptance and love as possible, until the young slither calmed with exhaustion.

We are partners, you and I, Slyn told him. *The way Erilya and Shyriel are partners. Bonded for life. Destined to rule together in the same way.*

"Rule?" Snake laughed. "I have no desire to rule. This place is not my home, these gods are not my gods, and I know less about slithers and life here than when I was six. I would be no fit ruler even if I desired it." The idea was ludicrous.

Or aberrant. Just thinking the word raised the hairs on Snake's neck.

You know I'm one of the most powerful prophets of the slithers. Would you like to hear the latest words shared with me by the gods? I have told no one yet, but I would share them with you.

No. Snake had no interest in more prophecy. Not even a little curiosity.

Slyn's black tongue flickered in silent laughter.

Snake's lips tightened in irritation. He wanted to order Slyn out of his house, but what could he do if the slither refused?

Violence to slithers would be punished by death. *That* he remembered clearly.

Slyn rose three feet above his coils, straight and formal. *Hear the words of the gods that were given me two days ago! The son of prophecy has come home, and the People will be rewarded for welcoming him. A new order is upon us, guided by the son of prophecy. The queen shall be cast down and a new ruler arise, bringing the promised prosperity to the People.*

Slyn settled back into his coils, signifying the end of the prophecy.

So you see, the gods intend for us to rule. And that is how prosperity will be restored. Beginning with the slaughter of the Wohim and rescue of the slithers they have taken.

21. War on Three Fronts

Jynx regained consciousness the next day. Snake knew as soon as Jonyl's runner arrived at the training grounds, before he even spoke. He could tell by the big grin on the young man's face.

Snake promptly turned the training over to Beyir. "Pair them up. Half strength or less; I don't want anyone injured. Work on yesterday's drills, then teach them what I showed you last night. Go to balance work if I'm not back by then. I'm not sure when or if I'll return today."

Beyir nodded, sympathy and understanding in his dark eyes. Snake remembered someone talking about the close bond between Beyir and his wife of twenty-four years and was grateful to the older man.

The messenger would rest and drink before returning, but Snake couldn't wait for him. He felt eyes on his back as he left, trying not to hurry. He managed to wait until he was out of their sight before he broke into a run.

This time he didn't feel the crunch of sand under his feet, or hear the wind in his ears. The warrior sun didn't touch him, and he even managed to sidestep a huge scorpion without breaking stride.

The young tanglecat half an hour later was a little harder. He saw it only as it leaped, but its inexperience helped him. It didn't twist and strike in midair, as an adult would, but Snake still took a stinging cut to his shoulder. He ducked away, spinning as he drew his blade and struck in the same movement. The keen edge sliced off two long, curved claws and the cat ran, screaming.

Snake slowed just before he reached the village to catch his breath, then forced himself to walk the rest of the way to his house.

Jonyl was still there. She bustled about, plumping pillows and cushions, and Snake smelled something cooking on the low fire just outside the back door.

She looked up as he came in. Her eyes still looked tired, but a spark glowed that hadn't been there for a while.

Jynx lay propped up by cushions to a half-sitting position, and her eyes opened as he approached.

He felt a smile stretch the corners of his mouth almost to the point of splitting his lips. This was still a sick room, though, and certain manners applied. He didn't race pell mell toward her and throw himself on top of her and the cushions. He didn't whoop with joy to see her brown eyes open. He didn't grab Jonyl for an impromptu dance around the room.

Instead he walked at a reasonable speed–as best he could– and dropped (decorously) onto a cushion next to Jynx. He covered one small, delicate hand with his and used the other to smooth walnut hair back off her face.

"Welcome back," he said, voice catching. "I've missed you. Where have you been?"

Jynx smiled, a tiny smile but a real one. "In the dark. Waiting to be enlightened. Waiting for you."

Jonyl spoke from behind him. "Slyn arrived shortly after she woke, so I asked him to send a runner to you." She sat down in her usual place. "I've gotten a little food down her, but she has no memory of what happened to her."

Disappointment hurt. "Perhaps some memory will return later. For now, she's awake and that's enough."

"I see no reason she shouldn't recover fully, nothing to cause concern, so I'm going home to rest. Send Lasyr if you need me, if anything changes. There's soup on the fire; she'll need the nourishment when she feels ready to eat." With a tired smile, Jonyl picked up her satchel and slung it over her shoulder. "I wish you health, peace, and happiness."

She turned and started for the door.

Snake squeezed Jynx's hand lightly, then got up and followed her. At the doorway they paused. "I don't know how to thank you," Snake said. "What's customary, to reward you for bringing her back from near death?"

Jonyl shook her head. "I do what I do because I must, as you are a warrior because you cannot help it. In this village, it is the way business is done. We help each other at need. One day perhaps you and your sword will save my life, and I will not pay you for that, either." She smiled, eyes tired and shoulders sagging.

Snake swallowed. "If ever you need anything from me, you have only to ask. I'm grateful for your devotion and persistence and care of Jynx, beyond words to give you."

She nodded and left.

He watched her for a moment, then turned back to Jynx.

The worry wasn't over yet. Mystery still cloaked the incident, and although he knew Jonyl would have already told him if Jynx knew more, he had to ask.

He sat again, holding Jynx's hand in both of his, a gentle cage to hold a delicate bird. He lifted her hand, kissed it, then returned it to the cushion. He kissed her brow. He kissed her lips, with love but without lust.

"How do you feel?" he asked.

"Fuzzy," she whispered. "As if there's a gauze curtain between us."

"What happened? We never figured it out."

She frowned in thought. "I don't know. I started down the steps outside the back door, and then I woke up here. I think something may have hit me in the head."

"We found no injuries. No knot that would suggest being struck."

"I... seem to remember a blinding pain in my head. Nothing else, except a bad dream or two, until I woke up."

"Did you see anyone? Anywhere? Doing anything?"

"I think... some children by the water, playing with small slithers." She shuddered lightly.

Jynx still saw slithers as exotic snakes in some ways, until she knew them as individuals. Snake suppressed a smile.

"There were a couple of larger slithers nearby, too, but they weren't part of the group, I don't think."

Snake thought about it. "Did any of the slithers speak to you?"

"No." Her voice sounded thin, a tired whisper.

"Did you recognize either of the adults?"

Her eyes were glazing over with weariness. "They all look alike to me." Except Ick, but that was understood between them.

"Sleep, beloved. Sleep as long as you like. I'll be here."

She obeyed before she finished nodding.

For a long time Snake sat thinking. If he knew who the children were, or the adult slithers, he could ask them what they saw. But there was no way to know.

He woke Jynx after a while to feed her a little soup, then ate a bowlful himself, though he wasn't really hungry.

Both relieved and worried, he lay down next to Jynx, gathered her into his arms, and fell asleep, the mystery still unsolved.

~~~

The Wohim raided in cool sun, while Snake trained his warriors far from the village. They snatched three youngens from the Acolyte precinct, killed a novice to steal two yearlings, and picked up several adult slithers caught hunting outside the village.

The villagers defended as best they could, but they had few weapons with the warriors gone. Jonyl and other healers spent the rest of the day tending the wounded, including one old man who lost most of his left arm to a Wohim sword and a girl of eleven raped by a Wohim with a long, red scar down one side of his face.

That one will die, Snake promised himself, jaw hard with anger.

It didn't help that Slyn brought up his prophecy again. This wouldn't have happened if he and Snake had been in charge, he assured Snake.

Shyriel was furious. "You're the war leader! You should have left enough men here to protect the village! Have you no common sense?"

Snake blazed right back. "I am *not* the war leader! I agreed only to train your warriors. Beyir is still their leader, Chief Priest of Protection."

"So you're trying to blame someone else. Someone who..."

Her words were lost in his shout. "I am *not* blaming Beyir! Focus on the Wohim, Shyriel. They're to blame for this!"

The gasps around them reminded him that they were in public—and that she was a queen and he'd broken protocol. Again.

He didn't care. She wasn't his queen!

They stood in the center of the village. He could just see the slither precincts off to his left and the People's hall off to his right, out of the corners of his eyes. Somewhere behind him a woman was crying, and so were all the village's children—mostly from fear, he thought. His shouting had just frightened them more.

He threw up his hands and walked away right in the middle of Shyriel's response, whatever it was.

Ick hissed a warning in his head just as Shyriel grabbed his arm and pulled him. He spun back to her, anger hazing his vision. "Do you think I enjoyed this any more than you did? Now leave me alone. I have work to do," he snarled.

He jerked away from her and left, seething. But his feet slogged through sand, ruining the effect of his intended long, powerful strides.

Jynx saw the whole thing, of course, from where she stood near Lasyr. And that's where Ick was, as well, coiled next to her feet. A thoughtful gesture, he realized, not to ask Jynx to carry her weight as she recovered from her ordeal.

He winced. More pain waited for Jynx when Ick made her decision. How could she be anything but what she was? She was a queen, and she'd make a queen's decision. He ached for Jynx, wondering if she realized yet.

He would give anything to keep her from the hurt of losing Ick for good. And then wondered if "anything" included fulfilling Slyn's prophecy. If they ruled instead of Shyriel and Ick, Ick would be free to go with Jynx.

Or dead. And Shyriel with her.

Could Slyn really be plotting against one or both of them? His warrior's mind took over. No. He'd kill Shyriel, perhaps, but not Ick. He'd mate with her "for the betterment of the slithers" and perhaps planned to co-rule with her, keeping Snake as their intermediary, a step down from both of them. Or perhaps he really did plot to co-rule with Snake, and still father babies with Ick. He'd always wanted to father a queen's babies.

Snake shook his head. Those scenarios were ridiculous. Not even Slyn would plot against the queens and the People. He shoved the thought away.

I've been in the Snows so long that I see plots and counterplots everywhere. These are simpler people, without all the conniving and backstabbing and manipulation of a Snows court. He longed to be in the Snows now, riding the Beast high into the mountains to hunt or race the Beast against all comers—except Kayde's horse, Wind Dancer, who always won, no matter what horses and riders ran against him.

The cool breezes of the lower peaks would feel really good in place of this dry, blazing heat. Or even the sharp, icy winds of the higher reaches.

He began to consider ways to speed up the training so he could go home. And he began to think in broader strategic terms, about ways to end this sooner. *Where can I find Beyir at this time of day?*

The Chief Priest, as anticipated, was in what Snake thought of as the tavern, although the People called it the "sampair," which meant something like "watering place" as best he could translate it.

Beyir saw him and waved him over, then waved at the attendant, who brought a pottery pitcher beaded with moisture and a cup.

"Ursaq," Beyir called it, pouring the blue liquid into a cup for Snake. "Manly nectar, sour and deadly for the unsuspecting." He grinned and handed the cup to Snake.

Snake had played this game before. A sniff would help him brace for the taste and effect, but it would also mark him as a cautious man rather than bold and daring.

He tossed it down in one huge gulp, banged the cup back onto the scarred wooden table, and grinned at the table full of men. Not bad. The flavor was certainly more sour than he was used to, with a dusty tang and no spices. But it wasn't as volatile and powerful as the joos he sometimes drank in the Snows.

Admiring, friendly laughter burst from the men at the table. He'd just become one of them, entering their society by way of the manly equivalent of a secret handshake.

Only two of the men were Beyir's warriors, one turned out to be the sampair owner, and he never knew the last one's place. One or two at a time the others left, until Snake had Beyir to himself.

The older man sobered. "Such an awful day here. Thank the gods no one died. The Wohim are truly evil people, to attack the weak and helpless when their warriors are gone."

"How would they know the warriors were gone?" Snake refilled his glass and sipped at it. He no longer needed a show, but he did need a clear head. He set the cup down and left it.

Startlement widened Beyir's eyes. "Do you think they knew that?"

"I think it's possible. Is there anyone in the village known to have ties to the Wohim? Or be sympathetic to them? Or who hates the slithers?"

"Hates the voices of the gods? I can't imagine." Beyir traced a moisture line down the side of the pitcher with his finger.

"What about the prisoner, Morinl? Could he have overheard anything? Do we still hold him? What disposition has been decided on?"

"No decision yet, that I've heard. In fact, I've not heard anything since the meeting."

Snake thought a moment. "Have the Wohim ever raided into the village before? Or only out in the dunes?"

Beyir shook his head. "They've never come into the village before—except once, probably ten years ago. They were repelled with the loss of two men—and three slithers they managed to snatch as they fled. We pursued, but they disappeared into the black sands, hidden by shadows, and we lost them."

"What about the magic of the white sands? Can it be used in some way to counter the black sand's magic?"

"The... white sand's magic?"

"I've been told every color of sand in the Rainbow Sands is magical but I've never heard what this sand's magic is."

"None that I know of," Beyir responded. He lifted his cup for a drink.

A pretext for not meeting Snake's eyes.

And that just made Snake more curious. *I'll ask Ick later. Or Slyn, if I have to.*

He shifted the topic—for now—and the two warriors talked strategies for over an hour longer, before Snake headed back to Jynx for the night.

22. White Sands

Jynx's fall, followed by the Wohim attack, put Snake in a foul mood. But those were just an excuse. Add to these an arrogant queen who, at sixteen, knew nothing but wasn't wise enough to know she knew nothing. His heart ached especially for the young girl who was raped, and he felt only uneasiness about Slyn's prophecies.

Slyn didn't help, either. His offer–thinly veiled as "prophecy," he suspected–was yet another form of manipulation, and Snake didn't like it. They were no closer to figuring out what happened to Jynx, but now that she was back to normal, everyone else had stopped worrying about it, even Jynx. And the Wohim raid abraded that deep part of him that believed his life's work was to protect the weak and helpless. The People had been both, with the warriors out at the training grounds.

Deep down, where he could usually avoid looking at it, he wondered if he were responsible for this raid, by killing the Wohim pursuers so savagely, so close to the white sands. Was any of that manipulated by the "prophecy"? *I'm just a featherball batted back and forth between players in a game I don't know the rules for.*

But the sharpest thorn in his foot right now was the Wohim raid. He and Beyir had taken the men on a "training run," trying to catch up before the Wohim reached the black sands. But Snake knew when they started they'd be too late. Once the Wohim reached the black sand, they couldn't be seen, and they seemed to leave no tracks. As if some great bird had swooped down and carried them off.

Couldn't anything go right? Just once? *Let's end this, so Jynx and I can go home.*

With that, his resolve stiffened. He went looking for Beyir and found him at the sampair.

The Chief Priest sat with three men Snake didn't know. When they saw him coming, they got up and left, all smiles but still in a hurry.

The cautious look in Beyir's eyes disappeared as Snake sat.

Just his imagination, then.

"Can you draw me a rough map of the black sands and the white sands?" he asked without greeting.

"I can, as of the last time I passed through. The sands shift constantly with the winds, so nothing stays the same for long." Curiosity replaced wariness in his expression.

"How long ago?" Snake was being very short but was in no mood for loquacity or explanations.

Beyir shrugged. "Within a year?"

Snake nodded. "That should work. It doesn't have to be exact."

Beyir rose. "Let's find smooth sand. I'll draw it there."

Snake chose an area next to his house that would be shaded by walls in the morning and by nearby palm trees in the evening, a place easy to keep an eye on.

Beyir squatted in the sand and drew two amorphous, adjoining shapes. "Black sands, very roughly," he said, pointing to the top shape. "White sands below. Here's our spring." He sketched it quickly. "Here's the river that runs past the Wohim village you found." His finger dragged through sand again. "Other known villages are much farther– here, here, and here that we know of, but their villages move from time to time. If one village is ascendant, I'm not aware of it. Here are mountainous dunes underlaid by rock, and also on the opposite side of the village, here." He marked the ridges with his finger. "There are many other dunes, mostly in north/south ridges, as you saw coming south, but these two are more solid. No reliable sources of water exist between their village and this one."

"Do you have any idea how many warriors they have? Or how many raiders?"

"Their village is known to be larger than ours. Assume a hundred fighters or more, although it could be half that many. I don't have a reliable count."

Snake frowned, thinking. "Are your men trained with bow and arrows? Do you have any distance weaponry?"

"Distance weaponry?"

"Bows, slings, crossbows, but especially catapults and other large equipment?"

"Bows, yes, and a few use slings to hunt or to protect against tanglecats. We've no one familiar with crossbows— except me, but I'm not that proficient, nor do I own one. A catapult or similar large weapon isn't very practical in deep sand."

No horses, either. Damn. But not unexpected. Snake scratched his stubbled chin. He needed to shave if he wanted Jynx to kiss him. And then his mind went back to the problems at hand.

He remained silent so long that Beyir finally broke into it. "What are you thinking?"

Snake glanced around. He saw no one in the vicinity, and no one paying any attention to them. He lowered his voice anyway. "I want to take the fight to them, become offensive instead of defensive. If we move quickly, we may get some or all of the slithers back."

"How? What would you suggest?"

"I don't know yet, but we're going to push hard on training from now on. No more easy tactics. In two weeks I want your men ready, and I'm going to be relentless to that end. I need you with me, to help me push and help me see possibilities and obstacles I normally haven't had to worry about. We're going to destroy the Wohim to the extent they never again consider raiding this village. We're going to make them pay for what they've done." In his mind he pictured a man with a long, red scar across his face.

And then I can be quit of this place with a clear conscience.

After Beyir left, Snake remained sitting in the sand, studying the map and reaching for his blurred memories of the Wohim village. Jynx could help him with its layout, but he needed more about the people themselves. Especially the warriors.

The thought hit him like a boulder. A spy was what he needed. Someone who could enter the Wohim village, observe for a few days, then return with an accurate report. Where would the Wohim warriors be found? Scattered on daily routines? Training in groups, or in one large group? Where? What were they training on? What were their weapons? Their techniques? How would they likely react to an attack–disciplined, with every man knowing his job? Or racing hither and yon, trying to get organized? One larger group? Several smaller groups? He needed to know the leaders and how they thought–especially now he'd killed their Malim, Nerom.

And who could infiltrate, or at least hide and watch effectively? He had two names in mind, but he wasn't happy with either of them.

He was still mulling the question when he went inside for the night.

The house was too quiet. For reasons of propriety Jynx had returned to her assigned dwelling, and he missed her presence terribly. He could almost catch a whiff of her scent... but it was just out of reach. Settling down to sleep was hard, and he finally curled up on the cushions where she had lain for two days. Here he did catch the faint scent of her hair and skin, and he at last fell asleep dreaming of her.

He awoke in the morning feeling empty and forlorn. And resigned to the spy he knew would agree to go.

Slyn.

~~~

Slyn agreed without hesitation when Snake talked to him in the morning.

I can hide under the sand, he suggested, *only my eyes and nose exposed. The magic of the black sand will keep me from being noticed. By timing my movements right and hiding properly, I can go anywhere in the village.*

"I don't need you going 'anywhere' in the village," Snake replied. "I need you in specific places, watching specific people for particular reasons."

I can create havoc and fear, unseen, the slither suggested. *Things can appear or disappear, small traps and trips can appear, unexplainable sounds can be heard. I will distract and confuse them, even frighten them.*

"Or alert them to your presence and get you killed. We can't risk the intelligence you could bring us." Snake tamped down his impatience. He couldn't realistically expect Slyn to understand espionage, but the worm seemed to brush aside Snake's attempt to coach him. "I'll send a human with you, too, if I can find the right person. I need to interrogate our prisoner before I decide who, but I'll want you on your way by day after tomorrow. Expect to observe for three days. Move around only after dark, the magic of the black sands notwithstanding."

Unease crept along the hairs of his forearms as he left Slyn. It would be just like him to leave before he was supposed to— without a human partner, and before he could interrogate the prisoner. A muscle in his jaw jumped. How to control such a slither, once the creature was out of sight and out of reach?

Abruptly he changed destination, crossing into the queens' precinct without hesitation. This slither queen wasn't twenty-five feet long, and he was no longer a little boy. Besides, he wore his sword every day now, with Beyir's approval.

For a brief instant his stomach clenched with the memory of Tchenya's raging charge out of the royal burrow. But then Ick came out to meet him. This queen bore no hostility, instead greeting him politely.

Welcome, Snake. What brings you to our home?

What a change from Tchenya, who had been highly offended by his encroachment! Or had she only been acting as required to manipulate the prophecy, as Ick claimed?

"I need to speak with you," he told her. "Without Shyriel."

He felt Ick's purr in his head. *Intriguing. Come in.*

He followed her through white halls to a small but comfortable room with scattered cushions. She coiled comfortably on one and pointed her forked tongue at one next to it for Snake.

You've been busy, talking with Beyir, planning, discussing. I like the idea of taking the fight to the Wohim. They must be stopped, no matter what.

"Have you been eavesdropping?" he asked, startled.

He felt the flutter of her laughter in his head. *Have I? Or do my people and slithers talk to me as they should?*

He exhaled heavily. Let her play coy. It didn't matter.

"Your information is good. I want to attack, rather than defend, catch the Wohim off-guard if I can. I'm sending Slyn to spy on the village, looking for specific information, and I want to send a human with him. I need a human perspective, as well as a slither one. Someone with Rapport to communicate with Slyn. Someone strong enough to control him, so that he doesn't make stupid decisions that could do us more harm than good."

Ah. Slyn does tend to go his own way, believing he knows better than anyone else. He's very intelligent and strong, but he has his own agenda. Ick was silent a few moments, thinking. *Have you met Lorm?*

"No. I haven't even heard the name."

I will send two humans with Slyn. Lorm is an old, old man. Once a warrior, but now beyond strength and agility. Wise in the ways of warriors and of men and slithers. Well respected by all and still very strong in Rapport. I will also send his grandson, Ahm, his caretaker. He has the physical strength that Lorm has outlived. Between them, they will help keep Slyn under control. Lorm will understand what Slyn needs to achieve and why, so you need not go yourself.

"Thank you, Ick," he said, then froze. Would she be offended that he still didn't use her real name?

You're welcome, Snake. What else do you need?

"Two things. First, I need to interrogate the prisoner, Morinl—myself, not just get reports from others who have spoken with him.

"And second, I need to know: What is the magic of the white sands?"

Ick turned emrel eyes on him.

Caught off-guard, he froze, trapped in immobility.

Faint menace underlay Ick's thoughts. *Why do you need to know?*

For a moment he couldn't think, his brain as constrained as his body, as if trapped in thick mud. He struggled through the thickness, pushed his tongue into the shapes he needed.

The tightness in brain and throat eased enough for a raspy voice. "I'm looking for an edge over the Wohim."

Ick loosed her hold a little more and he inhaled deeply. "Every color of sand has its own magic. The Wohim will take advantage of the concealment properties of the black sand. If we have magic that will offset that advantage, I need to know about it—everything I can learn, to give us the best chance to win."

She released him.

It was all he could do not to sag physically.

Unfortunately, the magic of the white sands will not help you. Its properties are very specialized and not likely to be helpful.

"If you're not a warrior yourself, you may miss a possibility that I would see. I can be very creative in war."

Ick remained silent, as if considering. *I must consult with Shyriel. Return at noon and we'll talk more. You will also be given access to the prisoner at that time. He will be yours to do with as you wish.*

Her tone had softened only slightly. What on earth was the magic of the sand, that she would protect it so fiercely? Even from him? He nodded, then as an afterthought bowed slightly. Maybe that would mollify her, at least a little.

Why the secrecy? Did the queens fear someone would steal sand instead of slithers if its magic were known? His mind sifted through ideas until his brain felt sand-scrubbed. In disgust he forced his thoughts elsewhere.

~~~

Jynx carried a hated blankness in her head. She banged her hand against the side of her skull in frustration, feeling as if a piece of her life were missing.

Why couldn't she remember? She saw the worry in Snake's eyes whenever he looked at her, but he had enough to worry about without this. He couldn't seem to let it go and concentrate on the things that mattered, increasing her guilt for the distraction when he least needed it.

Worse, she rarely saw him anymore. He spent all his time either training the men or strategizing with Beyir or the queens. What was the advantage of being so near when she didn't see him?

She saw Beyir walking toward the sampair, so maybe the queens, at least, were free right now. Specifically, Ick might be available. She didn't care about Shyriel. For that matter, she wasn't really comfortable with most of the People here—their concerns and ways of thinking were very different from hers—but Ick was an old friend.

A moment later she felt a comfortable buzz in her head. She

couldn't help smiling as she changed direction toward the queens' precinct, her mood already lightening.

Ick waited for her at the gold sand-edged border of the queens' precinct, her good humor and love clear through their Rapport. Jynx stepped across the border without even thinking about it. Not until Ick had wound about her waist did she realize that maybe she should have Shyriel's permission to enter, too. She didn't mention that to Ick. Despite her best efforts to keep her face smooth, she felt the corners of her lips quirk up, just a little. Flouting the human queen carried a certain satisfaction.

Cooler air wafted across Jynx's face as they crossed the jeweled threshold into the burrow. Ick guided her through a long hallway slanted gradually downward. Several adjoining branches crossed the main hall but Ick ignored them, leading her straight ahead.

They passed beneath a golden lintel set with seastones and turned at last. Here the corridor dropped more sharply before curving three times in quick succession. Another golden lintel was set with the largest skystones Jynx had ever seen—not that she'd seen many, living in the tallgrass far from "civilization."

She paused to admire the deep green emrels in the next lintel, then ducked underneath, into a cozy room of velvet cushions in bright jewel colors—emrel and seastone, but also godtears and lazh, pearls, and amber.

They settled on the cushions, relaxing in easy comfort.

"Your burrow is much larger than it appears on the surface," Jynx commented.

A placid buzz of appreciation vibrated lightly in her skull. *Few are aware that the surface of our precinct is very small, compared to its full size. It's not just a home but the seat of our government, with small meeting rooms and larger gathering spaces, in addition to specialized places like birthing rooms.*

"Birthing rooms? Ick, are you a mother?"

I have fourteen living offspring. I have lost eight more.

225

Jynx recognized the subtle feel of mourning in Ick's tone. "I'm sorry for your loss. What happened?"

Two died before they lived even one day. Their bodies did not adapt to their new world, or their food. Three died within a year, of accidents or illness. One was eaten by a tanglecat when she strayed outside the village. The others were stolen by the Wohim and I do not know their fates—only that they are forever gone.

Jynx remained silent for several minutes, absorbing what she'd heard. It seemed so strange! "Does the human queen also mate and bear an heir?" *Please let the answer be no!* She knew who Shyriel would choose, if she could.

No, not normally, Ick answered. *The human queen, traditionally, is a girl child born the same day as the next slither queen. They grow up together, bonding from birth to death. Only a few times in a thousand years has the next human queen been the daughter of the queen before her. They have not been our greatest rulers.*

A young woman appeared in the doorway, bearing a tray of figs, dates, long slices of coconut and cool melons, and the conversation turned to exotic food and some easy recipes that included them.

Only much later, after she'd left the queens' precinct, did Jynx realize she had no idea what special food was fed to the slithers who might become queens. Not that it really mattered.

~~~

Snake returned to the queens' precinct at noon. Beyir met him at the border and led him toward the doorway.

"Where's Ick? Uh... Erilya?" he asked. "I expected her to meet me."

Beyir's eyes flicked to the golden path and back to Snake's face. "Queen Erilya asked me to tell you that she and Queen Shyriel have spoken of your request and have declined it."

Bricks of disappointment dropped onto Snake's shoulders.

"I assume they already know, then, that if we fail I will attribute it to their lack of support. You'll tell them that for me?"

"It will make no difference."

"Tell them anyway." The more reluctant the queens were to share the white sand's secrets, the more he was convinced the magic was important to his goal. So why keep it from him? Surely Ick, at least, trusted him by now. Which meant Shyriel was the one objecting.

"You'll need to question the prisoner here," Beyir said. "I want no chance for him to signal any Wohim watching the village."

"I was promised he would be mine to do with as I wish. And I will." Snake's jaw hardened as he looked at Beyir. "It's not up to you."

"Why would you need to take him from here?"

Snake ignored him.

They stepped across the jeweled threshold and followed the white corridors down and down, to the room where Snake had met with the council previously. Morinl was there, as dirty and frightened as he had been before, hands bound behind him. Next to him, a protection guard with a spear snapped to formal attention as they entered.

Snake dismissed him and gestured the prisoner to a low cushion. "You can go, too, Beyir. I won't need you for this."

"You forget yourself, Kyr!" Beyir's eyes hardened. "*I'm* the chief priest of the Protection. Not you. Military matters are mine to decide!"

"Did Erilya consult you about my access to information and the prisoner? If not, you have no say in this. If that doesn't fit what you think is right, I'll call her to speak with you."

Beyir's face turned red and he glared.

Ah. Beyir had little or no gift of Rapport. His gift was combat—a gift great enough to become chief priest. But his conversations with Ick must include Shyriel—or at least someone from Prophecy with a strong gift. That could be important information, but Snake wished he'd realized earlier. He might have approached Beyir differently.

"Beyir, I respect your knowledge and skills. You know that. But this man must not think he can set one of us against the other. He must know there is no appeal, no recourse. And you do not want to be associated with what happens here." Snake firmed his gaze so Beyir could not mistake the depth of his intent.

He thought Beyir's face became a shade lighter. The older man stared for a moment, then nodded sharply and left without further comment.

Snake breathed a long, quiet sigh of relief. This would be difficult enough without the distraction of Beyir's presence.

Then he spun toward the prisoner and hit him on the jaw hard enough to snap a weak man's neck.

Morinl's head slammed back against stone with a loud crack and he dropped to his knees, stunned.

"Now. I know you speak this tongue. I've seen your eyes move from one person to the next, following a conversation. Don't bother pretending you don't understand my questions, or can't answer them in this language. You control how painful this discussion is going to be, by your cooperation or lack of it. I won't ask if you understand because I know you do."

Disgusted with himself for what he was about to do, he set to work.

He left hours later, weeping quietly in the darkness and covered with blood. None of it was his. He hid among white dunes until he was in control of himself again, then bathed in the spring as the flaming, bloody sun became engulfed by the desert. He scrubbed with sand until his skin burned, but it seemed he would never be clean again. No one should see him like this, and Jynx could never know what he'd done.

But in the twilight he saw Jonyl hurrying with her healer's satchel toward the queens' precinct. Jynx was with her, carrying her own satchel. Snake didn't have the courage to witness her reaction to what they would find and slunk into his house without calling to her. He lit no candles; let her think he was absent.

He allowed himself no sleep, knowing the nightmares he would face. When dawn came, he was both relieved and disappointed that Jynx had not come to him. Sand-eyed, exhausted, and self-excoriated, he didn't leave his house until well past midday—and then only reluctantly.

23. Love and Trust

"I think he's lost sight of why we came," Jynx said. "We were only going to see that Ick was returned here safely."

Jonyl smiled. "If that were true, you'd have started for home days ago."

Jynx and Jonyl had become fast friends almost immediately as Jynx recovered from her fall. Long discussions about remedies had led to more personal conversations, and they had discovered that they thought about their work and the world generally in much the same way, with just enough differences to make things interesting. Jynx already knew she would miss the People's best healer when she returned home.

"Snake got sidetracked by issues that have nothing to do with us, like training the Protection warriors. I don't know how he let himself get talked into that.

"Not to change the subject, but do you know what happened to the man we're going to see?" Jynx thought the queen's precinct an odd place for a man to be injured.

"I do not," said Jonyl, but her tone said otherwise. She seemed to carry a professional anger that, to Jynx, indicated sharp disapproval.

Why not share what she knew, if Jynx was going to see him for herself in another minute? She didn't press the matter.

They stepped onto the golden path leading to the queens'

burrow. Shyriel waited for them in the doorway ahead, haughty chin lifted high, as usual. Her mouth tightened and her eyes glittered when she saw Jynx. Jynx's backbone stiffened and she raised her own chin.

Her rival for Snake. Young. Beautiful. Powerful. How could she fight that, if Shyriel tried to seduce him?

Jynx took a slow, steadying breath and blew it out, along with images of Snake and Shyriel together. Too together!

Shyriel's look at Jynx was sharp but she only glanced at Jonyl.

"Jynx is highly skilled. I asked her to help me with the patient," said the healer.

"Erilya will take you to him," the queen told her. She didn't look at Jynx again. "We need him to live, to lead our warriors to his people. Beyond that, I don't care."

Jonyl nodded as Shyriel stepped aside. Behind her on the sandy floor, Ick uncoiled and came to Jynx, winding up her body and coiling around her waist.

Good morning, dear one, Ick greeted her. *Take the left branch ahead.*

Jynx followed her instructions, returning a cheerful greeting, glad to be with her friend again.

Jonyl has some gift of Rapport, Ick told Jynx as they walked, *but I'll likely speak only to you today. You can share what seems appropriate with her.*

Jynx nodded, wondering what Ick thought might *not* be appropriate to share.

Ick's contentment at spending time with Jynx was clear. Her tail came up to wrap around Jynx's arm, which she massaged with soft constrictions, her voice like a purr in Jynx's head.

It was only the underlying sense of sorrow that bothered Jynx.

What you face will be hard to see, despite your training, Ick said, *and harder when I tell you it's Snake's handiwork, performed with my permission.*

A trickle of cold ran down Jynx's spine. Maybe she shouldn't have come, after all. She'd seen Snake fight before, though. As long as *he* was uninjured, how bad could this be?

It's very bad. An interrogation to help in our fight against the Wohim. Brace yourself.

"Ick says it's bad. Brace yourself," Jynx said aloud.

The slither queen uncoiled from Jynx in a narrow corridor Jynx hadn't seen before and indicated a closed door with her flickering tongue.

Jynx opened the door and stepped inside. She caught her breath, then gagged at the hanging odor of blood. Jonyl stopped next to her, swearing.

Jynx decided not to tell her of Snake's involvement. Especially when she couldn't imagine her beloved might be responsible for this.

The walls were streaked with wide swaths of blood, some of the streaks going sideways instead of vertical. Shattered chair and table had been kicked or thrown aside into a corner. Both displayed bloody splashes.

A body lay crumpled on a cotton mattress in the center of the room. Morinl, the Wohim servant captured during the rescue of the slithers. He was alive, but only recognizable by the crescent-shaped scar on his left biceps. His features were bloody and broken, and so were several fingers and toes. Jynx didn't want to think about the long, straight red line running from below the notch in his throat to his birth knot.

Then there were the places he'd been skinned—like the captive slithers had been skinned. Only a few places on arms and legs, but the sight nauseated her. She wanted to turn to a corner and throw up, and Jonyl looked just as sick.

This was Snake's work? How? He was at heart a kind and gentle man, trained in violence but not naturally inclined toward it.

She needed to see him, to find out what happened.

To see what this work had done to him.

~~~

Snake's heart leaped when he saw Jynx coming toward his house. Then it constricted when he noticed her healer's satchel.

Her first words confirmed his worst fears. "Did you get what you needed from Morinl?"

Snake winced. The thought of Jynx seeing what he had done cramped his stomach. How could Ick ever allow that to happen? He stored up some unpleasant words to unleash on the slither queen later, when Jynx wasn't around.

"Not all, but I got what he knew." He watched her set her satchel inside his door and cross the room to where he sprawled on cushions with no energy to move. He braced, unable to tell from her calm, still face what she'd stored up to unleash on him. He wanted to avoid her eyes but found himself searching them instead, looking for a clue to how bad this was going to be.

His whole body stilled as she approached. What words could he possibly find to explain what he'd done?

To his surprise, her mouth didn't tighten. Her jaw remained relaxed. Her eyes showed... concern?

She leaned down, placing strong, cool hands on his cheeks, and kissed him.

Like honey. Or roses. Or something he couldn't name, sweet and beautiful and unbelievable.

She held the kiss for a long time. When she released his lips, her eyes filled with compassion. "I know you, Snake. I know your soul. And I know what it cost you to do this." She kissed him again, briefly and lightly.

And suddenly his arms pulled her down onto the cushions with him. He buried his face in the corner of her neck and cried. He clung so tightly she grunted, while he sobbed as if the entire earth relied on his tears to nourish it.

He'd thought he was cried out.

Jynx's eyes filled with tears, too, and compassion. And love.

As much as he hated himself right now, that was how much he loved Jynx.

They took comfort from each other, they mourned the events just past, they pushed out the dread and guilt and sorrow with their loving.

And when the sun rose again, they could continue normal living—changed forever somewhere deep inside, but closer than before.

~~~

The People were wretchedly healthy, Jynx reflected, and they had three healers of their own. She was bored, despite spending hours every day exchanging knowledge with all three—especially Jonyl. She worked alongside any of them whenever she could, but Jonyl remained responsible for the prisoner's wounds and Jynx always went with her. After all, her Snake had created these wounds; she should be involved in healing them.

Interestingly, the wounds were very painful but not so severe as she had expected. None were life-threatening or maiming—unless broken fingers didn't heal right. It was her job to see that they did. Still, once he'd been washed and treated, it wasn't as awful as she'd thought—although the next day she could still smell blood in the room.

They soon moved him. Jonyl insisted on a proper bed cushion for her patient in a clean room to avoid infections, although ointments and medications would help, too. For some treatments one of them remained with Morinl to be sure no side effects emerged, and Jynx usually took that duty. By now she didn't really expect any, but what else did she have to do, with Snake out training Protection's warriors?

Every evening some of those came back with pains, sprains, and even blood. Snake was drilling them in companies against each other and driving them hard. She and Jonyl left the treatment of those men to the other healers.

Mostly Jynx sat with the patient while Jonyl left to see other patients or mix up special concoctions. Since Morinl slept a good deal of the time, she was well and truly bored.

That's why she greeted Ick so cheerfully when the silver queen visited on the third day. Not that she expected the queen to visit, with all the queenly things she must have scheduled.

Come to think of it, what did Ick—and Shyriel, for that matter—do with their time? They didn't have lords and barons and court politics like Snake had described for the Kingdom of the Snows. She let her imagination run wild and was still lost in outlandish ideas of settling boundary disputes between precincts and between the burrows within them, or Shyriel deciding which of three outfits to wear that day, when Ick arrived.

Dear one, how is your patient doing? Ick coiled her tail comfortably around Jynx's wrist.

"Sleeping. I'm bored."

Ick's tongue flickered in silent laughter. *Come. I have something for you.* She released Jynx's wrist and wrapped herself about Jynx's waist instead.

With Ick directing her steps, Jynx walked through sandy corridors she'd not seen before. She updated Ick on the details of Morinl's health on the way, but in the back of her mind she wondered... did Ick mean a gift of some kind? Curiosity seized her—and she was a slave to her curiosity.

She only began to worry when they turned down a stone-walled corridor with only faint light—where there shouldn't be any. At least, Jynx certainly didn't see a source. She asked Ick about it.

Glow worms. If you look closely, just under the ceiling, you'll see them. Fuzzy creatures about three inches long, nibbling at the dusting of periman nectar there.

"Where does the light come from, though? The periman nectar?"

The nectar brings the glow worms. The glow worms crawl over each other to get to it. A glow worm glows when it's fuzzy back is stroked, which happens constantly as they crawl over each other.

Jynx stared in awe. By concentrating, she could just make out the small forms overhead, each hair tipped by a tiny bulb-shaped sac. Amazing! Then she began to think of how such worms might be able to help her work as a healer.

Turn right at the corner.

More glow worms lit this corridor. Jynx's shadow pooled at her feet as she pushed open the door a few feet down the hall.

Brighter, multi-colored light danced in the reflected brightness of the corridor's glow worms. Jynx blinked to adjust her eyes. The floor here was heaped with glittering gems in shades of red, blue, green, gold, white, black... every color she could think of. She heard her own indrawn breath at the dazzling display.

Tell no one of this room.

"The People are wealthy beyond kings!" Jynx began to comprehend the enormity of what she saw. Her view of the People began to shift. So many hidden things in the queens' precinct! "Where did all of this come from?"

This is the wealth of the People, in terms understood by all peoples. It is more than mere wealth, as well, but we have no need to speak of that now.

You have been my friend and my companion and are dear to my heart. Whatever comes, never forget that. Choose a single stone from this room as my token. If you ever have need, show it to one of the People and you will have whatever help they can give you. She unwound from Jynx and coiled on the floor near the door, watching her.

Choose? How, with thousands of stones? Dazed, Jynx walked among the haphazard piles, trying not to step on any of them—an impossible task. She touched a bloody ruby and withdrew her finger at once. Not that one. A golden tauz beckoned, until a pale green godtears caught the corner of her eye.

In her head she felt Ick's smug contentment. She was enjoying Jynx's reactions to the room and to individual stones. The love flowed outward from Ick, and Jynx turned it back on her.

Just when she thought her task impossible, a new gem caught her eye. Large, brilliantly faceted, it sat halfway up a pile of crystals as tall as Jynx was. Most importantly, it was the exact blue-green color of Snake's eyes, which she had studied at some length. She reached toward it, hesitated, then with a small sigh laid a finger against its largest facet. Comfort and peace. She'd found the right stone.

Without hesitation she picked it up and turned to Ick.

Approval and love filled her head—and a bit of amusement. *Do not forget, dear one. This is a token that will be recognized by anyone of the People, a pledge of help in whatever form you need it. For as long as you live.*

"How can they recognize the token if they weren't here to see it given to me?" Jynx's practical side had kicked in.

Ick's chuckle felt soft and warm. *Give me two days, and the story will spread of the tallgrass woman who saved my life and was gifted with a large, perfect seastone, the exact color of her lover's eyes, as a token of my gratitude. And the promise that I have made for aid to the woman bearing it.*

"This is a fabulous token, Ick. If I have helped you, you have also helped me, in ways I could never have guessed. Thank you." Jynx swallowed back sentimental tears. Ick's friendship far outweighed the value of the gem.

Overwhelmed, she slipped the gem into a pocket, wrapped Ick about her waist again, and left the room with one backward glance, as if to freeze the scene forever in her memory.

I have more to show you, Ick told Jynx, *and more to discuss, in confidence this time. You may not share even with Snake. Will you agree to that?*

How could she ever promise to keep anything from Snake? Jynx's curiosity overcame good sense. "Of course I agree. I will not speak a word to anyone without your permission. Not even Snake."

Then turn down this corridor, on the right.

Jynx did so, noticing at once that it descended more steeply than expected. It appeared to be a spiral path leading downward. Within a dozen paces she already dreaded trying to climb out of this hole. How deep did it go?

Ten minutes later, Ick directed her into a side tunnel that also spiraled downward. Interminably. Jynx's ankles started to ache.

Stop here.

Jynx stopped, but she saw nothing indicating a reason to. Just more stone walls and more sandy path.

Do you see that block that's slightly discolored on one edge? Above your head and to the left... yes, there. Press that stone firmly, right on the discoloration. Harder. It's an old and crotchety stone.

Jynx grunted with effort, leaning her body weight into the stone. Suddenly the block moved, receding under Jynx's palm so that she almost fell into the wall.

Inside that niche is a key. Please retrieve it.

"What else is in that hole? Scorpions? Mice?" Jynx wasn't sure which was worse.

Ick stretched upward and fluttered her tongue inside Jynx's ear. *No, silly. I'd have already eaten them.*

Jynx jumped at the tickling, then felt Ick's buzz of laughter in her head. Her face burning, she gingerly reached two fingers into the niche and found the key by feel.

We can leave the niche open for now. Come.

They spiraled down still farther, until Jynx began to be aware of just how much sand–and how much weight–lay above them.

Ick turned her into another corridor, and then another.

"You do know I'll never find my way back out without a guide, don't you?"

That's the whole idea. I'm about to show you the greatest marvel of the white sands, which is also our greatest secret. Such a treasure from the gods should be sacrosanct, protected from all but a few.

"Then why are you showing me?"

Ick wriggled as if she itched. *I've been told to, by one of our gods. No explanation, and not a prophecy, but perhaps the precursor to a prophecy. I'm uncomfortable doing this, but I won't disobey, either. That's why secrecy is so very important.*

"What secret could possibly warrant this kind of protection? If the gem room isn't this protected, I can't imagine what would require so many safeguards."

Ick was quiet for a long minute. Then she spoke again, her "voice" soft even in Rapport. *I'm going to show you the magic of the white sands.*

24. Back Door

Snake couldn't find Jynx anywhere. She had to be in the village somewhere, but he'd wandered through it three times now with no sign of her. He hated asking for help, but the third time through he started asking people if they'd seen her.

One older woman, gray and toothless, reported seeing her walking toward the queens' precinct, but that had been hours ago. If he understood her gummed words correctly.

He even checked the sampair, although she wouldn't have gone there—at least not by herself.

Ah! Maybe she was with Ick. He opened Rapport, reaching for the slither queen, but she was nowhere to be found. Odd, that. He guessed she and Jynx were together, perhaps in the queens' burrow. Maybe gossiping about the time they'd been apart over cups of fragrant iced cocomilk and plates of melons and dates.

With a sigh of frustration he turned back to his house. He'd given the Protection a day of rest. They needed time with friends and family to remember what they fought for, and to rebuild vigor after drilling hard all day every day. He'd hoped for some of that "family" time for him and Jynx, as well.

Feeling sorry for himself, he buckled on his sword harness. The blade itself was newly honed and oiled, but the leather grip was looking worn. He'd need a new one by the time he got home.

He looked out at rolling white dunes stretching as far as he could see and imagined it was snow instead of sand, cold as death instead of hot as Hestor's fires. Homesickness swept through him. How was his mother doing, without him there to help her? Was her husband home from his trading yet? He worried about his friend's heart, too—the broken heart Kayde denied. He hadn't bedded more than two women since returning from the tallgrass, and that was months ago. Come to think of it, what about Kahpur? She was responsible for Kayde's heart and didn't even seem to know it. Snake thought briefly about the Beast, but the gelding couldn't be in better hands than Kahpur's. He grinned to himself, thinking of the battles those two would have, then wondered how different his horse would be after so much time with such an expert horseman. The tallgrass was rural, and they had no "horsewomen," technically.

Snake's thoughts only sharpened his loneliness and he thrust them away impatiently. The best cure was to work it off. And he hadn't been through his sword forms for a long time, except the most basic as he taught and drilled the Protection.

He was overdue for a good workout on the more advanced forms, and with Resting Sun approaching, the air was cool enough to get some real work done. He just needed a place free of prying eyes. The full moon already floating above the dunes would provide sufficient light when the sun disappeared.

Slogging through the deeper sand outside the village felt good, a warmup before he even drew his sword. He guessed at a mile, then looked for a relatively flat space with decent footing. True, a warrior might have to fight the sand as well as the enemy—but not today.

Nothing suitable here. He changed his direction slightly and kept going.

Wallowing in loneliness, he wandered aimless for a long time. When he found the harder, shallower sand he sought, he removed obtruding rocks and hardy plants, just as the sun winked out below the horizon, leaving the moon in charge of the skies. Moonlight reflecting off the white sand provided more than enough light. His feet would know the patterns even if he was blindfolded.

On a whim, Snake removed his boots, bare feet curling into the warm sand. He'd forgotten how much he loved the feel of sand under his feet, squishing up between his toes. This wasn't the blistering sand of full daylight, but it was still warm under his feet this evening. For now. The longer he stayed, the chillier the sand would become. But his body—even his feet—would generate enough heat he probably wouldn't notice the cold. Especially when lost in his sword work.

Now if the venomous Canba beetles and sand snips would retire for the night, he'd be at peace. Just to be safe, he kept an eye out while concentrating on his sword. A hunting tanglecat could appear, but it wouldn't likely challenge the sword.

Snake settled into stance, controlled his breathing, and disappeared into the void where his sword awaited him. It was like settling into another world, where nothing existed but man and sword, sky and ground. When that world enveloped him completely, he began to move.

Slowly at first, body memory guiding his feet, his grip solid but loose from long habit, his weight centered exactly so. He concentrated on making each strike perfect, with foreblade or back blade, with point or pommel or hilt.

He moved smoothly on the shallow sand, toes gripping the surface as needed. The second time through this form, he adjusted better for bare feet in sand, and the third time he moved to deeper sand and began again.

He shifted from one form to the next seamlessly, without thought, as his body heated, never pausing between beginning and intermediate forms. Or intermediate and those advanced forms only useful to the most skilled swordsmen in the Kingdom of the Snows.

When he finished the warmup he paused, breathing hard. Now it was time for the real work. He began again, concentrating fiercely, flying through every move as fast as he could. No errors allowed, regardless of speed, unless he wanted to start over at the same speed. Relax to move for more speed, tight on impact for more strength. His arms and sword quivered as the tip stopped abruptly at his imaginary opponent's throat. Check, check, parry, slice, thrust. Twist on impact. He spun and stepped and rolled, advanced and retreated, "killed" the man before him and the one behind him in the space of two seconds. He fought from his feet, from his knees, from his back, from his belly, all under the red glare of Katinga's watchful Eye.

He took a break, swallowed five huge gulps from his waterskin, poured a little more on his head, and started again. Every move at top speed, blending from one form into the next, all with his eyes closed.

Lost. Another world, this one inside him. Nothing existed but man, sword, and sand.

By the time he had completed the work to his own satisfaction, Snake could see the quivering of his sword tip, caused by the exhausted trembling of arms and legs.

He collapsed on the sand, poured a little more water over his head, and drank what was left. He lay back on the chilled sand, aware of how cold the night air had become. He could close his eyes for just a moment...

...and when he opened them, the moon no longer rode the sky. The pale sand under icy starlight seemed no longer friendly. He'd slept much longer than intended, but there was no sign of impending dawn.

He stood up, his body protesting the insufficient recovery. His sword lay on the sand next to where he'd slept. He checked it over briefly and reached over his shoulder to sheathe it. Hooking the empty waterskin to his belt, he started walking. He'd walked less than an hour to get here, so he should reach the village before Rising Sun.

Sometime in the night, the wind rose. Not a storm by any means, but enough to shift sand between dunes, eat away small ones, and create new ones.

Two hours later, Snake climbed one of the taller dunes, chagrined to find how much his energy reserves had been depleted. From the top he turned in a slow circle, looking for signs of his tracks, or smoke from village fires, or anything that would point him back toward the village. "By Landir's tits!" he swore aloud. "Where's the village? I didn't walk that far! How could I get turned around?"

All he could do was wait for dawn and see if he could use the sun's position to get home. Back to the village, *not* home. Disgusted with himself, he sat down to wait, wishing he hadn't drunk the rest of his water after all.

So much for being born and raised in the sands.

The sun didn't come up quite where he expected it to, but it was close. He took his direction from where it rose and started back to the village. How embarrassing, to be lost so near his house! Of course, he could claim he'd trained all night, rather than admit being lost. He'd worked until the sun rose, right?

Better not to mention it at all. Just keep his mouth shut and explain nothing. Let the Protection make whatever assumptions they liked.

The night winds had rearranged too many sand dunes. He didn't recognize any of the unusual configurations or features he'd memorized on the way out. Not even when he turned around to view them from the opposite direction. He certainly didn't remember this broad curve along the belly of a ridge. He ground his teeth in frustration.

A few steps later he stopped to watch an enormous Canba beetle, recognizable by its six-inch length and the pattern of gold dots on its black carapace, arranged like a death's head. A good warning of its potent venom. He remained still as it scurried across the face of a dune. The things moved amazingly fast. At this distance, could he have his sword in his hand in time if it came for him? He didn't want to find out.

The beetle dug into the side of the dune and disappeared in seconds.

Snake went on, keeping a closer eye on his surroundings. And that was how he came to see something that shouldn't have been there.

~~~

The anomaly was faint, but there could be no mistake. Straight lines and right angles didn't really exist in nature–not on the smooth sides of sand dunes, at least. And this indentation was definitely rectangular, like a door.

Curious, Snake climbed the short, low ridge to the indentation. Even at close range it looked like a door. Way out in the middle of nowhere. What on earth...?

Without giving it much thought, he laid his hand in the center of the indentation and pushed it in.

A loud snap and sudden pain sent him reeling back with a howl. His fingers tingled, but a quick inspection revealed no damage.

Why would someone put a door in the middle of nowhere and booby-trap it?

A slow, gingerly examination revealed a thin cord had been stretched tight and his touch had released it to snap against his hand. It seemed designed to discourage, not prevent, exploration. Probably meant for wildlife, he decided.

Working carefully, almost as curious as Jynx would have been, he scraped away sand with his hands until a full-size wooden door, painted white, was revealed. Or was it a wall? Where was the latch?

He found it finally near the bottom of the door, to his surprise. It opened soundlessly onto a tunnel in the sand, one he couldn't stand up in but could navigate on hands and knees.

The wise choice would be to turn away. "Jynx, you're a bad influence," he muttered under his breath as he entered. He closed the door behind him; his mother had drilled that into him even into adulthood.

The tunnel turned three times before the ceiling receded. This corridor he could stand up in, even at an inch over six feet tall, without his sword hilt digging into walls or ceiling. He dusted the last grains of sand from his hands and strode forward more confidently. This had to be a construction of the People. No one else would be in the white sands. The only other place he'd seen corridors below the surface was in the queens' precinct. This corridor had to be part of that precinct, but why would it reach so far out into the dunes?

An emergency escape route for the queens, similar to what he and Jynx had traversed awhile back? It had to be. That meant that the corridor would eventually take him back to the village. It would be a bit awkward if he were caught, but not fatal.

He began to rest occasionally, but without water, he daren't rest long. His body was dehydrated and he had a war to fight soon. With no air circulating, the tunnels were hot and uncomfortable. Maybe he should worry more about survival and less about whom he might meet.

When he heard a voice in the distance, he froze mid-step, listening as hard as he could over the hammering of his own heart.

Only one voice? Someone talking to himself? He strained to hear a second voice, without success. The one he heard seemed to be coming his way. Maybe. He had no idea how far, though. Should he hope for someone to find him? Or hope no one did?

Whoever it was—even enemies—they were his best chance to survive this maze. He opened his mouth to shout. And stopped.

Before alerting a potential enemy, he reached out through Rapport.

Ick. Startled, maybe even angry.

Stay where you are and stay open, she commanded. *We're coming to you.*

"We." Who was with her? Shyriel? Jynx? One of the chief priests?

Snake sat down where he was and buried his face in his hands. He was so tired of being around slithers again. His throat felt like sand. He sucked on his tongue, hoping for moisture. Steeling himself, he reached out to Ick. "You wouldn't happen to have water, would you?"

Some of us are wise enough to carry water when we sneak into someone's home through the back door. Then silence.

He leaned his head back against the walls, elbows propped on knees, wondering if he was exhausted enough to sleep. That's when he smelled himself–the ripe aroma of a body gone stale after hours of strenuous activity. He needed a bath as much as he needed a drink of water.

Just as he realized he could scrub down with handfuls of sand, Jynx appeared at the far end of the corridor, Ick wrapped around her waist. Too late. She would smell him like this, and there was no way to prevent it. He sighed.

25. White Magic

Ick insisted on a leisurely lunch and, especially for Snake, plenty of water. Servers had brought three waterskins with lunch, but it didn't seem like enough. Snake resigned himself to careful rationing.

Trying not to think about why Ick and Jynx were so far underground, Snake bit into a succulent bite of Anigal goat, imported from the southern coast over two hundred miles away. This one had been cooked in coconut oil after soaking in rich cream. Wonderful! And exorbitantly expensive, he knew. The generous slice was the centerpiece of an artful wreath of sections of oranges interspersed with red pomegranate seeds.

"Uh, Snake?" Jynx whispered, "I've never eaten these red seeds before. Do I just eat the red part? Or do I eat the little white seed inside it, too?"

"Either way is acceptable, but it's easier just to eat the whole thing, fruit and seed. Sometimes the fruit is pulped for the juice, which is drunk alone or with added spices. They make pomegranate wine with the seeds, too, and it's very good."

He saw Jynx mouthing the word "pomegranate," as if memorizing it. Of course. She would never have encountered such a thing in the tallgrass.

The meal finished with a dollop of toasted meringue, a

perfect ending to an amazing meal.

Next time, Ick assured them, *I'll order pickled crocodile tongue. I think you would find it interesting and unique.*

Snake laughed aloud at the look on Jynx's face.

"She's teasing, right?" Jynx asked out of the corner of her mouth.

"Oh, no. It's quite a delicacy here. Rare, expensive, and delicious."

She shuddered visibly.

Thirst and hunger assuaged, Snake looked around at the heavy white sand walls shored up with sturdy timbers. For the first time, he realized that all the tunnels he'd followed and the room he sat in now had been dug and shaped by people–a gargantuan enterprise! How did they keep the maze of tunnels from collapsing?

Unable to resist, he asked Ick.

The queens' precinct is sacred, Kyr. A gift of the gods. Of course it would be safe for us.

He understood her tone to convey smugness and sighed. "You're saying all of this was done with magic?"

This time her laughter was distinct. *You have not noticed the stone? The solid white stone from which these sands have been scoured over time? They provide the base for the tunnels. Men spent decades building the tunnels and the rooms around them. They are not here because of the queens' precinct. The precinct is here because of the stones that underlay the area.*

Totally nonplused, Snake sat still, thinking back. Of course he'd seen the stone holding everything up. He just hadn't paid any attention. His head tilted ruefully. "I guess I wasn't that observant."

Lips thinned, Jynx stepped in. "You were exhausted and dehydrated, Snake, looking for a quick path back to the village. You had other concerns than what the walls were made of."

"Why are you here?" he asked Ick. "What brings you two into the depths of the white sands?"

Jynx turned to Ick, and he watched them "talk" without him.

Come, Ick told him. *I have something to show both of you.*

The corners of Jynx's eyes relaxed as Ick encircled her waist.

Snake gave her a hand up to her feet, trying not to get too close to Ick. Still, he took Jynx's hand as they left the room. Only a few minutes later they entered another room, this one with a large pool of water in the center.

Jynx's light laughter twinkled. "Ick says you're to bathe here, because you stink. Then you can join us, through that door." She pointed to an aged wooden door in the back wall.

Snake's face felt hotter than the sands they'd traveled to get here. He didn't move as Jynx walked through the door and closed it firmly behind her.

Embarrassed or not, he couldn't pass up this opportunity. The water was cool but not cold, and he scrubbed himself with the sand on the bottom. When he finally felt reasonably clean, except for needing to shave, he washed out his clothes without soap. With no alternative, he wrung the water from them as best he could and put them on again. He combed his hair with his fingers, took a deep breath and released it slowly, then walked through the wooden door.

What he found startled him, but not enough to let his reaction show.

Jynx sat on pure white sand, facing a row of colorful sands in piles of blue, red, gray, green, gold, black, copper, brown, and silver.

Slowly, wonder filling him, Snake sat next to her. He had no idea so many colors of sand even existed!

Ick coiled between them and the sandpiles.

Snake felt her in his head, a quiet buzz. He stilled himself to listen, to interpret the emotions that were her language.

What you see and hear may never be spoken of, to anyone, for any reason, upon pain of death, Ick told them.

With her flat reptile eyes, the statement felt ominous and

true. Snake shivered, knowing he would never reveal any of this to anyone. Not for fear; he had faced death many times. But because it was important and necessary. Jynx's light squeeze of his hand gave the same assurance.

Kyr. Jynx already knows what we do here. I believe you are here because the gods would include you, as well. She paused. *We are here to teach both of you the magic of the white sand.*

Flickering her tongue in laughter, Ick led them over to the piles of colored sand. Snake sat next to Jynx, facing the queen as if in a children's classroom. In a way, they were.

I'll start at the beginning, Ick said. *Some of this you may already know, some you won't, but first, a review of the magic of the various sand colors.*

When a new slither queen is born, pristine white sand is her first meal. It's what produces the silvered colors of a queen. It is the only time in her life she will eat of the white sands. This is a closely held secret that no other human knows, except the human queen and the chief priest of the Prophecy.

Blue sand is very different, being both brighter in color and larger-grained. Blue sand turns to water in the mouth— or when added to any moisture. Just give it a few seconds to convert. The Pomlo people live in the blue sand. They're friendly and non-violent, much like the People.

Black sand conceals. As little as a handful in the pocket will wrap an adult human in shadows. He'll be completely invisible if he avoids the sunlight. A Wohim can lie flat on the sand and remain still to avoid being seen, even if he wears red or yellow. Pay heed to this! They are our enemies.

Snake had already begun planning a way to acquire black sand to hide his warriors.

Red sand turns to blood when it gets wet. The Sett tribe's religion and rituals are built around this property. You don't want to know the details of their rituals, but know that red sand, wetted and rubbed on the skin, provides temporary invulnerability.

"Eeuuw!" Jynx scrunched her nose up in disgust.

Another useful property, Snake noted. He could smear some of his warriors with the bloody sand, making them appear vulnerable and enticing an attack by the Wohim that would result in Wohim deaths.

He'd worry later about the logistics of obtaining red sand.

Copper sand can be used to build temporary structures by pressing the grains together. In our village, we use it for low walls and boundary markers—and sometimes vessels to carry water. It also crumbles easily back to individual grains.

Gold sand... Ick hesitated.

Jynx finished it for her. "...is real gold that can be melted, formed into coins, and spent."

Yes. Ick moved on. *Green sand is for growth and healing. I don't know how it works, but Jonyl sometimes uses it. The other healers rarely do.*

Another bonus for Snake—a way to keep more warriors alive and healthy, to keep them fighting. He'd ask Jynx to get details from Jonyl later.

Brown sand grows things—primarily plants, I believe, but I'm unsure of its limitations. We have so few plants in our area that we don't use it much. Still, some think it might grow nonliving things, too, if anyone had time to experiment with it.

Snake made a mental note to arrange for experiments with brown sand. Perhaps it could "grow" the number of unbroken arrows, or mend broken shafts or something.

"I haven't heard you mention gray sand," said Jynx. "It clings to whatever it touches, and if you try to brush it off, it sticks to your hands. It's almost impossible to get rid of it."

Yes. It's not a sand I'd want to cross, Ick told them. *Purple sand is worse, though, and must be avoided at all costs, even purple sand that is simply blue and red sands mixed. It's acid and will eat through boards or cloth or flesh.*

For one flash instant, Snake thought of collecting the purple sand to use as a weapon, but not even he could bear the thought of what the acid would do to human flesh. "What triggers the sand to become acid?"

I don't know, Kyr. Nor do I have any desire to find out.

Silver sand has been used to make rudimentary mirrors, but I think that's due to physical properties, rather than magical ones. We can melt it to form a backing for glass, but it's not worth the trouble and expense to import the glass itself. It's easier just to buy mirrors.

White sand can do any of these things. The secret of how to trigger the property you want is the most closely guarded secret in the white sands.

"*Any* of them?" Snake gave her his full attention, his hands clammy with excitement. This would make the People's warriors invincible!

And Ick had said the white sand had no military application. He could hardly wait.

"How do we get the white sand to behave like a different color?" Jynx asked.

Do you remember the magic of the sands we discussed earlier?

She did.

And do you remember how to trigger the magic of each color of sand?

They looked at each other.

"Yes," said Jynx, "but some don't have a trigger. You just touch them."

Then that's what makes the magic happen. That's the trigger. The trigger you use for each sand, applied to the white sand, causes the white sand to manifest the same magic.

Snake thought about that for a moment. "That sounds almost too easy."

Ick's buzz in his head sounded like slither laughter.

Jynx, how does blue sand magic manifest?

"It gets wet."

More specifically, you put it in your mouth for a few seconds to turn it to water. Please put a handful of white sand in your mouth for a few seconds.

"Uh..." Her face showed the distaste of putting something in her mouth that could contain bugs, or dirt, or whatever.

Do you trust me?

"Of course." Taking a deep breath, Jynx scooped up a small handful of white sand from a nearby pile and put it in her mouth. A few seconds later her eyes widened and she swallowed. "Amazing! How..."

It's magic, Jynx. That's all we know.

"But... what about red sand?" asked Snake. "Isn't it also triggered by moisture? How does the white sand know the difference?"

Don't put it in your mouth. That turns it to water, like blue sand does. Pour a little water on it instead.

He did as she asked, watching the white sand turn to a thick, red liquid. He caught the faint scent of blood, even from so small an amount. He glanced up at Ick, startled.

Yes, it's really blood, with all the properties of any other blood.

Jynx, please form a small bowl by pressing white grains of sand together.

She did so, adding a fluted edge to the rim. "I see the grains remain white," she commented, "although the red sand magic changed color."

Yes. The color red is one of the properties of blood, so it can't be real blood if it's not red. That's why the color changed.

Without being told, Snake added some white sand to the small bowl. He started a fire in the cooking depression, then placed the white "copper" bowl over it. They watched in fascination as it melted into real gold.

"If that were assayed," said Snake, "it would test as pure, wouldn't it?"

Yes.

No wonder the People never seemed poor. They had only to melt white sand into gold, as if it were gold sand. Immeasurable wealth! And they seemed impervious to its lure.

Black sand is different, Ick told them. *Its magic is always there, without being triggered. For white sand to take on the properties of black sand, you can't simply put a handful into your pocket to be shadowed. Nor can you hide underneath the white sand and expect it to conceal you as black sand would. Any sand can be burrowed into for hiding; it's the shadows that you want the white sand to produce. To trigger the black sand's magic in our white sand, you'll need to seed the magic.*

Enfold a handful of white sand in black cloth, put it in your pocket, and it will cover you in shadows. As long as you're not in direct sunlight, your presence will be obscured.

"Obscured? Not completely hidden?" asked Snake.

It works the same as a handful of black sand does.

"So, to lie flat on—or under—white sand would hide me the same as black sand?"

To produce more shadows, enough to conceal your entire body, requires more sand. You may need to experiment since we've never considered it worth the effort—though now I wish we had. Perhaps a packet of white sand carried on your back? Or a black cloak covering any pack of white sand? I'm sure you'll find some condition that works.

"And gray sand?" asked Jynx. "It's triggered by touch."

We've never experimented with gray sand, given its clingy unpleasantness. Like silver sand, its properties may be physical, rather than magical.

Snake, of course, wished for an easy way to take gray sand on their raid. It could create havoc among the Wohim if flung into their faces or onto their weapons. Or maybe he could lure them to a wide, deep pool of the stuff. What a distraction! They'd be so busy fighting the sand, they would be easy prey. As long as his own men avoided it.

"What about green sand?" asked Jynx. "How is it triggered? How do we use white sand in its place?"

You'll need to ask Jonyl. But you may not tell her of the white sand's magic. Tell no one! Ick's emrel eyes stared at Jynx, then at Snake. *Or I will kill you myself, for treason.*

Jynx paled and Snake felt a wave of protectiveness toward her. "We owe you no fealty, Ick. We are not of the People. We can't commit treason, technically."

But I will kill you, nevertheless. Ick drew herself up, high above the seated Snake, and loomed over him.

He set his jaw, avoiding her eyes by staring into her hissing mouth. It brought back disturbing memories that he couldn't seem to push away.

"Ick, you know we would never deliberately harm you or the People," said Jynx. "Trust us to be your dearest friends. The white sand's secrets must be kept; we both know that. Threats are unnecessary. And unfriendly."

The queen subsided. *My apologies to both of you. If I did not trust you, you would not be here now. There's just so much at stake.*

To deflect Ick's worry more than anything, Snake began to share his ideas for using the white sand's magic. He found that both the slither and the woman expanded on his ideas, and Jynx's help was the most practical of all, shaping the ideas into workable plans.

He resolved to leave her in the village; he wouldn't risk her with the warriors, nor Ick–although Ick could be a valuable symbol to send them into war. And Shyriel. She'd have to be there, too. He sighed.

26. Disruption

Snake slept far too many hours. It felt self-indulgent, especially after such a long, luxurious swim in the oasis behind his house. But his energy had returned, bringing with it a shamefully good mood. He even laughed aloud as he set off to find Jynx.

The good mood faded when he couldn't find her. She must be with Jonyl, learning what she could, as usual.

He began to ask after Jonyl instead of Jynx. Two other healers offered to help him with whatever ailed him, but they hadn't seen Jonyl today. Or Jynx.

Why did he have to spend half his time looking for her? Couldn't she just stay in one place and wait for him? The way his mother stayed home to be available to her husband, instead of charging off hither and yon without telling him.

Jynx's imagined voice was not polite. If she'd heard that, she'd have remained calm and serene and said something to make him feel two inches tall. She had more important things to do than wait around for him; did he want a courtesan or a real woman, with a life of her own to live? He winced.

Maybe his mother could learn something from Jynx. Snake admitted to himself that Jynx's sense of adventure, purpose, and fun were a large part of his attraction to her. He wouldn't give up that part of her for anything. Certainly he didn't want a woman with nothing better to do than sit and wait.

He sighed and stopped complaining, even in his own head. She would come to him when she had something to tell him.

He touched Ick through Rapport to update her.

Not now, Snake. I'm in the middle of something. Her tone was impatient and unexpectedly sharp.

Feeling rebuffed, he dropped out of Rapport.

The warriors had had two days off instead of one, he mused, and should be well rested for hard training today. He turned his steps to find Beyir.

Finding Beyir was much easier than finding Jynx. He sent the Chief Priest to gather the warriors and run them through the dunes, stopping every half hour to train. Beyir didn't need him for these drills. If they didn't know how to do the exercises without him by now, his presence wouldn't help.

Nothing like heading up the defense and having nothing to do, he thought. Maybe he'd wait an hour or two, then join the warriors after all. They needed some work on coordinated fighting. Or maybe he could strategize with Beyir, although they'd just about exhausted that topic.

What he really needed...

Kyr! Come! Ick's imperative tone made him jump.

"Where are you?"

In the Pan.

He ran.

The Pan was an area just north of the village, circumferenced by dunes. Snake had considered using its dry, cracked floor of ancient mud for training—the flat-as-a-griddle surface would be ideal for beginning exercises—but the Pan was too close to the village. The men didn't need an audience as they trained, especially when learning new moves. Now he was glad of its proximity.

But what was Ick doing there? And what would create that urgent tone?

Snake dodged around an older couple arguing publicly. He ran straight toward the Pan, jumping a low wall of copper sand, and then another. Piled white sand snatched at his feet, slowing his progress. His heart pounded in his ears, his breath keeping time with his feet.

As he charged up the smaller dunes, buzzing filled his head—and this time it wasn't Ick.

Ah, Kyr! You're here after all!

Slyn. What was he up to now?

Snake topped the dune and looked down into the Pan, already scanning for Slyn and Ick.

Ick's mottled colors could blend into white dunes fairly well. Slyn's black couldn't. When Snake saw him, he found Ick, too, facing a slither at least three feet longer than she, and with a fierce, powerful presence.

He's only half sane, Snake reminded himself. Loose sanity and tightly-wound ambition were not a good combination. Snake plummeted down the dune, barely keeping his feet.

He'd watched these two fight before, when they'd caught up with the slither thieves. Ick had prevailed.

But that time, Slyn had been distracted by Snake's sudden appearance—the return of his first handler. The first that counted, anyway, after he'd gone through two other acolytes. The black slither had no distractions this time.

And being a queen didn't give Ick any advantage of size, strength, or magic. Only being chosen by the gods, if one believed in them.

Slyn had always thought the gods had chosen poorly. Even as a youngen, he proclaimed himself the equal of any queen. It was why he'd sought out Tchenya in her burrow, intending a mating.

No, that couldn't be. The size disparity was too great. What *had* he intended? A fight? Like the ones he'd been picking with increasingly large slithers? The size disparity was too great for that, too. Slyn might be aberrant, but he wasn't stupid.

Snake reached the two slithers and stepped between them.

Ick's temper didn't worry him; she was no danger to him.

Slyn was another matter. He'd been born aberrant and powerful both. Even when Slyn had been part of his acolyte nest, Snake could seldom predict what he would do. The adult creature was smarter, more experienced, and just as much an enigma. A confrontation would not be a good idea.

He turned to the slither queen, remembering Slyn's assignment. "Ick, do you have an immediate need for Slyn? I need to get his report." He asked openly, so both could hear him.

Ick's wry tone indicated she'd forgotten, too. *You may have him for as long as you need him. Report to me later with details.*

"As you wish." Snake smiled at Slyn. "Welcome back, Slyn. Would you join me for refreshment while you report?"

Perhaps I should report here, directly to Erilya. I'm wearied from my long journey.

"The queen has other duties awaiting her. I'd be pleased to carry you on my shoulders. We should have refreshments waiting at my house when we arrive." Surely Ick was already using Rapport to arrange for food and drink.

I am not your servant. Just get him away from me, Ick grumbled privately. *Go.*

He tried not to smile, knowing refreshments would be waiting for them.

He took his time carrying Slyn home. The black slither grew heavier with every step, and it was almost a mile back to the house. He felt Slyn's pride as they entered the village. Apparently the slither assumed a certain status from his "friendship" with the "son of prophecy" for all to see.

Some people smiled at the sight, while others didn't notice. One or two even looked away. That said a lot about Slyn's reputation here, Snake thought. Surely it wasn't his!

A young girl was just leaving Snake's house as they arrived. She smiled at Snake, her eyes as flirty as the subtle movement of her shoulders. A scrawny little thing, far too young to be arching her back at men she didn't know. He gave her a disinterested half smile, then widened it to a warm grin as Jynx appeared in the doorway.

One hand was extended as far in front of her as possible, holding a small cage woven of reeds. Her face screwed up in disgust as she looked at it. "They made me carry Slyn's refreshments," she said.

Snake had to laugh. "What's in it?"

"I told them I didn't want to know and covered my ears when they tried to tell me anyway. I won't stay long enough to watch him dine."

Canba beetles! Slyn clearly thought the creatures were a special delicacy. *And still alive*!

Jynx shuddered. Slyn had spoken to both of them. Her eyes widened and she looked from Snake to Slyn and back.

Snake followed her into the house. "Have you ever watched a slither hunt? It's really interesting. Traditionally, courtesy requires that you open the cage, and when the prey emerges, the slither hunts them."

"So I was told. That's why I won't be staying. I was also told these creatures are deadly!"

Snake laughed as he kissed her cheek–carefully avoiding the wooden cage. "Slyn will protect you by eating them."

Something in her eyes changed briefly, but he couldn't put his finger on what it was. He let it go; she'd tell him later, if it mattered. Most likely, she just didn't like Slyn.

"Here," she said, "you take these. I'm on my way." She glanced at Slyn from the corner of her eye, a light tension radiating from her body.

She *really* didn't want to watch Slyn hunt and eat! Snake held his grin inside as she walked wide around them, handing him the crate as Slyn crawled from his shoulders to the floor. She left without her usual kiss.

Snake set the small crate on the floor and opened it. Three large Canba beetles skittered out, each at least five inches long. The black carapace bore a golden death mask, and each leg bore spikes, shorter versions of the venomous tails. Their heads were tiny compared to their bodies.

They scattered in different directions and Slyn launched himself after them.

Despite his words to Jynx, Snake had no interest in watching him hunt. He was focused on the refreshments of cocomilk, coconut flesh cut into stars, pastries coated with cinnamon and honey, and crisp, cool green melon. These must have come from the queens' own stores. And when he saw delicate slices of redfish and bluegill, he knew it for sure.

By the time he'd eaten the redfish and three coconut stars, Slyn had gulped down the last of the Canba beetles, carefully squeezing it in his coils until it popped, to get the ultimate flavor from its juices.

At least, that was the explanation given to Snake.

"Report while I eat, Slyn."

The slither took a moment to sip from a saucer of cocomilk left on the floor for him, then coiled up across from Snake. The first thought he shared with Snake caught him by surprise: *Have you discovered the magic of the white sands yet?*

Snake took a moment to select one of the cinnamon pastries and take a bite to hide his reaction. He chewed slowly, thinking hard. "I was hoping you could tell me about it," he said after swallowing. "Especially how we can use it against the Wohim."

Slyn's hiss revealed his frustration. *Why would our magic be a secret, when all other colors of sand are easily understood?*

"That's not a question I know the answer to. Tell me about your mission. I want a full report."

Slyn nipped one of the bluegill slices, working it into his mouth by alternating top and bottom rows of teeth. *The village isn't where you told me it was. No tents, but a lot of disturbed sand. I saw where the tents had been, found a few pieces of debris—a pot, or a bit of cloth, or whatever—so it was the right place. The only thing still there was a wooden shed nearby. It smelled and tasted of slither blood.*

Slyn paused for a sip of cocomilk.

Most of their trail had been covered by the wind, but I traced it far enough to determine where the village is now. They placed it in a canyon on the west side of the black sand, near the mountains, and surrounded it with man-made black dunes.

"Surrounded it? Why? What are they up to?" If they wanted black dunes around them, why stop in a canyon in the first place?

They're trying to hide from us. Slyn's tone was impatient, as if he explained the obvious.

"If that's true, they must know we're planning an attack. And that means they've been spying on us."

Or perhaps we have a traitor in our midst, someone who warned them.

Snake fingered a pastry without picking it up. That thought disturbed him; it was hard to imagine any of the People betraying the village.

"Who?" he asked aloud. "Who would be willing to do something like that?"

Slyn picked up another slice of Snake's bluegill and swallowed it whole. *Someone not of the People would be the logical suspect.*

Jynx. She was the only one in the village not of the People. "No. Jynx wouldn't do that." He'd have laughed, if Slyn hadn't been so serious about it. "She would have no reason, and no opportunity anyway."

She's an outsider. She may not be who you think she is.

"You're seeing what isn't there. It's not Jynx."

You're too close to her to see what I see.

"Enough! Before you make me angry." Snake's jaw clenched. The slither couldn't be that stupid. Not this one! What was he up to?

How did Slyn think this accusation would help him in the goal of replacing the slither queen? That was the real question. Did he see Jynx as a threat to his ambition? How? Why?

He turned the conversation back to the Wohim, but his mind was only partly on the topic as he picked Slyn's brain for details of his reconnaissance.

~~~

Jynx couldn't stop her hands from shaking. Fear slid up her spine in tiny tingles. Her mind wasn't on her footsteps, let alone her destination, but she still hurried through the white sand. Truthfully, she didn't care where she was going. As long as it was away.

But where would she be safe? Would anywhere in the Rainbow Sands be safe for her?

She had to go home. Now. She had to get out of here! Even if it had to be without Snake. Even alone. Her breath came in short, sharp gasps until she began to feel light-headed.

Still she refused to slow, as close to panic as she'd ever been in her life.

The memory of a voice in her head didn't relent. She recognized it though she didn't know whose it was or where she'd heard it before. Then memory came flooding back—a memory of darkness and whispers and exploding pain.

Memory of the night she fell.

She'd accepted that she would never remember the details of the fall, and so had everyone else. Why now? And why so... jumbled? More feelings than memories, more impressions than specifics.

She remembered walking toward Snake's back door, the one facing the spring. She remembered... maybe... feeling someone in the dark house. She didn't remember who, or anything about him, but someone had been there. Her certainty firmed.

She had taken a step down in the black night, and when she opened her eyes, she'd been on Snake's cushions with Jonyl by her side. She'd lost days.

No, there was another scrap of memory. Something

between stepping and waking up. It was nebulous, unfocused; she couldn't quite...

The horrible pain had been in her head, as if a spike had been driven into it. She'd felt herself start to fall...

Laughter. Someone had laughed as she fell. Whoever had been in the house. But she couldn't put a sound to the laughter, only the knowledge of its existence.

Another scrap. Redness. Lights, perhaps. Like rubies in the darkness. She didn't know what that meant.

She gasped, found herself in her own house, grabbing her possessions and cramming them into her satchel. Water. She'd need to take water. Plenty of it.

She'd have to navigate by Katinga's Eye, as Snake had done.

Food. Was there anything in the house? Her panic didn't abate. If anything, it increased.

She didn't really need food. There would be villages on the way where she could beg or steal. That would get her out of here faster.

She grabbed a full waterbag, slung her satchel across her chest, peeked out the door, and darted out into the sand. She knew north from here. Without Ick weighing her down, she would make good time—especially if the Slipaway Trail appeared, to give her a ride.

Heart pounding, she ducked behind a white dune and started north. She couldn't get home fast enough to suit her. The laughter in her head followed her away from the village.

~~~

Slyn chuckled.

Snake frowned. "What's so funny?" That was the second time Slyn had laughed for no reason. In fact, his entire behavior was a bit "off" today, starting with his implied threat to Ick. He didn't seem to be serious about it now, but Ick had certainly taken it seriously or she wouldn't have summoned him.

Just remembering how much Erilya fears me. She called you, rather than taking me on herself. And I hadn't even threatened her.

"You're lucky she hasn't ordered your execution. What were you thinking? Even an implied threat is stupid!"

She's too weak to be a good queen, Kyr. A strong queen would have slapped me down instead of calling for help.

"It didn't occur to you that queens don't do their own fighting? Or that she simply called me to come get your report? You have an inflated opinion of yourself, Slyn. You always have."

He felt Slyn's anger, felt him throttle it. Some.

Do you believe she's more intelligent than I? Stronger? Braver?

"It doesn't matter what I think. She's gods-chosen, for the gods' reasons. I believe they make queens instead of kings for a reason. I also think this foolishness needs to stop. You can't become a slither queen. You can't rule here. The People would never accept you unless you're gods-chosen, which can never happen. We need unity right now, not division among our strongest slithers. So accept your place and help the People. You can't survive if the People don't."

Snake's irritation verged on anger. Why did Slyn have to complicate things unnecessarily?

Surely he didn't expect to depose—or kill—Ick and take her place. He had to know better than that.

Then the back of his neck chilled. Whatever had possessed him? He'd said "our slithers!" The distaste in the back of his throat was real.

"Back to the subject. Did you look for the things I sent you to observe?"

I looked at everything.

"What about their warrior strength? How are they organized? How many warriors do they have?"

Their warriors look like any other humans. I could not tell which are warriors and which are not. Nor could I discern a specific leader. They appear not to be organized in any particular fashion that I could see. I did not have an opportunity to watch them train. If they train at all.

Snake cursed under his breath. This was as futile a reconnaissance as he'd ever encountered. "How many men are in the village?"

Better to ask how many humans. The women could fight alongside their men in an attack such as we plan.

How lazy could this slither be? He hadn't even bothered to count the men separately. "How many adult humans, then?" And Snake had no intention of sharing his plan with Slyn.

Over a hundred. Close to a hundred and fifty.

Snake ground his teeth. He'd requested a specific count. "Did you enter the village as I asked?"

Oh, yes. I saw some men sharpening weapons near the center of the village. They sang songs as they worked, as if performing a ritual.

The kind of rituals warriors might perform before battle.

Nothing like Wolf Guard rituals, of course. No Tears of Heroes to be dipped in their own blood and eaten, to produce ferocious berserkers on the field of battle.

Snake sighed. A few Wolf Guard would be nice to have right now. Why hadn't he at least invited Kayde on this adventure? One good warrior he could rely on. He felt the weight of responsibility and inevitability settle onto his shoulders like an anvil.

27. Flight

Jynx's blind panic carried her through the sands for hours. She told herself it wasn't panic. She just wanted to put as many miles behind her as she could before the sun came up and turned the sands into a skillet. True, the dunes weren't flat enough for a skillet, but maybe a big pot over the fire. Or...

She shoved these thoughts out of her head. Focus. Focus on getting home, no matter what. A pair of blue-green eyes flashed through memory, puncturing her equilibrium. She pushed that away, too. No distractions. No temptations.

She ran. When her breath snatched, she fought the temptation to stop–and ran. She wasn't a runner, but she ran.

She couldn't find Katinga's Eye. And the moon wasn't up yet.

Could anything else go wrong?

She glanced behind her, almost afraid to look. Something was back there. Following her. If it was a tanglecat, she was as good as dead already. Worse, she was dinner!

Her rational mind disagreed, but she ignored it. Her breaths came in gasping pants now, and she felt a vague trembling throughout her body.

And then she stopped and threw up. Running often did that to her.

She made it perhaps another quarter mile before she

vomited again.

She couldn't keep throwing up! She'd soon be dehydrated, at the mercy of sun and wind.

As if she wasn't already.

Jynx forced herself to take a break, trying to ignore the pressure in her mind to keep moving, no matter what. She tried to limit how much water she drank. Two swallows only.

So why was she pouring the entire contents of her waterbag over her face?

Jynx fought a sudden urge to weep. She never cried! Not for herself, at least, although sometimes in sympathy for others who suffered. Out here, in the middle of the Rainbow Sands, she couldn't spare the moisture for tears. She was still a long way from the blue sand and its magic.

She hugged herself with trembling arms as tears rolled down her cheeks.

And in her head, laughter. Again. She almost recognized the raspy voice.

~~~

"Has anyone seen Jynx today?" Snake licked the last of the creamy sugar tart off his fingers. "I seem to have lost her, or maybe I turn right when she turns left. I've seen neither hide nor hair of her since yesterday afternoon." And she usually sleeps with me, he didn't add, being considerate of the People's customs.

"I haven't," said Shyriel. "But then, I prefer not to mingle with foreigners." She tucked her legs closer to her body, leaning on one hand to reach for her own sugar tart from the tray. This one was filled with berries and no cream.

"Nor I," said Beyir from his place in the circle. Three others shook their heads as well.

Jonyl's thick brows lifted in mild surprise. "That's odd. She said she'd join me bright and early to talk about the green sand, but I haven't seen her."

"I'm sure she'll show up," said Shyriel. "Eventually. Perhaps she's enjoying a brief dalliance; I've seen several young men watching her."

Bitch. Snake looked at her from beneath lowered brows, wishing he could poison her with a look. He drew breath for a sharp retort.

Easy, Snake. Ick's buzz, sharp in his head. *Don't give her the satisfaction. I'll see if I can reach Jynx.*

But Ick couldn't reach her, either. That meant Jynx was sleeping, or... his thoughts stuttered... or she wasn't in the village, or even close to it.

Snake's worry level bumped up several notches. If Ick couldn't reach her she must be... what, a mile or more away? He didn't know the distance limitations of Rapport.

When lunch ended, Snake didn't stay for the discussion of preparations for battle. Beyir could handle that. Instead he went straight to where Jynx was staying, with some thought of tracking her footsteps from there.

What he found sent him into a near panic.

The place was littered with Jynx's things—a stray bit of clothing wadded up by the back wall. Cups and utensils strewn about randomly. Cushions no longer neatly stacked but flung about as if she'd been searching for something.

Her satchel of herbs and medicines still lay near the door and he sighed with relief. She wouldn't go far without that!

Then he noticed that her waterbag was missing. And her head covering wasn't—the one she wore to protect her head from the sun.

Where on earth...? What was she doing?

His stomach rolled into a tight, painful ball.

Jynx had left in a hurry, maybe been carried off. Something was terribly wrong.

For a brief moment he thought about his obligations to the People and the upcoming battle.

Obligations? This wasn't really his fight. Not his concern.

But Jynx *was* his concern. Even if he didn't love her with all his heart—which he did—he'd brought her here. He was responsible for her safety. He *had* to find her, no matter what.

He hurried back to his house. Food. Waterbags. He buckled on his harness and sword, added knives to his boots, and stuffed a sizeable bag of white sand into his light pack.

Where would she go? Why?

Which direction?

Home. She had to be going home.

He left the village without bothering to tell anyone. Nothing mattered except Jynx.

And the answer to one big question: Why?

~~~

Jynx threw up again. Running away home wasn't any fun if she couldn't run without heaving and home was halfway around the world.

In the darkness, the white sand seemed to shine like a faint moon. There was something she needed to remember about the white sand, if she could just think of it. Something important.

No, no. It couldn't be more important than going home. No time to stop. She swallowed the vomit's dregs, her throat burning. She couldn't afford to waste water—or time—cleaning out her mouth.

Were those clouds overhead? Wispy, faint—maybe a pale veil of stars instead? She couldn't be sure, with her eyes blurring like this.

Come to think of it, she couldn't be sure of anything anymore. Laughter where there should be no laughter. A voice in her head, not in her ears. No direction for sure, without Katinga's Eye. No Snake. No, snakes were everywhere out here. Why did she want another one?

Her head ached, as if her brain banged against prison walls. Why couldn't she think straight?

Her toes began to catch in the sand. She was dragging her

feet so badly she could have tripped and fallen!

And then she did, as if the thought had triggered the deed. Her hands came down flat on the sand but couldn't stop her from rocking forward and burying her nose in it.

Jynx pushed up on her hands, gasping a lungful of air and a few white grains. She swallowed water, to her surprise. But she couldn't think how she got water in her mouth.

Half panicked, she coughed. She struggled not to inhale again, coughed harder. Inhaled carefully through her nose, to the background music of a raspy laugh that terrified her.

What was that new sound? She almost gasped in alarm, caught herself just in time. And recognized the frightened mewing as her own voice. She sat back on her heels, shivering.

Her shivering made her aware of the sweat on her face. From running? From fear?

She sat still, waiting for her face to dry in the moisture-free desert air. Listening for the voice in her head that she couldn't quite hear, but that never really seemed to be gone. As if it lived there now.

That meant it had to be her imagination, right? Or she was going crazy.

Get out! she screamed at it silently. *Get out of my head*! She pushed at it.

The voice disappeared.

Jynx began to breathe normally again. Slowly she relaxed. When her hands stopped shaking, she stood up and began walking again. A few steps later she turned back, picked up her forgotten waterbag, and started forward again.

She never did see Katinga's Eye, but a couple of hours later she became aware that the sand beneath her feet no longer shone like soft moonlight, but like a starless night–deep and black and shadowed.

There was something about the shadows she should know... if she could just think of it.

As the fear sifted away, a neutral blankness invaded her mind. She felt safer like this, with a cottony cushion separating her from the world. Like a cocoon, maybe, or a frail wall separating her from danger. She lurched forward again, her feet clumsy but moving.

Black sand meant she was going the right direction, at least. She remembered that much. They'd come through black sands to reach the white sands.

She'd relax more if the black sand were a little less... intimidating. Danger seemed to lurk unseen in the shadows that curtained every dune. It had been scary when she and Kahpur had traveled through over a year ago, but this was worse. The darkness felt thicker, and whatever frightened her now could remain hidden. Danger identified could be faced, but this?

Still, she felt better already. Even facing her fear in this way gave her more control. Or at least the feel of it. She lifted her chin in defiance. Fear could kill, but she wouldn't allow that to happen to her.

Squaring her shoulders, she stepped forward boldly, despite the faint trembling in her fingers.

Fear energy kept her moving. The urgency to get home clawed at her. She drank a few sips of water as she walked. When she became tired enough, she would take proper breaks, but she wouldn't waste the time until she had to.

The sun rose, but the day didn't get much brighter. Even the sunlight couldn't penetrate the shadowed dunes completely, so that Jynx seemed to stumble through a perpetual haze. If she couldn't see well, she also couldn't be seen well. She took comfort from that.

With the coming of light, however dim, she began to feel stronger, more confident. Maybe she really could do this! She could orient on the strongest light so she wouldn't walk in circles, and eventually she would reach the blue sands.

When the wind first came up, she was annoyed. Sand whispered as it swirled, forming and reforming wind patterns in the sand. As it rose, it peppered her hands and face. She tucked her chin to her chest to protect her eyes and kept moving. If it didn't get any worse, she'd be fine.

Strange, how the shadows above the sand also seemed to twist and writhe. And deepen.

Within minutes the pale sunlight no longer reached her. She was enveloped in a storm of sand and blackness.

This wasn't her first sandstorm. She knew what to do. Still, she plowed forward as long as she could, looking for a good place to wait out the storm.

She found one, an unexpected wall of stone alongside a dune. She slid down the nearby sand to reach the bottom, then tucked herself against that bulwark. The whistle of the wind softened a bit. She took a quick drink from her waterbag, because she might not have another chance for a while. Then she covered herself completely with the sheet in her pack and hunkered down to wait.

~~~

Sand slashed Snake's face as the wind picked up. He'd been following soft indentations in the sand that could be footsteps, but they were filling up faster as the wind rose.

How big a lead did Jynx have? Were these even her tracks?

He drew cloth from his shoulder across his lower face and held it there with one hand to filter out the worst of the white sand. Fine grains still collected in the corners of his eyes, no matter how much he squinted.

Whistling wind threw sand into his ears; more sand pooled about his feet, burying them so that he had to shorten each stride to pull a foot loose for the next step. At this rate, how would he ever catch up?

He set his jaw and leaned harder into the wind, tucking his chin against his chest. The step from white sand to black wasn't clear cut; the grains mingled and danced in the breeze together, blurring the line where they met. With no visible light in the swirling blackness and no view of the sky at all now, he couldn't be sure which direction he was going. Somewhere on the long, long black and white border...

No indentations preceded him anymore. He needed to hole up and wait it out before he became totally lost. Just a few more steps...

He leaned into the wind, ducking his head against the onslaught. He could manage a few more... He halted, body wavering as he sought to keep his feet.

Jynx. Jynx. Jynx. Holding her name like a prayer, he pushed forward.

And solid black shapes rose before him, darkness and shadow and enmity. They leaned toward him, reaching.

By the time he realized they were real, it was too late to reach his sword. His forward movement halted. He went down into the sand, borne by the weight of the specters.

~~~

They found her. In the midst of a sandstorm big enough to be visible from twenty miles away, how did they even know she was there to be found? Surely it wasn't her white sheet. So much black sand covered it now that she should have been invisible.

At first Jynx thought it was just the hot desert wind tugging at her sheet. But when one edge came up and stayed up, she knew it was more than that. The face that appeared was shrouded in black cloth that covered everything but the eyes. Fierce, dark eyes stared at her for one interminable moment.

She recognized him. That large mole beside his right eyebrow identified him as Nerom, the Malim of the warriors of the black sands.

Fear shivered through her. There was nowhere to go to avoid him. No space to move, to resist. Her mouth dried.

So much for screaming. She didn't even have a weapon with her—one small knife for harvesting herbs, and it wouldn't damage him at all, unless she stabbed him in the eye. And even then he'd only be blind in one eye, still capable of killing her.

He reached in, clamped his hand around her wrist, and pulled.

She tried to resist, but he simply dragged her, belly down, out of her shelter, out into the whistling wind and needling sand. She clutched her satchel hard, hoping it wouldn't slide off her shoulder and be lost. Especially Kahpur's magic bowl that had to be returned. It was her friend's most valuable possession–besides her horses, at least.

Sand slid down the back of her tongue and caught in her throat. She coughed it up, frantic.

What had ever possessed her to run? She shouldn't be here at all! She should still be in the white sands, where she had friends. Where Snake must be wondering where she was. And where Ick would help protect her.

Here, she felt helpless. She'd prepared in a panic, relieved that she remembered the sheet. But she wasn't prepared for this.

The storm had abated, but wind still whistled around her ears and tossed sand against her face. She tried to duck her head, but the sand's swirling brought it into her face anyway.

More figures appeared behind the Malim, just enough obscured that she couldn't make out how many.

How did they find her in this storm? Sheer happenstance? Or were they looking for her–or someone else? Jynx hated not having answers to basic questions. For that matter, why would warriors be out in the storm looking for anyone? They certainly couldn't be looking specifically for her!

The attack. The one Snake was leading against the Wohim. Perhaps it had already started, and she was caught up in the war now! Dread shriveled her spine, but only for a moment, before fear for Snake drove it out.

And then she had no time for fear or dread or anything else, as they bound her hands with stiff rope, pulling the bonds so tight they cut her skin. She bit her tongue against the pain. Another, longer rope was tied around the one binding her hands and used as a lead, as if she were a horse, forced to follow meekly where they led.

Her captors began walking, not looking back to see if she followed. They would know if she fell or tried to run. She had the distinct feeling that if she fell, they'd simply drag her, so she made it a point to keep her feet even in deep drifts of black sand. No matter how many clumsy steps it took to keep her balance.

They walked a long time. The storm stopped. Only the lightest grains of sand still hung in the air. Dull sunset glowed through it. The wind died, and Jynx thought she might, too. Fear had stolen her energy and her self-confidence, leaving her as dull as a cornfield in winter. She partitioned off the fear as best she could, hoping to avoid being touched by it. In so doing, she separated herself from the world, allowing nothing to touch her.

Time passed, and she didn't feel it. Wohim voices jabbered, but it was background noise and she didn't hear it.

She didn't think about the future—not even a few minutes into the future—for fear she didn't have one. If it ended, she'd rather not see it coming. Time and the world slid past, as if she slogged in place.

28. Shadow Sands

He fought the specters. Black on black, they moved within shadows, as ethereal as the wind lashing him, unseen.

Deep, soft sand trapped Snake's feet, slowing him and holding him almost in place. His lightning quick reflexes couldn't help him if he couldn't use them. He couldn't tell how many he fought; they blended with the whistling wind and stinging sand so that he barely saw them move, and never in time.

A heavy blow on the back of his head buckled his knees. He almost held to his feet, but when he stumbled forward, the sand caught his toes and he splashed into it.

A knee landed in the middle of his back as he inhaled. Sand grated the back of his tongue and he desperately controlled his breathing enough to cough it out without allowing any into his lungs.

The man on his back stretched Snake's head back and laid a knife to his throat.

He froze.

A harsh command stopped the knife's movement. Snake held as still as possible, feeling the faint trickle of blood down his throat. No real damage, he thought. But it had been close.

The man wrenched his arms behind his back and tied them with harsh rope, then dragged him to his feet.

His attacker was huge. Even bigger than Kayde!

Snake could defeat someone that much bigger than he, but not muscle for muscle. He began cataloging moves that would defeat this—monster. About half of them he discarded when someone took his sword.

Then he could do nothing but go where they pushed or dragged him. Resistance wouldn't help him, but it would anger his captors.

Why didn't they kill him outright and leave his body for burial by the sand?

He couldn't let that happen. Jynx was out here somewhere. If he died, who would find her and protect her? *I can't do anything to help her right now, but I will get loose and I will find her.*

Why did she run? Why was she so determined to leave the white sands? Surely she wasn't leaving him!

But he couldn't know that. He wasn't good with women, like Kayde was.

That didn't matter. He still had to find her, find out why she left. No matter what. Just leaving, without a word, wasn't like her. Jynx would have told him to his face if she was done with him. She would have considered it the ethical, honest thing to do.

The big man pushed him again, a jolt rather than steady pressure. Snake stumbled. Unable to catch himself, he fell, burying his face in sand. He jerked his head up, started to roll onto his back to trip up his enemy.

He caught himself. They'd be on him so fast he wouldn't get anything from it but satisfaction. And maybe a beating. Frustrated, he subsided and struggled back to his feet, watched intently by the Wohim.

This time a tall, slender man took Snake's elbow and guided him into a straggled line with the others. The big man still slogged along behind the group, like a guard moving prisoners. Except Snake was the only prisoner.

He ducked his chin against his chest to protect his eyes

from stinging sand. The march became interminable, a lifetime of wind and sand and moving forward.

Was this a regular patrol that had chanced upon him? How many such patrols did the Wohim have? Or were they on their way somewhere else—a group of raiders on the way to the white sands? He needed information, to put things into perspective and see the whole picture.

He cursed Slyn with every step. The slither should have brought him all the information he so badly needed, but he had brought nothing! Anger roiled in his stomach.

He forced himself back to a semblance of calm. Slyn had been deliberately unhelpful. A slither of high intelligence, he wouldn't have done this by accident. A deliberate act, then, against Snake's orders, detrimental to the People, and dangerous for those who would soon go to war against the Wohim.

It made no sense. If Slyn wanted to rule the slithers, why would he *not* want to help Snake overcome the Wohim, who would destroy the slithers that Slyn wanted to rule?

No helpful answers came to him, although he spent the rest of the journey thinking hard enough to make his head ache.

They stopped once, in the lee of a rocky outcropping, to rest and drink water they carried with them. Even Snake was given a few swallows by the giant, at the leader's nod.

"Morinl." The big man's black eyes fastened intently on Snake.

What? Snake recognized the word but couldn't place it.

"Morinl," he said again. He placed a hand over his heart. "Morinl."

The captive. The one Snake had tortured for information. Sick dread filled his gut. Clearly the captive was important to this man, who was big enough to snap Snake's spine like a twig.

He shook his head. "I don't know what you're saying," he said aloud. "I don't understand."

"Of course you do," said the group's leader. Black eyes

glared at him. "You recognized the name when Changn first spoke it. Morinl is his brother, captured as we transported snakes through the sand. Changn is asking about him. I hope you have a good answer. For your sake."

"You speak our language," Snake blurted.

The man shrugged. "Does Morinl live?"

Snake hesitated. "So far as I know." Visions of blood and horror flashed through his memory. He swallowed, hard.

The leader spoke briefly to the giant, who seemed to relax the tiniest bit. And then he got the men to their feet and on their way again, without another word.

To Snake's relief, the wind whistled past his ears on a lower note. The sandstorm was less fierce now, and perhaps it would soon give way entirely. But with his luck today, that wasn't very likely.

The journey continued for at least another hour. During that time the wind diminished until finally, near the end of the trek, the world lay calm and peaceful, as if nothing had ever disturbed the black sand. Nearby, a single tiny cascade of sand trickled down the side of a small dune, disturbing the delicate curve of a sand wave. The only breeze Snake felt was the wind of his own passage.

The Wohim spoke among themselves but translated none of it to Snake. In fact, they generally ignored him.

That changed when the colorful tents of the Wohim village came into view. Grins appeared on the faces around him, and then the warriors thrust spears and swords toward the sky, ululated wildly, and raced madly for the village, dragging Snake with them.

People poured out of the tents—women, children, and old men—to greet the returning warriors with cries of gladness, childish shrieks, and ululations of their own.

Snake began to hope they would be caught up in reunions and forget his presence long enough for him to escape.

As if reading his mind, Changn's huge hand gripped his arm so tightly Snake thought it might break.

The giant pushed him toward a large red and blue striped tent near the center of the encampment. As they drew near, a woman emerged and stepped out to meet them. She spoke briefly to Changn, cut a sharp look at Snake, and walked away.

Dread knotted Snake' stomach. This didn't look good for him. Her eyes said she knew something he didn't, and he wouldn't like it.

Or he could be imagining things, a captive in a hostile camp.

Changn snarled, baring big, square brown teeth, black eyes glaring fury at Snake.

The stomach knots tightened. Snake tried to twist his hands within the confines of the sisal rope but found no give in them. Why had Changn suddenly become so hostile?

He thought he knew but hoped he was wrong. If he guessed right, they'd somehow discovered what happened to Morinl. If they had, his own death would arrive soon.

The giant strode to the red and blue tent, dragging Snake with him. He flung open the flap and hurled his prisoner inside.

Snake twisted to land on his shoulder blade, the firm sand giving way so that he wasn't harmed.

Changn spat just outside the flap, still glaring at him, then dropped the flap. Through its translucence, Snake saw him turn to face outward, powerful arms crossed over his chest.

And then he heard a long, slow hiss, and felt a buzz of triumph in his head.

He already knew, but he rose to his knees and turned toward the center of the tent.

Amid bowls of cocomilk, melon slices, and smoked kangapak ribs, Slyn lay half coiled, red eyes glittering and black tongue flickering.

Welcome, Kyr. This moment has been long in coming.

~~~

Jynx's journey through black sand ended at last. The Wohim treated her with more dignity than she expected, but she wasn't surprised to find herself once again standing before Srika, Malim of the Caretaker Guild. At least Srika spoke her language, though the grim set of her mouth and her hard eyes warned of little welcome this time.

The first thing Srika did was take Jynx's satchel and hand it to a woman standing nearby.

"Destroy everything in this." Her gaze remained on Jynx.

Shock flashed through Jynx. "No! Please, no! My herbs are in there! Everything I use for healing!" And Kahpur's magic bowl.

The woman spilled the contents of her satchel on the ground. She watched as beardtongue, paperflower, hawkweed, chicory, yucca roots, downy milkweed, and bright orange butterfly milkweed blew away in the breeze, lost forever.

Then they shredded the hareem, the spare clothes she'd brought, the muslin and cloth she used for bandages and for storing herbs. They shattered the healing implements she'd brought—mortar and pestle, digging tool, half a dozen tiny jars, and stir sticks. Scissors. Her small herbal knife. Everything. Gone.

When they brought out Kahpur's bowl, Jynx cried out and surged forward, stopped by her bindings. "It was my mother's," she lied, voice choking. "It's all I have of hers!"

A large sword destroyed the magic bowl in two blows. Jynx bowed her head—not to hide tears that she refused to shed, but to cover her rage. They had just wronged the wrong person. This would *not* go unanswered! She had to bide her time, wait for the right moment, but there *would* be a reckoning.

If only Snake were here. He'd set this to rights quickly! But he remained in the white sands, preparing the warriors for war. Her heart surged at the thought of these—fiends!—being destroyed by the People they had so wronged.

Only later, sitting in a small tent with hands still bound behind her, did her rage settle to a cooler anger. Their time would come. If not now, then eventually. The One would handle this in His own time, and in His own way. Although she'd love to be His instrument in this. Or Snake. He'd be a truly lethal instrument.

What would they do with her, while she waited for Snake to find her? No doubt he would. No doubt he searched for her even now. If he would just search a little faster!

How soon would he notice she was gone? She sighed. It could be awhile, if he yet trained the warriors. But surely he'd missed her by bedtime last night. And so she prayed that he was on his way, that he would find her soon.

When he rescued her, they could just go home from here, without backtracking to the white sands. But without her medicines and herbs, and without the magic bowl to provide food, how would they get home safely? Unless, of course, the Slipaway Trail appeared.

Best not to rely on the Trail. Best to rely on themselves only.

So why had she left so precipitously? She couldn't remember what had convinced her to go, with no word to anyone, not even Snake. Something dark and dangerous. But her memory kept slipping sideways, away from the moment she knew she had to leave immediately.

Well, if she let it alone instead of worrying at it, she'd be more likely to remember.

She'd had memory problems almost from the moment they'd arrived in the white sands. She sighed heavily, irritated at herself.

And then she settled down to pick at the ropes as best she could, looking for a way to ease their grip on her wrists—or remove the bindings all together.

~~~

"You *planned* this?" Snake burst out. "*You* arranged my capture by the Wohim?"

Slyn's voice was smug. *I'm more than you've ever given me credit for, Kyr. Unlike slithers not chosen by the gods, I can listen without you being aware of it.*

Snake knew better. Or thought he did. He'd never heard of such a thing, and he didn't believe it." So you listened to see where I might be, and sent enemy warriors there to find me." He kept his tone flat, although he did try to hide his animosity.

You've never appreciated me, Kyr. I always thought you understood me better than anyone else, but understanding isn't enough. You never really wanted me in your nest, and you treated me accordingly. Every chance you got, every time I tried to prove myself, you held me back.

"Held you back? I tried to protect you, to keep you safe and out of trouble. Do you know how much trouble I was in because of you?" Snake snorted.

I heard you ask to hand me off to someone else, to wash your hands of me.

"No. I never did that." Then a memory caught him, of his younger self, when he overheard a conversation between his father and his mother:

"This youngen has caused terrible nightmares for two acolytes already, and one of them may lose his place in the priesthood because of the damage to his mind. Neither was ready for such a... different... slither. Eccentric. Perhaps beyond eccentric."

"What does that mean? Beyond eccentric?" Mother demanded. "And different how? If they place him with Kyr, what is the danger to our son?"

"Slyn is very intelligent, but he's a social misfit. He's clumsy and awkward, physically and mentally. A human like him would become an artist or criminal; his thoughts are that different."

Could Slyn have heard that? How? Who would have told him, and why?

Meaningless questions that he would never know the answers to. But if he had heard–or learned of–those things, how might they have warped him? True, Slyn had always felt unloved and unwanted–but he'd seemed content with the young Kyr.

Except for wanting more for his life. Always more. That's why he'd picked so many fights with larger slithers. For status. For reputation. To be more, in everyone's eyes.

And breaking protocol to enter the queens' precinct? Not for mating at all, despite Slyn's curiosity about it at the time.

For status. To be seen as bold and powerful, a fit leader for all the slithers. To take Tchenya's place, to be the first slither king.

Worse, Slyn expected Snake to rule alongside him. As Shyriel and Erilya ruled together, so he expected himself and Snake to be partnered.

Snake's chest tightened. A power-hungry slither, one who truly saw himself as superior. He'd always said that, but Snake had dismissed it. It could never happen, so it wasn't worth thinking about.

He'd been embarrassingly short-sighted, not to see that Slyn set no limitations on what he would do for the power and status he craved.

And then there had been that recent prophecy Slyn had shared with him, just the other day... He struggled to remember.

"A new order is upon us, guided by the son of prophecy. The queen shall be cast down and a new ruler arise, bringing the promised prosperity to the People."

Slyn's next words had filled him with a dread that had never fully abated: *"So you see, the gods intend for us to rule, and that is how prosperity will be restored. Beginning with the slaughter of the Wohim and rescue of the slithers they have taken."*

Presumably, the "new ruler" would be Slyn, and Ick would be the one cast down. And if she died, Shyriel would die.

Did Slyn expect to rule alone, unable to communicate with humans who had no Rapport? Or did he think Snake would fulfill that role?

Could this situation become any more snarled?

Like a black cloud, one question hovered over everything. Why would Slyn ally with the Wohim, when he'd already stated his intent to rescue the slithers from them? Any that still lived, at least. It made no sense, and Snake soon got lost in the tangled explanations Slyn gave him.

He drew the only logical conclusion he could find: Slyn wasn't aberrant after all. He was insane.

To Snake's relief, Slyn turned back to his interrupted meal, ignoring him. The warrior took advantage of the time to review everything he thought he knew. But the problem nagging him the hardest wasn't Slyn, though it probably should be. Once again he came back to Jynx.

The rest didn't matter, except to those who lived in these two tribes. He'd done what he'd promised, and more. Their prophecy had been fulfilled where it concerned him. More than anything, he needed to get free and find Jynx. They had no reason to be in the Rainbow Sands anymore.

If Jynx had started for home, as he believed, she would likely have gone through the black sands—and become caught in the storm. She could be out there still, buried in sand.

Damn. From one worry to another. He hated the Rainbow Sands! Nothing good ever happened to him here. Except his growing closeness to Jynx, and making love to her. As long as she was there, everything else was fine. When she wasn't, nothing went right.

"Slyn?"

No response, although he could see the black slither sipping cocomilk twenty feet away.

Exasperated, he tried Rapport.

Slyn stopped eating and looked at him.

"Is Jynx within reach of your Rapport? Can you listen and find her?"

Jynx! I've never understood your interest in her! You should have let her die in the sands before you ever reached the People.

"Slithers choose their own mates. Why wouldn't humans?" Snake's jaw tightened in anger.

Because humans aren't bright enough to make good choices. Why bother with a farm girl, when you could have a queen? Shyriel is younger, more beautiful, and more powerful than Jynx. You could have her for the asking; when my prophecy is fulfilled, you can take her for wife or concubine. Jynx will only lead you into disaster.

Words. Snake ignored them, keeping his face and body relaxed and neutral. "Jynx is the one I want. Can you find her by listening? Or were you just bragging?"

Slyn stared at him for a long moment. Slither eyes didn't blink. Then he turned his head away from Snake and ignored him.

The silence between them continued, and Snake settled himself to out wait his opponent.

He stretched his fingers and wrists, trying to relieve the pressure of the harsh ropes that bound him so tightly.

"I'm starting to lose feeling in my hands," he said in a low voice. Slyn would hear it, if he was listening. And if he wasn't, shouting might not help.

Slyn still didn't look at him, even when two men came in to take the dishes and left-overs from Slyn's repast. As they started to leave the tent, one of them detoured to cut Snake's ropes and retie his hands in front of him.

Snake looked at the black slither. "Thank you, Slyn."

He waited until the men had gone. And then he relaxed the fists he'd been holding so tightly closed. Relaxed, his wrists weren't as large and he had a bit of space—what Jynx would call "wiggle room." If he could just have the tent to himself for five minutes!

Surely Slyn had a burrow somewhere, where he would soon retreat to sleep. Slithers didn't usually sleep surrounded by so much open space. At least, he thought he remembered that from his childhood lessons.

"How long have you been an ally of the People's enemies?" he asked.

Slyn's mouth opened wide in a loud hiss in Snake's direction.

"Have you been spying for them all this time? Have you been leading the slithers into captivity and death? How much loss of life has been your work, Slyn? And why?"

Slyn hissed again, exposing double rows of needle-sharp teeth. His deadly tail lashed. But he said nothing.

Power. Somehow, the aberrant worm expected to gain power through his betrayals. Now that he understood Slyn better, that was the only explanation that made sense.

Had his betrayals been selective, aimed at the slithers who opposed his will? Or just whoever had been handy? Or weak?

He felt a fresh surge of fury from Slyn.

Quiet! Or Jynx will die!

29. The Truth

Her face anvil-hard, Srika removed Jynx's bonds so she could eat, then sat as far away as she could and watched every bite disappear into her mouth.

Eating with her hands made Jynx feel childish and stupid. The sticks of bread didn't bother her, but consuming a thin gruel by drinking it didn't appeal to her. Nor eating juicy meat with her fingers. She had nothing to wipe the grease from her fingers so, with a mental shrug, she wiped them on the floor of the beautiful tent.

Srika's gasp of outrage provided a certain satisfaction. What was she supposed to do? Wipe the grease onto her own clothes? She'd have used a cloth, had Srika provided one.

Twice Jynx thought Srika would speak, but she did not. After they'd stared at each other awhile, a young girl came into the tent to collect Jynx's supper things.

As the girl left, Srika spoke briefly to her, then returned her hard gaze to Jynx. She had probably requested a cloth or napkin for the next time, Jynx guessed.

"You have damaged me," Srika finally said in Jynx's own tongue, when they had the tent to themselves again. Srika had grown up in the tallgrass but married into the Wohim. "I spent years proving myself! Showing my people I can be trusted! That the tallgrass people are not to be feared or hated! And now my people once again say that I cannot be trusted after all, that I am like you, that I bide my time to seek their downfall! Do not expect my sympathy or my pity, or my assistance.

"After the foolishness you exhibited when you were last here, no one from the tallgrass will ever again be tolerated in the black sands but will be killed on sight! How many other people will die because they are mistaken for your countrymen? Their deaths, and possibly mine, will be on your head!"

Jynx lowered her eyes in submission. "I'm trying to return to the tallgrass. I travel alone, wanting only to go home. The sandstorm caught me, and then men from your village. *They* brought me here. I did not seek this place, having enough of sand for a lifetime."

"And yet here you are, despite your protests. Saying a thing does not make it true, and yet you expect me to believe your story despite the obvious lies."

"Obvious lies?" Jynx tried to think of any lie she'd told. Surely, if she'd told one, it wouldn't have been obvious. She'd had better practice than that!

"You claimed to be traveling alone, which was easily disproved when they found your companion."

Companion? Ick wasn't traveling with her this time–and couldn't be expected to, with war approaching so fast. It couldn't be anyone else, though, with Snake so busy with the warriors. This made no sense.

So she asked. "What companion would that be? I can think of no one who would have been free to accompany me, even if I'd asked–which I didn't. I want only to return home, as swiftly as I may."

Although, come to think of it, she didn't remember exactly why she'd been in such a hurry. She'd left Snake! Even when he would soon look death in the eye again! Why did she have to fall in love with a warrior! He could give her nothing but heartache.

She thrust away the irrational thought.

Srika studied her, an odd look on her face. "You deny traveling with your love, Kyr?"

How did the Malim know Snake's birth name? Caught off-guard, Jynx could only gape at Srika.

Sometimes nothing in the world seemed to make sense. This seemed to be one of them.

What was she supposed to say? *He doesn't have time to come with me because he's preparing a surprise attack on the Wohim?*

Maybe the Wohim already suspected and hoped to gain some advantage from what Jynx knew.

When she said nothing, Srika snorted in a very unfeminine fashion, then rose and left the tent. A man entered and wordlessly tied Jynx's wrists behind her back again, then took up a position outside next to the door, where she could see his shadow.

With a sigh, she went back to work on her ropes, more determined than ever. If even a faint chance existed that they had caught Snake, she had to get loose. She had to find him, to let him know she was here and in a real jam.

Even though she didn't make much progress—why couldn't they use a soft cotton rope, instead of tough sisal?—Jynx kept at it. She couldn't think what else to do to get out of this pickle.

And then she burst out laughing. Was she in a pickle or in a jam? The image of a pickle slice smeared with strawberry jam... eeuw! But she still laughed.

Not hysteria. Jynx never succumbed to hysteria. She laughed because the very idea of a pickle in a jam tickled her. Tickled by a pickle.

Maybe she did have just a touch of hysteria.

The shadow of the guard outside the tent door didn't twitch. Jynx shoved away the thought of pickles and jam and watched him. Too bad he wouldn't be distracted.

She spent the next hour thinking of distractions and trying

to guess the results she would get, until the ideas became too bizarre for even her imagination. Worst of all, nothing she had come up with could work.

The sun was sinking fast toward the horizon. She would welcome the cover of darkness for an escape, except that darkness in black sand meant she'd probably be lost before she even got out of the village.

She gave up on her bonds. With no perceptible change in the ropes after so much work, it seemed unlikely she could pick them apart enough to get free. And she might need the energy for something else. Assuming she could think of something else to try.

She had to get loose! She had to find Snake. If Srika told the truth, he was here, in this village. Somewhere. And that meant that he'd come looking for her and been caught, probably after the sandstorm, as she was.

If she screamed, would he hear her, through all the tents? Was he close enough? And what were they doing to him?

The Wohim knew he was a formidable opponent. They couldn't afford to let him live long. In fact, he could already be dead!

Her heart clutched in her chest and for an awful moment she couldn't breathe. No. Not Snake. He wasn't dead. He couldn't be. She would have known.

Jynx calmed herself as best she could. They were two parts of one soul. If he died, it would kill her. She was still alive, and therefore so was he.

No, it wasn't logical—and she was a very logical person. But it was true. She felt it in the depths of her bones, in heart and soul.

So. Snake was alive. That meant he would be coming for her. She just had to keep the faith and be ready.

Readiness can only be maintained for so long, though, and at some point Jynx let herself down onto her side and slept lightly.

When warm air touched her cheek she awoke. In the

darkness she could no longer see the guard's shadow, but he remained in place. He or someone like him.

The flap dropped back into place, enclosing her once more in stifling air, but it opened again a moment later. The guard entered–the same man, to her surprise–and set a candle on a low table well away from her. Then he held the flap open for someone entering before leaving to take up his post again.

Only no one entered.

Oh, wait. The faint flicker of the candle caught movement near the flap. She squeezed her eyes half shut, trying to see.

A slither. A big one, judging by the height of the red eyes.

Jynxxx... A sibilant whisper filled her mind with amusement and animosity.

"Slyn?" And suddenly she couldn't breathe. The pressure against her mind increased, tightening into a brutal headache. Laughter inside her head.

Laughter she recognized. The same voice that had urged her abrupt departure for the tallgrass.

And before that...

She just had time to brace before something heavy and dark slammed into her mind. A sudden inflation inside her skull threatened to burst it from the inside. Pain, terror, nightmare. She would have clutched at her head, if her hands had been free, but she couldn't even pull her arms up over her head to shield it.

It wouldn't have helped. The attack was inside her skull, not outside it.

She caught a whimper in her teeth, ground them together to hold her screams inside.

But they remained inside her head, where Slyn heard them and laughed.

She'd felt this laughter before.

Yesss. The night you fell. You are very strong, Jynx. You should have died that night but you refused to. You surprised me then, or I'd have been rid of you. That won't happen again. You're a distraction to Kyr, and that cannot continue.

And so I drove you from the white sands.

Jynx couldn't catch the moan that escaped. Her thrashing only rolled her over her own elbow, threatening to pull her arm from her shoulder. She couldn't think. She "heard" Slyn's voice but it carried no meaning now. Only sound. Only a roaring hiss. Only pain, and unbearable pressure.

You will not be the first I have killed. When I was but a youngen, I burned an acolyte's mind from him. With no mind, he could only sit stupidly while his mother tried to feed him. He didn't even remember how to swallow! You will die like that, too. Your interference will end, and Erilya's protection will be gone with it. She will die soon after you, and Shyriel after that.

Jynx couldn't think, couldn't breathe. She wanted to ask why but couldn't remember the word.

Slyn picked up on it anyway. *Without you to distract Kyr, he and I will replace Shyriel and Erilya, becoming the true rulers of the People of the white sands, fulfilling a prophecy given me by the gods.*

He crushed her mind with his.

And at last she screamed, long and loud, before she lost consciousness entirely.

~~~

Grayness swirled aimlessly. No sound, no feeling, just... existing inside the fog. Jynx drifted, riding the mist, wandering through nothingness. Like the Slipaway Trail—beyond the impenetrable brush between the trees that lined it.

Just being...

No sound, except perhaps the faint throb of her own heartbeat.

Some self-awareness still existed. She knew she lived, surprised that it surprised her. But this place was fine and she felt no impulse to be elsewhere. This place—inside her own skull?

It hurt to think, as she released the thought. She let go of everything, allowing the world–if it still existed–to take her where it would.

Perhaps she slept. That might explain the jumbled images, at least. But the images were too blurred to mean anything. Sleep healed, so she relaxed into its nothingness, into the soft blanket of gray where she drifted...

Time had disappeared with the world.

She had nothing. She was nothing. She wanted nothing. Except to sleep, to stay in this place without feeling. Without pain and confusion.

Jynx opened her eyes and blinked against the brightness. Faint sounds came from outside, the everyday voices and movements of people going about their business.

The pounding pain in her skull urged her to ooze away again, but it was already too late for that. Her shoulder ached and she remembered rolling over her own elbow.

And she remembered Slyn.

She sat up with a gasp, clumsy as she hadn't been since childhood. Her wrists burned, proving that her hands remained bound, and boomers went off inside her skull. She groaned, wanting the peaceful, pain-free grayness again, but now that she knew what it was, she wouldn't return there willingly.

She had the tent to herself. Thank the One, Slyn had left sometime in the night. Even the thought of the aberrant slither brought fear crawling up into her throat.

Morning sun outlined the shadow of her guard against the tent wall. The Wohim outside cheerfully went about their day, while she lay here in pain. While Snake languished in confinement and possibly pain–if they hadn't killed him already.

That thought catapulted her fully back to herself. Somewhere in the Wohim village, Snake still lived. And would not be killed, she realized. Slyn couldn't allow the Wohim to kill him; it would destroy his own prophecy. The jolt of panic dissipated. As long as Snake lived, they both could survive this. No better man lived for rescuing maidens in distress—even if Jynx herself couldn't claim maiden status. Widows deserved valiant rescues, too, and she trusted to Snake to see to it.

Unless Slyn hadn't told him she was here. No predicting what the slimy-souled worm would do. She needed to get free and find Snake; they'd be stronger together than apart. Perhaps even unstoppable.

She reviewed Slyn's sins to herself—the childhood trouble he'd caused Snake, the death of Snake's father and the upheaval of Snake's life, burning out a child's mind and attempting to destroy hers, the attack on the night she fell, coercing her to run for home—right through the enemy villag... oh, and his fight with Ick, and his betrayal of the People to the Wohim... Her anger grew with the list of his misdeeds.

The angrier she grew, the more determination accumulated between her shoulder blades.

If she ever got close to Slyn again, she'd cut his damn head off! If she had a knife.

Her oath revealed the extent of her anger. She never used that kind of language! Almost never. She had to be honest, at least with herself.

The guard outside the tent changed in midmorning and the new guard came into the tent. He removed her ropes and handed her a half-full waterskin. She took a long, sweet drink of leather-impregnated water and he left the 'skin with her, retying her hands in front of her this time. So she wouldn't need his help to drink, she was sure.

As he tied, she glanced quickly to see where he wore his knife.

How strange! It hung down his back in a scabbard, the hilt reaching up to the knob at the back of his neck. Snake and Kayde wore their swords across their backs, but she'd never heard of a knife carried behind like that.

She couldn't think of any way to get to it, to steal it without being noticed.

If she still had her satchel and its contents it might be possible... a bit of the right herb in the waterskin, plus a flowery herb for sweetness, and the offering of a drink. And then keeping him with her until he passed out.

If wishes were whistles, she'd have music all day. She snorted.

She glanced around the tent for anything to help her get free. Nothing. A few cushions and a blanket or two, but nothing else.

Determined, she fought up to her feet and planted herself, pausing until her faint dizziness passed. Then she examined every inch of the tent, hoping for something that could help her.

Nothing. Unless she counted that small rip in the floor halfway between the center and the back wall, and it wasn't even as long as her hand.

Movement did feel good, though. She stayed on her feet, walking around the tent's interior twice, then reversing direction to walk around a few more times.

Not only could she not escape, she was likely to die of boredom!

She thought about asking if Srika had any needlework she could be doing, or herbs that needed crushing, but she couldn't bear the thought of aiding her enemies in any way— even something so insignificant. Besides, Srika wouldn't likely trust her with a needle.

Jynx sat once more, bored rather than tired. She could try making up stories in her head, to share with Sayvil's children when she got home. But her mind wouldn't settle into the effort.

She pulled her knees up to her chest, holding them there with bound arms wrapped around them and rested her chin on top.

She'd sat down next to the rip in the tent floor. For a while she studied it, wondering how hard it would be to tear the tough material–cotton, she thought, instead of the silk she might have expected.

A quick glance at the door showed that her guard hadn't moved. She turned her back to the door to obscure her movements and inserted her hands into the tear, ripping it longer in the process. Maybe she did have a chance...

The ripping sound seemed small, but if it continued, it could draw attention. And it would be easily seen when they brought food.

The cushions weren't large and she moved them easily, scattering them and the blankets between the rip and the wall, careful not to be too obvious. The guard would have to walk clear past the center of the tent, winding his way through cushions and stepping over blankets, even to see the rip now. She could keep most of the rip covered, if no one looked too closely.

The tent wall itself would be the problem, but she had a little time to think about it.

Bracing the more fragile end of the tear against her ropes, she pulled the rip longer, grunting with the effort of the awkward movements. She thought about chewing the ropes off, but a single mouthful of stiff fibers changed her mind.

By the time the guard entered with her lunch, the rip was almost as long as Jynx was tall, and she was working on an idea that might hasten her escape. If it didn't get her killed.

This time the guard sat nearby while she ate a spicy stew from a small bowl. The flavor was wonderful, but the spice left her struggling to breathe.

The guard chuckled, his eyes lighting up, clearly enjoying her discomfort, although he seemed proudly amused rather than vicious. Perhaps his wife had made it? An old family recipe, maybe?

Jynx gave him a sheepish smile when she handed the bowl back to him. He nodded vigorously several times, still grinning, before he left with the empty bowl.

He *could* be a nice man, when not guarding prisoners. Or skinning live slithers. Her jaw locked in anger and as soon as she could she returned to the rip in the tent floor.

Walking about her prison seemed a good idea, and she felt restless anyway. They wouldn't be as surprised to see her moving around later, and they'd pay less attention when she did. Besides, walking around the tent kept her muscles loose and ready.

She slept fitfully that night, dreading another visit from Slyn, but he didn't appear.

Two of the cushions would assure better sleep than last night, at least, and a blanket covered her head to toe. They were part of her escape plan, which she reviewed relentlessly.

A guard came in to check on her twice, a different one each time. One stood over her for a long time before he left. She didn't see the friendly guard again.

She waited only a few minutes after the second guard left before throwing off her blanket. The arrangement of cushions and blanket only took a moment. It would do–she hoped–in the darkness of the tent.

This wouldn't be easy with her hands tied, but as Kahpur would say, she had it to do.

Taking a deep breath, she eyed the rip in the floor. In the darkness, she saw only a jagged black line longer than she was.

Much depended on how tightly the tent hugged the ground. Pegged too tight, it would trap her and she might be unable to get out *or* turn around!

Getting into the rip only took a moment. Crawling under the tent floor from there took forever, with her hands bound. The tent was pegged tight, but she could move. An inch at a time, then two inches at a time, and that seemed to be her top speed. Did she have enough of the night left to get out?

She'd better have! This would be her only chance. Her passage wrinkled the tent floor above her. It would be unmistakable how she got out.

When she reached the tent wall, she worried again. Would anyone be out there to see her emerge? What a foolish idea this had been! Snake's presence and her own would have the Wohim on full alert. She had little chance of succeeding, and if she did, they'd likely kill Snake for it.

She hesitated at the wall, listening. Nothing. No sounds, nothing human out there.

Picking up the edge of the tent an inch or two, she laid her cheek against the sand and strained to see.

Again, nothing.

Now or never.

She dug her fingers into the sand as far as she could, pulling while she pushed with her toes. The exertion left her panting before even her head emerged, and she couldn't quiet her breath enough to listen.

Crawling out from under the pegged tent took probably half an hour as a guess, and every passing minute shot more panic into her nerves. She swallowed the mewling sound that threatened to push past her lips.

Her shoulders pushed into the night. Seeing no one, she emerged on her knees.

Still clear.

Grabbing two handfuls of concealing black sand, she staggered to her feet and slogged her weary way to the edge of the village, staying as close to the tents as she could. Looking back, she saw a large tent in the center of the encampment, where no less than six armed guards patrolled.

That's where Snake is. She had no way to help him, though. She was so depleted she could barely move.

She walked away from the village, found Katinga's Eye to guide her, and started back toward the white sands and help.

~~~

White sand had never looked so good. Jynx saw it first as a pale line across the horizon, recognizable only because she remembered it from her initial arrival.

"Ick?" She tried Rapport, hoping she could reach so far.

Jynx! Where are you? Snake is missing, too, and the warriors are in an uproar over his desertion.

"He didn't desert. He was captured. I have much to tell you, and it's all important."

Where are you?

Jynx described the location as best she could, given the featureless black sands. Then she brought her friend up to date on recent events. "I have no water," she concluded, "and I'm still in the black sands. I don't know how to find water out here." Somehow she'd neglected that detail in planning her escape, for which she had chastised herself with every step. A feeble sun hung over the dark dunes, inhibited by the perpetual shadows hovering over the sand. That had so far saved her from extreme dehydration, at least. She wondered idly if the Wohim ever had to contend with the sun's full strength.

Help is on the way, dear one. Stay strong.

Over the hours, the line of white sand thickened and finally resolved into the distant peaks of dunes. Jynx's heart sank. Still so far! Her body trembled with fatigue and despair.

She needed to rest, but she didn't dare. The Wohim would know by now that she'd escaped and how. They still had Snake, and they could make him suffer for her actions. Slyn wouldn't let him be killed, but she knew better than most how much damage a body could sustain and still live. Worse, they could send warriors after her, and she had little chance of avoiding recapture. The quiet air didn't disturb her footprints, so they would find her easily.

The third time she fell from exhaustion, she stayed down. Only for a few minutes, of course, just long enough to regain some energy—with neither food nor water to replenish it. For the thirteenth time she scolded herself for not stealing supplies on her way out.

By the time she could see how tall the white dunes really were, her body wanted to give up. She wouldn't allow it. Thankfully, soon after that she saw movement in the distance.

Jynx? Can you see them yet? Help should be getting close.

"Yes, I think I do." Jynx fought the sand to get to her feet. Here, at least she didn't have to shade her eyes to see. She did anyway, out of habit. "It looks like they'll miss me, though. They're headed too far west. Let me try something."

Jynx shut down Rapport, stuck two fingers in her mouth, and whistled a loud, shrill whistle that could be heard a mile away in clear air. Of course, this shadowy air wasn't really clear, so she whistled again.

Either they heard her or Ick was talking to them—or both. The movement turned toward her. She whistled once more, waving her free hand to catch their attention.

Then she sat down to wait.

It took them longer than expected to reach her. They were on foot, pulling a low wagon on runners that slid smoothly over the sand.

The sledge contained barrels of water, as well as food. Someone handed her a most welcome cup of cool water, which she drained twice, and helped her into the sledge to ride.

Then they turned around and took her back to the white sands and her beloved Ick.

30. Preparing for War

Jynx dozed on the way back to the white sands, grateful for the constant murmur of voices that suggested all was well. Her body complained that dozing wasn't enough. She agreed, but she had much to do yet before she could allow herself any real sleep.

The water, the rest, and dates, melon slices, and some kind of salted fish restored her more than she'd have believed possible.

Ick met them at the border between black and white sands and rode back with them, coiled next to Jynx.

Shyriel waited for them at the border of the queens' precinct, Beyir at her side. Ick and Jynx left the wagon, Jynx expressing profound appreciation to those who had brought her back.

"I'm pleased to see you well, Jynx," said Shyriel by way of greeting. "Erilya has shared with me what you told her. I'm sorry this cannot wait, but I would ask that you join us, and Beyir, to speak more of these events and to plan. We cannot allow the son of prophecy to remain a prisoner. He must be brought home. Now."

"Or as soon as we can manage it without endangering him further," Beyir amended.

They retreated to a secluded room within the queens'

precinct, where a simple meal had been set out on a low table surrounded by comfortable cushions.

Jynx paid more attention to a bright orange-colored juice than to the food. Anything liquid sounded so good! It proved every bit as sweet and good as she'd imagined, and a servant stepped forward to refill her cup as soon as it emptied. Already energy surged through her.

At Shyriel's request, she recounted her experience again, beginning with the night she fell and ending with her escape from the Wohim tent.

Did you see any slithers while you were there? Ick asked.

"No. None except Slyn. Nor did I see a shed such as we saw at their prior location. Was there another raid while I was gone?"

No. But we seem to have fewer slithers. We have servants trying to do a census, to see who, if anyone, we're actually missing.

This didn't make much sense to Jynx. The "missing" slithers could be hunting or in their burrows. But then, what did she really know about slithers? Not much.

Beyir asked her a question and she forgot about the missing slithers. Instead, she answered questions, and more questions, and even more questions. With no sleep the night before, her energy started to sag in spite of drinking enormous amounts of the orange juice.

Ick finally stopped the discussion for Jynx's sake, insisting they had plenty to discuss that didn't require her presence.

Grumbling, Shyriel acquiesced, and Beyir excused himself to walk her out. Thank the One, because she was too tired to get all the twists and turns right, on the way out of the burrow.

To Jynx's surprise, he walked her all the way to her door, chatting of inconsequential things. And then he stood a little longer.

Shoulders and knees sagging, Jynx wanted nothing more than to go inside and collapse. Would it be rude if she pushed past him into the house without a word?

"Say what you have to say, Beyir," she told him. And knew her guess was right as she watched him search for words.

"I have to ask," he said. "You never saw Kyr but took Slyn's word for it that they have him?"

"Yes." They'd talked about this in the meeting.

"He is the strategist, the planner for the war we will take to the Wohim. Is he truly a prisoner? Is there any chance, even the slightest, that he only pretends, that he will betray us to our enemies? That he and Slyn, with whom he bonded a lifetime ago, are colluding to set themselves up as co-rulers, regardless of the cost to the People?"

Jynx's mouth dropped open. She felt the blood drain from her face and her head spun slowly. Then blood suffused her face again, in anger. Her fist swung toward Beyir's face but she caught herself.

And a good thing, too, as his arm had already started up to block her.

"Snake would never betray the People!" she spat. "If he did, who could blame him, after all that he endured here. And yet here he is, training your warriors, coming up with a plan, and working his tail off to help the People with whom he severed all connections twenty years ago! He owes the People nothing! *You* owe *him*! And when he gifts you with his knowledge and his leadership, from the largeness of his heart, you *doubt* him? You don't deserve what he's done for you! You have no idea what it cost him to come here, to open old wounds, to expose himself to fears created in his childhood! You give no thought to what he's suffered, only to your own needs! And now, on the brink of war, you *doubt him*?" She clenched and unclenched her fists, wondering if she could still punch him and get away with it. "How dare you!" Jaw aching with restrained fury, she pushed past him into the house.

At the last moment, she turned back, last words on her lips. "You will never find a man more loyal and true, braver, stronger, more willing to do the right thing no matter the cost. He *promised*! And Snake keeps his promises!"

She turned her back and slammed the door in his face.

Then she stood still, listening to Beyir's footsteps die away, before throwing herself onto the nearest cushions and sobbing her heart out.

That man had better still be alive! He'd better survive, or she'd kill him herself.

~~~

When will the People come for you, Kyr? Slyn coiled well out of Snake's reach, his tone tight and hard.

Snake, chin almost on his chest, didn't look up. He hadn't responded to any of Slyn's attempts at conversation since learning that Jynx had been here, in this camp, and escaped.

He'd found out when Changn came into the tent and beat him, while Slyn spat angry questions at him. As if he'd helped her, tied and guarded as he was! He ignored the body blows from the giant, having fought enough battles to know these were survivable. The blows to his head worried him more, but unless one of the powerful blows broke his neck, he'd live through them. No individual blow, he reminded himself, hurt worse than the Beast throwing his head back into Snake's as he mounted. Damn horse. Snake wished the damn horse were here now. The warhorse would make short work of Changn and then chew Snake's rope off.

Ah, well. The Beast was probably behaving properly under Kahpur's strict requirements, and even learning some manners. Just so she didn't take the edge off enough to spoil him for combat alongside Snake.

He actually missed the Beast, to his surprise.

But then, anything he could find to take his mind off Changn's fists would be a good thing right now.

So he turned his thoughts to Jynx, his favorite subject. He had to believe she'd escaped cleanly, that she'd be able to bring help. And worrying about her long trek back to the white sands served no good purpose. Instead, he remembered the times they'd spent together. The day he and Kayde had abducted her and Kahpur. The time they'd spent on the Slipaway Trail, searching for a healer. They'd found a Little Man named Sprig, as fine a healer as any in the world. The time Jynx had told him off roundly. He found himself smiling at that memory!

Until Changn snatched him halfway to his feet by his hair and slammed a boulder-sized fist into his gut. He saw it coming in time to tighten up so the blow couldn't go deep enough to damage his insides. Even so, he barely held it off, and the sisal ropes binding his wrists behind his back deepened the furrows they made in his wrists.

As long as he kept his mind elsewhere, he could get through this.

The time they'd dropped into a ravine to shelter from a cyclone. He'd actually had to touch Ick, to peel the unconscious slither from around Jynx's waist! His skin prickled with the memory. And being rescued from the tripwire by the women! And making love to Jynx for the first time...

The world disappeared.

When he opened his eyes again, he was alone. His face was wet and smelled of blood, in a tent dark as the underbelly of a stoat, lit only by a small oil lamp across the tent from him. Its tiny flame drew the eye, but he could see little else.

Silence surrounded him. He didn't see Slyn and received no answer to his tentative touch through Rapport. Slyn seemed to be sleeping, somewhere beyond the tent.

He hurt all over. Searing pain in his right eyebrow. A dull ache in his bound arms and a sharper one in his abraded wrists. His nose hurt abominably—worse when he tried to breathe through it, so he breathed through his mouth. His head seemed to take a hammer blow with every heartbeat.

He hurt so much that even thinking became excruciating. He worked to distract himself.

Had he ever been in so much pain before? Maybe that time the Beast kicked his thigh and almost broke his leg? Falling off that mountainside in the Kingdom of the Snows? Well, no, not that; he'd landed in a deep snowdrift that King Brace had pulled him out of, but the snow had cushioned most of the impact. His fight with Kayde when they first met? Even then Kayde had been bigger, but no, that was normal roughhousing, nothing unusual.

He gave up trying to think and lay still, just existing and trying to ignore the pain—until he realized the tiny flame of the oil lamp could be his friend.

Crawling took a long, slow time, especially with almost every inch of his body hurting, but Snake needed to be out of here before Slyn returned. And that meant he needed to be free of his bindings.

Had Changn left any of his body free of bruises, broken skin, swollen flesh? The tiny flame of the oil lamp and grim determination drew him forward. His left calf came into contact with something he didn't see in the darkness and he left a bit of flesh behind on whatever it was, clenching his teeth to hold back a roar of pain.

He turned his back to the flame and tried blindly to maneuver his wrists into position for the flames to devour the rope. His lower back took the first burn; he hissed through clenched teeth. The second burn came not from the flame but from the hot metal of the lamp pressing against his forearm.

Sweat poured down his body from the effort, but he couldn't seem to line up his ropes with the flame. The smell of burning excited him—at last, freedom within reach!—until he realized the smell was the hair on his arms crisping. Still he forced himself to hold his arms in place, determined to take the pain in exchange for his freedom.

He heard the tent flap open, but it was already too late.

In three strides, Changn reached him, wrapped a huge

hand around his throat, and flung him away from the tiny flame.

Snake tried to scramble away on his back but he already knew it for a futile effort.

Changn beat him again, and Snake had no way to fight back, or even to avoid the blows. When he passed out from the pain, a dash of water in his face woke him, until he passed out again. And woke again. And again. Until he didn't.

~~~

Dear one.

Jynx struggled up from the depths of dreamless sleep. As she re-entered the world, she realized she felt rested, for the first time in days.

Dear one.

"Ick?" She sat up. "I'm awake."

I need to speak with you privately. I will arrive, with breakfast, in a few minutes.

"Breakfast! Thank you, Ick. I'll be here.

She washed, but she had no fresh clothes to change into. Everything she owned except the clothes on her back had been destroyed by the Wohim. All the work of gathering, drying, crushing–all for nothing. All the hours spent sewing her clothes–wasted. The beautiful hareem and her plans for her wedding night–destroyed. And Kahpur's magic bowl smashed. Guilt washed through her, even knowing Kahpur would forgive her immediately. Losing her friend's bowl violated her own code of honor. If you borrowed something, you returned it in the same condition. That was just good manners.

She tried to shake out her britches–still scandalous back in the tallgrass–and her one remaining shirt, both dirty and ripped from crawling under the tent floor in them. With luck, no one would see her but Ick. Maybe Ick could arrange a change of clothes for her, too.

When Ick arrived, three women arrived with her, bearing breakfast breads, juices, water, and a thick porridge.

Ick took one look at her—and probably a sniff—and sent one of the servers for fresh clothes for Jynx, even if they had to be sewn. The woman wanted to take measurements but retreated from Ick's glare, promising something clean immediately and a new wardrobe by day's end. What a relief! Jynx's shoulders relaxed.

As they ate, Jynx answered a few questions about what she'd seen in the Wohim encampment, but she suspected that wasn't Ick's purpose for coming. Curiosity plagued her, a disease from which she had no immunity.

The women cleared the dishes just as Jynx's clean clothes arrived. No britches, but an ankle-length red skirt accompanied by a finely sewn white blouse. That wouldn't stay clean long. But the clothing fit well enough, and it felt good to be clean again.

Then all the women left and Jynx settled in for a real conversation with Ick.

Ick seemed quite pleased with herself. Maybe even a little smug, and it certainly had nothing to do with clothes. Jynx's head tilted, brows raised in question.

The People prepare for war, Ick told her. *Beyir works the warriors up, emphasizing the heroism needed, the strength and courage trained into them. He has finalized the battle plans he and Snake agreed upon. All is in readiness for war.*

"Beyir seems to think Snake may have betrayed the People after all," said Jynx.

No. He would never do that. Beyir doesn't know him as I do. Would you like me to reassure him?

A little sheepish, Jynx related last night's conversation with the chief priest of the Protection.

He's being careful, Jynx. He's getting older and relying heavily on Snake—and now Snake isn't here, so he's feeling a little vulnerable. Beyir wants to keep the son of prophecy safe, too, but responsibility for all of us weighs on him.

Jynx hesitated. "Is he jealous of Snake, do you think?"

No. I don't think so. He's in awe of Snake's knowledge and skill, and I think relieved to share his burden, rather than jealous of the help prophesied for us.

Jynx digested that, re-evaluating the memory of Beyir's words the night before. "Then that's not really what you want to talk to me about, is it?"

I have something important to tell you, and it must be kept in the strictest confidence.

"I'm good at keeping secrets."

Yes, dear one. You are. Let's go out into the sands for a bit.

Mystified and intrigued, Jynx knelt to give Ick easy access to wrap around her waist. They left by the back door, telling no one where they went.

To Jynx's surprise, their destination was the hard, flat Pan. They had little protection from the sun here, but no one could approach without being seen well in advance. Fortunately, the Pan sat amid ridges of rock and hardened, dry mud, so they could find a place out of direct sunlight to sit and speak somewhat comfortably.

"Do you worry about eavesdroppers, Ick? Spies? Is that why we're out here?" Jynx swept a few small pebbles aside so the slither queen would have a smooth place to coil up for their talk.

Most of the People are absolutely trustworthy and would never deliberately speak to the detriment of all. But only one person speaking without thought could create problems for all of us. Especially since we have a spy among us.

"A spy? Here?"

Ick's gentle laughter fluttered softly in her head. *Slyn, silly. He comes and goes, generally unnoticed unless someone wants to speak to him. And now we know where he goes and why. Few have ever trusted him, for good reason. But he feels the lack of trust as animosity, and so it has shaped who he is.*

Jynx nodded. She certainly didn't trust him, especially after hearing his confessions, spoken with pride! "I doubt he'll return here. He'll know that I've shared everything."

We have a secret weapon of which he knows nothing. Nor does Snake, nor even Beyir. It is a weapon that I have constructed, a fighting force that the Wohim will not understand or easily counter.

Suddenly a picture formed in Jynx's head. A river of black slithers, biting and holding, envenomed tails stabbing... Her eyes widened in horror.

Yes. A disciplined force of slithers, trained to act as a unit. I have worked on this since my return, secretly, to see whether such a thing is possible. It is.

"What does Shyriel think of this idea?"

I haven't told her. She's not that bright, you know. Better that she learn after the fact, not before.

"You think she would betray you?" Jynx, for all her dislike of the human queen, couldn't see that happening.

No. Not on purpose, at least. But I do think she would object, perhaps even put obstacles in our way.

"You could tell her this strategy came as a prophecy from the gods."

Laughter fluttered again. *It did. Along with the suggestion that it be kept private.*

Oh, my. Slither prophecy turned out to be much more complex than Jynx had ever dreamed. "So you planted the idea of missing slithers, freeing them to retreat into the dunes to drill."

Yes. Shyriel is convinced that slithers out hunting have been stolen by Wohim raiders, despite no visible sign of them. She is both fearful and angry.

"I don't like the idea of you at the head of the slither attack. You're much too valuable to the People, and the Wohim are greedy to get their hands on you for breeding."

I will not lead them into battle, Jynx. Their leader is Henth, a mild and gentle slither from Snake's childhood nest. They were very close, I believe. She endured capture by the Wohim and escaped, but the emotional scars remain. Hate for them fills her, and a desire for revenge. She is intelligent and determined and the slithers will follow her.

I've also chosen a human leader with a strong gift of Rapport to work closely with the slither force. Human hands and human ways of thinking will be invaluable against human enemies.

"But Snake is a captive himself. And wouldn't he be leading the human warriors if he were here?"

Exactly. A smug buzz filled Jynx's head. *That's why you'll be the human leader of the slither contingent.*

~~~

Jynx met Henth in the warriors' training area, where Snake had drilled Beyir's men relentlessly. Wearing new leather britches with a sheathed knife strapped to her thigh, Jynx carried Ick around her waist. She stepped through an opening between two rocks.

A long, venomous tail struck toward her face. She jerked her head back.

Stop! Ick's mental bellow left Jynx's ears ringing, but the venomous tail stopped, quivering.

Jynx hadn't even seen the slither until it moved. It lay coiled neatly on a small shelf of rock, black tongue flickering at Jynx.

Henth, said Ick, broadcasting, *I've brought you the human leader I promised. This is Jynx, who is very dear to my heart and Kyr's beloved. You will find her intelligent, stubborn, and fearless. She has just escaped the Wohim and can lead your cadre and the human troops there, and she can show you where Kyr is being held. You are the commander of the slither cadre, but Jynx will be your co-commander. She must learn quickly all that you can teach her of how the slithers will fight, so that she can help in ways that only a human can—only a human with experience of the Wohim.*

Beloved of Kyr? The longing in Henth's voice immediately melted Jynx's reserve.

"I remember Snake speaking of you," she said. "I remember how enraged he was, to learn of how the Wohim treated you. And how he grieved for those slain. I think, of all the slithers in his nest, his fondest memories are of you."

She felt Henth relax, felt her acceptance. *Welcome, Jynx. As two who love Kyr, we must of course be the best of friends. Whom he loves, I will love.*

"And I the same, Henth. I will learn from you, and together we will defeat the Wohim so life for all of us can return to normal." To their separate versions of normal, but it seemed impolite to say so.

Jynx, are you comfortable enough that I can leave to return to the queens' precinct? I don't want Shyriel wondering where I am.

"I'm fine, Ick. I think Henth and I will get along very, very well."

Good. I leave you in her care, then. Oh, and we're moving up the date of our attack. We'll leave for the black sands day after tomorrow. Snake is our first priority, as we'll need him to lead the troops in battle, alongside Beyir. Or in his place, if necessary.

"I need to look through his house, too, to see what weapons we can take to him. The Wohim will have taken whatever weapons he had with him," Jynx said.

Go, Erilya, Henth broadcast. *We can handle everything without interrupting your day.*

Jynx watched Ick leave, a little forlorn. The possibility existed that after the war, when she and Snake left the sands, she might never see Ick again. She still hoped for the best. Ick had enjoyed adventuring together, as well as living with her in the tallgrass, although sand wasn't readily available there. She took hope from Ick's bald statement that Shyriel wasn't bright. Surely that boded well for Ick's choice.

Then she chose not to think about it anymore. It was Ick's choice, not hers—she knew what she'd choose!—and Jynx had no say in it. Worrying about it was a useless waste of time.

Instead, she needed to put her mind to what lay ahead and the task of getting Snake out of the Wohim village alive. A quick prayer to the One followed, nothing formal but certainly heartfelt. And she planned to do a lot of those, because the coming days would be the most dangerous of her life.

"I'm ready, Henth. Show me what I need to know."

31. War

The Wohim didn't bring in a healer or offer any succor at all, except a cup of water twice a day. Snake took it as a clear sign they meant to kill him. So why didn't they just get it done?

At this point he would welcome it, if he could just see Jynx one more time first.

Not that he wanted her here. She'd escaped; she was safe. That was what he wanted most. But Jynx wouldn't just send help. Not her! She'd come with his rescuers, convince them they couldn't find the village without her.

By Landir's tits! How in the Bearslayer's name could he protect her like this! He could barely move, five days—at his best guess—after her escape. His left arm was broken for sure. His nose, too. He'd carry burn scars on his forearms the rest of his life. His entire body was one enormous bruise, and he might never be able to sire children. Cold sweat drenched him at the thought of what Changn had done. Everything hurt. To the point of nausea.

Despite bone weary exhaustion, he couldn't sleep for the pain. If his time sense was right, the People would be leaving in a couple of days to attack the Wohim. He doubted they could leave any earlier, given the preparations needed.

He drifted again, lost in a blue fog, where tiny boomers sent sparks shooting across his vision. He worried vaguely about time spent here, and especially about the sparks, feared he might be losing his eyesight. But even the fear felt vague, as if he were separated from reality by the fog.

Someone—it had to be Changn—grabbed him by his throat and jerked him to his feet, but Snake couldn't root his legs root to the tent floor enough to stay up. He hung limp in Changn's fist. Changn squeezed, and Snake felt a vague relief. Changn would kill him now and the pain would end.

The giant released him and he crumpled to the floor. The lilt and crash of voices washed over him.

Kyr. Do you yet live?

Adjusting his perception took a moment. Slyn. "What do *you* want?" Surprised it came from his mind, not his mouth.

Jynx is dead. She tried to bring Beyir's warriors into the black sand. We found their bodies covered in blood. The People have renounced you for the evil you've brought upon them. You have nowhere to go but back to the Snows. If you leave now, the Wohim will not stop you, but it must be now!

"They'll let me go?"

You're no threat, Kyr. Alone, badly injured, weaponless... go home while you can. Rescue is not coming. Jynx no longer lives. There is nothing to keep you here.

Because you cannot hurt them now, the Wohim will give you food and water for your journey. I suggest south, to the coast, to take ship for the Snows. It will be an easier journey.

Little of the news sank in. Only six words made sense. You can go. Jynx is dead.

Jynx is dead. Not true. Couldn't be true. The world hadn't exploded; it still existed, so she had to be alive. *He* was still alive, so Jynx lived. If she didn't, he'd be dead now.

He tried not to see her torn, bloody body, but it was there, in his head. How? Who? How? How? He repeated himself because he couldn't find any words that made sense.

Tears dripped from his chin, slid down his neck.

He'd sleep. He'd wake up, and it would all be a dream. A nightmare. Not real.

Then Slyn showed him, through Rapport, the picture of devastation, fifty bloody bodies of the men he'd trained. And in the center, as if they'd died trying to protect her, Jynx. Long walnut hair spread on the sand. Bloody gashes over her entire body. She wore new leather britches he hadn't seen before, and a dagger on her thigh, also new.

Stone. He became stone. Nothing was real. Nothing mattered. That couldn't be Jynx. No. Never. No. No. No.

And then he closed in on himself, immune to whatever the Wohim could do to him. He cuddled his rage, cradled its fires, imagined the pain he would bring to each and every one of them. It became his goal in life, his only goal the complete and utter destruction of the Wohim.

~~~

Snake felt Slyn's smug satisfaction and added a small branch to the flames that ate him from inside. He began to understand how the Wohim could bring themselves to skin living slithers. No death would be too awful for that evil creature. He pictured a slow, ugly death, the kind of leisurely skinning that would keep Slyn alive and in maximum pain. Cut off his deadly tail. Yank out his merciless fangs. Spit him on a long rod and roast him still living, over a hot fire.

But even in the throes of a hatred he'd never believed possible, Snake shied away from the thought of eating slither steaks. His past was too much a part of him.

"I'll go," he called after the men leaving the tent with Slyn. "I'll be on my way at once and never look back, never return. I accept your offer. Just bring me food and water, as promised."

Even Snake didn't expect the rancid bitterness of his words. "You know your prophecy of co-ruling the white sands can never happen now, Slyn. If I ever catch you away from help, you will die the most horrible death I can devise."

319

Me? I didn't kill her, Kyr. I had nothing to do with it. As I said, they were found like that. I'm only the messenger, because you do not share a language with the Wohim. Somehow he managed to sound hurt. *You must understand that I am here to pave the way for peace. If we will pay a small tribute, they will promise to leave our slithers alone, and you and I can co-rule in the peace and prosperity foretold.*

And then he left the tent, riding on Changn's shoulders, while Snake's anger seethed and boiled.

Snake gritted his teeth. He had to get free. Had to! Even if he died in the process, he'd put an end to the evil of that insane slither!

But struggle as he might, his bonds only deepened the now-bloody grooves in his wrists. The lamp had been removed, so even its tiny flame was no longer available to help him. Nor did he see anything else in the tent that might help—but then, he might not, with vision in his right eye so blurred from the beating.

Time dragged with nothing he could do to help himself. He saw over and over the image Slyn had shown him: Jynx, lying dead and bloody amid the People's warriors. The turmoil in his heart dragged him down into the darkest place he'd ever been. Tears stung his eyes but he blinked them back, pushing his anger forward to cover the grief. There would be time to grieve later, after Slyn was dead.

He started working his way along the tent floor, toward the door, until he noticed a huge shadow standing outside. Changn was on guard. He slumped back, not discouraged but knowing he had no chance to escape right now. He could only hoard his body's resources and wait. He needed time to recover, but luckily for him time was all he had right now. That, and a warrior's trained patience and determination. Right now the only thing he could do while waiting was heal. He closed his eyes, slowed his breathing, and slept, trusting his ears to awaken him if anyone entered.

They gave him water when they fed him–his first food in two days. A terrified young woman spooned porridge into his mouth, glancing often over her shoulder to assure Changn still guarded her. Then she helped him drink a cup of water and scurried from the tent.

Changn scowled at him and turned to go, then spun and backfisted him across the face before turning and marching out.

Bearslayer help him, if Changn ever learned exactly what Snake had done to his brother!

As dusk fell, they fed and watered him again, and one of the guards took him to the slop pit, to his relief. Then they left him alone, except that there were two guards now–one outside the door, the other on the opposite side of the tent.

The guards changed somewhere near midnight, at Snake's best reckoning. They'd probably change again near dawn. Again he settled to sleep, senses still monitoring for change in the world around him.

He awoke on high alert, halfway to dawn. He couldn't tell what woke him, but something had. Careful not to move, or even open his eyes, he strained his other senses for information. Nothing routine, he knew.

His eyes flipped open at a gentle touch on his mind.

Kyr.

Even in Rapport he heard only a whisper. He held his breath. It didn't feel like Slyn, but who else could it be?

Henth, Kyr. It's Henth.

He caught a sob before it escaped, slapped with an unexpected relief. A friend! And a very brave one, considering what she had suffered at the hands of the Wohim. "What are you doing here?" His mouth formed the words but he kept them behind his teeth. Henth would still hear him.

Rescuing you, silly!

"How did you find me?"

Jynx led me to this tent. She marked it during her own escape.

Pain left Kyr almost breathless, and this time part of his sob escaped. He'd never known such searing hurt. "Impossible! Jynx is dead!"

Certainly not! She and I will co-lead the slither contingent of our attack on the Wohim, while Beyir leads the human contingent.

"But... I saw her... Slyn showed me... all dead... covered in blood..."

Magic, Kyr. Some magic that Jynx has, from the red sands.

Stunned, Snake needed a moment to reorient. Of course! The magic of the white sands! The white sand had taken on the properties of the red. He had thought to use the same tactic himself, to pretend injury and death to lure the Wohim! He started to laugh silently.

Hush! Let me work in peace!

He almost managed that, except for the shaking of his body with laughter. He'd rather have laughed out loud, but this wasn't the time.

Sit still, Kyr, so I can chew your bonds off.

And she did, while Snake beheld the wonder and glory of the world, and how beautiful everything was, and Jynx especially, whom he could hardly wait to see, because he needed to see for himself that she was all right...

Hold still! Henth's tone felt stern, despite its thread of amusement.

Her upper fangs pierced his wrist once, but that remained the only mishap, at least until he stood up.

He wavered, staggered once trying to keep his balance, then stood spraddle-legged to catch himself.

"I couldn't see anything here that would make a good weapon," he told her.

Except me.

Henth? Sounding smug?

He lifted her. She wrapped his arm once, and they walked toward the door, Snake only half balanced.

He ducked through to the outside.

The surprised guard whirled toward him, mouth opening to shout.

Henth's tail whipped over her head and struck into the guard's throat. A slight convulsion near the tail signaled the release of venom.

The guard froze, eyes wide, and collapsed.

Glancing around, Snake pulled the body inside the tent and fastened the door from the outside.

Henth opened Rapport wide and signaled.

Warriors began to slip among the tents, slitting the throats of sleeping Wohim men. Every other warrior carried a full-grown slither on shoulders or arms, and more slithers wound through the black sand, invisible except for their red eyes.

With a grunt, Snake dropped to his knees. The deep sand dragged at his feet and he had no strength to push forward. Despite the battle energy infusing him, his body wouldn't obey.

"Go, Henth. I've got him." Beyir was there, lifting him up as Henth shot away, hungry for more prey.

The chief priest pulled Snake's arm across his shoulders and lifted him back to his feet, then wrapped Snake's waist with the other arm. "Let's get you to safety, where the healers can tend your wounds. You're not part of this fight, my friend."

Snake allowed most of his weight to rest in Beyir's strong arms. "Jynx?"

"She's fine—and furious that I wouldn't allow her to assist in your rescue. You've got yourself a full-blood tanglecat there, Kyr!" He chuckled, clearly an admirer. "The sooner I get you to her, the less likely she'll find a way to jump into the middle of this."

Even wounded, Snake could smell blood in the air now, mingling with the screams of frightened women and dying men. He looked back over his shoulder at the swords and other weapons flashing, even household items swinging through the air.

"This isn't your fight, Kyr. Not anymore. It's ours." Beyir's voice took on a no-nonsense sternness. He meant what he said.

So Kyr turned his attention to staying on his feet while Beyir half-carried him back to the supply sledges and the healers. And Jynx.

~~~

The cacophony of battle faded behind him as Snake leaned on Beyir and made his way toward Jynx. It was done. The People's warriors had trained hard and knew what to do. Their cause would inspire them. Surprise gave them a sizeable advantage. They should triumph quickly.

He stopped, no longer leaning on Beyir, who looked at him in surprise. Snake wobbled but stood on his own feet. "They need leadership and guidance, Beyir. Go. I'll make it to Jynx, never fear, if not quite as fast."

Beyir searched his face briefly and gave him a curt nod, then told him how to get to the healers before turning back to the battle, curved sword already in his hand.

Snake never had gotten the hang of those swords. A little curve could be a good thing, but these? Shaking his head, he started forward, slow and clumsy without Beyir's support. He wouldn't be much good in a fight right now, anyway.

Jynx would expect him, would be watching for him. Anticipation quickened his steps and he fell, feet trapped by sand, and rolled down a short incline.

When he regained his feet, he didn't know which way to go. The shadows hanging over the sand looked the same in every direction. He cursed, looked around for clues. This way. He was sure of it.

He slowed his pace further, careful not to trip. Sand

scoured all the bruises Changn had inflicted, and he'd rather avoid more of them.

The first shouting Snake heard seemed to be physical and he almost started to run. Slyn's voice stopped him. Slyn's—and Henth's?

He oriented on the sounds in his head and ran as best he could, given his condition and the abysmal footing. Slyn and Henth, about the same age and therefore similar size, would be well-matched physically, but how could Slyn's insane rage *not* give him an advantage over gentle, quiet Henth?

And this was a fight to the death, insults and fury filling the air. Over him.

Snake's hands and cheeks went almost numb at the thought.

Slyn wanted him dead, which seemed fair, since Snake wanted the same for him. But Henth would die to defend him, and she intended to kill Slyn now to assure Snake's safety.

Weaponless, what could he do? He surged over the top of a black dune and slid down the far side on the seat of his pants.

He almost landed on Henth. Black slithers blended into black sand, and the shadows rising like a mist above the sand obscured even the slither's red eyes and open mouth until he came within inches of her.

The fight had just started, with lots of hissing, red mouths agape, and long bodies weaving above the ground like dancers. No strikes yet, at least.

Snake had dealt with numerous slither fights as a child, as Slyn sought increasingly larger slithers to attack, to prove his worthiness to rule. But full-grown slithers were much more dangerous than youngens. Their venom had long since come in, where the youngens had been far too young to have venom. Nor did they have this kind of strength and power. Still, even the youngens needed a handler each, to separate them simultaneously so no one got hurt.

Snake, battered and alone, couldn't possibly stop this fight. But he had to, somehow, to protect Henth.

He charged in between them, thrusting a hand toward each of them. "Stop!" he roared in his best Command voice. He'd been one of the best at Command as a child. But now? With adult slithers focused on killing each other? What the hell was he thinking?

Fangs struck his arm, and the pain dropped him to his knees in the sand.

Henth took advantage of Slyn's focus on Snake, her tail barely visible in the darkness as she arrowed its tip at Slyn.

Slyn's tail swung up and wrapped Henth's. They struggled to control each other with tail and fang, drawing blood with several strikes in quick succession.

Snake stumbled to his feet, ignoring the stinging burn, and fell back a few steps. Youngens were one thing. But how did one control two adult slithers at once? Even two adult humans would be hard-pressed to separate these combatants.

Henth strained to unwrap her tail from Slyn's, and he strained to keep her trapped. Once he'd wrapped her several times, his control would be decisive. He'd only have to leave enough of his tail free to stab and inject.

Which was all Henth had to do, too, but to Snake it seemed that Slyn, not Henth, controlled at the moment.

Henth bit her opponent, again and again.

Slyn responded with bites of his own, on the defensive now, trying to bite while unwinding his tail enough to stab.

As Slyn's tail came loose, Snake leaped to grab it well back from its tip. The taper made it hard to hold onto, and before he could set his grip it jerked free.

Henth stabbed at Slyn during the distraction, but the wily slither flicked his tail to smack against her coils and wrapped her in his tail again.

Then Slyn hit Snake with his tail—not a stab but a swat that lifted him from his feet and flung him into the sand.

Snake felt the blood retreat from his face as memory struck: Tchenya, her huge tail swatting his father, slamming him to the ground and killing him.

For a moment he couldn't breathe. For a moment he felt the queen's coils wrapping around him and squeezing, the sound and feel of bones breaking.

But he was Wolf Guard now, and that was a child's memory, not a warrior's. He'd been hurt worse many times since then. Nor did it matter what wounds he already carried. Scowling fiercely, he thrust pain aside as unimportant and scrambled up.

Henth bit Slyn twice more, dodged his weaving head, and bit him again.

His teeth struck her three feet below her head and ripped out a chunk of flesh.

Her scream echoed through Rapport as Slyn gulped down the chunk as if it were kangapak instead of slither.

While Henth's pain and fear echoed through his head, while Slyn's extreme aberration roiled his stomach, Snake ran.

Hoping he was right, he threw himself onto Slyn's tail, pinning it down close enough to the tip it couldn't be lifted. At the same time, he opened to Rapport with Henth.

"Now, Henth! Now, my beautiful warrior! Strike, and have done!"

She heard.

Her tail arced over her head and stabbed into Slyn just behind his head. A small convulsion delivered the venom, and then she threw herself away from her enemy.

Slyn's scream echoed in the world and in Rapport. Every slither within five miles had to hear him scream!

And then he convulsed, his entire spine rippling as he bucked, screaming.

Snake rode the bucking spine for two convulsions before being flung into the air. He landed face first in deep sand and came up sputtering and spitting.

Slyn thrashed violently, his tail landing within a foot of Snake, and then swatting the narrow part of Henth's tail.

His death throes seemed to go on forever, and his screams reverberated through Rapport as if they'd never stop.

Snake watched for a moment, then turned away. A job well done, he told himself. But this had once been a special youngen with high intelligence and great promise. A life that young Kyr had been responsible for. And now a death. He could feel no satisfaction or relief, only a deep, heartfelt sadness.

When he looked up, he and Slyn and Henth were surrounded. A ring of slithers joined through Rapport kept watch as one of their own died. And with them were the humans—the ones with the gift of Rapport, who had also heard the screams and come running.

No one spoke. No one moved, until Slyn lay still on the black sand.

32. Decision

The battle had decimated the Wohim. Three of the Malim made the trek to bring gifts signifying peace to Queen Shyriel and Queen Erilya. Srika was not with them.

Jynx heard later that her husband had been killed in the battle and she was on her way back to the tallgrass, to a small village named Ashlock, far distant from Sayvil.

Shyriel returned Morinl to them, and the Wohim returned three surviving slithers, none in good shape but all alive. Rhodor, the Malim of the Merchant Guild, promised the Wohim village would be relocated farther from the white sands.

Peace accords were written over a period of three days and signed. Never again, said the accords, would the Wohim bother the People, neither human nor slither. They had, they claimed, been led astray by Slyn's boasts and promises. Only Rhodor had been able to converse with him directly, but he immediately shared with his village whatever information Slyn had provided.

The only snag in the formalities came when Rhodor revealed that the Wohim had specifically sought Erilya, and also planned to snatch Shyriel and wed her to Rhodor, so that more Wohim with Rapport could be bred.

They got past it because both sides wanted to avoid further

hostilities.

And then they celebrated with food and drink, with song and dance and story, and with vivid displays of skill by warriors and performers from both sides.

They feasted on Anigal goat and pickled crocodile tongue, dates and pomegranates, coconut meat and milk, and other delicacies. Jynx refused seconds on the crocodile tongue.

Snake looked at her and she looked back. Their fingers intertwined. His mischievous smile flipped her heart over and she followed, docile as a lamb, when he led the way out into the dunes, where no one would disturb them.

Apparently a few other couples had the same idea, though, so they wandered for almost an hour before finding what they wanted—even though one couple offered to give up their special place for the celebrated son of prophecy and his beloved.

"Just in time," Snake murmured when at last they sank down at the foot of a tall dune that sparkled quietly in the moonlight. He held in a moan as he eased himself down, but Jynx still heard it.

His injuries hurt her almost as much as they did him. If only she still had her satchel and its contents, so she could treat his wounds properly... She pushed the thought aside. "If-onlies" were worthless and she refused to spend time on them.

Snake still hurt. He moved like an old man, limping from the damage to his leg but careful with all movements. Most of them would heal eventually, but he would always carry scars from his time in captivity.

Mostly they talked quietly, holding each other as if they had each become the other's anchor in a wind-blown world.

As dawn edged the horizon at last, Jynx whispered, "I want to go home, Snake."

He squeezed her shoulders. "So do I, Jynx."

Neither of them mentioned either the tallgrass or the Kingdom of the Snows, and Jynx wondered where home was now. And if their expectations of home were too different to make a life together.

They'd have to talk about it as they traveled by ship back to their own continent.

But not now.

Sudden fear clutched at her heart. One thing more, before they could leave. One more thing she regarded with longing, even as she dreaded it.

As if she'd heard, Ick's soft voice reached her. *It's time, dear one.*

She must have broadcast it, because Snake also sat up, as if he'd heard. He squeezed Jynx's hand and helped her to her feet.

By rights, she should be helping him up. He was the injured one.

They made their slow way back to the village, Jynx wondering if Snake knew the depth of her anxiety. Surely he did.

Jonyl, Jynx's friend, met them at the border of the queens' precinct. After a moment's hesitation she allowed Snake to accompany her into the precinct. She supported Jynx by her staunch presence, although she barely spoke as they crossed golden sand into the burrow.

Would this be the last time Jynx entered these beautiful hallways?

Jonyl led them into a large chamber Jynx hadn't seen before, squeezed her hand, and left her there. Then she touched Snake's shoulder and beckoned him away with her. He hesitated, but when Jynx nodded he touched her cheek lightly and followed Jonyl out.

A choice is necessary. Ick spoke to Jynx and Shyriel only after the others had gone and the door closed. *The time has come. The son of prophecy has fulfilled his duty and the slithers are no longer in danger from the Wohim.*

Jynx stole a quick glance at Shyriel. The queen's face was stone, empty and controlled. Not calm, no. Hidden. She revealed neither worry nor anticipation. Jynx wondered how much practice that took.

Shyriel.

Ick talked to Shyriel first. Was that a good sign or a bad one? Jynx's heart pounded.

We were born on the same day and bonded from birth. We have been like sisters for all of our lives. When one of us dies, the other will follow. Our bond is unbreakable for as long as we live. Whatever happens, I will always love you.

She turned to Jynx.

Tears welled and Jynx blinked hard to erase them. How could she compete with what she'd just heard?

Dear one. Ick's tone softened. You saved my life, despite a complete revulsion for snakes—which you thought I was. You adopted ways that weren't yours to accommodate me, at least in part, and we bonded through the dance, when you wore Isyr's hareem. We faced danger together many times and you introduced me to Snake—our Kyr, the son of prophecy. Nothing can ever break the bond we share. You are my dear one, and whatever happens, I will always love you.

Jynx felt hot tears rolling down her cheeks but made no effort to stop them—as if she could!—nor would she give in to sobs to open her constricted throat.

She felt Ick's heartbreak. Having to choose had to be wrenching, but slithers couldn't cry.

Shyriel, if I leave with Jynx, we will never see each other again. This has been told me by the gods.

Jynx, if I stay with Shyriel, we may see each other again someday, under specific conditions, but there is no certainty of this. This has also been given to me.

Either decision will break my heart, but the gods have told me that I must choose for myself. I can be with only one of you.

Jynx thought her heart would break alongside Ick's. "Dear one," she whispered, "I also love you, with an unbreakable bond. What you choose must be what's right for you, and I will live with your choice and love you no less, whatever you choose." And then a huge sob betrayed her. So much for stoicism.

Shyriel's face remained stone. The woman had incredible self-control! Or perhaps she just didn't return Ick's love full force.

My duty is clear, as is my choice. I must remain here with Shyriel and rule our People. There can be no other way.

THE END

About the Author

Martha Gilstrap's life is filled with stories: the ones she reads, the ones she writes, and the ones she lives. Her family's oral tradition claims descent from the legendary Leif Erickson, the discoverer of America–a tale of which she is inordinately proud, although her mother always wondered why she'd claim "that old pirate."

She used to ride a Kawasaki motorcycle, eventually earned a black belt in RyuTe Karate, owned her own dojo, trained on the grounds of an Okinawan castle destroyed in WWII, and edited and published an international karate newsletter. She has taught Latin to grade-school children, worn a bite sleeve for a Rottweiler "attack," got thrown by the same horse twice within five minutes, and spent New Year's Eve on the Puerto del Sol in Madrid. She's been in the pen with wolves (well socialized, of course), played with horny toads, petted snakes, ridden an elephant, and once sang with the band on a yacht in Acapulco Bay.

She lives in a suburb of Kansas city with a sweet-natured mutt who was driven 1000 miles in one day to bring her to her new home, by the wonderful people who rescued her from abandonment near their home.